Siren's Spring

For lifelong friends Skot Larson and David Bennett, their biannual "thrill tour" was a sacred ritual—a desperate pact against the slow, inevitable creep of middle age. But as they approached fifty, the aches were deeper, the exhaustion came faster, and the time between adventures felt longer. Their hearts were willing, but their bodies were beginning to fail.

On a dangerous cave-diving expedition deep in the Colombian jungle, a catastrophic collapse traps them hundreds of feet beneath the earth. In a desperate, final search for a way out, they discover what mankind has only ever dreamed of: a hidden grotto, illuminated by a pool of glowing, turquoise water. Water that doesn't just quench their thirst, but rewinds the clock.

They surface from their ordeal not just alive, but reborn. Their old injuries are gone, their bodies are stronger, and they look and feel decades younger. Back in civilization, with the help of their media-savvy friend, Buzz, they commit a fatal error in judgment. They share their unbelievable story online. The post goes viral, a modern-day miracle for a world starved for hope.

But their newfound fame becomes a siren's song, luring in predators far more dangerous than any they faced in the jungle. A shadowy corporation, led by a brilliant and dying man, will stop at nothing to possess their secret. Skot and Dave soon learn that the greatest discovery in human history is also the world's most dangerous commodity.

They cheated death only to find themselves hunted, their miracle now the very thing that might get them killed.

Hearthstone Press Trade Paperback ISBN

979-8-218-73781-8

"In the end, we only regret the chances we didn't take, the friends we didn't meet, and the adventures we didn't share"

~Unknown

"What happens here, stays here"

~Las Vegas Convention and Visitors Authority

~ Jason Hoff and Jeff Candido, R&R Partners

This book is dedicated to lasting friendships, shared adventures and the living stories created.

Prologue

1718

Off the Coast of Colombia

Aboard The Scourge, A dying pirate ship

The stink of death had its own bunk on The Scourge, and by now it was sleeping in the captain's quarters.

It was a thick, sweet smell, a permanent resident in the humid air that clung to the becalmed galleon like a wet shroud. It was the smell of scurvy-rotted gums, of dysentery, of hope festering in the oppressive Colombian heat. For two weeks they'd been anchored in this nameless cove, a mosquito-infested purgatory, and every day the stink grew a little more confident, a little more certain of its eventual victory.

Captain Gideon Crowe, a man who had once sacked Campeche with nothing but a stolen longboat and a crew half-mad on rum, now found himself a prisoner of his own decaying flesh. He lay in his sweltering cabin, the ornate brocade of his coat stained with sweat and God knows what else, his world shrunk to the throbbing, relentless agony in his left leg. Gangrene. He didn't need the ship's drunkard of a surgeon, Cobb, to tell him. He could see the black lines crawling up from his ankle, a dark tide of corruption consuming him from the ground up.

Cobb, to his credit, had tried. He'd stumbled in a few days prior, reeking of cheap grog, and offered to saw the leg off. "A clean cut, Cap'n," he'd slurred, brandishing a rusty hacksaw he used for butchering pigs. "You'll be hoppin' about in no time."

Crowe had calmly drawn the flintlock pistol from his bedside table, cocked the hammer, and suggested that if Cobb didn't make himself scarce, the only thing hopping would be his own head into the shark-infested waters below. A captain of The Scourge did not die in pieces. He would be renewed, or he would die whole. It was a matter of pride, the only currency Crowe had left.

He dragged his gaze from the peeling varnish on the ceiling to the map spread across the table. It was his obsession, his final, desperate wager against the inevitable. A brittle sheet of vellum, stolen from a dead Spanish navigator whose ship they'd taken months ago. It wasn't a treasure map in the traditional sense. It didn't lead to chests of gold or jeweled goblets. It promised something far more valuable. A riddle, scrawled in the Spaniard's spidery hand, spoke of a cenote, a sacred well hidden from the sun, a Fuente de la Vida whose waters could wash away disease and grant a man the vigor of his youth.

A bloody fairy tale. But it was the only one he had.

A sharp rap on the cabin door broke his trance. "Enter," he rasped, his voice dry as sand.

The door creaked open to reveal Silas, his first mate. Silas was a rock, a man whose face was a testament to a life lived at the sharp end of a cutlass. Scars crisscrossed his leathery skin, but the one that mattered now was the deep line of worry etched between his brows. He stepped inside, his presence filling the small cabin, bringing with it the slightly less putrid air from the deck.

"Captain," Silas said, his voice low. He didn't look at Crowe's leg, but they both knew it was the third person in the room. "The men are restless. We've buried three since sunrise. The water barrels are low, the mood is lower. They're talking of mutiny. Not to me, not yet. But the whispers are there."

Crowe pushed himself up, his knuckles white as he gripped the edge of his bunk. A wave of dizziness washed over him, the pain in his leg a searing counterpoint. "Whispers die when men have a purpose, Master Silas. Are the preparations made?"

Silas sighed, a sound of profound weariness. "Aye. A party of ten. Myself included. We have the torches, the water, what little food we can spare. But Gideon..." He took a step closer, his voice dropping further. "This is a fool's errand. A ghost story on a dead man's map. Let us weigh anchor and try for Tortuga. We might lose half the men, but the other half will live."

"To what end?" Crowe shot back, a spark of the old fire in his eyes. "To limp back into port, a crew of broken beggars on a half-rotten ship? To watch me waste away while the rest of you drink yourselves into oblivion? No." He pointed a trembling finger at the map. "That map is our purpose. That map is my salvation. And what saves the captain, saves the ship. Now get out. We make for the jungle at dawn."

Silas held his gaze for a long moment, a silent argument passing between them. Finally, he gave a curt nod. The rock had been worn down by the tide of the captain's will one last time. As the door clicked shut, Crowe fell back onto his sweat-soaked pillow, the effort having cost him dearly. He was steering his crew by the Siren's song of his own hope, and he knew, with a chilling certainty, that they were sailing straight for the rocks.

The jungle journey was worse than any hell he could have imagined. It wasn't a battle of cannon and steel, but a slow, grinding war of attrition against an enemy that never tired. The heat was a physical weight, pressing down, squeezing the air from their lungs. Insects with a taste for human misery swarmed them, leaving welts that swelled into weeping sores. A young cabin boy named Pip was snatched by a crocodile in a murky swamp, his scream cut short with a sickening crunch. Two more men succumbed to fever, their bodies left to the jungle's indifferent embrace.

Crowe drove them onward, a hobbling tyrant fueled by sheer, bloody-minded desperation. He leaned heavily on a driftwood crutch, every step a fresh explosion of agony. The men followed, not out of loyalty anymore, but out of a morbid, fearful curiosity. They wanted to see if their captain's mad quest would lead to a miracle or a grave.

On the seventh day, they found it. A jagged fissure in a rock face, half-hidden by a curtain of thick, green vines. It looked like a wound in the earth. Silas wanted to turn back. The place felt wrong, cursed. But Crowe could feel it—a faint, cool breeze wafting from the darkness, a promise of relief. It smelled of wet stone and clean earth, and something else... something ancient and pure.

"Light the torches," Crowe ordered, his voice barely a whisper.

The descent was a journey into another world. The oppressive heat of the jungle gave way to a subterranean cool. The narrow passage, slick with moisture, opened into a cavern so vast and beautiful it silenced them all. It was a cathedral built by a patient, forgotten god. Stalactites, thicker than a man's waist, hung from the ceiling like glistening, stone chandeliers. The walls shimmered with veins of quartz and other minerals they couldn't name, catching the torchlight and fracturing it into a thousand glittering shards.

And in the center of it all, a pool.

It was perfectly circular, its water so clear it seemed invisible, save for the soft, internal luminescence that pulsed from its depths. It wasn't a reflection of their torches; it was a light all its own, a ghostly turquoise glow that seemed to breathe with a slow, hypnotic rhythm. The men stared, their faces a mixture of fear and awe. This was a place of power. A place where the rules of their world might not apply.

Crowe felt a tremor of something he hadn't felt in years: genuine hope. He let his crutch fall to the stone floor with a clatter. Leaning on Silas, he hobbled to the edge of the pool. He peered into the glowing water and saw his reflection. It was a stranger, a gaunt specter with the haunted eyes of a dying man. This was his last chance.

He knelt, the pain in his leg a final, sharp reminder of his mortality. With a hand that shook, he scooped the living water and brought it to his lips.

It was cool, sweet, and tasted of life itself. A jolt, more powerful than any lightning strike, coursed through him. It wasn't just a drink; it was an unwinding of time. The agony in his leg didn't just vanish, it was annihilated. He felt the fever lift from his mind like a parting fog.

Strength, pure and potent, flooded his limbs. He felt the knotted muscles in his shoulders loosen, the ache in his back from years of hard living simply dissolve.

He pushed himself to his feet. He took a step, then another, his movements sure and strong. He looked at his men, their faces slack with disbelief. A laugh, deep and triumphant, erupted from his chest, the sound echoing through the sacred cavern. He had done it. He, Gideon Crowe, had stared into the abyss and spat in its eye. He had conquered death itself.

The laugh hitched, catching in his throat on a knot of sudden, inexplicable terror.

He looked down.

The black lines of the gangrene were not gone. They were moving. With a horrifying, unnatural speed, they surged from his knee, no longer crawling, but sprinting across his thigh like black lightning on his pale skin. He watched, frozen in a paralysis of ultimate horror, as the dark corruption slithered over his hip, across his stomach, a web of black death consuming his flesh in seconds, the life-giving water acting not as a cure, but as a terrifying catalyst.

The scream that finally tore from Gideon Crowe's throat was not one of victory. It was the sound of a soul realizing, in its final moments, that it has been lured by the most beautiful promise in the world, only to discover it was a curse with a quicker, hungrier appetite than his own.

Chapter 1 : The Idea

The problem with paradise is that it's usually designed for people half your age.

David Bennett came to this profound realization while staring at a margarita glass the size of his head, currently in the possession of a college kid who looked like he'd have trouble growing a respectable mustache. The kid was laughing, a loud, obnoxious bray that echoed across the turquoise water of the resort pool. He was surrounded by a gaggle of equally young, equally tanned, and equally loud friends. They were flawless, drunk, and stupid, radiating the kind of effortless immortality that you only possess when you've never had to seriously consider your own deductible.

Dave, meanwhile, sat under the relative shade of a thatched palapa, trying to discreetly prick his finger. He watched the bead of blood well up, a tiny red pearl of his own mortality, and fed it to the glucose meter he held cupped in his hand. 148. A little high, but not terrible, considering the celebratory beer he'd had an hour ago when they'd finally checked in. Still, it was a number. Another data point in the slow, inexorable decline of the machinery he called a body. At forty-seven, life had become a game of managing numbers: blood sugar, cholesterol, 401(k) contributions, the ever-dwindling balance of his accrued vacation days.

He was a CPA. Numbers were his life, both professionally and personally. He spent ten months of the year wrangling the chaotic finances of small businesses into neat, orderly columns, a job that was equal parts accounting and therapy. He made good money. He had a wife he still loved, two kids who were expensive but mostly wonderful, and a life in the suburbs that was comfortable to the point of being suffocating. Twice a year, he cashed in his vacation days, his good-husband-and-father points, and let his best friend, Skot, drag him to the edge of the world to feel something other than comfortable.

This trip, it was the coast of Colombia. The promise was of adventure: pristine coral reefs, and more importantly, a newly-discovered system of inland, flooded caves that were supposed to be some of the best diving on the planet. The reality, so far, was a sprawling, all-inclusive resort where the greatest danger seemed to be slipping on a spilled piña colada.

"If you stare at that thing any harder, it's going to file a restraining order."

The voice, a familiar baritone blend of sarcasm and bonhomie, belonged to Keith "Buzz" Walker. Buzz didn't walk; he materialized, usually in a cloud of expensive cologne and misplaced confidence. He flopped into the lounge chair next to Dave, his ample frame straining the limits of his hibiscus-print swim trunks. He was already clutching a brightly colored drink, complete with a tiny paper umbrella that looked absurd in his meaty hand.

"It's called managing my health, Buzz," Dave said, zipping the meter back into its case. "A concept you might want to look into before your liver unionizes and goes on strike."

"Nonsense," Buzz declared, taking a loud slurp of his drink. "My liver and I have a perfectly symbiotic relationship. I provide it with premium spirits, and it provides me with the courage to talk to women like that." He gestured with his chin toward a pair of bikini-clad women by the swim-up bar. "Besides, I'm on a strict vacation diet. It consists of anything I can point to on a menu."

Buzz was, and always had been, their glorious, trust-fund-enabled anchor. While Skot and Dave spent their youth figuring out how to make a living, Buzz had been figuring out how to spend the small fortune his grandfather had made in commercial real estate. He was their court jester, their social director, and, more often than not, the guy who paid for the top-shelf tequila. He joined them on these trips not for the adrenaline, but for the amenities. For Buzz, adventure was something you watched from the comfort of a hotel bar while flirting with the waitress. His only social media was a carefully curated feed of parties, exotic locations, and selfies with a rotating cast of beautiful, temporary women. He was Peter Pan, if Peter Pan had a dad who left him a portfolio of dividend stocks.

"So, what's the plan, Davey?" Buzz asked, adjusting his sunglasses. "You and Captain Ahab gonna go poke a shark tomorrow? Or is it something more exciting, like competitive napping?"

"Cave diving," a new voice said.

Skot Larson approached their little encampment, his stride easy and athletic. Even at forty-nine, Skot still looked like he was carved out of wood and wire. He had a wiry strength, a full head of unruly brown hair that was just starting to show threads of silver at the temples, and an artist's restless energy. He was carrying a mesh bag filled with regulators and dive computers that he'd just finished rinsing in the gear-washing station. For Skot, the resort was just a base camp. The real destination was always somewhere wild and untamed.

"Ah, of course," Buzz said, not bothering to sit up. "Confined spaces, underwater, with a limited air supply. Sounds delightful. You two have fun with that. I'll be here, beta-testing the structural integrity of this lounge chair."

Skot grinned and dropped the bag next to his chair. "You don't know what you're missing, Buzz. They say it's like flying through another world down there. We've got the permits, a great map of the system. It's gonna be epic."

Skot was a freelance graphic designer, a career choice that perfectly suited his temperament. He was a dreamer, a man with a thousand brilliant ideas and a bank account that perpetually hovered just above zero. He was the kind of guy who took the "C" out of his name just to be different and unique. He chased experiences, not paychecks. It was Skot who had convinced Dave to try dirt biking in Moab, surfing in Costa Rica, and that one terrifying, ill-advised motorcycle trip through the mountains of Vietnam. Dave was the brakes, Skot was the accelerator, and Buzz was the guy in the back seat asking if they were there yet.

"I know exactly what I'm missing," Buzz countered. "Panic. And mud. I'm pretty sure I saw a documentary where a guy got stuck in one of those things. No thank you. The only tight squeeze I'm interested in is at the tequila bar during happy hour."

Dave watched the easy banter, a ritual honed over three decades of friendship. This was the rhythm of their trips. Skot would propose the insane, Buzz would mock it, and Dave would reluctantly agree, caught somewhere between his fear of dying and his deeper fear of not having truly lived. Lately, the first fear was starting to gain a bit more ground. His body just didn't bounce back the way it used to. The Harley he and Skot rode back home was starting to feel heavy. His knees ached after a long run. The numbers on his glucose meter were a constant, nagging reminder that his warranty was running out.

"We'll be careful," Dave said, as much to himself as to Buzz. "Don't forget, Skot mastered the art of diving in the murky waters of water hazards of more golf courses than I can count. Made a pretty penny off those golf balls, too. He knows what he's doing."

"Damn right I do," Skot said, pulling a dive computer from the bag. He fiddled with the settings, his face lighting up with genuine excitement. "I've been reading the dive reports for this system for months. They call the main chamber 'The Cathedral.' Divers who've been there say it's life-changing."

Life-changing. The phrase hung in the air. Dave thought about his life. It was a good life. A safe life. But was it a life that had been changed recently? Or had it just been... managed? He looked from Skot's face, alive with the promise of adventure, to Buzz, who was already trying to catch the eye of a passing cocktail waitress, and felt a familiar pang. He was the man in the middle, the fulcrum on which their strange, three-way friendship balanced.

Later that evening, after a mediocre steak dinner that cost more than their rental car, Skot and Dave were back in their shared room, the floor covered with the guts of their adventure. Air tanks lined the wall like miniature bombs. Wetsuits hung in the bathroom, dripping onto a pile of towels. The air smelled of neoprene and salt. Buzz had, predictably, disappeared in the direction of the resort's nightclub, a place he'd referred to as his "command center."

Skot was meticulously checking the O-rings on his regulator, holding it up to the light. "You seem quiet," he said, not looking at Dave.

"Just tired," Dave lied. "Long flight."

"You're thinking about the dive," Skot stated. It wasn't a question.

Dave sighed and sat on the edge of his bed. "It's just… deep, man. And enclosed. We've done reef dives, a couple of shallow wrecks. This is different. It's more risky than Palm Point Country Club… even with the gators."

Skot finally looked up, his expression softening. "Hey. We've got a solid plan. We lay the guideline. We watch our air. We stick to the turn pressures, no exceptions. We've done a hundred gear checks. I would never take you anywhere I thought we couldn't handle. You know that."

"I know." And he did. In all their years of thrill-seeking, Skot had never been reckless. He was meticulous in his planning, a side of his artistic brain that most people never saw. He respected the danger, which is what made him a good partner.

"It's not just that," Dave admitted, looking at his own hands. They were hands that spent most of their time on a keyboard, soft and pale. "It's… I don't know. Getting old, I guess. Everything just feels like more of a risk."

Skot put down the regulator and came over, clapping him on the shoulder. "That's why we do this, man. To prove we've still got it. To push back. Look, we'll do the first dive tomorrow. We'll stick to the main chamber, keep it simple. If you don't like it, we scrap the rest of the cave dives and spend the week drinking cocktails on a catamaran. No harm, no foul."

Dave nodded, a genuine smile finally reaching his face. "Okay. Deal."

"Good." Skot grinned. "Now help me check this inflator hose. I'd rather not find out it has a leak when we're a hundred feet down."

As they worked, their hands moving with practiced familiarity, Dave felt some of the anxiety recede, replaced by the quiet hum of anticipation. This was the part he loved, the ritual. The calm before the storm. The quiet focus of two old friends preparing to step off the edge of the map together, one last time. Or the time after that. As many times as they had left.

He just hoped the numbers would be on their side.

Chapter 2: The Cathedral

The rental jeep was a rattling metal box of misery. It had no air conditioning, a suspicion of a suspension, and a smell that suggested a small, damp animal had recently used the glove compartment as its final resting place. Every rut and pothole on the jungle road—which was less a road and more a theoretical path someone had once carved with a machete—sent a jarring shockwave through the vehicle. It was perfect.

For Skot, the bone-jarring ride was a sign of authenticity. They had left the pampered world of the resort behind and were now entering his territory: the frontier. He gripped the steering wheel, a wide, boyish grin on his face as he navigated a particularly nasty stretch of mud. "See? This is what it's all about! Earning it!"

Dave, riding shotgun, just grunted and tightened his grip on the door handle. Earning it, for him, felt suspiciously like acquiring a mild concussion. He'd already popped two ibuprofen, and the day's adventure hadn't even truly begun. In the back, their scuba gear, carefully packed in crates, clanged and shifted with every lurch, a metallic chorus of impending doom.

"I'm earning a bruised kidney," Dave muttered, wiping a sheen of sweat from his brow with the back of his hand. The air was a humid blanket, thick with the smell of damp earth and blooming things he couldn't name. "I didn't think I would ever say this, but this ride is worse than that yellow VW bug you drove in college.

So remind me again why we couldn't just find a nice, accessible reef like normal people?"

"Because normal people don't get to see The Cathedral," Skot said, his eyes bright with the fervor of a true believer. "Buzz doesn't get to tell stories about this. The kid with the head-sized margarita doesn't get this. This one's just for us."

That, Dave had to admit, was a compelling argument. The idea of having something that belonged only to them, an experience untainted by tourism and Instagram filters, was a powerful lure. It was the core of their decades-long pact against the mundane.

After another hour of punishment, Skot pulled the jeep into a small, overgrown clearing. He killed the engine, and the sudden silence was deafening, broken only by the chittering of unseen insects and the distant cry of a tropical bird. This was it. The entrance to the underworld.

It wasn't a gaping maw or a dramatic chasm. It was a simple, unassuming pool of startlingly clear water at the base of a limestone cliff, no bigger than a backyard swimming pool. It was fed by a small, trickling waterfall that cascaded down the moss-covered rocks, creating a serene, almost sacred atmosphere. It was beautiful, and Dave's anxiety eased a fraction.

They worked with the practiced efficiency of a team that had done this a hundred times before. They hauled the heavy tanks from the jeep, assembled their regulators, and wriggled into the tight embrace of their neoprene wetsuits. The pre-dive ritual was a comfort to Dave, a checklist of familiar tasks that grounded him in the technical, knowable aspects of what they were about to do. They checked each other's gear, the hiss of tested regulators a reassuring sound. Skot went over the dive plan one last time, his finger tracing a line on the laminated map.

"We descend here," he said, pointing to the center of the pool. "The passage opens up quickly. We'll follow the main line down to about ninety feet. That's where we'll hit the entrance to The Cathedral. We do one slow, easy circuit, keeping the guideline in sight at all times, and then we head back. Air is turn-around point. If either of us hits eighteen-hundred PSI, the dive is over. No arguments. Got it?"

"Got it," Dave confirmed, his mouth suddenly dry.

Strapping on the heavy tank and buoyancy compensator, Dave felt the familiar transformation from clumsy land mammal to awkward, lumbering beast. He waddled to the edge of the pool, Skot right behind him. They sat for a moment, fins dangling in the cool water.

"Ready to go to church?" Skot asked, a grin flashing behind his regulator.

Dave gave him a thumbs-up, took a final breath of the hot, sticky jungle air, and pushed himself forward, tumbling into the silent, weightless world below.

The shock of the cool water was a welcome relief. All the weight, all the sweat and anxiety of the surface world, vanished in an instant. There was only the gentle pressure of the water and the rhythmic, meditative sound of his own breathing, a slow, steady inhale… exhale… that was the soundtrack to this alien planet. He followed Skot's fins down into the blue, equalizing the pressure in his ears with practiced ease.

The small surface pool was a lie. Ten feet down, the world exploded. The bottom dropped away into a vast, sun-dappled cavern. Beams of sunlight pierced the surface, creating shimmering, ethereal curtains of light that danced in the water, illuminating the rock formations in breathtaking detail. It was like flying through a liquid sky. Dave felt the last of his apprehension melt away, replaced by a profound sense of awe. Skot was right. This was magic.

They followed the thick, white nylon guideline deeper, their powerful dive lights cutting sharp cones through the deepening blue. The sunlight faded, and they were in a world of their own making, a bubble of light moving through an infinite, silent darkness. They were explorers on a new frontier.

At ninety-four feet, they saw it. The guideline led to a wide, perfectly arched opening in the rock. It was a doorway. Skot paused, turned to Dave, and made a grand, sweeping gesture with his hand, like a master of ceremonies presenting the main event.

They swam through the archway, and Dave's breath caught in his chest, a bubble of pure wonder escaping his regulator.

Cathedral was the only word for it. They had entered a chamber so immense it seemed impossible. The beams of their lights couldn't find the walls or the ceiling. It was like floating in the center of a hollowed-out mountain. And everywhere, suspended in the blackness, were colossal, ghostly white formations of limestone. Stalactites, thicker than ancient trees, hung from the unseen ceiling above. Stalagmites rose from the depths below like the spires of a submerged city. Some met in the middle, forming massive, fluted columns that soared through the void. It was a silent, magnificent, and deeply humbling place.

For twenty minutes, they flew. They drifted through this majestic, sleeping world, their movements slow and deliberate. They were insignificant specks in the face of its geological grandeur. Dave felt a sense of peace he hadn't felt in years. The numbers, the worries, the endless management of his life on the surface—it all seemed petty and meaningless here. This was real. This was eternal.

It was on their return circuit, as they neared the archway back to the main passage, that the world ended.

It started not as a sound, but as a feeling. A deep, resonant vibration that pulsed through the water and into Dave's bones. It was a low, guttural thrum, like a giant tuning fork had been struck somewhere deep in the earth. He saw Skot stop ahead of him, turning, his posture instantly changing from relaxed awe to rigid alarm.

Then came the sound. A horrifying, grinding roar that seemed to come from everywhere at once. The water around them shimmered and shook. Dave saw a cloud of silt bloom from the ceiling above the archway. Small pebbles and chunks of rock began to rain down around them, tumbling slowly through the water.

Skot frantically signaled to him—GO! GO NOW!

They kicked hard, swimming for the exit with a sudden, desperate burst of adrenaline. But it was too late. With a final, deafening CRACK that vibrated through Dave's entire ribcage, a huge section of the ceiling directly above the archway gave way. A slab of rock the size of a minivan sheared off and plunged downwards, triggering a catastrophic chain reaction. The archway, their only way home, imploded.

An avalanche of rock and silt cascaded down, a thunderous, rolling cloud of destruction. The pressure wave hit Dave to his bones, sending him tumbling head over heels into the blackness. His dive light was ripped from his hand, and he was plunged into absolute, terrifying darkness. He didn't know which way was up, down, or sideways. Silt filled the water, thick and choking. He couldn't see his own hand in front of his face. He could only hear the roar of the collapsing rock and the frantic, panicked rasp of his own breathing.

This is it. This is how I die. The thought was cold and clear in his mind.

He slammed into something hard—a column—and the impact knocked the wind out of him. He clung to it, trying to fight the vertigo, trying to slow his breathing, trying to get his brain to work. Don't panic. Panic uses air. Don't panic.

The roaring subsided, replaced by an eerie silence, punctuated by the occasional trickle of falling sand. The once-clear turquoise water was now a thick, brown soup. Visibility was zero. He was blind, alone, and trapped a hundred feet beneath the earth.

A light. Faint, diffuse, but there. He turned his head and saw a blurry, wavering glow through the soupy water. It moved, bobbed, and then grew stronger as it approached. Skot. He'd held onto his light. Relief, so powerful it was nauseating, washed over Dave. He wasn't alone.

Skot grabbed his arm, his grip like iron. He pulled Dave close until their helmets almost touched. Dave could see his friend's eyes behind his mask, wide with fear but also burning with fierce determination. Skot pointed his light at their pressure gauges. Dave's read 1600 PSI. Skot's was even lower. They had maybe twenty minutes of air, tops.

Skot pointed his light at the wall of rubble where the exit used to be. A solid, impenetrable mass of rock and silt. Then he shook his head. No way out.

For a moment, Dave felt the black terror threaten to swallow him. But then Skot did something else. He pointed his light away from the collapse, toward a small, dark crack in the wall of The Cathedral they hadn't noticed before, a fissure barely wide enough for a man to fit through. He looked at Dave, and through the frantic bubbles of his own breathing, Dave understood the question.

Do we die here, or do we take the one-in-a-million chance?

Dave nodded.

What followed was ten minutes of pure, claustrophobic hell. Skot went first, pushing his tank ahead of him to squeeze through the tightest spots. Dave followed, trying not to think about the millions of tons of rock above them. The passage was a tight, winding tube, scraping their tanks and tearing at their wetsuits. They were swimming on borrowed time, every breath a precious, finite resource.

Just when Dave was sure they were just swimming deeper into their own tomb, he saw Skot stop ahead. He saw the beam of his light spill out into a larger space. They had found something. He kicked his way out of the narrow tube and into a new chamber.

It was small, no bigger than a large living room. But it was different. The water here had a strange, shimmering quality. And as their lights played across the ceiling, they saw it wasn't a ceiling at all. It was a surface. An air pocket.

With the last of their strength, they kicked for it, hope surging through them. They broke the surface, sputtering and gasping, ripping the regulators from their mouths. They were alive. They could breathe. The air was cool and clean, with no trace of the jungle's humidity or the cave's mustiness.

They floated in the center of the grotto, their exhausted bodies treading water, their minds reeling. The source of the strange light wasn't their torches. It was the water itself. From the depths of the small pool, a soft, ethereal turquoise light pulsed, illuminating the entire cavern. It was the color of life, the color of magic.

Their tanks were nearly empty. They were exhausted, dehydrated, and trembling with adrenaline. They kicked over to a shallow ledge and dragged themselves out of the water, their bodies feeling impossibly heavy. They lay on the smooth stone, panting like beached whales.

"We're alive," Dave croaked, the words tasting strange in his mouth.

"Yeah," Skot breathed, staring at the glowing water. "But where the hell are we?"

The water was their only option. Their canteens were back in the jeep, in another lifetime. Skot, ever the leader, went first. He knelt at the edge of the pool, scooped the glowing liquid in his hands, and drank deeply. Dave watched him, his heart pounding.

Skot's eyes went wide. "Dave..." he whispered, his voice filled with a strange wonder. "You have to try this."

Wary but desperate, Dave crawled to the edge. He drank.

It wasn't just water. It was like drinking pure energy. A cool, clean vitality spread through his body, erasing his exhaustion in an instant. The ache in his back, a constant companion for the last ten years, simply vanished. The throbbing in his knee from an old motorcycle accident disappeared. He felt... clean. He felt a clarity in his mind that he hadn't experienced since he was a teenager.

He looked at his hands, then at Skot. He felt a surge of strength, of wellness, so profound and instantaneous it was terrifying. It wasn't just a drink. It was a reset. A miracle.

They were trapped, lost, and soon could be presumed dead. And they had just stumbled upon the biggest secret in human history. The Siren had sung her song, and they had just taken the first, intoxicating sip of her curse.

Chapter 3: Command Center Ops

The key to a successful vacation, Keith "Buzz" Walker had long ago decided, was establishing a solid base of operations. A command center. For soldiers, this might be a fortified bunker. For spies, a safe house. For Buzz, it was a specific, strategically chosen stool at the swim-up bar of a five-star resort, preferably one with a clear sightline to the sunbathing area and a bartender who understood that "the usual" was a standing order, not a suggestion. The stool had to be perfect—close enough to the action to hold court, but just far enough away to create an air of exclusive, magnetic detachment. It was a science.

Today, operations were proceeding beautifully.

The Colombian sun was a warm, liquid gold, the water was a perfect, crystalline blue that smelled faintly of chlorine and expensive coconut sunscreen, and the two young women to his left were laughing at his jokes. Success. He'd already nicknamed them "Sunshine" and "Moonbeam" in his head, a private joke based on their Californian auras, and they seemed to be enjoying the attention. They were his audience, his focus group, the vital human element in his carefully curated tableau of relaxation.

"And so I told the guy," Buzz said, leaning in conspiratorially, his voice a low, rumbling monologue that was just loud enough to be heard over the salsa music pulsating from the speakers. "I said, 'Look, a yacht is not an investment. An investment is a thing that makes you money. This is a hole in the water you throw money into.

It's a beautiful, majestic, fiberglass hole, but it's a hole. But if you're gonna have a hole,' I told him, 'it might as well be a big, sexy one with a hot tub and a guy named Jean-Pierre who can make a killer martini.' He bought it the next day. A beautiful thing. A beautiful, beautiful thing."

Sunshine, the blonde one, giggled and playfully splashed him. "Oh my god, Buzz, you're terrible."

"I'm a facilitator of joy," Buzz corrected her, raising his glass in a toast. "A cruise director for the human spirit. I see a problem, like a distinct lack of fun, and I solve it. It's a gift. A terrible, wonderful gift." He took a long, slow sip of his drink, a perfectly crafted concoction of rum, pineapple, and something blue that the bartender called a "Blue Macaw." He savored the synthetic, sugary taste. It was the flavor of a problem-free existence. He was in the zone.

Moonbeam, the brunette, swirled the ice in her glass. "So, these friends of yours you were telling us about," she said. "They're really, like, in a cave right now? As we speak?"

"An underwater cave," Buzz clarified, a theatrical shudder running through his ample frame. "It's madness. Beautiful, beautiful madness. I'm over here trying to achieve maximum relaxation, a state of pure, blissful nothing, and those two knuckleheads are actively trying to get claustrophobia. They left at the crack of dawn, all excited, talking about 'laying guidelines' and 'turn pressures.' Sounds like a corporate retreat, if you ask me. A very wet, very dark corporate retreat with a much higher chance of drowning."

"Why do they do it?" Sunshine asked, her brow furrowed with genuine confusion.

"Because they're crazy," Buzz said with a grin, gesturing for the bartender. "They're chasing something. Adrenaline, youth, I don't know. They think it keeps them young. They think that staring death in the face and giving it the old finger-wag is the key to vitality. Me? I think a steady diet of premium tequila and good company is the real fountain of youth. It's a philosophical difference, you see. They want to conquer nature. I want to build a very comfortable, very well-stocked fort in the middle of it and let nature do its own thing."

He launched into a series of embellished stories about their past adventures, casting himself as the witty, sophisticated voice of reason and his friends as lovable, thrill-seeking maniacs. He told them about the time Skot tried to rig a sail to a dirt bike in Moab ("A total disaster, a beautiful disaster! He had this whole theory about wind power and torque, it was very scientific. Ended with him in a cactus and the bike looking like a piece of modern art."). Then he moved on to the legendary raccoon story.

"So there's Dave," he began, leaning in, painting the picture. "The numbers guy. The man has a spreadsheet for everything—his retirement, his cholesterol, the optimal walking speed to the mailbox. He's meticulously calculated the precise caloric intake required for a three-day hike, right down to the last almond. He's got it all in this high-tech, bear-proof canister. First night, he ties it up in a tree, just like the book says. But he didn't account for the variable. The chaos factor. The raccoons. These weren't your friendly, neighborhood trash pandas, these were like a little SWAT team. They worked in formation. It was incredible. They got the canister down, and I swear I saw one of them using the spreadsheet as a napkin. So there's Dave, with nothing but a bag of granola and his principles, trying to reason with them…"

It was in the middle of this particularly good story that his phone buzzed. It was in its waterproof pouch, a high-tech amulet around his neck. He glanced at it. A text from his sister, Sarah.

"Have you heard from Skot or Dave? Jen just called me, a little worried. Said she hasn't heard from Dave all day, which is weird for him."

Buzz rolled his eyes. He felt a flicker of annoyance, a tiny pinprick in the perfect, hermetically sealed bubble of his afternoon. Worry was the opposite of vacation. It was an invasive species. He had a duty, a sacred duty, to protect his own state of bliss.

"Ah, a dispatch from the mainland," he announced to the girls, holding his phone up. "The committee on worrying is holding an emergency session, it seems. They're worried. Of course, they're worried. It's their job. Me? My job is to make sure you lovely ladies don't go a single second without a premium cocktail. It's a question of priorities, you see. You have to triage the fun."

He typed back a casual reply, his thumbs moving quickly across the screen.

"Relax. They're fine. They're in a cave in the middle of nowhere. No cell service. You know how they get. Tell Jen not to worry. I'm on the ground, running point. The situation is under control."

He hit send and immediately dismissed the thought, a practiced mental maneuver. The "situation" was that he was three Blue Macaws deep and considering a strategic shift to margaritas. His friends were fine. They were always fine. They'd roll in later that afternoon, smelling of sweat and self-satisfaction, and he'd have to listen to a thirty-minute monologue about some stupid fish they saw. The horror.

He turned his attention back to the girls. "Now, where was I? Ah, yes. The lead raccoon. Let's call him 'Bandit Prime.' He looks Dave right in the eye, holding a single almond…"

The evening bled from gold to purple. Buzz kept the drinks flowing. He convinced Tiffany and Brooke (he'd finally gotten their names straight) to move the command center from the pool to the resort's high-end steakhouse. He booked them a prime table on the terrace overlooking the ocean, ordering a bottle of champagne that cost more than Dave's monthly car payment. He loved the little gasp the girls made when the sommelier presented the bottle. It was all part of the performance, the curation of a perfect, enviable experience.

He was in his element, the lord of his manor. He checked his phone again, just to clear the notifications. Nothing new from the worry committee. He swiped over to his own social media, admiring a selfie he'd posted an hour ago of just himself at the swim-up bar, a triumphant grin on his face. The caption was perfect: "Holding down the fort while the cats are away. It's a tough job, but somebody's gotta do it. #ToughLife #Colombia #SoloMission" The likes were rolling in. The brand was strong. His life was a carefully edited highlight reel, and this was prime content.

"Everything okay?" Brooke asked, her brow furrowed with what looked like genuine concern as she saw him looking at his phone.

Buzz flashed his most charming, carefree smile, a masterpiece of practiced nonchalance. "Never better," he said, raising the champagne bottle to refill her glass. "Just checking the market. And the market for fun is at an all-time high." He topped off his own glass. "The night is young, the company is exquisite, and tomorrow is someone else's problem."

He truly believed it. As he clinked his glass against theirs, the sound a cheerful, crystalline chime against the gentle roar of the ocean, he had no way of knowing that tomorrow was already here. And it was a problem that was going to be bigger, darker, and more terrifying than his money or his motor-mouth could ever solve. His friends were a hundred feet underground, fighting for their lives, and the party was just getting started.

Chapter 4: Body and Stone

For a long time, neither of them spoke. The only sounds in the grotto were the gentle lapping of the glowing water and the ragged, unsteady rhythm of their own breathing. They lay on the smooth stone ledge, two men who should have been dead, their bodies thrumming with an impossible, terrifying energy. The soft, turquoise light of the pool painted shifting patterns on the cavern ceiling above, a silent, beautiful light show for an audience of two.

It was Dave who finally broke the silence, his voice a hoarse whisper. "I don't have a headache."

Skot turned his head, his face illuminated by the eerie blue-green glow. "What?"

"The jeep," Dave clarified, sitting up slowly. He ran a hand through his wet, thinning hair. "The ride out here. I had a monster of a headache starting. It's gone." He paused, doing a mental inventory. "My back doesn't hurt. My knee... Skot, my knee feels... normal." He bent his right knee, the one that had been a source of grinding, chronic pain since a motorcycle spill five years ago. He bent it again, this time putting weight on it. Nothing. Not a twinge. The ghost of an ache that had lived with him for half a decade had been evicted.

"My shoulder," Skot said, his voice full of awe. He rotated his left arm in a full circle, a motion that would have sent a bolt of fire down his arm just an hour ago, the legacy of a dislocated shoulder from a long-ago climbing fall. "It's... perfect."

They stared at each other, their faces a mixture of wonder and disbelief. This was impossible. It had to be a trick of the mind, a shared hallucination brought on by a lack of oxygen and the trauma of the cave-in. Adrenaline could do strange things, dull the pain, create a false sense of well-being. That had to be it.

Dave, the man of numbers and logic, needed proof. He needed a data point that wasn't subjective, that wasn't based on feelings. He unzipped a small waterproof pouch on his belt, his hands moving with trembling purpose. He pulled out the familiar black case of his glucose meter.

"What are you doing?" Skot asked, watching him.

"I'm checking the facts," Dave said, his voice tight. He pulled out a test strip, inserted it into the meter, and reached for the lancing device. He pricked his finger, the tiny, familiar sting a small anchor to reality in this sea of madness. He squeezed a bead of blood onto the strip and held his breath, waiting for the meter to count down. Five... four... three... two... one.

The number that flashed on the small screen made his blood run cold.

92.

It wasn't just a good number. It was a perfect number. The kind of number a healthy twenty-year-old would have after a balanced meal and a light jog. It was a number Dave hadn't seen on his own meter, not without a week of brutal dieting and a cocktail of medications, in fifteen years. Before dinner at the resort, after one beer, he'd been at 148. Now, after the most stressful, physically demanding ordeal of his life—a situation that should have sent his blood sugar skyrocketing—it was 92.

He stared at the number, his mind refusing to process it. He checked it again. It was real. This wasn't adrenaline. Adrenaline didn't rewrite your body's metabolic code.

"Skot," he said, his voice barely audible. He held out the meter.

Skot crawled over and looked at the number. He didn't understand the specifics of Dave's condition, not really, but he understood the look on his friend's face. It was the look of a man whose entire understanding of the world had just been shattered.

"Is that… good?" Skot asked gently.

"It's impossible," Dave breathed. "It's a miracle. Or something else."

They sat in silence again, the impossible number hanging in the air between them. The initial shock began to wear off, replaced by the slow, creeping tendrils of a far more practical and terrifying reality. Dave looked around the cavern. It was beautiful, yes. The glowing water was magical. But it was also a cage. A beautiful, magical cage carved out of solid stone.

"So, what now?" Dave asked, the pragmatist in him finally wrestling back control from the awe-struck child. "We feel great. Fantastic, even. But we're still trapped a hundred feet underground with no food, no way to communicate, and about ten minutes of air left in those tanks."

The weight of their situation settled back over them, heavier this time because of the cruel irony. They had been given a gift of impossible vitality in a place where it was utterly useless. It was like being handed the keys to a brand-new Ferrari at the bottom of the ocean.

Skot, ever the optimist, was already in motion. He stood up, his body moving with a newfound grace and power. "We explore," he said, his voice firm. "This grotto is here. The air is fresh. There has to be another way in or out. Water got in here, air got in here. We just have to find out how."

He was right. Sitting here and marveling at their own wellness was a death sentence. Action was their only hope. They took stock of their gear. They had two dive lights, one of which was Skot's powerful primary torch. They had their dive knives, their masks, and fins. Their tanks and regulators were now just dead weight.

"Okay," Skot said, thinking out loud, his designer's mind mapping the space. "The cave-in is behind us, through that tight passage. That's a dead end. So, the exit has to be in this room."

The grotto was roughly circular. The walls were smooth, worn by eons of water, offering no obvious handholds or passages. The only feature was the pool itself. It took up most of the floor of the cavern, a deep, glowing heart.

"The water," Dave said, realization dawning. "It's the only way. If there's another way out, it has to be through the pool."

They slipped their masks on and submerged their faces, peering into the glowing depths. The turquoise light seemed to emanate from the very center of the pool, which looked to be about forty feet deep. The source of the light was obscured, a pulsating, bright spot in the center of the floor. And leading away from the bottom, on the opposite side from where they had entered, was a dark, uninviting hole. A tunnel.

It was their only chance.

"No way," Dave said, pulling his head out of the water. "Skot, we can't. We have no idea where that goes, how long it is, or if it even leads anywhere. We can't just free-dive into an unknown, underwater tunnel. That's suicide."

"What's the alternative, Dave?" Skot shot back, his voice echoing in the chamber. "Sit here and wait? We drink the magic water until we starve to death? I don't know about you, but I feel stronger than I have in twenty years. If there was ever a time to bet on ourselves, it's now."

Dave looked at his friend. Skot was right, and he hated him for it. His own pragmatic brain, the one that calculated risks and advised caution, was screaming at him that this was insane. But the new, vital energy coursing through his veins was whispering something else. It was whispering that maybe, just maybe, they could do it.

"We'd have to hold our breath," Dave said, thinking through the logistics. "We have no idea how long the tunnel is."

"So we test it," Skot said, his mind already three steps ahead. "We use the guideline from your reel. We tie it off here. One of us goes in, as far as he can on one breath, unreeling the line. Then he comes back. We see how far he got. We see what it's like. We make a plan based on actual data." He even used Dave's language. Data. The bastard was good.

The plan was terrifying. But it was a plan. And a plan, any plan, was better than sitting here waiting for the end.

"Okay," Dave said, his heart pounding a hard, steady rhythm in his chest. "Okay. Let's do it."

They spent the next hour preparing. They stripped off their heavy tank assemblies, leaving them on the ledge. They would be faster, more agile, without them. They secured their knives and lights. Dave took the small, plastic reel of guideline—a piece of emergency gear they'd almost never used—and tied the end securely around a knob of rock on the ledge. He handed the reel to Skot.

"I'll go first," Skot said. It wasn't a question.

"No," Dave said, surprising himself. "I will."

Skot looked at him, confused. "Dave, I'm the stronger swimmer, the more experienced diver…"

"And you're the guy with the ideas," Dave interrupted. "You're the one who's going to get us out of here. I'm the guy who follows the plan. Let me be the yardstick. I'll go as far as I can. You time me. You see how far the line goes out. Then the smart guy can figure out what to do with that information. It makes sense."

Skot studied his friend's face for a long moment. He saw the fear there, but he also saw a new kind of resolve, a steely determination he hadn't seen in Dave for years. This wasn't the cautious CPA. This was the man who had ridden beside him through the mountains of Vietnam, the man who had faced down his fears time and time again.

The water hadn't just healed his body; it had reminded him of who he was.

"Alright," Skot said, clapping him on the shoulder. "Be careful. The second you feel like you need to turn back, you turn back. Don't be a hero."

"Wouldn't dream of it," Dave lied.

He stood at the edge of the glowing pool, the reel in his hand. He put on his mask and took a series of long, slow, deep breaths, hyper-oxygenating his system, just like they'd taught him in his first scuba class. The air felt cool and clean in his revitalized lungs. He looked at Skot, who gave him a sharp, encouraging nod.

Dave gave a final exhale, then drew in one last, massive breath, filling his lungs until they burned. He put the reel in his mouth to hold it, grabbed the light, and plunged headfirst into the silent, glowing world, kicking hard for the dark, waiting hole at the bottom. The line began to unspool behind him, a thin, white thread leading back to his only friend in the world. He was a human probe, diving blind into the heart of the earth, his body and his will the only things he had left.

Chapter 5: The Long Breath

The world dissolved into a silent, blue-black tunnel. The moment Dave plunged into the dark opening at the bottom of the grotto, he left the realm of the known. The soft, turquoise glow of the spring vanished behind him, swallowed by the oppressive darkness. His universe shrank to the size of the beam cast by his dive light, a frantic, probing cone of white in an infinity of black.

His body, however, was a revelation. He kicked with a strength and efficiency that felt alien. His lungs, which should have already been starting to burn with the need for air, felt calm and capacious. The water, which should have felt cold and menacing, felt slick and energizing against his skin. He was a torpedo, a human arrow fired into the heart of the earth. The thin, white guideline unspooled from the reel in his mouth, his only connection to the single point of safety in the entire world.

The tunnel was narrow, a rough-hewn tube of rock that seemed to have been bored out by some ancient, subterranean river. The walls were smooth in some places, jagged in others, covered in a thin layer of dark, velvety silt that puffed up into clouds as he passed. He kept one hand out in front of him, fending off the rock, his knuckles grazing the coarse texture. He forced himself to stay calm, to focus on the task. Kick, glide, breathe. No, don't breathe. Just kick, glide, stay calm.

His analytical mind took over, a defense mechanism against the primal terror that was trying to claw its way up his throat. He started counting his kick cycles. One, two, three, four… It was a way to measure distance, a way to impose order on the chaos. He estimated he was moving at about two feet per second. At ten kick cycles, he'd gone about forty feet. His lungs still felt fine. It was an unnerving, unnatural feeling. He should be hurting by now. The absence of pain was almost as scary as the darkness.

Twenty kick cycles. Eighty feet. The tunnel remained straight, a relentless, dark corridor. He scanned for any side passages, any openings, but there were none. This was a one-way street. The question was, to where? He resisted the urge to look back. Looking back was pointless. The grotto was behind him; safety, if it existed, was somewhere ahead.

Thirty kick cycles. One hundred and twenty feet. Now he felt it. The first, gentle squeeze in his chest. The first whisper from the primitive part of his brain, the part that didn't care about plans or data, the part that only cared about air. Air. Now. He ignored it. He had more in him. The water had given him more. He had to trust it. He had to trust the miracle.

He pushed onward, the guideline now a steady, reassuring weight against his lips. It was his anchor. As long as the line was there, he wasn't lost. He was just… remote.

It was at forty-five kick cycles—maybe one hundred and eighty feet into the black—that he felt something new. It wasn't something he saw; it was something he felt against his entire body. A current. It was subtle, a gentle but persistent pressure pushing against his face and chest.

The water wasn't stagnant. It was flowing, moving from whatever was ahead to the grotto behind him.

His heart hammered in his chest, a wild drumbeat against the silence. A current meant a source. It meant this tunnel wasn't a dead-end pocket; it was a conduit. It connected their little grotto to a larger body of water. A lake? The ocean? It didn't matter. Any large body of water was better than the stone-walled tomb they were in.

The squeeze in his chest was an insistent fist now. The calm was gone, replaced by a frantic, buzzing urgency. The whispers for air had become a roar. His diaphragm spasmed, an involuntary, painful contraction. This was his body's final warning. The point of no return.

He had to get a little farther. He needed more data for Skot.

He kicked another ten times, his movements now fueled by a desperate, adrenaline-laced surge of will. The current was slightly stronger here. And then he saw it. Or rather, he saw the absence of it. The beam of his dive light, which had been reflecting off the tunnel walls, suddenly seemed to get swallowed by the space ahead. The tunnel was opening up. He was coming out into something bigger.

His lungs were on fire. Black spots danced at the edges of his vision. This was it. The absolute limit.

He stopped, planting his fins against the floor of the tunnel. He let go of the reel, letting it float on the end of its tether, and fumbled for the dive knife strapped to his calf. His fingers felt thick and clumsy. He pulled out the knife and, fighting the pressure in his chest, jammed it into a crack in the rock floor, creating a physical marker at the end of his journey. He gave the guideline a sharp tug, three times, the signal he and Skot had agreed upon: I've reached my limit and I'm coming back.

Then he turned and swam for his life.

The journey back was a blurry, heart-pounding nightmare. He reeled the line in with a frantic energy, his arms burning with the effort. The fear was a physical thing now, a coppery taste in his mouth. The tunnel, which had seemed merely oppressive on the way in, now felt like a throat, actively trying to choke him, to hold him back. Every foot felt like a mile. His vision narrowed until it was just the thin, white line in front of him, his only path back to life.

Just when he thought his lungs would rupture, he saw it. A faint, beautiful, turquoise glow ahead. The grotto. The sight was so beautiful it almost made him weep. He kicked with the last, explosive vestiges of his strength, rocketing out of the tunnel mouth and toward the shimmering surface.

He broke through into the air with a savage, desperate gasp, a sound that was half-sob, half-roar. He ripped the mask from his face and took in huge, shuddering gulps of the cool, clean air. It was the best thing he had ever tasted. He felt Skot's hands grab him, pulling him toward the ledge.

"Dave! You okay? Talk to me!" Skot's voice was tight with worry.

Dave couldn't talk. He just lay on his side on the smooth stone, his body trembling, and drank in the air, glorious air. After a full minute, he managed to sit up.

"I'm okay," he rasped, his throat raw. "I'm okay."

He looked at Skot, who was holding the reel. "Your knife is gone," Skot said.

"I left it," Dave said, his breathing starting to even out. "I marked the end of the line."

Skot's eyes went wide. "You made it to the end of the reel?"

"No, not even close." Dave looked at the reel in Skot's hands. A significant amount of the thin white line was still spooled around it. "How much line is that?"

Skot squinted at the reel. "This is a three-hundred-foot reel. I'd say... you maybe used two-thirds of it? Maybe two hundred feet, two-twenty at the most."

Dave's heart sank. Two hundred and twenty feet. It had felt like a journey to the center of the earth, an impossible distance. And it was only two-thirds of the way. The tunnel could go on for another hundred feet, or another thousand.

"It's too far, Skot," Dave said, the hope draining out of him. "We can't make it. I barely made it back from that distance. We can't swim the whole length of the tunnel on one breath. It's impossible."

"No," Skot said, his eyes gleaming with an intensity that startled Dave. "No, it's not. Don't you see? You just did something that should be impossible. A two-hundred-and-twenty-foot swim into an unknown passage and back, on one breath? After the day we've had? A week ago, you wouldn't have made it fifty feet. The water, Dave. The water is changing us. It's making us better."

"It's not enough," Dave insisted, shaking his head.

"Did you see anything?" Skot pressed, his voice urgent. "Anything at all?"

Dave's mind raced, replaying the dark journey. "The tunnel opens up at the end. Into a bigger space. And… there's a current. A real one. I felt it pushing against me. The water is flowing from that end to this one."

Skot slammed his fist into his palm, a sharp crack that echoed in the grotto. "That's it! That's everything! It connects to something! A subterranean river, a lake, something! It's a way out!"

"It might as well be on the moon, Skot! We can't reach it!"

"Yes, we can!" Skot knelt in front of him, his face inches from Dave's. "You went in cold. You went in cautious. Now we know the route. We know there are no side tunnels. We know what we're facing. We go together. We swim not to explore, but to escape. We swim with everything we have. We drink more of the water. We charge ourselves up and we go for it. It's a race. All or nothing."

Dave looked from Skot's blazing eyes to the softly glowing water. The idea was insane. It was a suicidal, desperate gamble based on a feeling and a sliver of hope. It went against every cautious, calculating instinct in his body.

And it was the only plan they had.

He thought about his wife, Jen. He thought about his kids. He thought about the comfortable, suffocating life he had been so desperate to escape from for just a few days. Now, he'd give anything to go back to it. To manage his numbers. To sit on his couch. To be bored. To be alive. This tunnel was the only path that led back to that life.

He looked at his hands. They felt strong. He took a deep breath. His lungs felt clear and powerful. The water hadn't just healed him. It had prepared him.

He looked at Skot and nodded slowly. "Okay," he said, his voice steady now. "All or nothing."

A grim smile spread across Skot's face. "That's my man."

They didn't speak again for a while. They moved to the edge of the pool, the source of their curse and their only hope. They cupped their hands and drank deeply, letting the cool, energizing liquid wash through them, a silent sacrament before the final, desperate act. They were no longer just two friends on an adventure. They were something else. Something more. They were survivors, about to take one last, long breath and gamble everything on the impossible.

Chapter 6: All or Nothing

There was a quiet solemnity to their final preparations, the kind of focused calm that settles over men who have accepted that their next action might be their last. They moved with a shared purpose, a silent understanding that passed between them in glances and nods. Words were useless now. The time for discussion and debate was over. There was only the plan, the water, and the will to see it through.

They strapped their fins on, the familiar slap of rubber against their heels a small, grounding ritual. They secured their dive lights, ensuring the lanyards were tight around their wrists. Dave watched Skot coil the remaining guideline and tuck the reel into a small pouch on his weight belt. It was useless for navigating the way out, but it was a record of their journey, a souvenir from hell they couldn't bring themselves to leave behind.

It was Dave, the pragmatist, who paused. He was standing at the edge of the glowing pool, poised for the final, desperate plunge. He looked from the dark, waiting tunnel mouth at the bottom of the pool to the two heavy, discarded BCDs lying on the ledge. An idea, born of pure, forward-thinking terror, sparked in his mind.

"Wait," he said, his voice sharp in the quiet grotto.

Skot, who was already at the water's edge, turned. "What is it? We have to go."

"I know," Dave said, his mind racing, the CPA in him calculating a new kind of risk. "But what happens when we get out? If we get out. We'll be in the middle of the jungle. No food, no gear, no clean water. We'll be back to square one." He gestured to his own body, to the impossible strength he could feel humming in his muscles. "This feeling? This is because of the water. What happens when we're out there for a day? Two days? It's not going to last forever. We'll be just as broken as we were before, only now we'll be lost, too."

Skot's face went grim as the logic of Dave's words settled over him. He had been so focused on the immediate, life-or-death problem of the escape that he hadn't dared to think about the survival that would have to come after. Dave was right. To escape the grotto only to die of exposure or infection in the jungle would be the cruelest irony of all.

"We have to take some with us," Dave said, his voice low and urgent. He pointed at the BCDs. "They're bladders. Durable, heavy-duty bladders. We can fill them."

The idea was brilliant, and it was a terrible, time-consuming risk. The process would be awkward. It would deplete their energy right before the most physically demanding swim of their lives. But it might be the one thing that kept them alive in the days to come.

"Okay," Skot said after a moment, his decision made. "Okay. We do it. Fast."

They moved with a new, frantic purpose. They dragged the heavy buoyancy compensators to the water's edge. The plan was simple in theory, clumsy in practice. They had to submerge the vests, force all the air out of the bladders by pressing the deflation buttons, and allow them to fill with the glowing, miraculous water.

Skot went first, wrestling his BCD into the pool. The vest, designed to be buoyant, fought against him. He had to put his full weight on it, pushing it under the surface, his arms straining as he held down the valves. Dave watched as the last of the air bubbled out and the vest began to sink, growing heavy and water-logged. Skot carefully sealed the valves, trapping the precious liquid inside, and then hauled the now incredibly heavy BCD back onto the ledge. It sloshed with contained power. They repeated the process with Dave's vest.

By the time they were done, they were both panting, their muscles burning from the effort. They had their insurance policy, but they had paid for it with their own dwindling reserves of strength.

They stood at the edge of the pool for the last time, two mortal men about to attempt something immortal. The turquoise water pulsed with its soft, living light, a silent, beautiful monster. It had healed them. It had given them this one, desperate chance. And now, they were stealing its fire.

Skot looked at Dave, his face grim but resolute in the blue glow. He raised a hand, three fingers extended. On three. Dave met his gaze and nodded, his heart a steady, heavy drum in his chest. He felt a strange clarity, a preternatural calm that had settled over him after his test dive. The fear was still there, a cold stone in the pit of his stomach, but it was no longer in control. He was.

Skot raised one finger. One.

Dave began the breathing cycle, a long, slow inhale that filled every corner of his lungs, held for a beat, and then a slow, controlled exhale that emptied him completely. He felt the energy from the water, a clean, humming power that seemed to be waiting for his command.

Skot raised a second finger. Two.

Another breath, deeper this time. He could feel his heart rate slowing, his body entering a state of focused readiness. He looked at Skot, his friend, his brother, the man who had led him into this mess and the only man who could possibly lead him out. He saw his own determination reflected in Skot's eyes. They were in this together, to the end.

Skot raised his third finger. Three.

Dave took one final, enormous breath. He pulled the air in until his lungs felt like they would burst, a life-giving hoard of oxygen to sustain him in the dark. He held it, put his mask in place, and without a moment of hesitation, he and Skot plunged into the water as one.

They didn't waste an ounce of energy. They kicked in perfect, powerful synchronization, their bodies angled down toward the dark mouth of the tunnel. This wasn't a dive; it was an assault. They were two projectiles aimed at freedom, and the tunnel was the barrel of the gun.

They entered the blackness, Skot in the lead, his more powerful light cutting a path. Dave followed just behind and to his right, his own light adding to their small bubble of vision. The first hundred feet were a blur of focus and power. Dave felt incredible. The water seemed to part before him. His muscles, humming with the spring's strange magic, worked with a flawless, piston-like efficiency. The burning in his lungs he'd expected was absent. There was only a calm sense of purpose, a feeling of immense, contained power.

They passed the 150-foot mark, the halfway point of Dave's previous journey, and he still felt strong. He saw the beam of Skot's light momentarily illuminate the hilt of his dive knife, still jammed into the crack in the rock. Skot didn't slow. He swooped down, plucked the knife from the rock with a smooth, practiced motion, and tucked it back into the sheath on his calf without breaking his rhythm. The message was clear: We're not stopping. We're not even slowing down.

This was uncharted territory now. Every kick forward was a kick into a place neither of them had ever been. And it was here that Dave's body began to remember the rules of being human. A dull, persistent ache started to build in his chest. It wasn't the frantic, panicked burn of before, but a deep, powerful pressure, as if a giant hand were slowly closing a fist around his lungs. He forced the feeling down, concentrating on the hypnotic rhythm of his kicks, on the reassuring sight of Skot's fins just ahead of him.

Just when Dave thought he couldn't possibly go on, that he would have to give in to the screaming, primal need to breathe, he saw Skot signal. He raised a fist, then pointed forward, his movements sharp and urgent.

Dave peered past him, his eyes straining. The beam of Skot's light was behaving differently. Ahead, the water was filled with tiny, glittering particles, like a cloud of submerged dust motes dancing in their lights. And the darkness… it wasn't as absolute anymore. There was a faint, grayish tinge to it, a subtle shift from pitch black to a deep, featureless charcoal. They were getting closer.

The sight gave him a new surge of energy, a fresh dose of adrenaline that temporarily silenced the agony in his lungs. He kicked harder, closing the distance to Skot until they were swimming side-by-side. The current he had felt before was stronger here, a tangible river pulling them forward. It wanted them to escape.

The end of the tunnel wasn't a clean exit. It was a jagged, fractured maw, as if a giant had taken a bite out of the rock. They burst through it, leaving the claustrophobic tube behind and entering a vast, open, and deeply disorienting space. It was a cavern of immense size, filled with dark, murky water. But it wasn't a sealed chamber. Far, far above them, so far it seemed like a distant star, was a single, tiny pinprick of pale green light.

The surface. It was a hundred feet above them. Maybe more. It was a lifetime away.

And this is where their bodies, pushed beyond every conceivable limit, finally betrayed them. Dave's vision began to tunnel. The black spots he'd seen before returned, swarming in from the periphery. His powerful kicks faltered, becoming clumsy, desperate strokes. The need to breathe was no longer a request; it was a violent, physical command that threatened to rip him apart from the inside.

He saw Skot start to drift, his movements slowing. He was losing the fight.

No. The thought was a bolt of lightning in Dave's mind. Not here. Not after all this.

He reached out and grabbed the strap of Skot's buoyancy vest, yanking him close. He looked into his friend's eyes behind his mask and saw his own terror reflected there. He shook his head fiercely, a silent, desperate command. We go. Now.

What happened next was not swimming. It was a pure, vertical flight, fueled by the last dregs of their will. They kicked with no form, no grace, just a frantic, clawing scramble for the surface, for life itself. Their lungs were screaming, their muscles were cramping, and their minds were fraying at the edges.

The pinprick of light grew, expanding into a shimmering, emerald ceiling. They could see the tangled roots of trees hanging down into the water. It was real. It was there.

Thirty feet. Their bodies screamed.

Twenty feet. The light was blinding.

Ten feet. They could see the sky.

They broke the surface together in a chaotic explosion of foam and desperate, ragged gasps. They ripped their masks off, tilted their heads back, and inhaled. The air was thick, wet, and smelled of mud and chlorophyll, and it was the most glorious, wonderful thing in the world. They floated on their backs, two exhausted, broken men, and just breathed, their chests rising and falling in deep, shuddering convulsions.

After an eternity, Dave managed to roll over and take in their surroundings. They were in the center of a large, circular cenote, identical to the one they had entered what felt like a lifetime ago. The walls were sheer cliffs of limestone, draped in vines and moss. Towering jungle trees formed a dense canopy far above, creating a cathedral of green.

They were out. They were alive.

Chapter 7: Signal to Noise

The steakhouse had been a triumph. The champagne had been crisp, the filet mignon had been flawless, and the company had been attentive. By all metrics Buzz used to measure an evening, it was a resounding success. But success was a moving target, and a true master of leisure knew that momentum was everything. To go from a five-star dinner back to a hotel room would be a catastrophic failure of imagination. It was an amateur move.

"Ladies," Buzz announced, pushing his chair back and dabbing his mouth with a linen napkin, "I hope you've conserved your energy, because this evening is entering Phase Two."

Sunshine... or was it Moonbeam, looked intrigued. "Phase Two? I'm almost afraid to ask."

"Don't be," Buzz said with a grin that felt like it was powered by high-octane tequila. "Phase Two is where we introduce a little chaos into the system. A little structured risk. We, my friends, are going to the casino."

The resort's casino was exactly what Buzz needed it to be: a loud, glittering temple of distraction. It was a cavern of a different kind, one where the only darkness was in the tinted windows that blocked out the natural passage of time and the only risk was financial. The air was thick with the scent of expensive perfume, faint cigar smoke, and the metallic tang of money. The constant, chiming symphony of a hundred slot machines was the room's heartbeat, a frantic, greedy rhythm. This was Buzz's kind of wilderness.

He strode through the aisles of flashing lights and spinning wheels like a returning king, Tiffany and Brooke flanking him. He led them not to the mindless slot machines, but to the green felt oasis of the blackjack tables. This was a game of nerve, of perceived skill, of personality. It was his stage.

He slid onto a stool at a twenty-five-dollar-minimum table, pulling a thick wad of cash from his pocket that made the dealer's eyes widen almost imperceptibly. "Let's get into some trouble, shall we?" he said to the table at large, buying in for an amount that made Tiffany let out a low whistle.

For the next hour, Buzz was the star of his own show. He wasn't just playing cards; he was performing. He was charming, loud, and impossibly lucky. He flirted with the dealer, a stone-faced woman named Elena who he was slowly managing to crack. He ordered rounds of drinks for the entire table, paying for them with a hundred-dollar bill and a casual "keep the change." He won, lost, and won again, his stack of chips growing into a chaotic, multicolored mountain. The cards didn't matter. The money barely mattered. What mattered was the atmosphere. He was the sun, and everyone else at the table was a planet caught in his glorious, gravitational pull.

His phone, resting on the felt beside his chips, buzzed. He ignored it. It buzzed again, a persistent, annoying vibration against the felt.

"Someone's popular," Sunshine said, leaning over to be heard above the din.

"It's the burden of being a man of international importance," Buzz said without looking down. "Probably my broker, wanting to tell me we've cornered the market on soy futures or something equally tedious."

But the phone didn't stop. It buzzed a third time, then a fourth, a frantic, insistent staccato. The performance was faltering. The other players were looking. Even Elena's professional mask seemed to flicker with a hint of curiosity. The noise was interfering with his signal.

With a theatrical sigh of annoyance, he scooped up the device. "Excuse me for one moment, folks. The world apparently cannot function without my input."

He slid off the stool and walked a few feet away, turning his back to the table to create a small pocket of privacy. He swiped the screen open.

The screen was a wall of worry.

Five missed calls from his sister, Sarah.

A dozen text messages.

SARAH: Keith, Jen is freaking out. She called the hotel. They're not there.

SARAH: She called the dive shop. The guy said the tanks were due back hours ago.

SARAH: The police in that area won't do anything for 24 hours unless the hotel files a report. Can you PLEASE just go to the front desk and ask them to do it?

SARAH: KEITH, ANSWER YOUR DAMN PHONE. THIS ISN'T FUNNY.

Then, a series of messages from a number he recognized as Dave's wife, Jen. Her texts were shorter, more frantic, each one a tiny digital dagger.

JEN: Buzz, please. I'm scared.

JEN: The hotel says the jeep is gone.

JEN: Dave would have called. He always calls.

JEN: Please, just do something.

He stood there for a long moment, the cacophony of the casino fading into a dull roar in his ears. The cold spike he'd felt earlier at the dinner table was back, sharper this time. It wasn't fear, not yet. It was rage. A hot, potent anger. How dare they? How dare they ruin this? How dare their drama and their stupid, reckless hobbies bleed into his perfect night?

His mind, a master of self-preservation, immediately began building a fortress of rationalizations. They're fine. They've done way crazier stuff than this. Skot probably found some other cave he wanted to explore and lost track of time. His phone is dead, Dave's is dead, it's no big deal. They're sitting around a campfire somewhere, laughing about this. He constructed the narrative in seconds, a story so plausible and convenient that he almost believed it himself. The alternative—that they were hurt, or trapped, or worse—was an ugly, inconvenient truth he refused to entertain.

But he had to do something. The girls were watching. His sister and Jen were blowing up his phone. He had to perform the part of the concerned friend.

He walked back to the table, his face arranged into a mask of somber responsibility. "Apologies, everyone," he said, his voice a smooth, controlled baritone. "A little situation with my friends. It seems they've misplaced themselves. I need to go have a chat with the front desk. Don't let Elena take all my winnings while I'm gone."

He strode out of the casino, his long-practiced swagger feeling hollow and fraudulent. He walked through the opulent, marble-floored lobby, his mind racing. He wasn't thinking about what might have happened to Dave and Skot. He was thinking about how he was going to manage this intrusion. This was a public relations problem, not a crisis.

He approached the front desk, where a different clerk from the afternoon shift was on duty. The man had a crisp uniform and a polite, plastic smile.

"Good evening, sir. How may I help you?"

"Yes, my name is Keith Walker," Buzz said, leaning against the polished counter. "I'm here with my friends, Skot Larson and David Bennett. Room 412. I'm getting some... worried calls from back home. A bit of an overreaction, I'm sure. Could you just confirm for me if they've checked in or left any messages?"

The clerk tapped a few keys on his computer, his smile never wavering. "I'm sorry, sir. I see no new messages, and their keys have not been returned. We do show that they took one of the resort's rental jeeps this morning and it has not yet been returned to the motor pool."

"Right," Buzz said, nodding as if this was all perfectly normal. "Right. See, that's what I figured. They're adventure types. Always pushing the envelope. They probably found a great spot and decided to camp overnight. They do it all the time." He was selling it now, trying to convince the clerk, and by extension, himself.

The clerk's smile tightened a fraction. "I see, sir. Their registered checkout is in four days. However, given that their families are concerned and they are overdue, would you like the resort to contact the local authorities? The Policia Nacional? We can file a missing persons report on your behalf."

This was it. The moment of decision. The fork in the road. One path led to flashing lights, grim-faced officials, endless questions, and the complete and utter annihilation of his vacation. The other path led back to the casino.

Buzz sighed, a carefully crafted performance of a man burdened by his friends' lovable irresponsibility. "No," he said, shaking his head. "Let's not call in the cavalry just yet. That's the last thing they'd want. It would be a huge fuss over nothing. Let's give them until, say, noon tomorrow. If we haven't heard from them by then, we can… re-evaluate."

"As you wish, sir," the clerk said, his professional mask back in place. "Please let us know if there is anything else we can do."

"You've been a great help," Buzz said, turning away before the man could see the flicker of something—relief? guilt?—in his eyes.

He walked back toward the casino, his stride feeling lighter. He'd handled it. He'd contained the situation. He'd bought himself another night of freedom, for himself and for them. He owed it to them not to overreact, he told himself.

He rejoined the girls at the blackjack table, where his mountain of chips sat waiting for him.

"Is everything okay?" Tiffany asked, her voice soft.

Buzz flashed a reassuring smile, a masterpiece of deceit. "Everything is under control. My friends are just extending their little dirt-worshipping adventure. Seems we have another night to ourselves." He slid back onto the stool and picked up a heavy, hundred-dollar chip, its weight cool and solid in his hand. "Now, where were we?"

He pushed a large stack of chips into the betting circle, a bet far more reckless than any he'd made before. He needed the noise. He needed the risk, the lights, the laughter. He needed to be anyone but the man who had just rolled the dice with his best friends' lives. He needed to drown out the tiny, cold voice in the back of his head that was whispering, for the first time, that he might have made a terrible mistake.

Chapter 8: The World of the Living

Dave woke to the sensation of a thousand tiny needles pricking his skin. He opened his eyes to a world of brilliant, dappled green. The sun, now high in the sky, was filtering through the dense jungle canopy, painting the mossy ground in shifting patterns of light and shadow. The needles were ants—a busy, indifferent column of them, marching across his arm as if he were just another feature of the landscape. He sat up with a jolt, brushing them off, his heart hammering with a momentary, disoriented panic.

Then it all came rushing back. The cave-in. The grotto. The desperate, breathless swim with their precious, water-filled BCDs clutched to their chests. The final, frantic scramble to the surface.

"Skot?" he called out, his voice a dry croak.

"Right here." Skot's voice came from the edge of the cenote. He was sitting on a rock, shirtless, staring into the crystal-clear water. His wetsuit, peeled down to his waist, lay in a heap beside him.

Dave pushed himself to his feet. Every muscle in his body screamed in protest. The adrenaline from their escape had worn off, leaving behind a deep, profound ache. He felt like he'd been run over by a truck. He hobbled over to Skot, his bare feet tender on the damp earth.

"Anything?" Dave asked, his eyes scanning the impenetrable wall of green that surrounded them on all sides. The jungle wasn't just trees; it was a solid, vertical mass of life, a chaotic tangle of vines, ferns, and broad-leafed plants, all competing for a sliver of sunlight.

"Just more of this," Skot said, gesturing to the wilderness. "And a lot of noise." The air was alive with a symphony of sound—the buzz of insects, the screech of parrots, the low, guttural call of something he hoped was a monkey. It was vibrant and alive, and it made Dave feel very small and very out of place.

They were alive, but they were profoundly lost. They had no food, no fire, no shelter, and no map. They had the clothes on their backs, two dive knives, two dive lights, and the two heavy, sloshing BCDs filled with the most valuable substance on Earth. They were two suburban dads who played at being adventurers, dropped into a situation that would test a seasoned survivalist. The odds were not in their favor.

"We need a plan," Dave said, his pragmatic mind kicking into gear, searching for a problem it could solve. "We should stay here. Near the water. Someone will come looking for us eventually. The dive shop, Buzz…"

"Will they?" Skot asked, turning to look at him. There was a strange intensity in his gaze. "Will they look for us here? Does anyone on Earth know this place exists? We didn't even know it existed until we washed up in it. We're off our own map, Dave."

Skot was right. Their jeep was parked at the entrance to another cenote, miles away. Any search party would focus their efforts there. They would search the main cave system, find the collapse, and assume the worst. They would be presumed dead, their bodies lost forever in the flooded caves. No one was coming. The realization landed in Dave's gut like a cold stone.

"So what do we do?" Dave asked, his voice betraying a sliver of the despair he was trying to keep at bay. "Just start walking? In which direction? It's a 360-degree wall of 'we're screwed.'"

"First," Skot said, standing up, "we take a look at the facts." He pointed down at his own reflection in the still water of the cenote. "Look."

Dave shuffled to the water's edge and peered in. He saw his own face staring back at him, framed by the blue sky and the green canopy. But it wasn't his face. Not exactly. The deep-set lines around his eyes, the ones he'd earned from years of squinting at spreadsheets and worrying about mortgages, were... softer. The tired, puffy bags under his eyes were nearly gone. And his hair—his thinning, receding hair—looked fuller, darker. It was subtle, but it was undeniable. He looked rested. He looked healthy. He looked, to his own astonishment, like he had ten years ago.

He looked over at Skot. The effect was even more pronounced on his friend. Skot had always been wiry and energetic, but now he seemed to radiate a new kind of vitality. The silver threads at his temples were gone, replaced by his natural brown. The network of fine lines that crisscrossed his face from years of smiling and squinting in the sun had vanished. He looked lean, powerful, and young.

"This is real," Dave whispered, touching his own face, his fingers tracing the smoother skin. "It wasn't just the adrenaline."

"No," Skot said. "It's real." He held up his hand, clenching it into a fist. "I feel it. I feel… strong. The ache is gone, Dave. Underneath the bumps and bruises from yesterday, I feel clean. Like a brand-new engine."

They stood there for a moment, two men staring at their own ghosts, their own younger selves returned to them by some impossible, subterranean magic. They were seeing the evidence with their own eyes. The effects of the grotto's water weren't just a first-aid kit; it was a time machine running in reverse inside their own bodies.

The discovery shifted something in Dave. The cold knot of despair in his stomach began to loosen, replaced by a strange, unfamiliar warmth. Skot was right. They were in a desperate situation, but they weren't the same men who had entered the cave yesterday. They were better. Stronger. Faster. They had an advantage, a secret weapon sloshing in the BCDs at their feet.

"Okay," Dave said, his voice stronger now. "Okay. We move. Which way?"

Skot's face broke into a grin. He was the leader again, the explorer with a map to chart. "The sun," he said, pointing up through the canopy. "It's past noon, so it's starting to head west. Our resort, the coast, is east of the jungle. So if we walk away from the sun in the afternoon, we're generally heading in the right direction."

It was a crude compass, but it was a compass nonetheless.

"We'll need to find a river," Skot continued, his mind already working on the logistics. "All water flows to the sea.

We find a river, we follow it downstream. It's our best bet of finding a road or a village."

The plan was simple, almost laughably so, but it was a plan. And for Dave, a plan was everything. It was a shield against the overwhelming chaos of their situation.

Their next task was to figure out how to carry their precious, life-giving cargo. The water-filled BCDs were impossibly heavy and awkward. Using their dive knives, they cut long, tough strips from the neoprene of their wetsuits. Skot, with his artist's hands, was surprisingly adept, weaving and tying the strips to create a pair of crude, uncomfortable, but functional backpack harnesses for the heavy bladders. It was a clumsy solution, but it would have to work.

Finally, they were ready. They stood at the edge of the jungle, two modern men stripped of everything but their wits and a strange, miraculous secret. They were about to step into a world that did not want them there, a world of biting insects, venomous snakes, and predators they couldn't even imagine.

Skot turned to Dave, his face serious. "Ready for a little walk?"

Dave took one last look at the tranquil, beautiful cenote that had served as their gateway back to the world. Then he looked at his friend, his brother. He felt the impossible strength in his limbs, the steady, powerful rhythm of his own heart. He was terrified. And he had never felt more alive.

"Let's go home," he said.

And together, they turned their backs on the water, shouldered their heavy, sloshing burdens, and stepped into the suffocating green embrace of the jungle.

Chapter 9: The Price of the Ticket

Buzz woke up because a tiny, persistent man was trying to split his skull open with a tiny, persistent hammer. The hammer was located somewhere behind his right eye, and its rhythm was brutally in sync with the dull, thumping bass of the music still echoing in his memory from the night before. He groaned, a sound that felt like it scraped its way up his throat over a bed of gravel, and attempted to roll over. It was a mistake. The movement sent a tidal wave of nausea through him, and the tiny man with the hammer redoubled his efforts.

He cracked one eye open. The hotel room was a disaster zone, a testament to the fact that Phase Two had bled into an unsanctioned, and largely unremembered, Phase Three. An empty champagne bottle lay on its side next to the television. A high-heeled shoe, not his own, was perched precariously on a lampshade. Brooke, or was it Tiffany, had left behind some delicates. His own clothes were scattered across the floor in a trail leading from the door to the bed, suggesting he'd undressed with the urgency of a bomb-disposal expert.

He was alone. Thank God for small mercies. Post-party post-mortems were not his strong suit.

He fumbled for his phone on the nightstand, his hand clumsy and uncooperative. He found it, squinted at the screen, and saw the time: 11:04 AM. He also saw the notifications. A wall of them. So many that his phone had simply given up on displaying them individually and summarized them with a single, damning line: "99+ notifications."

He let his head fall back onto the pillow, which smelled faintly of chlorine and someone else's perfume. Denial. It was a powerful and underrated tool for happiness. For a few blissful moments, he could pretend the notifications weren't there. He could pretend his head wasn't trying to secede from the union of his body. He could pretend that the only pressing issue on his agenda was deciding between room service pancakes or room service eggs benedict.

But the real world, the world outside his carefully constructed bubble of fun, was a patient and relentless beast. It was knocking.

With a monumental effort, he swung his legs out of bed and sat up, the room giving a sickening lurch. He staggered into the palatial bathroom, avoided looking at his own reflection in the mirror—a cardinal rule of post-bender mornings—and turned the shower on, twisting the knob all the way to cold. The icy spray hit him unsympathetically, and he gasped, his system jolting into a state of shocked, shivering awareness. It was punishment, but it was a necessary one.

As the water sluiced over him, washing away the sweat and regret of the night, his mind began to clear. The fortress of rationalizations he had built so carefully in the casino lobby last night now seemed flimsy and absurd in the harsh light of day. They probably found a great spot and decided to camp overnight. Did they? Neither Skot nor Dave had packed any camping gear. They were meticulous planners. An impromptu night in the jungle wasn't their style. They do it all the time. No, they didn't. Not without telling anyone.

He turned off the water, toweled off, and wrapped a fluffy hotel robe around himself. He felt marginally more human. He walked back into the main room and, with the grim determination of a man about to read his own sentencing, he picked up his phone and opened it.

The messages from his sister, Sarah, had escalated from worried to furious.

> SARAH (3:14 AM): I can't sleep. This is wrong, Keith. I have a bad feeling.
>
> SARAH (5:22 AM): I'm calling the consulate in the morning if I don't hear from you. I'm not kidding.
>
> SARAH (7:30 AM): You're a selfish, useless bastard. Are you even awake yet? Jen is beside herself.

The texts from Jen were worse. They were shorter, stripped of all anger, leaving behind only the raw, throbbing nerve of pure fear.

> JEN (4:00 AM): I keep calling Dave's phone. It just rings. I know the battery is dead but I can't stop.
>
> JEN (6:15 AM): I told the kids he was having fun. I told them he was fine.
>
> JEN (8:00 AM): Please. Buzz. Please just tell me what's happening.

The words hit him harder than the cold shower. For the first time, he felt the situation not as an inconvenience or an intrusion, but as a crisis centered on real people. Jen, a woman he'd known for twenty years, a woman who treated him with a kind of amused tolerance, was terrified. And he was the reason she was still in the dark. He was the man on the ground. The one who was supposed to be there. He was their friend.

He scrolled through his call log. Twelve missed calls from his sister. Eight from Jen. He deserved every ounce of their anger.

He started to pace the room, his bare feet sinking into the plush carpet, his mind a whirlwind of guilt and a still-potent desire to be wrong. He needed one more hit of denial, one last piece of evidence that would let him off the hook.

He found the number for the dive shop on a crumpled brochure on the desk. He dialed, his heart pounding a nervous rhythm against his ribs. A man with a thick local accent answered.

"Buenos días, Caribbean Dive Adventures."

"Hi, yes," Buzz said, trying to keep his voice casual. "My name is Keith Walker. My friends, Skot Larson and David Bennett, rented some gear from you yesterday. I was just wondering if you'd heard from them? They're running a bit late, and you know how it is, folks back home start to worry."

There was a pause on the other end of the line. "The two Americans? For the cenote dive?"

"That's them," Buzz said, his hopes rising. Maybe they'd stopped by. Maybe it was all fine.

"No, señor," the man said, his voice flat and professional. "They did not return the equipment yesterday. The tanks and the regulators are now one day overdue. My boss, he is not happy. This is very expensive gear."

"Right," Buzz said, his stomach twisting. "Right. Of course. Well, I'm sure they'll be along soon. Thanks." He hung up the phone before the man could ask any more questions.

The last pillar of his fortress had crumbled. The dive shop owner wasn't worried about his friends; he was worried about his gear. To the rest of the world, Skot and Dave weren't missing. They were just irresponsible. Because of him. Because he had told everyone not to worry, to stand down.

He looked at the clock on his phone. 11:41 AM.

He had less than twenty minutes. The arbitrary deadline he'd plucked out of thin air last night to save his own skin had become a finish line. He could let it pass. He could call his sister, lie, tell her he'd just gotten back from checking the dive site himself and there was no sign of them. He could buy himself more time. More time for what? To order pancakes? To hit the pool? The thought was suddenly disgusting.

He thought of Dave, his quiet, steady friend, the bedrock of their trio. He thought of Skot, his wild, brilliant, dreamer of a friend who pushed them all to be more alive. He remembered a time, years ago, when his car had broken down in the middle of the night, two hundred miles from home. He had made one call. And at four in the morning, Skot and Dave had pulled up in Skot's beat-up pickup truck with a thermos of coffee and a set of jumper cables, no questions asked. They hadn't mocked him. They hadn't told him to wait until morning. They had just come.

And what had he done for them? He'd ordered another round of drinks.

The shame was a physical thing, a hot flush that spread from his chest to his face. He walked back into the bathroom and stared at his own reflection, really looked this time. He saw a puffy, hungover, middle-aged man with fear in his eyes. A spoiled child in a grown-up's body. The king of a kingdom of one.

"You're an idiot," he said to the man in the mirror.

He walked out of the bathroom with a new sense of purpose. The lethargy was gone, replaced by a cold, clear, and terrifying resolve. He threw on a pair of shorts and a wrinkled polo shirt, shoved his feet into a pair of loafers, and grabbed his wallet and room key. He didn't bother to comb his hair. The performance was over.

He strode through the lobby, his focus absolute. He didn't notice the families heading to the pool or the couples checking out. He walked straight to the front desk, to the same polite clerk from the night before.

The clerk's smile was as bright and plastic as ever. "Good morning, Mr. Walker. I trust you have good news about your friends?"

Buzz leaned against the counter, his hands flat on the cool marble. He looked the clerk dead in the eye. "No," he said, his voice low and steady. "I don't. They're missing. I was wrong last night. I was a fool. We need to call the police. Right now."

The clerk's professional smile finally faltered, replaced by a look of genuine seriousness. "Of course, sir. Right away."

The clerk made the call, speaking in rapid, hushed Spanish. Buzz stood there, his heart a leaden weight in his chest, and waited. He had finally done the right thing. But he knew, with a certainty that chilled him to the bone, that it was twelve hours too late. The ticket for his perfect night had just come due, and the price was going to be higher than he could ever have imagined.

Chapter 10: Green Hell

The jungle did not welcome them. It consumed them. The moment they stepped away from the relative sanctuary of the cenote, the world became a wall of suffocating green. The air, which had seemed merely humid before, was now a thick, wet blanket that clung to their skin and made every breath feel like they were drinking from a straw. The symphony of unseen creatures was no longer a charming backdrop; it was a constant, unnerving chorus of clicks, buzzes, and screeches that scraped at the edges of their nerves.

Progress was measured in feet, not miles. Every step was a battle. Thick, thorny vines snagged their clothes and tore at their exposed skin. The ground, a treacherous carpet of decaying leaves and tangled roots, seemed designed to trip them, to twist an ankle, to send them sprawling. They quickly learned that walking in a straight line was a fantasy. They were forced into a constant, meandering zigzag, seeking the path of least resistance through the unforgiving terrain.

The BCDs, which had seemed like a brilliant solution back at the grotto, were now instruments of torture. The water-filled bladders were heavy and awkward, sloshing with every movement and throwing them off balance. The straps dug into their shoulders, and the bulky shapes caught on every low-hanging branch. But they were also their lifeline, their only source of the miraculous water, so they bore the weight without complaint.

After what felt like hours, Skot called a halt. They slumped to the ground, their backs against the trunk of a colossal tree whose bark was as rough as ancient stone. They were drenched in sweat, covered in a latticework of scratches, and breathing in ragged, painful gasps.

"We're not making any time," Dave panted, wiping a stream of sweat from his eyes. "At this rate, it'll take us a month to get out of here."

"I know," Skot said, his chest heaving. He looked exhausted, but underneath the grime and the sweat, Dave could see a flicker of that same intense focus he'd had in the cave. "But we're not the same guys who hiked in, remember?"

It was true. As miserable and exhausted as he felt, Dave had to admit that his body was holding up in ways it shouldn't. Normally, a hike like this would have his back screaming and his diabetic body crying out for a careful balance of sugar and rest. But the deep, chronic aches were absent. He was tired in his muscles, but he felt a core of strength, a reserve of energy he hadn't tapped into yet.

"Let's try some," Skot suggested.

They carefully unstrapped the heavy BCDs. Dave fumbled with the oral inflator valve on his, pressing the button to release a stream of the clear, magical water into his cupped hands. It wasn't glowing anymore, not in the bright light of the jungle, but he knew the power was still there.

He drank. The effect was immediate and astonishing. It was like pouring coolant over an overheating engine. The exhaustion didn't just recede; it vanished. The superficial aches and pains from their struggle through the undergrowth disappeared. His mind, which had been foggy with fatigue, snapped back into sharp focus. He felt a surge of clean, cool energy spread through his limbs.

He looked at Skot, who had also just drunk from his own supply. The weariness was gone from his friend's face, replaced by a renewed vigor.

"Holy hell," Dave breathed. "It still works."

"Never doubted it," Skot said, though the look of profound relief on his face told a different story. He stood up, stretching his arms over his head. "This changes the game. We're not limited by normal endurance. We're limited by daylight. We can go longer, harder."

And they did. The water was a cheat code for survival. Whenever their strength began to wane, whenever the crushing fatigue threatened to overwhelm them, they would stop, drink a few precious mouthfuls from their BCDs, and be instantly restored. They became a relentless, two-man machine, pushing their way through the jungle with a stamina that was both a gift and a deeply unnatural secret.

They developed a rhythm. Skot, with his better sense of direction and his boundless, water-fueled optimism, took the lead, using his dive knife to hack at the most stubborn vines. Dave followed, his analytical mind constantly scanning their surroundings, looking for dangers Skot might miss, his eyes peeled for the telltale signs of snakes or the flicker of movement that might signal a predator.

Their senses felt... sharper. Dave noticed things he never would have before. The iridescent blue of a butterfly's wings against a green leaf. The intricate, geometric pattern of a spider's web. He could hear the faint rustle of a lizard in the undergrowth from twenty feet away. The world seemed more vibrant, more detailed, as if a filter had been removed from his perception. His body wasn't just healing; it was optimizing.

Late in the afternoon, their luck changed. Skot, who was a few yards ahead, suddenly stopped and raised a hand. "Listen," he whispered.

Dave froze, straining his ears past the cacophony of the insects. And then he heard it. A sound so faint it was almost subliminal, but it was there. The gentle, musical murmur of moving water.

A river.

They abandoned all caution and plunged through the undergrowth toward the sound, their hearts pounding with a renewed, desperate hope. The sound grew louder, a steady, promising gurgle. They burst through a final curtain of thick, broad leaves and found themselves standing on the muddy bank of a small, fast-moving river.

It was maybe thirty feet across, its water the color of milky coffee, but it was the most beautiful sight Dave had ever seen. It was a path. A dynamic, living line carved through the static, suffocating green.

"Downstream," Skot said, his voice thick with emotion. He pointed to the right, where the current was flowing. "That's the way home."

They followed the riverbank, their progress infinitely easier now that they were out of the thickest part of the jungle. As the sun began to dip below the canopy, casting long, dramatic shadows across the forest floor, they found a small, sandy clearing a few feet from the water's edge. This would be their camp for the night.

They didn't have a fire, but they had their wetsuits. They unrolled them on the sand, the thick neoprene a welcome barrier against the damp ground. As darkness fell with the startling speed of the tropics, the jungle transformed. The familiar sounds of the day were replaced by a new, more menacing chorus. The air grew cooler.

They sat side-by-side in the dark, the black, rushing water of the river their only companion. They were two men, alone and vulnerable in a world that was not their own. But they were not without hope. They had a direction. They had a supply of a miracle. And they had each other.

"You think Buzz is worried yet?" Dave asked, breaking a long silence.

Skot let out a short, humorless laugh. "He's probably just cracking his third bottle of champagne. He'll assume we're fine until the hotel manager tells him we've racked up a bill he has to pay."

Dave smiled. The thought of Buzz, in his own world of self-indulgent bliss, was a strange comfort. It was a reminder of the world they were fighting to get back to. A world of trivial problems, of comfort, of safety.

"We'll make it back, you know," Skot said, his voice quiet but certain in the darkness. "We will."

Dave looked out at the impenetrable blackness of the jungle across the river. He thought about the near-death experience in the cave, the impossible strength flowing through his veins, the long, brutal day they had just survived. He felt a profound shift within himself. The fear was still there, but it was no longer the dominant emotion. It was being overshadowed by a fierce, primal, and exhilarating will to live.

"Yeah," Dave said, and he was surprised to find that he believed it. "I know."

Chapter 11: The Machinery of Worry

The resort lobby, which had seemed so opulent and full of promise just the night before, now felt like a gilded cage. The morning sun streamed through the massive floor-to-ceiling windows, illuminating the dust motes dancing in the air and throwing the vibrant patterns of the expensive tile into sharp relief. To the other guests, families laughing as they headed to the pool and couples holding hands on their way to breakfast, it was another perfect day in paradise. To Buzz, it was a waiting room. Purgatory with a better class of furniture.

He sat in an oversized armchair, a cup of coffee growing cold on the table beside him. He hadn't touched it. He'd been sitting there for forty-five minutes, a self-imposed exile from his trashed hotel room. He had showered again, dressed in the cleanest clothes he could find, and combed his hair, but it was a pointless charade. He felt like a ghost haunting the scene of his own greatest failure, invisible to the happy, living people flowing around him. Every laugh felt like an accusation. Every cheerful "Buenos días" from a passing staff member felt like a twist of the knife.

He had done what he was supposed to do. He had set the wheels in motion. And now, he was discovering a truth that was completely alien to him: the real world did not operate on his timetable. It did not care about his urgency. It had procedures.

A man in a crisp, beige uniform approached him. He was older than Buzz had expected, maybe in his late fifties, with a neatly trimmed mustache, iron-gray hair, and a face that was a roadmap of long days spent under a hot sun. His eyes were tired but sharp, and they missed nothing. He carried himself with a quiet, unhurried authority that was somehow more intimidating than any display of force.

"Mr. Walker?" the man asked. His English was excellent, with only a slight, musical accent.

"Yes," Buzz said, standing up, his palms suddenly slick with sweat.

"I am Lieutenant Morales of the Policia Nacional," the man said, offering a firm, dry handshake. "The hotel manager informed me of your situation. I understand your friends are overdue from a diving excursion."

"Yes. That's right," Buzz said, his voice sounding thin and weak to his own ears. "Skot Larson and David Bennett."

"Let us sit," Morales suggested, gesturing to the chairs. He pulled a small, worn notebook and a pen from his breast pocket. He moved with a deliberate slowness that was maddening to Buzz. "Can you please provide me with their full names and dates of birth?"

Buzz recited the information, feeling like a schoolboy reporting a lost pet. Morales wrote it down with neat, precise letters.

"And their planned itinerary for yesterday?"

"A dive," Buzz said. "In a cenote. An inland cave. Skot—Skot's the experienced one—he had a map. He left a copy in their room, I think."

Morales nodded slowly. "And when were they expected to return to the resort?"

Here it was. The question he'd been dreading. "Yesterday afternoon," Buzz mumbled, his eyes fixed on a meaningless pattern on the rug. "Maybe three or four o'clock."

Morales made a note. He didn't look up. "And you are reporting this to us now, at approximately noon the following day. Can you explain the delay, Mr. Walker?"

The question was gentle, professional, but it landed like a body blow. Buzz felt a hot flush of shame creep up his neck. He could lie. He could say he'd been out looking for them himself. But the thought of constructing another lie was suddenly exhausting. The truth, as ugly as it was, was the only thing he had left.

"I... I thought they were fine," he said, the words tasting like ash. "They're adventurers. They do this stuff. I assumed they'd lost track of time. I didn't want to overreact, to cause a scene over nothing. I made a mistake. A bad one."

Lieutenant Morales finally looked up from his notebook, and his tired eyes held Buzz's for a long moment. There was no judgment in them, no anger. There was something worse: a quiet, profound understanding. It was the look of a man who had seen this exact brand of human foolishness a thousand times before. He had seen fear curdle into denial. He had seen selfishness masquerade as patience.

"I see," Morales said, and with those two simple words, Buzz felt the full, crushing weight of his failure settle over him. "Mistakes can happen. Now, we must work with the time we have. You mentioned a map. I would like to see it. And their room."

Buzz led him to the elevator, the silence between them heavy and thick. They rode up to the fourth floor. Buzz's hand trembled slightly as he inserted the key card into the door of room 412.

The room was just as they'd left it two days ago. It was a stark contrast to Buzz's own chaotic suite. This room was a space of preparation and purpose. The two beds were neatly made. On the desk, surrounded by charging cables and a few paperback novels, was a laminated map of the coastline and the jungle beyond. Skot had marked a route in red dry-erase marker from the resort to a specific point labeled "Cenote Escondido."

Morales picked up the map, his eyes tracing the route. "This is our starting point. We will dispatch a unit to this location immediately to look for their vehicle."

Buzz's eyes scanned the room. It was like a museum exhibit titled "The Day Before." He saw Dave's dopp kit on the bathroom counter, his toothbrush sitting next to a bottle of prescription medication. On the nightstand beside what was clearly Dave's bed, there was a framed picture that must have been tucked into his suitcase. It was a photo of his wife, Jen, and their two smiling kids. They were at a beach, squinting in the bright sun, a perfect little family frozen in a moment of ordinary happiness.

The sight of it was another wake-up call for Buzz. These weren't just his adventure buddies, his foils, his audience. They were real people with real lives, with people who loved them, with children who were waiting for their father to come home. And he, Buzz, had been at the casino, buying drinks for strangers. The tiny man with the hammer was back in his skull, only this time he wasn't wielding a tool of pain, but of guilt.

"Did your friends have any special equipment?" Morales asked, pulling Buzz from his spiraling thoughts. "Anything that might help us?"

"Just… dive gear," Buzz said, his mind foggy. "Tanks, masks… lights. Skot—he films everything. He has one of those little GoPro cameras. He mounts it on his helmet. He never dives without it."

Morales's interest piqued. "A camera? This is good. The footage could show us what happened."

They left the room, and Morales posted a junior officer at the door, instructing him to allow no one to enter. The room was now part of an official investigation. As they walked back to the elevators, Morales outlined the next steps in his calm, measured voice. A team would secure the jeep. Another team, including expert cave divers, would be assembled to search Cenote Escondido. He explained that these things took time. That the terrain was difficult. He was managing expectations. He was telling Buzz, in the kindest way possible, to be prepared for the worst.

They reached the lobby again. "Mr. Walker," Morales said, turning to him. "We will do everything we can. I need you to stay at the resort. Do not try to go to the site yourself. You will only interfere. We will need to ask you more questions later. For now, the best thing you can do for your friends is wait."

Morales gave him a final, brief nod and walked away, already speaking into a radio he'd produced from his belt. Buzz watched him go, a man in his element, a man moving with purpose.

And Buzz was left alone again in the center of the lobby, adrift. The waiting was supposed to be the hardest part, but Buzz knew the hardest part was yet to come. He pulled out his phone, his thumb hovering over Jen's contact information. He had to make the call. He had to tell her that their husbands were officially missing, that a search was underway, and that it was his fault they were only starting now.

He took a deep breath, the air in the pristine, air-conditioned lobby feeling thin and useless. He pressed the call button. The silence as it rang felt like an eternity. He had entered the machinery of worry, a complex and brutal engine powered by fear and regret, and he knew with a sickening certainty that he would not be leaving it for a very, very long time.

Chapter 12: The Agony of Guilt

The silence on the other end of the line was a vast, empty canyon, and Buzz felt like he was screaming into it and hearing no echo. He had just finished explaining the situation to Jen, Dave's wife, his words clumsy and inadequate, each one a small, painful stone he was forced to hand her. He had stumbled through the timeline, the call to the front desk, the arrival of the police. He had apologized, the word tasting like rust in his mouth, so flimsy and pathetic it nearly choked him. He braced himself for anger, for accusations, for the hot, righteous fury he so richly deserved.

What he got was worse.

When she finally spoke, her voice was unnervingly calm, stripped of all the frantic energy from her texts. It was the calm of deep shock, the quiet of a landscape after a bomb has gone off, the air still and heavy with unspoken devastation.

"A search party," she repeated, the words toneless, hollowed out. "Like on the news."

"Jen, they're doing everything they can," Buzz said, his own voice sounding thin and desperate in the crushing silence. He was trying to reassure her, but he knew he was really trying to reassure himself. "The lieutenant, Morales, he seems like the real deal. He's organized. He's already got people on the move."

"Okay," she said. Just, okay. The word was a universe of pain. It was the 'okay' of someone who has been told the test results are bad. The 'okay' of someone who realizes the life they were living five minutes ago no longer exists. "Okay. The kids… I need to… I need to figure out what to tell the kids."

"Tell them… tell them their dad is on an adventure," Buzz offered, the words turning to ash in his mouth. What a cruel, facile joke. An adventure.

"I already did that yesterday," she replied, and the quiet crack in her voice, a tiny fissure in her wall of shock, did more damage to Buzz than an hour of shouting could have. "When they asked why he didn't call to say goodnight. I need to go. I need to… think." She paused, and for a moment Buzz thought she had hung up. Then, her voice returned, a bare whisper. "Keep me… just… call me. Don't text. I need to hear a voice. Call me the second you hear anything. Anything at all. Even if it's nothing."

The line went dead.

Buzz stood in the opulent hotel lobby, his phone feeling like a fifty-pound weight in his hand. He had done it. He had made the call. And the crushing guilt he had felt before now had a new and terrible companion: a share of her pain. He sank back into the oversized armchair he now considered his personal cell, the soft cushions offering no comfort. He was now the designated point of contact, the field marshal in a war of waiting, a job for which he was uniquely, catastrophically unqualified.

Lieutenant Morales had been true to his word. The machinery of worry, once engaged, moved with a surprising and terrifying speed. Within the hour, the lobby of the resort began to feel less like a vacation spot and more like a forward operating base. Two more uniformed officers arrived, their polished boots clicking with grim purpose on the terracotta tiles. They didn't smile. They didn't engage with the curious tourists. They spoke in low, clipped tones with the hotel manager, who now wore a strained, anxious expression that had replaced his usual polished hospitality. The manager kept wiping his brow with a handkerchief, his professional bonhomie having evaporated in the heat of a real-world crisis that couldn't be solved with a complimentary fruit basket.

The atmosphere in the lobby curdled. Guests began to notice. A couple in matching floral shirts on their way to the brunch buffet stopped and stared, whispering to each other behind cupped hands. A family with young children gave the officers a wide berth, the parents instinctively steering their kids away from the intrusion of real-world trouble, their vacation bubble pierced. The resort was no longer a haven; it was a fishbowl, and Buzz was the strange, ugly fish floating in the middle, the object of every whispered speculation.

He saw the junior officer who had been posted outside Skot and Dave's room come down and hand Lieutenant Morales a large, sealed evidence bag. Inside, Buzz could clearly see the laminated map and Skot's GoPro camera case. The sight of it sent a fresh jolt of acid into his gut. That little black box, wherever it was, probably held the truth. It held the last images of his friends. It might contain the silent, terrible footage of their final moments, a truth he was not sure he could bear to see. He imagined Morales finding only the camera and settling in a quiet room somewhere, watching the footage, seeing what his friends had seen, and the thought made him feel physically ill.

He stayed in his chair, a prisoner of his own making. To leave would feel like an abandonment. To go back to his ravaged hotel room would be to surrender to the spiraling, venomous thoughts in his own head. So he sat, a sentinel of guilt, and watched the resort's carefully curated illusion of paradise crumble around him, one suspicious glance at a time.

The leak, when it came, was not a dramatic explosion. It was a quiet, digital trickle that quickly became a flood. It started with a woman sitting two armchairs away, a tourist from Ohio in her late forties with expertly highlighted hair and a penchant for scrolling loudly through her social media feeds. She had been watching the police activity with undisguised curiosity. Buzz saw her lean over and say something to her husband, her eyes flicking toward him. Then her thumbs began to move with startling speed across the screen of her phone. She was composing a post for her community Facebook group back home.

"You guys will not BELIEVE this, so crazy, we're at this resort in Colombia and there's a huge police presence. Apparently two American guys went missing on a scuba dive yesterday. One of their friends is sitting right here in the lobby, looks totally devastated. So scary! Praying for their families."

An hour later, a freelance journalist in Bogotá, whose entire livelihood depended on a finely tuned network of digital alerts for keywords like "American tourist," "missing," and "Colombia," got a ping. The Facebook post was public. He made a few calls. He cross-referenced flight manifests. He called the resort, pretending to be a concerned family member, and a harried new clerk at the front desk, overwhelmed by a situation not covered in her training manual, confirmed that yes, there was an ongoing situation involving two missing American guests, but she couldn't provide any further details.

That was all he needed. He typed up a short, dramatic article and filed it to a US-based news wire service, adding a touch of color about the region's treacherous, unexplored cave systems.

Buzz knew none of this. He only knew that the atmosphere in the lobby was growing more tense. His phone, which had been blessedly silent since his call with Jen, suddenly buzzed against the arm of the chair. It was a news alert from a major network.

"Two American Tourists Missing After Cave Dive in Colombia."

Buzz's blood turned to ice. He tapped the notification, his thumb trembling. A short, sparse article appeared. It named them. Skot Larson, 49, a freelance graphic designer. David Bennett, 47, a certified public accountant. It mentioned their hometown. It mentioned the resort. It mentioned that a friend traveling with them had reported them missing late the following day.

A friend traveling with them. The phrase was anonymous, but it felt like a brand on his forehead.

Then his phone began to melt down. It was a digital avalanche. It wasn't just Jen or his sister anymore. It was everyone. Text messages from cousins he hadn't spoken to in years. Missed calls from old college roommates he hadn't seen since graduation. A frantic voicemail from his mother, her voice high and panicked. And then the social media notifications began, a tidal wave of them. People were tagging him in the news articles being shared on Facebook. His own "fun in the sun" posts from the day before—the poolside selfies, the casino chips—were suddenly flooded with comments.

"Is this your friends?? OMG I hope they're okay!"

"Keith, what is happening? We just saw this on the news!"

"Praying for them and for you."

His private nightmare was now a public spectacle, a piece of shareable, clickable content. He was trending.

The final, definitive blow came from his sister. She called, and when he answered, he could hear the distinct, dramatic music of a cable news network in the background.

"Keith," she said, her voice shaking with rage and disbelief. "It's on CNN. Right now. They're showing their pictures. They're showing Dave's family photo. They're showing your damn Instagram posts from the casino. They're talking about you, Keith. They're asking why you waited so long to call for help."

He felt the floor drop out from under him. He was no longer just the friend. He was a character in the story. The irresponsible one. The partier. The one who had let them down. The narrative was being written without him, in real time, on a global stage, and he was being cast as the villain.

As if on cue, the phone at the front desk rang, its shrill tone cutting through the lobby's nervous quiet. Buzz watched as the clerk answered it, listened for a moment, and then looked over at him, his eyes wide with a new kind of deference and alarm. He placed his hand over the receiver.

"Mr. Walker?" the clerk called out, his voice a little too loud. "It's… it's a producer. From the American news. They want to know if you are available to make a statement."

Buzz stared at the clerk, the hum of the air conditioning, the distant chatter of guests, the frantic buzzing of his own phone all fading into a single, overwhelming roar. He had lost control. Completely. The story was now a runaway train, and he was tied to the tracks. The unblinking eye of the world had found him, and he knew, with a gut-wrenching certainty, that it would not be looking away anytime soon.

Chapter 13: The Depreciating Asset

Morning did not arrive in the jungle; it seeped in. It was a slow, gray dilution of the oppressive, absolute black of the night, a reluctant transition from one kind of misery to another. Dave woke up shivering, a deep, bone-rattling chill that the humid air did nothing to warm. He was curled on his side on the lumpy, uncomfortable bed of his rolled-out wetsuit, and he could feel that the dampness from the ground had worked its way through the neoprene, infusing his very marrow with cold. Every joint was a universe of pain. His back, a landscape of dull, familiar aches for the better part of a decade, was now screaming in protest. His knees, the right one in particular, felt like they were filled with ground glass. His shoulders throbbed with a deep, punishing ache from hauling the makeshift water bladder. He felt a hundred years old, and badly cared for at that.

He tried to sit up, and a groan escaped his lips, a sound that was part animal, part rusted hinge. The movement sent a fresh wave of agony through his system. The jungle looked different in the gray morning light. The shapes that had been menacing, hulking shadows in the dark were now just trees and vines, but they seemed to hold a quiet, brooding indifference to his suffering, their leaves dripping with a mist that felt as heavy as mercury. The air, thick and cloying, smelled of decay and wet earth. Beside him, the river rushed on, a dark, muddy torrent, completely unconcerned with his plight.

Skot was already awake, sitting cross-legged on his own wetsuit, staring into the mist as if he could divine their future in its shifting patterns. He looked as miserable as Dave felt. His face, usually so animated, was pale and drawn in the half-light. His hair was plastered to his forehead with sweat and dew. Dave watched him wince as he tried to rub some life back into his left shoulder, the old climbing injury having returned with a vengeance. The miracle of yesterday had worn off. The bill had come due. They were just two broken, middle-aged men, lost in a world that was actively trying to dismantle them piece by painful piece.

"Morning, sunshine," Dave croaked, his voice so raspy it felt like it was scraping his throat raw.

Skot turned, and his attempt at a smile was a pathetic, grim caricature. "If you call this morning," he muttered. "I think I was personally bitten by every mosquito in Colombia last night. And a few of their cousins from the wrong side of the tracks." He winced again as he tried to push himself to his feet, hissing in a sharp breath. "I feel like I went ten rounds with a cement mixer. And lost. Decisively."

This was their new reality, a brutal, exhausting cycle. They were slaves to the water, their bodies now completely dependent on the very substance that was the root cause of all their trouble. It was a Faustian bargain they hadn't even realized they'd made.

Without another word, they crawled to their precious, sloshing BCDs. The ritual was no longer a moment of wonder; it was a necessity, as vital and unglamorous as a diabetic taking his insulin. Dave fumbled with the oral inflator valve on his, his fingers stiff and clumsy from the cold. He pressed the button, and a small stream of the clear, magical water trickled into his cupped, dirty palm. He looked at the precious liquid, their entire stock of hope. He did a quick, mental calculation, a CPA's habit he couldn't shake. They had maybe five or six quarts left between the two of them. It suddenly felt like a pitifully small amount, a tiny inheritance they were forced to squander just to make it through the day.

He drank.

The effect was even more profound this time because the starting point was so much lower. It was like a light switch being flipped in a dark, decrepit room. The pain didn't fade; it evaporated. The deep, grinding ache in his joints vanished in a puff of smoke. The fiery itching of a hundred insect bites subsided to a dull tingle and then, blessedly, to nothing at all. Warmth flooded his limbs, chasing away the bone-deep chill. The fog of exhaustion lifted from his brain, replaced by a crystalline, startling clarity. He felt the machinery of his body reset, reboot, and come online, better than new. The world snapped back into high definition.

He watched the same transformation happen to Skot. The grimace of pain on his friend's face softened, the lines of exhaustion smoothed out, and the light of life returned to his eyes. Skot stood up, this time with the fluid grace of a trained athlete, and stretched his arms wide, a look of pure, unadulterated wonder on his face.

"I will never, ever get used to that," Skot said, his voice now strong and clear. "It's like being reborn. Every single time."

"We're junkies, Skot," Dave said, his own voice steady, though the thought was unsettling. He was looking at their dwindling water supply with a cold, professional eye. "This stuff is keeping us alive, but we have a finite supply. A depreciating asset. Every time we take a drink, we're draining the bank account. What happens when it runs out?"

Skot's renewed good mood faltered slightly. He looked from the life-giving BCDs to the vast, unforgiving jungle that surrounded them. "Then we'd better be somewhere else by the time it does," he said, his tone sober. "Come on. We're burning daylight."

They packed their makeshift camp with a new efficiency, their revitalized bodies moving with purpose. They shouldered the heavy water bladders and set off, following the muddy bank of the river downstream. But today, the jungle felt different. The background noise of insects was still there, a constant, high-pitched hum, but it was punctuated now by other sounds. Sounds that made the hair on their arms stand up.

A rustle in the dense undergrowth to their left, too heavy and deliberate to be a lizard or a bird. They would freeze, their eyes wide, and listen to the sound of something large moving parallel to them, just out of sight. A few minutes later, a guttural, coughing roar would echo from the canopy far downriver, a sound that was definitively feline and terrifyingly large. They were not alone. They were being watched. They were being stalked. The Green Hell now had teeth.

They moved with a new, nervous energy, their heads on a constant swivel. Their enhanced senses were a curse, making every snapped twig sound like a gunshot, every shadow look like a predator about to pounce. The feeling of being prey was a primal fear that no amount of magical water could erase.

It happened near midday. They were navigating a particularly treacherous stretch of the riverbank, a jumble of large, slick rocks covered in a thick, slimy green algae. Skot, ever the more agile of the two, leaped from rock to rock with a goat's confidence. Dave followed, more cautiously, his mind on the precious BCD sloshing on his back. He planted his foot on what he thought was a stable surface, but the algae gave way.

His foot shot out from under him. For a terrifying, weightless moment, he was airborne, his arms pinwheeling for a balance that wasn't there. He crashed down hard, his right leg twisting and plunging into the murky water between two large rocks. A sharp, searing pain, white-hot and absolute, shot up his leg from his shin. It was a pain unlike any of the dull aches he had become accustomed to. This was the pain of acute, catastrophic damage.

He screamed, a raw, ugly sound that was swallowed by the jungle.

Skot was at his side in an instant. "Dave! Are you okay?"

"My leg," Dave gasped, his face pale with shock. "Oh God, my leg."

Skot helped him pull his leg from the water. The sight made them both sick. The river water, brown and muddy, was suddenly stained with a shocking, brilliant crimson. Blood was pouring from a deep, ragged gash that ran half the length of his shin. It wasn't a cut; it was a canyon. The rock had sliced through his pants and flesh with the clean, brutal efficiency of a dull saw, leaving a gaping wound that revealed the shocking white of the bone beneath.

"Oh, Jesus," Skot breathed, his face losing all its color.

Real panic, cold and sharp, set in. This wasn't a pulled muscle or a twisted ankle. This was a life-threatening injury. In this environment, with no medical supplies, a wound like this was a death sentence. Infection would be rampant in hours. And he was losing blood at an alarming rate.

Skot, his own hands trembling, tore a long strip from the sleeve of his tattered shirt and tried to fashion a crude tourniquet, but the blood soaked through it instantly. He tried to apply pressure, but the flow was too heavy. Dave lay back against the rock, his head spinning, a cold sweat breaking out all over his body. He could feel his own life pouring out of him into the muddy banks of the Colombian river.

"This is it," Dave whispered, his vision starting to tunnel. "This is how it ends."

"No!" Skot yelled, his voice a frantic bark. "No, it isn't!" He was looking around wildly, at the useless jungle, at Dave's pale face, at the ever-widening pool of blood. And then his eyes landed on the BCDs. A desperate, insane idea sparked in his mind.

"The water," he said, his voice a hoarse whisper.

"What?" Dave mumbled, his consciousness starting to fade.

"The water!" Skot repeated, scrambling for Dave's BCD. "We have to try the water!"

"No... Skot, don't..." Dave protested weakly. "It's for drinking... we can't waste it..."

"What good is drinking water if you're already dead?" Skot yelled, fumbling with the valve.

He had no idea if it would work. Would it just wash the wound? Would it do nothing? Or worse, would it somehow poison him through an open wound? He didn't have time to consider the possibilities. He tipped the BCD and poured a small, precious stream of the clear, magical water directly into the horrifying, gaping gash.

The effect was instantaneous and utterly, supernaturally terrifying.

The bleeding didn't just slow; it stopped. One moment, blood was flowing freely; the next, it simply ceased, as if a tap had been turned off. Dave, roused from his shock by the strange sensation, stared at his own leg in stunned, horrified awe. The water wasn't just cleaning the wound; it was doing something.

They watched, mesmerized, as the edges of the deep laceration began to pull together. It was a slow, visible, and deeply unnatural process. It looked like a time-lapse video of a healing wound, but it was happening in real time. Tiny, pink threads of new flesh seemed to weave themselves across the chasm, knitting the separated tissues back together. The raw, exposed muscle and bone were slowly covered. The skin drew taut. Over the course of a single, breathtaking minute, the six-inch, bone-deep gash closed, sealed, and vanished, leaving behind only a thin, faint, pink line of brand-new skin, as if the injury had happened years ago and had healed perfectly.

Dave tentatively touched the spot. The skin was smooth, warm, and whole. There was no pain. None.

He looked at Skot. Skot looked at him. The sounds of the jungle, the heat, the danger—it all faded away. They were two men staring at a miracle so profound, so impossible, it shattered their understanding of reality for the second time in three days. They had felt the water's effects inside their bodies, but to witness its power from the outside, to see it perform an act of instant, perfect creation… it was godlike.

The awe was quickly replaced by a new, more practical terror. Skot picked up Dave's BCD. It was noticeably lighter. The single, life-saving act had cost them dearly. They had used nearly a third of Dave's remaining supply. Their depreciating asset had just taken a massive, catastrophic hit.

They got to their feet, the adrenaline of the moment leaving them shaky and weak. The sounds of the jungle returned, the unseen predators in the trees, but now there was a new fear, one that was far more immediate. The fear of running out.

"We need to talk about something else," Dave said suddenly, needing to break the hypnotic, maddening rhythm of the hike. "Anything. My brain is starting to feel like it's full of bees."

"Okay," Skot said, swatting at a fly that was buzzing near his ear with a new, startling speed. "You pick a topic."

"Buzz," Dave said.

Skot laughed, a genuine, hearty laugh that sounded strange and wonderful in the oppressive silence. "What about him?"

"What do you think he's really doing right now?" Dave asked. "I mean, really. Let's break it down."

Skot considered this for a moment, a small smile playing on his lips. "Okay. It's about one o'clock in the afternoon. My guess is he slept until eleven. He ordered an obscene amount of room service, probably charged it to our room, including something ridiculous like a 'wellness shot' that he will complain about. He's now parked on a lounge chair by the pool, wearing sunglasses that cost more than my first car, and he's telling some poor, unsuspecting tourist a story that is at least seventy-five percent bullshit about the time he almost invested in Bitcoin in 2010."

"That sounds about right," Dave agreed, a smile tugging at his lips. The image was so vivid, so perfectly Buzz, that it felt like a dispatch from another universe. A universe of comfort and inconsequential lies. "He's probably just starting to get worried, though."

"Oh, for sure," Skot added. "He's probably sent us an angry text demanding to know where we are because our disappearance is interfering with his vacation schedule. Something like, 'Hope you guys are having fun dying. The blondes from California are asking about you and it's killing my vibe.'"

"He'll do the right thing, though," Dave said, a statement that was also a question. "Eventually."

"Yeah," Skot said, his voice softer now. "He will. When his back is against the wall, and there's absolutely no other option left that allows him to continue partying, Buzz comes through. He just has a very long and scenic definition of 'last resort.'"

The conversation helped. It was a tether to their old lives, a reminder of the world they were fighting to reclaim. They trudged on, their spirits momentarily lifted.

It was late in the afternoon when they saw it. They came around a bend in the river and Skot, in the lead, stopped dead in his tracks. Dave came up beside him, following his friend's gaze.

On their side of the river, almost completely swallowed by a thick curtain of vines, was a small, man-made structure. It was a crude dock, built of heavy, dark wood that had been bleached gray by years of sun and rain. Most of the planks were rotted through, but the main posts, thick as telephone poles, were still standing, defiant against the jungle's relentless campaign to reclaim everything. At the back of the dock, a narrow, barely-there path led away from the river and into the trees.

It wasn't ancient. It wasn't a Mayan ruin or a pirate relic. It was newer than that. Maybe twenty years old? Thirty? It was the first sign of human activity, other than their own, that they had seen in two days.

They approached it cautiously, their enhanced senses on high alert. Skot nudged one of the main posts with the toe of his boot. It was solid. He stepped onto the few remaining planks near the shore. They groaned under his weight but held.

"Who the hell would build a dock out here?" Dave whispered, his eyes scanning the opposite bank, half-expecting to see a hidden cabin or a plume of smoke. There was nothing. Just more jungle.

Skot pointed to the path. "Someone who wanted to go that way."

The path was more of a suggestion than a trail, but it was undeniable. Someone, at some point, had repeatedly walked this route, beating down the undergrowth. Their hope, which had been a flickering ember, flared into a bonfire. A path led somewhere. A dock was for a boat. A boat meant people.

"We follow it," Skot said, his voice tight with excitement. "We leave the river. This has to lead somewhere."

Dave felt a surge of hope so powerful it almost made him dizzy. But as he looked from the derelict dock to the dark, narrow path leading into the unknown, a sliver of his old, cautious self returned. The risk-assessment part of his brain began flashing warning lights.

"Or," he said quietly, "it leads to whatever happened to the people who built it."

Skot looked at him, and the excitement in his eyes was tempered by a new understanding. This wasn't just a sign of hope. It was a sign of a story. And out here, in the green hell, stories rarely had happy endings.

They had a choice to make. Follow the safe, slow, known path of the river, or gamble on the mysterious, unknown path that cut into the heart of the jungle.

"We've been betting on the impossible for two days now," Skot said, as if reading his mind. "No reason to stop."

He took the first step onto the overgrown path. After a moment's hesitation, Dave followed. They left the river behind, turning their backs on the one landmark that had guided them, and plunged once more into the green labyrinth, drawn forward by a rotten dock and the ghost of a forgotten trail.

Chapter 14: The Ghost of the Trail

The decision to leave the river felt monumental, a deliberate step off the one path that made logical sense. The river was their lifeline, a flowing, dynamic entity that was guaranteed, by the simple laws of physics, to eventually lead them to a larger body of water, and from there, to civilization. It was their map, written by the hand of God himself. To turn their backs on it felt like a special kind of hubris, like tearing up the only page of instructions they had.

This new path was different. It was a gamble, a whisper of a forgotten story leading into the suffocating, green unknown. The moment they stepped onto it, leaving the relatively open space of the riverbank behind, the world changed. The jungle closed in around them, a claustrophobic embrace. The canopy above was thicker here, filtering the already weak afternoon light into a dim, greenish twilight. The air grew still and heavy, losing the faint breeze that had followed the water. It was like walking from an open field into a sealed room.

The trail itself was less of a path and more of a memory. It was visible only to their newly enhanced senses. Dave could see the subtle, unnatural depression in the earth, the way the undergrowth grew just a little less thickly in a meandering line. He could spot the occasional snapped branch on a tree, now covered in moss, a sign that someone had passed this way long ago. It was a ghost of a trail, and they were following it deeper into the gloom.

Their progress was even slower than it had been along the river. They had to stoop under low-hanging vines thick as a man's arm and push their way through giant, waxy leaves that slapped against them with a wet, percussive sound, showering them with droplets of stale water. The air was filled with the rich, loamy smell of decay. Everything was either growing or rotting with a ferocious, silent energy.

"Whoever made this path, they weren't taking a scenic stroll," Dave muttered, wiping a spiderweb from his face that was as thick as thread.

"No," Skot replied, his voice a low grunt of exertion from a few feet ahead. "They were trying to get somewhere. Or get away from something." He used his dive knife to slash at a curtain of vines blocking their way, the blade making a satisfying thwack. "The question is, did they make it?"

It was a question that hung in the thick, still air between them. They were following in the footsteps of ghosts, and the thought sent a cold shiver down Dave's spine that had nothing to do with the dampness.

They drank from their water supply more frequently now, not just to fight off the physical exhaustion, but to sharpen their senses, to keep the encroaching dread at bay. Each sip was a shot of pure, clean confidence, a reminder that they were not ordinary men. They were stronger, more aware. They needed that belief to keep going, to keep putting one foot in front of the other on a path that could be leading them to their salvation or to the same forgotten end as its original trailblazers.

After an hour that felt like a lifetime, the character of the jungle began to change again. They started seeing signs that were undeniably human. First, it was a rusted machete blade, its wooden handle long since rotted away, half-buried in the black mud. Skot nudged it with his foot, then left it where it lay. A little farther on, they found a small, unnatural clearing, where a few massive trees had been felled, their colossal stumps now serving as giant, moss-covered thrones for ferns and fungi. Someone had cleared this land for a reason.

The path grew wider, more defined. And then, it opened up.

They stepped out of the thick undergrowth and into a large, circular clearing. It was like stepping into a ruined cathedral. The jungle formed the walls, but the clearing itself was a space of profound and eerie silence. It was clear this had once been a significant human encampment, but the jungle was in the process of swallowing it whole.

In the center of the clearing were the skeletal remains of what might have been a large tent or a crude lean-to, its canvas rotted away to nothing but a few tattered, greenish-brown rags clinging to a collapsed frame of moldy poles. Rusted, unidentifiable pieces of machinery lay scattered about like the bones of strange metal animals. A small, cast-iron stove, miraculously intact, sat askew, a tree sapling growing up through its rusted grate.

And there, on the far side of the clearing, sat the ghost.

It was a vehicle. An old Land Rover, the kind you saw in documentaries about Africa from the 1970s. It was an icon of rugged exploration, and it was completely, utterly dead. Its tires were flat, the rubber cracked and perished. A thick coat of rust covered every metal surface, so deep and pervasive that it had turned the original paint into a mottled, brownish-orange skin. The windshield was a spiderweb of cracks, and a thick, woody vine had snaked its way through the passenger-side window, wrapped itself around the steering wheel, and was now working its way out the other side. The jungle was not just covering the vehicle; it was consuming it, digesting it.

Dave and Skot walked toward it slowly, as if approaching a sleeping beast. It was both the most beautiful and the most heartbreaking thing they had ever seen. It was a symbol of everything they were trying to get back to—technology, civilization, escape—but it was a corpse.

"Well," Dave said, his voice flat. "There's our ticket home."

Skot didn't reply. He ran a hand over the rusted hood, his touch gentle, reverent. He was an artist, and this was a sculpture of profound and tragic failure. This was the end of someone's story. The final, silent testament to a dream that had died in this suffocating green place.

They spent the next half hour exploring the derelict camp, a grim archaeological dig. They found little of use. A few empty, rusted cans. A broken glass bottle. The rotted leather of a pair of work boots. Whoever had been here had either left in a hurry or had been taken by the jungle, leaving almost nothing behind.

Their last hope was the Land Rover itself. Maybe there was something inside. Skot wrestled with the driver's side door, the hinges groaning in protest before giving way with a loud, metallic shriek. The inside smelled of mildew and time. The seats were just springs and rotted foam. The dashboard was cracked and faded.

Dave went around to the passenger side and peered in. He reached for the glove compartment, his fingers fumbling with the rusted latch. It was stuck fast.

"Got your knife?" he asked Skot.

Skot handed him the heavy dive knife, and Dave used the thick, serrated spine to pry at the latch. With a final, sharp crack, it broke open. He reached inside, his fingers brushing against something that felt like damp, pulpy leather. He pulled it out.

It was a journal. A small, leather-bound book, the kind someone might use to log their thoughts or keep records. It was in terrible condition, swollen and warped by years of humidity. The pages were fused together in a solid, moldy block.

"Anything?" Skot asked, leaning in to look.

"I don't know," Dave said. He handled the journal with the care of a bomb disposal expert, carrying it over to the flat hood of the Land Rover. He used the tip of the knife to gently, painstakingly peel back the top page. It tore, but a large section of it came away, revealing the page beneath.

The paper was yellowed and stained, the ink a faded, blurry blue. Most of it was illegible, a wash of watery marks. But some words, where the pen had pressed harder, were still readable. They weren't full sentences, just fragments, islands of coherence in a sea of decay.

"…water from the black creek… tastes of iron…"

Dave felt a chill. He carefully peeled away another layer of fused pages. More fragments emerged.

"...third day of the fever... Ramirez is delirious... talking to his dead brother..."

"Skot, look at this," Dave whispered.

Skot leaned closer, his eyes scanning the faded script. The next legible fragment was on the following page.

"...not a fever... it's the water... the bad water... it makes the rage come..."

Dave's blood ran cold. This wasn't a log of a successful operation. It was a record of a descent into madness.

He managed to separate one final, larger piece of a page. The writing here was spidery and frantic, the pen having dug deep into the paper.

"...Javier tried to leave... said the spring was a demon... we stopped him... the gold is so close... but the water... the water is making us gods and monsters... can't tell which... saw Javier by the river... his eyes..."

The final word was just a blurry, incomprehensible smudge.

They stood there in the silent, decaying camp, the cryptic journal lying between them on the rusted hood of the dead machine. The story of this place was becoming terrifyingly clear. Other men had come here, chasing a different kind of treasure. And they had found a different kind of spring. A spring that didn't heal, but infected. A spring that didn't grant vitality, but madness.

Dave looked at the BCDs lying on the ground, their precious, life-giving cargo suddenly seeming infinitely more valuable and infinitely more dangerous. They hadn't just been lucky to find their grotto. They had been impossibly, miraculously lucky to have not found this one.

They had traded the simple, honest problem of being lost for a much more complex one. They had found a potential way out, but it was a dead machine in a haunted place. And they had just learned that the jungle held more than one kind of secret, more than one kind of water. Theirs was a miracle. But just a few miles away, flowing from a black creek, was its evil twin. A Siren of a different sort, one whose song led not just to death, but to damnation.

Chapter 15: The Unblinking Witness

The Land Rover was a monument to failure. It sat in the center of the clearing, a rusted, vine-choked tombstone marking the final resting place of someone else's dream. After the initial, chilling discovery of the journal, Dave and Skot had approached the dead machine not as a potential escape, but as a problem to be dissected.

Dave, the pragmatist, was the first to voice the obvious. "It's hopeless, Skot." He ran a hand over one of the tires, a cracked and flattened pancake of rubber that had long since fused with the damp earth beneath it. "The tires are shot. The battery, if there even is one left, has been dead for twenty years. The engine is probably a solid block of rust. We'd have better luck trying to build a helicopter out of bamboo."

He was right, and they both knew it. This wasn't a simple mechanical failure; it was a case of terminal decay. The jungle had been working on this vehicle for decades, its slow, relentless processes of moisture and growth doing more damage than a sledgehammer ever could.

Skot, however, refused to surrender to the obvious. His optimism, a trait Dave usually found endearing but now found maddening, was in overdrive. "We don't know that for sure," he argued, trying to wrestle the hood open. It was rusted shut. "We just have to take a look. Maybe the engine block is protected. Maybe we can patch the tires. We have neoprene from the wetsuits…"

"Patch them with what, Skot?" Dave shot back, his voice sharper than he intended. The grim reality of their situation was pressing in on him, and his patience was wearing thin. "And inflate them with what? Wishful thinking? We don't have tools. We don't have parts. We have two knives and a couple of flashlights. It's over. This thing is a coffin."

The word hung in the air, ugly and final. Skot stopped struggling with the hood and turned to face him, his face a mixture of frustration and hurt. He kicked at the rusted front bumper, a loud, unsatisfying clang that echoed in the quiet clearing. He was a man of action, a man of solutions, and for the first time, he was staring at a problem he couldn't charm, out-think, or out-maneuver. The sheer, immovable physics of their predicament had finally cornered him.

Defeated, he slumped down onto the ground, his back against the petrified front tire. He ran a hand over his face, smearing the grime. He looked at his dive helmet, which he'd set down on a patch of moss nearby. It was a relic from the other world, their world, a world of high-tech gear and planned adventures.

He reached for it, his movements slow and dejected. He picked it up, his thumb tracing the familiar contours of the molded plastic. It was a habit, a comforting, tactile motion. His thumb brushed against the hard, rectangular shape mounted on the side, just above the ear. The GoPro.

He froze. His eyes went wide. He looked at the camera, then at Dave, then back at the camera. A new kind of light, a frantic, dawning electricity, began to burn in his gaze.

"What?" Dave asked, seeing the sudden shift in his friend's demeanor. "What is it?"

"The camera," Skot whispered, his voice barely audible. He held the helmet up as if it were a holy relic. "I was so busy not dying, I completely forgot."

Dave stared at it. The little black box with its unblinking, fish-eye lens. It seemed absurd, a trivial piece of electronics in a place where only the most primal survival skills mattered. "So what? The battery's been dead for days. It's a useless brick."

"No," Skot said, shaking his head, his excitement building. "No, you don't get it." He scrambled over to his BCD, which lay on the ground like a discarded carapace. He fumbled with a small, zippered pocket on the side, a pocket they hadn't bothered to check because it didn't hold anything vital for their immediate survival. "I always pack it. Always. For emergencies."

His fingers closed around a small, hard object. He pulled it out. It was a waterproof pouch, no bigger than a wallet. He struggled with the ziplock seal for a moment, then tore it open. He tipped the contents into his palm.

Out fell a small, dense, black rectangle and a coiled-up USB cable.

A power bank. A waterproof, shockproof, high-capacity power bank. The kind of over-the-top, absurdly prepared piece of gear that only a gear-head like Skot would think to bring on a simple day-dive.

Dave stared at the little black brick as if it were the most magical object he had ever seen. It was. In this context, it was Excalibur. It was the Holy Grail. It was a miracle of a different sort — a miracle of obsessive compulsive preparedness.

"You have got to be kidding me," Dave breathed, a slow smile spreading across his face.

The mood in the clearing had transformed in an instant. The crushing despair was gone, replaced by a giddy, frantic hope. They were no longer two exhausted survivors staring at a wreck; they were archaeologists who had just found the key to a lost tomb.

They huddled together on the ground, the Land Rover forgotten for the moment. Skot carefully detached the GoPro from its helmet mount. He plugged the cable into the power bank, then into the camera's tiny charging port. A minuscule red light on the camera flickered to life. It was charging. It was working.

They waited for what felt like an eternity, though it was probably only ten minutes, watching the little red light as if their lives depended on it. Finally, Skot decided they had enough of a charge. He unplugged the cable and held the camera in his trembling hands.

"You ready?" he asked, his voice hushed.

Dave just nodded, his throat too tight to speak.

Skot pressed the power button. The small LCD screen on the back flickered, went blue, and then an image appeared. It was a shot of the jungle floor, upside down. Skot navigated the simple menu, his fingers surprisingly nimble. He found the playback option and selected the last file recorded. The file was huge, nearly two hours long. He pressed play.

They leaned in, their heads almost touching, and stared into the tiny, two-inch screen. And the world fell away.

The first thing they saw was their own descent into Cenote Escondido. The footage was breathtakingly clear, the sunbeams piercing the water, the sense of flying through a liquid sky. Dave felt a pang of nostalgia for the men they had been just a few days ago, so full of naive excitement.

Then came The Cathedral. Even on the tiny screen, its scale was awe-inspiring, the massive, ghostly columns drifting past the lens. It was beautiful, serene. It was the "before."

And then came the "after."

The footage suddenly shook, a violent, nauseating vibration. The audio, which had been only the gentle sound of their breathing, was now a deep, grinding roar, a terrifying, distorted sound coming through the waterproof casing. They watched, mesmerized and horrified, as the archway ahead of them imploded in a silent, billowing cloud of silt and rock. The screen went black for a moment as Skot was thrown by the pressure wave, then it was a chaotic, spinning blur of brown and gray. They were reliving their own near-death, but this time from the cold, objective perspective of the unblinking witness.

They watched their desperate, terrifying squeeze through the escape passage, the lens so close to the rock walls that they could see every scrape and scratch. The audio was a frantic, ragged rasp of their own panicked breathing.

And then, the moment.

The lens broke the surface of the water, and the screen was flooded with an impossible, brilliant, turquoise light. It wasn't a reflection; it was a source. The grotto was alive with light, pulsating with it. The footage showed them surfacing, ripping their masks off, their faces pale with shock and exhaustion. They watched themselves drink the water. They watched their own expressions change from terror to pure, dumbfounded wonder.

It was real.

They had known it was real, of course. They had felt it in their own bodies. But seeing it on a screen, captured as objective data, was something else entirely. It was undeniable proof. It wasn't a shared hallucination. It wasn't a trick of the mind. It was a physical, documented phenomenon. They had captured a miracle.

Skot stopped the playback. They sat in silence, the sounds of the jungle rushing back in to fill the void. The little camera in Skot's hand was no longer a toy. It was the most important object on the planet. It was their story, their proof, their power.

Dave looked at Skot, and he saw the same realization in his friend's eyes. A profound shift had occurred. Seeing what they had survived, seeing the irrefutable evidence of the magic that now flowed through their veins, it changed the equation. The despair was gone, burned away by the glowing light from the tiny screen.

"Okay," Dave said, his voice quiet but infused with a new, steely resolve. He looked from the camera in Skot's hand to the dead, rusted Land Rover. It no longer looked like a coffin. It looked like a challenge. "So. The battery is probably dead."

Skot grinned, a real, full-throated grin of pure, unadulterated audacity. The artist, the dreamer, the madman was back. "Probably," he said. "So I guess we'll have to find a way to charge it."

Chapter 16: The Lazarus Machine

The tiny screen of the GoPro went dark, plunging the clearing back into its own dim, green twilight. For a long moment, Skot and Dave didn't move. They remained huddled on the ground, the silence between them thick with the aftershock of what they had just witnessed. It was one thing to live through a traumatic event, to have the fractured, subjective memories of it rattling around in your skull. It was another thing entirely to watch it play out from a third-person perspective, a cold, digital record of your own impossible survival. The footage wasn't a memory; it was evidence. It was truth.

And that truth changed everything. The rusted Land Rover, which had been a symbol of hopelessness just minutes before, now looked different. It was no longer a tombstone. It was a challenge. A dare.

Dave was the first to speak, his voice quiet but infused with a new, steely resolve that had been forged in the glowing light of the tiny screen. "Okay," he said, looking from the camera in Skot's hand to the dead machine. "So. The battery is probably dead."

Skot looked up, and a slow, audacious grin spread across his face. It was the grin of a man who had just been reminded that the normal rules of the world no longer applied to him. The artist, the dreamer, the madman was back. "Probably," he said. "So I guess we'll have to find a way to charge it."

He didn't mean with electricity.

What followed was not mechanics. It was a resurrection. They descended upon the Land Rover not as two men, but as a force of nature in reverse. The jungle had spent decades slowly, patiently digesting this machine. Now, they were going to make it regurgitate it.

Their first obstacle was the hood. It was rusted shut, the metal fused together by years of moisture and oxidation. Skot, fueled by a fresh sip of the miraculous water and a surge of manic energy, grabbed the lip of the hood with both hands.

"Together," he grunted.

Dave grabbed the other side. On a count of three, they pulled. It wasn't a delicate operation. There was a hideous, groaning shriek of tortured metal, a sound that echoed through the quiet clearing. The hinges, which should have held firm, bent and then tore away from the frame with a sharp crack. They lifted the entire hood off the vehicle and tossed it aside, where it landed in the undergrowth with a dull, final thud.

They stared into the engine bay. It was a horrifying sight, a mechanic's nightmare. It was a tangled mess of rotted hoses, frayed wires, and rust. A thick layer of composted leaves and animal nests covered everything. It looked less like an engine and more like a geological formation.

"Well," Dave said, his newfound optimism taking a slight hit. "That's... not great."

"It's a canvas," Skot declared, his eyes gleaming. He was already at work, plunging his hands into the leafy grime, pulling out handfuls of debris with a gardener's enthusiasm. "We just have to find the engine underneath."

For the next two hours, they worked with a frantic, focused energy. They were a perfect team, their movements economical and intuitive. Skot was the brute force, tearing out the larger nests and rotted components. Dave, with his CPA's eye for detail and his supernaturally enhanced focus, followed behind, meticulously cleaning the smaller, more delicate parts. He could see things he never would have before—a tiny crack in a distributor cap, a frayed connection on a spark plug wire. His mind, which was used to finding errors in complex spreadsheets, was now debugging a complex, three-dimensional system of decay. He found he understood it, in a way. He could see the flow, where the energy was supposed to go, where the blockages were.

They used their dive knives to scrape away the thickest layers of rust. They used strips of neoprene from their wetsuits as rags to wipe down the engine block. They drank from their BCDs whenever they felt their energy begin to wane, each sip a fresh wave of power and clarity.

They found the vehicle's toolkit in a rusted-out box in the back. Most of the tools were useless, fused into a single, solid lump of rust. But they managed to salvage a heavy, solid wrench and a tire iron. These became their primary instruments.

The battery was, as predicted, a complete loss. It was a swollen, corroded brick, its terminals blooming with a pale green crust. Skot unbolted it and unceremoniously dropped it to the ground. There was no saving it.

"So how do we start it without a battery?" Dave asked, stating the obvious, impossible problem. "We can't push-start it with four flat tires."

"We don't need the battery to run it," Skot said, tapping the distributor cap. "We just need it to turn the engine over. To get the alternator spinning. Once the alternator is going, it generates its own electricity. We just need to give it that first kick."

"With what?"

Skot's eyes scanned the engine bay, then the tools in his hand. He looked at the massive crankshaft pulley at the front of the engine. "With that," he said, pointing with the wrench. "We turn it ourselves."

Dave stared at him. "You're insane. Skot, that's not possible. It takes hundreds of foot-pounds of torque to turn an engine over, especially one that's been sitting for twenty years. We'd need a ten-foot breaker bar. We'll snap that wrench in half and probably break every bone in our hands."

"A week ago, you would have been right," Skot said, his voice low and intense. He held up his own hands, turning them over. They were grimy and scratched, but they were steady. "But we're not the men we were a week ago. We swam two hundred feet through a solid rock tunnel on a single breath of air. Don't tell me we can't turn a stupid crank."

The sheer, breathtaking audacity of the idea was infectious. It was a challenge thrown at the feet of the gods, of physics, of logic itself. It was insane. And it was the only thing they had.

But first, the other problems. The fuel tank was mostly empty, containing only a few inches of a foul-smelling, sludgy brown liquid that was more varnish than gasoline. But it was flammable. The fuel line was clogged solid. Dave spent an hour meticulously working a thin, stiff wire he'd pulled from a rotted seat spring through the line, clearing the blockage one painstaking inch at a time.

The tires were their biggest physical challenge. They were beyond repair. So, they decided to improvise. They spent the rest of the day and into the twilight hours engaged in the most brutal manual labor of their lives. Using their knives, they hacked at the tough, fibrous jungle plants, cutting down armfuls of the stuff. Then, using the tire iron as a lever, they pried one side of each rotten tire off its rim and began stuffing the plant matter inside.

It was grueling, punishing work. They packed the tires so tightly that they became solid, unyielding masses of green. Their hands were raw, their bodies were screaming, but every time they faltered, they took another sip of the water, and the pain vanished, replaced by a fresh wave of tireless, miraculous strength.

They worked through the night, their two dive lights casting long, dancing shadows across the clearing. The jungle came alive with the sounds of the dark, a chorus of clicks, hoots, and growls, but they were too focused to be afraid. They were men possessed by a singular, impossible purpose.

By dawn, it was done. The four tires were stuffed solid, bulging like over-full sausages. The engine was as clean as they could get it. The fuel line was clear. They were ready.

They stood before the open engine bay, two grimy, sweat-soaked gods of the junkyard. Skot took the heavy wrench and managed to fit it over the large bolt on the crankshaft pulley. It was a snug fit.

"Okay," Skot said, his voice a low, gravelly rasp. "This is it. We get one shot. We both get on this thing. We pull with everything we have. Everything the water gave us. We need to get it to make one full rotation. Just one."

Dave positioned himself next to Skot, his hands gripping the smooth, cold steel of the wrench. He could feel the raw power humming in his own muscles, a deep, resonant energy that was waiting to be unleashed. He looked at his friend's face, taut with concentration, and he nodded.

"On three," Dave said.

"On three."

They took a deep, shuddering breath.

"One."

They tightened their grip, their knuckles white.

"Two."

They leaned in, putting their entire body weight into it, their muscles coiling like springs.

"THREE!"

They pulled.

The wrench didn't move. It was like trying to pull a mountain. The resistance was absolute. Dave felt a scream of frustration build in his throat. It was impossible. He had been right.

"AGAIN!" Skot roared, his voice a raw, primal cry of defiance.

They pulled again, but this time it was different. They didn't just pull with their muscles. They pulled with their will. They poured every ounce of the miracle inside them, every bit of their desperation, every memory of their fear and their hope, into that single, focused point of effort.

There was a sound. A deep, groaning, cracking sound from the heart of the engine, the sound of twenty years of rust and neglect finally surrendering. The wrench moved. An inch. Then another.

They roared, a single, unified sound of pure, savage effort. They were no longer thinking. They were pure force. The wrench moved faster, a quarter turn, a half turn. They could hear the pistons inside the engine block groaning, scraping against the cylinder walls.

They gave one final, convulsive heave, putting the last of their strength into it. The crankshaft completed a full rotation.

And from the depths of the dead machine, there came a sound.

A cough.

A single, sputtering, pathetic cough, followed by a puff of black, acrid smoke from the exhaust pipe.

It was the most beautiful sound they had ever heard.

Chapter 17: Presumed Dead

The single, sputtering cough from the Land Rover's engine was the most beautiful sound they had ever heard, but it was followed by a profound and discouraging silence. The puff of black smoke dissipated into the humid air, leaving behind only the smell of burnt, ancient fuel and the quiet, indifferent hum of the jungle. The miracle had been fleeting. They had proven the machine wasn't entirely dead, but it was still a long way from being alive.

"Well," Dave said, his voice a ragged whisper, his hands still trembling from the monumental effort of turning the crank. "That's something."

"Something isn't enough," Skot grunted, wiping a slick of grease and sweat from his forehead with the back of his arm. He was breathing in deep, shuddering gasps, the superhuman strength they had summoned for their single, heroic pull now completely spent. The familiar, deep ache was already beginning to seep back into his muscles, a reminder of their body's new, cruel cycle of debt and payment.

They were back to square one, only now they were exhausted. The problem was no longer one of brute force, but of finesse. They had managed to turn the engine, but it hadn't caught. That meant a failure in one of two fundamental systems: fuel or spark.

"It's not getting a spark," Dave said, his analytical mind taking over. The brief, heady rush of god-like power was gone, and he was a CPA again, albeit a very dirty one.

He was looking at the engine not as a single entity, but as a system, a ledger of interconnected accounts. "We turned it over, the carburetor probably managed to suck a little of that fuel sludge up, but the spark plugs never fired to ignite it."

He leaned over the engine bay, his newly sharp eyes scanning the tangle of old wires. He pointed to the distributor cap, the plastic hub from which the spark plug wires radiated like the legs of a dead spider. "That's the brain. If it's not sending the signal, nothing else matters."

Skot followed his gaze. "Cracked?"

"Or just corroded," Dave said. He gently unclipped the cap. The inside was a horror show. The metal contact points were covered in a pale green, crusty corrosion, a cancerous bloom of oxidation that would prevent any electrical current from ever completing its journey.

For the next hour, they worked with the meticulous focus of surgeons. They took another small, precious sip of the water, the familiar, cool rush chasing away the aches and sharpening their minds. They used the edge of Skot's dive knife to painstakingly scrape the corrosion from each tiny metal contact point inside the distributor cap and on the rotor. They pulled each spark plug, cleaning the fouled, grimy tips with strips of neoprene. It was delicate, frustrating work, their large, clumsy hands struggling with the tiny, fragile components. But their focus was absolute. Their shared desperation had forged a non-verbal bond between them; they moved and worked as a single, eight-limbed organism, driven by one unified thought: make it work.

....

Miles away, in a world that operated on procedure and probability, another team was working with a different kind of focus. The official search for Skot Larson and David Bennett had reached its grim, logical nexus: Cenote Escondido.

Lieutenant Morales stood on the muddy bank, his arms crossed, his face an impassive mask. The scene was one of controlled, somber activity. Two police vehicles were parked in the clearing, their presence a harsh, official intrusion in the wild green. The rental jeep was there, exactly where Skot and Dave had left it. It had been dusted for prints and searched. Inside, the officers had found two wallets, two cell phones, and a pile of dry clothes. Men on a simple day-trip. Men who had expected to come back.

The real action was at the water's edge. Two men, both local legends in the international cave-diving community, were preparing to enter the water. They weren't police officers; they were civilians, volunteers who were always called upon when the jungle's watery underworld claimed a victim. They were lean, weathered, and deeply serious, their movements economical and precise as they assembled their complex rebreather units. They spoke to each other in low, technical Spanish, their conversation a quiet litany of gas mixtures and decompression times.

Morales watched them, his expression unreadable. He had seen this scene play out too many times. The hopeful beginning, the methodical preparation, and the inevitable, grim conclusion. He knew what they would find. Or rather, what they wouldn't.

"The entry point is stable," one of the divers, a man named Mateo, reported to Morales. "The guideline is still in place from the last survey team. We will follow it to the entrance of the main chamber, 'La Catedral.'"

"Be careful," Morales said, his voice quiet. "The friend, Mr. Walker, he said they were experienced, but not with this kind of system. They can make mistakes. Get disoriented."

Mateo nodded, his face grim. "The caves do not forgive mistakes, Lieutenant."

With a final gear check, the two divers slipped into the water and vanished, leaving behind only a trail of slow-rising bubbles. Morales was left on the bank with two junior officers and the oppressive, waiting silence of the jungle. He pulled out his worn notebook and began to write, documenting the time, the conditions, the names of the divers. He was a man who believed in order, in procedure. And the procedure for this kind of tragedy was well-established. Now, all they could do was wait for the inevitable, official word.

....

"Okay, try it now."

Skot and Dave stood over the engine, their hands braced on the fenders. They had cleaned every contact point they could reach. They had reconnected the spark plug wires in what Dave prayed was the correct order. The moment of truth had arrived again.

"We can't pull it by hand all day," Dave said, his breath misting in the humid air. "We'll kill ourselves."

"We just need it to catch," Skot insisted. "Just for a second."

They took their positions at the wrench again, their bodies screaming in protest. They drank another mouthful of water, the effect slightly less potent this time, as if their bodies were becoming accustomed to the miracle. The asset was depreciating.

"One... two... THREE!"

They heaved, pouring their renewed strength into the pull. The engine turned, groaning its protest. It coughed once, then twice. It sputtered, a ragged, promising rhythm. A small flame shot from the carburetor, a startling WHOOMP that made them both jump back.

"It's trying!" Skot yelled, his face wild with a manic grin. "It wants to live! Again!"

They threw themselves at the wrench, pulling with a desperate, frantic energy. The engine sputtered, caught, and then, with a sound like a dragon clearing its throat, it roared to life.

It was the loudest, most violent, most beautiful sound in the world. The engine ran not with a smooth hum, but with a rattling, shaking, ear-splitting clatter. It spewed a thick cloud of blue-black smoke that filled the clearing with a toxic, glorious smell. It was a wounded, angry beast, but it was alive. It was running.

They stumbled back, staring at the shaking, rattling engine in disbelief. They were covered in grease, grime, and sweat. Their hands were bleeding from a dozen small cuts. They looked like madmen, like wild things born of the jungle. And they were laughing. A hysterical, joyous, triumphant laughter that echoed through the clearing, momentarily drowning out the sound of the resurrected machine.

....

Forty minutes later, two figures broke the surface of Cenote Escondido. The divers emerged with a slow, weary deliberation, pulling their masks off to reveal faces etched with grim finality. They swam to the bank, where Lieutenant Morales was waiting.

"Report," Morales said, his voice flat.

Mateo, the lead diver, pulled himself onto the bank, water streaming from his gear. "It's as we feared, Lieutenant," he said, his voice heavy. "There was a major collapse. The entrance to La Catedral is completely gone. Sealed. Tons of rock and silt."

"Is there any way through?" Morales asked, though he already knew the answer.

Mateo shook his head. "Impossible. We probed the edges of the collapse. It's unstable. No one could have survived being caught in that. And there is no other way out of that chamber. We searched for any sign of them, any equipment that might have been blown clear. Nothing. No bodies, no tanks, no lights." He looked at Morales, his eyes filled with a weary sympathy. "They are in there, under the rock. There will be no recovery. I am sorry."

Morales stood in silence for a long moment, the sounds of the jungle pressing in around him. He had his answer. It was the answer he had expected from the beginning. Clean, logical, and tragic. He made a few final notes in his book, his neat letters a stark, orderly contrast to the chaotic violence of the event he was recording.

He looked at his junior officers. "Pack it up," he said quietly. "Our work here is done."

He walked back to his vehicle, pulling out his radio to contact the main office. He would have to call the consulate. And then, he would have to make the drive back to the resort. He would have to find Mr. Walker, the loud, foolish, guilt-ridden friend in the lobby. He would have to sit him down and tell him, with official certainty, that the search was over. That there was no hope. That his friends were gone, their bodies entombed forever in the dark, silent heart of the jungle.

Chapter 18: The Road Back

The roar of the resurrected engine was a violation. It tore through the sacred quiet of the clearing, a vulgar, mechanical scream that sent birds scattering from the high branches of the canopy. The Land Rover shuddered and shook, its entire frame vibrating with the violent, protesting convulsions of its own rebirth. Thick, blue-black smoke billowed from the exhaust, filling the air with a rich, acrid stench that was, to Skot and Dave, the most beautiful perfume in the world. They had done it. They had performed a miracle of grease and rust and sheer, bloody-minded will.

Their laughter, wild and hysterical, eventually subsided, leaving them in a state of giddy, adrenaline-spiked disbelief. They stood there, two grimy, sweat-soaked gods of the junkyard, and stared at their creation. It was alive. But it was not well.

"Now what?" Dave asked, shouting to be heard over the rattling din.

"Now we drive it out of here!" Skot yelled back, his eyes wild with triumph. He scrambled toward the driver's side door, his movements infused with a manic, unstoppable energy.

Getting the Land Rover moving was nearly as difficult as starting it. Skot climbed into the driver's seat, which was mostly just springs and rotted foam, and surveyed the cracked dashboard. The gearshift was stiff, resisting his attempts to move it. He had to slam it with the heel of his hand, a brutal act that was met with a hideous grinding of unseen gears before it finally lurched into what he hoped was first.

He pressed the accelerator. The engine roared in protest, the vehicle shaking violently, but it did not move.

"The tires!" Dave yelled, pointing to the wheels. "They're sunk into the mud!"

Of course. After decades of sitting in one place, the earth had begun to claim the vehicle, pulling it into its soft, damp embrace. They were stuck.

For a moment, despair threatened to overwhelm them again. To have come so far, to have achieved the impossible, only to be defeated by a few inches of mud, seemed like a uniquely cruel cosmic joke. But the water was still singing in their veins. The miracle was not yet finished with them.

"We lift it," Skot said, his voice a low growl of determination. It was an insane suggestion. A two-ton vehicle. But they were fresh from the miracle of the engine, and the word "impossible" had lost some of its power.

They didn't have a jack. They had their bodies. They wedged themselves against the rear quarter panel of the truck, found what purchase they could on the rusted frame, and pushed. It was like trying to move a building. Their feet slipped in the mud, their muscles screamed, but they pushed with a synchronized, superhuman force.

Slowly, agonizingly, the corner of the vehicle lifted. An inch. Then another. It was enough. With a wet, sucking sound, the tire broke free from the mud's grip. They repeated the process on the other three wheels, a brutal, exhausting, and utterly miraculous feat of raw power. By the time they were done, they were gasping, their bodies trembling on the verge of collapse. They took another deep drink of their water, the world snapping back into sharp, clear focus.

Skot climbed back behind the wheel. Dave got in the passenger side, the door shrieking its protest. Skot revved the engine, and this time, when he eased off the clutch, the Lazarus machine lurched forward, its strange, plant-stuffed tires bumping and squelching over the uneven ground. They were moving.

The drive was a special kind of hell. There was no suspension to speak of, and the solid, lumpy tires transmitted every single bump, rock, and root directly into their spines. They were bounced and thrown around the cab, their teeth rattling with every jolt. The steering was a vague suggestion at best; Skot had to constantly fight the wheel to keep them moving in a generally straight line. The brakes, they quickly discovered, were more of a theoretical concept than a functional system.

But they were moving. They bumped their way out of the clearing and onto the ghost of a trail, the Land Rover's wide body carving a new, more definitive path through the undergrowth. Branches scraped and screeched against the metal sides. Leaves slapped against the cracked windshield. It was like driving through a car wash that used trees instead of brushes.

"How are we doing on water?" Skot yelled over the engine's roar.

Dave checked his BCD, which he was clutching in his lap like a nervous passenger holding a carry-on bag. He sloshed it around. "Maybe two quarts left," he shouted back. "Yours?"

"About the same!"

Their depreciating asset was becoming critically low. They had enough for maybe two more "recharges" each. After that, they would be on their own, just two normal, aching, middle-aged men in a broken-down truck. The ticking clock of their own mortality had returned.

The trail was a nightmare. It was narrow, winding, and overgrown. Twice, they had to stop, get out, and use their knives to hack away a thick, fallen log that was blocking the path. At one point, the trail dipped suddenly, and the front left tire plunged into a deep, muddy hole, bringing the truck to a jarring halt. It was stuck again.

"I've got an idea," Skot said, a familiar, mad glint in his eye. He rummaged behind the seat and found a length of rusted, heavy chain. He climbed out, slogged through the mud, and wrapped one end of the chain around the trunk of a thick, sturdy tree a few yards in front of the truck. He hooked the other end to the front bumper.

"Get behind the wheel," he instructed Dave. "When I tell you, give it gas. Gently."

Skot then positioned himself at the front of the vehicle. He grabbed the chain with both hands, planted his feet, and began to pull. Dave watched in stunned disbelief. It was a one-man tug-of-war against a two-ton machine. Skot's muscles bunched, the veins in his neck standing out like cords. He was pulling the Land Rover, inch by painful inch, out of the mud, using nothing but his own two hands and the strange, miraculous fire in his blood.

"Now!" he roared.

Dave stomped on the gas. The engine screamed, the rear wheels spun, and with a final, heroic pull from Skot, the truck lurched out of the hole and back onto the path.

Skot collapsed against the hood, panting, his strength completely spent. Dave cut the engine, the sudden silence a blessing. He jumped out and handed his friend the BCD. Skot drank deeply, his body visibly recovering, the exhaustion receding from his face.

"You're a lunatic," Dave said, a statement of pure, unadulterated awe.

"We're alive, aren't we?" Skot shot back with a grin.

They drove on. Hours passed in a blur of green, brown, and jolting, bone-jarring motion. The jungle began to change. The thick, primordial density started to thin out. They saw more signs of human activity—a discarded plastic bottle, a newer, less-rotted machete mark on a tree. The path was becoming wider, more defined. The ghost trail was becoming a real road.

And then, they saw it. Through a break in the trees, they saw a flash of movement. Another vehicle. A battered, blue pickup truck, kicking up a plume of dust as it drove along a road perpendicular to their own path.

They had found it. A real road.

With a whoop of pure joy, Skot slammed the accelerator. The Land Rover burst through the last curtain of foliage and onto a wide, well-worn dirt road. They were out. They were free from the green hell.

They drove for another twenty minutes, the ride on the dirt road feeling as smooth as glass compared to the jungle floor. The sun was low in the sky, casting a warm, golden light over the landscape. And then they saw it ahead, shimmering in the heat haze. Civilization. Or a reasonable facsimile thereof.

It was a small, dusty outpost, barely a town. It consisted of a single, cinder-block building with a corrugated tin roof and a single, ancient-looking gas pump out front. A hand-painted sign hanging crookedly over the door read "GASOLINA Y COMESTIBLES."

Skot steered their monstrous, mud-caked, barely-held-together vehicle toward the gas pump and brought it to a rattling, sputtering stop. He cut the engine, and the silence that followed was the sound of salvation.

For a long moment, they just sat there, their hands trembling, their bodies buzzing with the aftermath of their ordeal. They had made it.

The screen door of the small store creaked open, and a man stepped out. He was old, his face a leathered roadmap of wrinkles, and he was wiping his hands on a greasy rag. He looked at the Land Rover, then at the two men climbing out of it. His jaw went slack. His rag slipped from his fingers and fell to the dusty ground.

He was staring at two ghosts. Two men who looked like they had been dragged through the jungle for a week, their clothes in tatters, their faces covered in beards and grime. But underneath the filth, there was something else. An impossible vitality. A startling youthfulness in their eyes that did not belong on men who looked as they did.

They stood there, two living, breathing contradictions. Skot took a step forward, his legs unsteady on the solid ground.

"Hola," Skot said, his voice a raw croak. "Do you have a telephone?"

The old man didn't answer. He just stared, his eyes wide with a mixture of fear and pure, dumbfounded awe, at the two men who had just driven out of the jungle in a machine that had no right to be alive. The men who the whole world knew were dead.

Chapter 19: Ghosts on the Wire

The inside of the gas station was a cool, dusty haven from the oppressive afternoon heat. It smelled of stale beer, motor oil, and the faint, sweet scent of chewing tobacco. The old man, whose name they learned was Mateo, had recovered from his initial shock with the quiet resignation of someone who had lived long enough to know that the world was a deeply strange place. He looked at Skot and Dave not as aberrations, but as a particularly bizarre story he would one day tell his grandchildren.

He gestured to the phone. It was a rotary, a heavy, black plastic relic from an era before satellites and screens, and it sat on the cluttered wooden counter next to a jar of pickled eggs that looked equally ancient. Its coiled cord was hopelessly tangled and coated in a thin film of grime.

"A collect call?" Mateo asked in slow, careful Spanish.

"No, no," Skot said, pulling a damp, crumpled bill from the pocket of his tattered shorts—emergency cash he'd forgotten he even had. "For the call. Por la llamada."

Mateo nodded, accepting the money. The problem now was one of memory. In a world where every important number was stored in a device that was currently sitting in an evidence bag miles away, they had to dredge the recesses of their minds.

"What's the number for the resort?" Dave asked.

Skot just stared at him blankly. "I have no idea. I booked it online three months ago. The number is in my email."

"Your phone is in a plastic bag in a police station," Dave stated flatly.

"Okay, plan B," Skot said, thinking. "My sister, Sarah. Jen knows her. We call Sarah, she goes to your house, gets the 'Disaster Folder' with the itinerary, and calls us back with the resort's number."

It was a convoluted plan, but it was a plan. They spent the next five minutes trying to remember Skot's sister's phone number, a mental exercise that was surprisingly difficult. They pieced together most of it but were stuck on the last four digits. Was it 4587 or 5487? The harder they tried to recall, the more uncertain they became.

Dave, the pragmatist, finally held up a hand, stopping the frustrating back-and-forth. "This is ridiculous. We're overthinking it." He turned to Mateo. "Señor," he said in his halting, high-school Spanish. "Por favor... operadora internacional?"

Mateo's weathered face broke into a smile, understanding immediately. He took the receiver from Skot, spoke a few rapid words into it, and then handed it back to Dave. A new voice was on the line, a woman speaking clear, crisp English.

"International operator, how may I direct your call?"

Relief washed over Dave. It was so simple. "Yes, hello. I need the number for a hotel, please. A resort. It's called... El Santuario. Near Santa Marta, Colombia."

There was a pause and the faint clicking of a keyboard. "I have a listing for El Santuario Beach & Golf Resort. Is that it?"

"That's it!" Dave nearly shouted. "Can you connect me, please?"

"One moment."

The line clicked and whirred, and then they heard the familiar, soothing hold music of the resort, a gentle pan-flute melody that was grotesquely out of place with their current reality. Finally, a cheerful receptionist answered.

"Good afternoon, El Santuario, this is Isabella speaking."

"Hello," Dave said, his heart pounding. "I need to be connected to a guest's room, please. The name is Keith Walker. Or just 'Buzz' Walker."

"Of course, sir. One moment while I connect you."

The phone began to ring, a shrill, old-fashioned brrrring. Dave handed the receiver to Skot. "You're up," he whispered. "Try not to give him a heart attack."

. . . .

Keith "Buzz" Walker was conducting a funeral for himself, and the guest of honor was a bottle of scotch that cost more than most people's monthly rent. He was in his hotel room, the blackout curtains drawn tight against the afternoon sun, creating a tomb-like gloom. The television was on, the volume muted, but the images were loud enough. It was an American cable news channel. A professionally concerned anchorwoman was talking to a "security expert" via satellite. On the screen next to them was the photo of Dave and his family that Buzz had seen in their room, and next to that, a rugged, smiling selfie Skot had taken on a past motorcycle trip. And in the corner, a smaller, infinitely more damning picture: Buzz himself, grinning like an idiot, a drink in his hand, a photo he had posted from the casino two nights ago.

The chyron at the bottom of the screen read: "TRAGEDY IN COLOMBIA: WHAT HAPPENED TO THE MISSING DIVERS?"

He had watched for an hour, a form of self-flagellation. He had seen himself painted as the villain, the "irresponsible friend," the hedonist who partied while his friends were dying. They didn't use his name, not yet, but it was him. Every word was a lash. The security expert was talking about the "golden hours" after a disappearance, the critical window for a successful rescue. A window Buzz had spent cementing his reputation as the life of the party.

He had just finished a call with Lieutenant Morales. The official news was grim and final. The search divers had found the cave-in. There was no way through. No signs of life. The search was being scaled back, moving from a rescue operation to a recovery one, though recovery was deemed impossible. It was over. Skot and Dave were gone.

The guilt was no longer a sharp spike; it was a vast, suffocating ocean. He was drowning in it. The expensive scotch sat on the table beside him, its amber liquid glowing in the gloom. He hadn't touched it. Drinking felt like a betrayal. Partying was what had gotten him into this mess. To drink now would be to toast his own damnation.

The phone on the nightstand rang, its shrill, old-fashioned brrrring a violent intrusion into his silent, self-loathing wake.

He ignored it. It had to be a reporter. Someone from the network had probably figured out his room number. Let it ring.

It stopped, and the silence was a relief. Then, thirty seconds later, it started again, just as loud, just as insistent. A cold fury began to bubble up through the guilt. The audacity. The sheer, ghoulish nerve of them.

He snatched the receiver from its cradle. "WHAT?" he roared into the phone, his voice a raw, broken thing. "What do you want? There's no comment! There's no statement! Leave me the hell alone!"

There was a pause on the other end, a crackle of static over a long-distance line. Then a voice, weak and thin, but achingly familiar.

"...Buzz? It's me. It's Skot."

The world stopped. The sound of the muted television, the hum of the air conditioning, the frantic beating of his own heart—it all just ceased to exist. Buzz stood perfectly still, the phone pressed so hard against his ear he thought it might break his skull. He didn't breathe. It had to be a hallucination. Grief did strange things to the mind. He had read that somewhere.

"No," Buzz whispered. "No, you're not."

"Yeah, I am," the voice on the phone said, a little stronger this time. "Well, most of me. We're… we're okay, man."

And then the dam broke. The ocean of guilt inside him erupted, not as sorrow, but as pure, undiluted rage. It was the rage of a man who had been dragged through hell and back, only to find out the reason for the trip had been a clerical error.

"YOU SON OF A BITCH!" he screamed, the sound ripping from his throat. "They told me you were DEAD! I just got off the phone with a cop who told me you were buried under a mountain! They're showing your face on CNN! I'm watching your damn funeral on TV right now! Where the HELL ARE YOU?"

"It's a long story," Skot said, his voice strained. "A really long one."

"Look, can you just let me talk to Dave?"

There was a shuffling sound on the other end of the line, and then a new voice, calmer, steadier. "Buzz. It's Dave."

Buzz sank to his knees on the plush hotel carpet, the phone still clutched in his hand. Tears, hot and uncontrollable, streamed down his face. He was sobbing, a deep, ugly, gut-wrenching sound he hadn't made since he was a child. "Dave," he choked out. "Oh, God. Dave."

"I know, buddy. I know," Dave's voice was a calm anchor in the storm of Buzz's emotions. "Listen to me. We're okay. We're alive. But we're in trouble, and you are the only person on the planet who can help us."

Buzz scrubbed at his face with the sleeve of his robe, trying to get a grip. "Where are you? Are you hurt?"

"We're at a gas station. In the middle of nowhere. A place called... I don't know, Puerto-something. We don't have any money, any phones, any ID. We have the clothes on our backs and a story you are not going to believe." There was a pause. "And we need you to be very, very smart right now. We need the fixer, not the party animal. Can you do that?"

The question was a bucket of ice water. The hysteria receded, replaced by a sudden, sharp clarity. His friends were alive. They were in trouble. And they needed him. The guilt wasn't gone, but it had been transformed, reforged into a new and powerful fuel: purpose.

"Yeah," Buzz said, his voice no longer choked with sobs, but low and steady. He stood up, his legs still shaky. "Yeah, Dave. I can do that."

"Good," Dave said, a wave of palpable relief in his voice. "Get a pen. I'm going to tell you exactly what you need to do."

Buzz scrambled for the hotel stationery on the desk. He listened as Dave laid out the plan, a series of logistical steps that were both simple and incredibly complex. A wire transfer. A rental car. A set of coordinates. Discretion.

When Dave was finished, Buzz read the instructions back, his mind, which was usually occupied with guest lists and drink orders, now completely focused on the intricate details of a rescue operation.

"I'm on my way," Buzz said. "I don't know how long it will take me, but I am on my way. Just… stay there. And don't talk to anyone."

"Don't worry," Skot's voice came back on the line. "We're not exactly in shape to be chatty. And Buzz?"

"Yeah?"

"Thanks, man."

"Don't thank me," Buzz said, a bitter edge to his voice. "I'm the idiot who was playing blackjack while you guys were… doing whatever the hell it is you were doing. Just stay alive until I get there. That's an order."

He hung up the phone.

He stood in the center of the dark, silent room, the frantic energy of a moment ago now replaced by a cold, humming focus. He looked at the muted television, at the faces of his friends being eulogized by strangers. He looked at the bottle of scotch, a monument to his own self-pity. He walked over, screwed the cap on tight, and shoved it to the back of the minibar.

He strode into the bathroom and splashed cold water on his face. He looked at his reflection in the mirror. The puffy, guilt-ridden ghost of a man was gone. In his place was someone else. Someone with a dangerous light in his eyes. Someone with a mission. The party was over. The real work had just begun.

"Okay," he said to the man in the mirror, his voice a low, determined whisper. "Let's go get our boys."

Chapter 20: Running Silent

The man who walked out of the El Santuario resort lobby bore only a passing resemblance to the Keith "Buzz" Walker who had been its unofficial social director for the past three days. The flashy, oversized sunglasses were gone, replaced by a pair of simple, dark aviators that hid the frantic, newly-focused energy in his eyes. The loud, hibiscus-print shirt, a staple of his vacation persona, had been traded for a plain, dark polo that absorbed the light rather than reflected it. He moved with a coiled, purposeful tension, a predator's gait that was utterly alien to his usual bon-vivant saunter. He ignored the curious stares of the other guests and the sympathetic, pitying glances from the hotel staff. He was no longer a performer playing to the crowd; he was a ghost, slipping through the spaces between people, his mind a whirlwind of logistics, lies, and a cold, burning rage at his own stupidity.

His first priority was money. Dave's instructions had been clear: they needed cash, and they needed a vehicle that couldn't be easily traced back to the resort. Buzz couldn't just put a rental car on his credit card, not with his name now plastered across international news. Every transaction he made could be a breadcrumb. He had to become invisible, a concept so foreign to his nature it was almost laughable. His entire life had been about being seen.

He bypassed the resort's concierge, a man he'd been on a first-name basis with an hour into his stay, and walked straight to the taxi stand out front. He slid into the back of a slightly battered sedan, the vinyl seat hot from the sun. He leaned forward and showed the driver a crisp American fifty-dollar bill, a down payment on discretion. The driver's eyes widened in the rearview mirror.

"Santa Marta," Buzz said, his voice low and steady. "And I need a bank. The biggest one you know. And then... I need to find a place that rents cars for cash. Not a big company like Hertz. A local place. A place where they don't ask for a passport. Understand?"

The driver, a man with a weathered face and a deep, intuitive understanding of the universal language of money, understood perfectly. He gave a single, sharp nod, tucked the bill away, and pulled out into traffic with an aggressive skill that left the pristine, manicured grounds of the resort behind in a cloud of dust.

The drive into the city was a descent from a fantasy world into a loud, vibrant, and chaotic reality. The palm-lined boulevards gave way to narrow, bustling streets choked with a cacophony of car horns, vendors shouting their wares, and the vibrant, pulsing rhythm of cumbia music spilling from open doorways. Buzz stared out the window, his mind a cold, calculating machine. This was not his world. He was a tourist here, a conspicuous one. He pulled his cap lower on his head and slid down in his seat, feeling the irrational paranoia of a wanted man. He felt like every person on the street was watching him, recognizing the face of the irresponsible American from the television.

The driver dropped him in front of a large, modern bank building that seemed out of place amidst the colonial architecture. "Aquí," the driver said. "Banco de la República. The biggest." He then pointed down the street.

"For the car, I will wait. You call me when you are done." He handed Buzz a small, worn business card with his number on it.

The bank was an ordeal. It was a cavern of cool, conditioned air and polished marble floors, but it operated on a rhythm that was completely alien to Buzz's world of instant gratification. There were lines, roped off with velvet cords. There were forms, filled out in triplicate with pens that were chained to the counter. There was a languid, unhurried pace to every transaction that set his teeth on edge. He wanted to scream at the people in front of him, to tell them that his friends' lives might depend on the speed of this transaction, but he couldn't. He was a character now, playing a part. The concerned friend of the tragic American tourists. He had to be calm. He had to be patient.

When he finally reached the front of the line, he was met by a young woman with perfectly manicured nails and an expression of bored professionalism. He explained, in his rudimentary Spanish supplemented by a lot of pointing and hand gestures, that he needed to make a wire transfer to a small, rural business and then make a large cash withdrawal.

The process took an eternity. The teller had to get a manager's approval. There were phone calls. There was the slow, deliberate typing of information into a computer system that seemed to run on steam power. He could feel the teller's curious eyes on him, and he knew she probably recognized him from the news reports. He was a local celebrity of the worst kind. To her, he must have looked like a man trying to move money around after a tragedy, and her suspicion was a palpable thing. He smiled, he nodded, he filled out the paperwork with a steady hand, wiring a substantial sum of his own money to a man named Mateo who owned a gas station in a town that didn't appear on most maps.

An hour later, the transfer was complete. He walked out of the bank, blinking in the bright, hot sun, a thick envelope of cash tucked into the inside pocket of his jacket. The paranoia was worse now. The envelope felt like it was burning a hole through his shirt. He called the taxi driver.

The car rental was a different kind of challenge, a descent into the city's gray market. The driver took him to a dusty, sun-baked lot on the outskirts of the city, tucked behind a tire repair shop. It wasn't a Hertz or an Avis. The sign was a faded, hand-painted affair that just said "AUTOS." A dozen dented, mismatched vehicles sat shimmering in the heat, looking like they had been abandoned after a long, hard life. The proprietor was a wiry man with oil stains on his shirt, a cigarette dangling from his lips, and a suspicious squint that seemed to be his default expression. He looked like a man who had seen everything and was impressed by nothing.

This was a world of unspoken rules. Buzz knew his usual charm and bravado would be useless here, even counterproductive. He pointed to a dark gray Toyota pickup truck, old enough to be anonymous but new enough, he hoped, to be reliable. The proprietor grunted, walked over, kicked one of the tires, and named a price for a week's rental that was utterly extortionate.

Buzz didn't even blink. He pulled out the thick envelope of cash and peeled off the bills, the proprietor's eyes following the movement with a hawk's intensity. Buzz added a few extra hundred-dollar bills to the pile—a silent, non-negotiable fee for the man to forget his face the second he drove off the lot. No paperwork was signed. No ID was shown. A set of keys was slapped into Buzz's palm. It was a transaction between two men who both understood the value of absolute discretion.

Finally, he was on the road, the anonymous truck's air conditioning blasting his face with cool, blessed air. He was a ghost. A man with a mission. He pulled out his phone to plug Dave's coordinates into the GPS, and as the screen lit up, he saw it. A missed call and a new text message. From Jen.

His heart seized in his chest. He pulled the truck over to the side of the busy road, the traffic roaring past him in a blur of color and noise. He knew he had to read it. He had to know. His thumb trembled as he opened the message.

JEN: Buzz, I'm sorry if I was short with you. I'm just… I'm not thinking straight. Thank you for being there. Did Lieutenant Morales say anything else? Any timeline? Anything at all? I keep looking at the news, and it's making me sick.

He closed his eyes, the simple, heartfelt words a fresh torment. The lie he had to tell was a physical weight in his throat. He had to maintain the fiction. He had to protect the mission. He had to protect her from a hope that was still fragile, that could still be extinguished in a hundred different ways between here and that dusty gas station.

He typed back, each word a betrayal, a small act of necessary cruelty.

"No news yet, Jen. Morales just said it's a slow process. The jungle is tough. But you have to hold on. We have to be strong. Don't watch the news. It's all just speculation from people who don't know anything. I'll call you the second I have anything real. I promise."

He hit send, and the word "promise" felt like a shard of glass in his soul. He had promised to call her with news, and he already had the most important news in the world, and he was keeping it from her.

He threw the phone onto the passenger seat as if it were contaminated and pulled the truck back into traffic with a sharp, angry jerk of the wheel. The guilt was a fire, but he couldn't let it consume him. He had to use it as fuel.

He followed the GPS out of the city, leaving the coastline behind. The landscape began to change dramatically. The roads grew rougher, the towns smaller and farther between. The lush, coastal green gave way to a dryer, more rugged terrain of hills and scrub brush. He was driving into the interior, into the heart of the country, a world away from the five-star resorts and the swim-up bars. This was their world. The world of dirt roads and unforgiving landscapes, the world they had chosen. And for the first time in his life, he was willingly, desperately, trying to enter it.

Hours passed. He drove with a relentless, focused intensity, stopping only for gas. He ate nothing. He listened to nothing but the hum of the tires on the asphalt and the frantic, determined beating of his own heart. He was running silent. He was running on a promise. He was the fixer, the operator, the man with the most precious, painful secret in the world, and he was driving as fast as he could toward the one thing that could redeem him.

Chapter 21: An Outpost of Ghosts

The phone receiver clicked back into its heavy, black cradle with a sound of profound finality. For a long moment, Skot and Dave just stood there in the dusty, silent interior of the gas station, the ghost of Buzz's hysterical, relieved, and furious voice still echoing in their ears. They had done it. They had cast a message in a bottle into the vast, indifferent ocean of global telecommunications, and their one-man rescue party had received it. They were no longer entirely alone, and the sheer, staggering relief of that fact was a physical thing, a wave that washed over them, so potent it made their knees feel weak. The tension they had been carrying for days, a weight so constant they had stopped noticing it, suddenly released its grip. Dave leaned against the cluttered counter, the adrenaline that had fueled him for the last 48 hours draining away, leaving behind a deep, cavernous exhaustion that felt bottomless.

The old man, Mateo, who had been watching the entire exchange with a look of quiet, baffled curiosity, seemed to understand the shift in their energy. He had seen men at the breaking point before; it was a universal language. He shuffled behind the counter and pulled two dusty glass bottles of Coca-Cola from an ancient, humming refrigerator. He popped the caps off on the edge of the counter and slid them toward Skot and Dave. He said nothing, but the gesture was clear. It was an offering of shared humanity, a simple welcome back to the world of the living.

"Gracias," Dave said, his voice thick with an emotion he couldn't name. He picked up the bottle. It was cold and slick with condensation. The sugar and the caffeine would be a shock to his system, a system he was only just beginning to understand again. He took a long drink. It was the most incredible thing he had ever tasted—sweet, sharp, and blessedly, beautifully normal.

They took their Cokes outside, away from the stuffy confines of the small store, and sat on a low, crumbling concrete wall that bordered the dusty patch of land. The monstrous, mud-caked Land Rover sat ticking and cooling by the gas pump, a monument to their impossible journey. The sun was beginning its slow descent, painting the sky in soft hues of orange and purple. The heat of the day was finally starting to break.

"So," Skot said, after a long silence, taking a swig of his own Coke. "The fixer is on the move."

"The party animal is on the move," Dave corrected him, a small smile playing on his lips. "Let's just pray he doesn't get distracted by a karaoke bar or a pretty face on the way here."

"He'll get here," Skot said with a confidence Dave wasn't sure he actually felt. "He sounded... different. Scared. I've never heard him scared before. Not really."

"We all were," Dave said quietly. He looked down at his own hands. They were caked in grease and dirt from their work on the engine, the nails broken, the knuckles scraped raw. But underneath the grime, the skin looked smooth, healthy. It was a bizarre contradiction. He was a wreck, and he was in the best shape of his life.

The silence settled over them again, but it was a different kind of silence now. It wasn't the oppressive, menacing silence of the jungle. It was the quiet, anxious silence of waiting. The silence of the bus stop after you've just missed your ride and you have no idea when the next one is coming.

Mateo shuffled out of the store again, his initial shock having settled into a kind of weary acceptance of the strangeness of his day. He pointed toward a spigot on the side of the building, connected to a coiled, green hose. "Agua," he said simply. He made a washing motion with his hands.

It was another gift, another small act of kindness that felt monumental. They took turns at the spigot, the water blessedly cool, though it felt strangely inert and lifeless compared to the stuff they had been drinking. They scrubbed the layers of sweat, mud, and grease from their faces, arms, and hair. And as the filth washed away, the miracle was revealed in the soft, forgiving light of dusk.

Dave watched as Skot splashed water on his face. The graying temples he had known for the last few years, the ones he and Buzz had relentlessly teased him about, were gone. Skot's hair was a uniform, vital brown. The deep crow's feet that usually crinkled at the corners of his eyes when he smiled had been replaced by the smoother skin of a man a decade younger.

"Your hair," Dave said, his voice hushed with awe. "The gray is gone."

Skot stopped, touching his own temples as if he could feel the missing color. He looked at Dave, really looked at him in the fading light. "Your face," he said, his voice equally stunned. "The lines... you look... rested."

Rested was the last word on earth Dave would have used to describe how he felt, but he knew what Skot meant. He walked over to the grimy side mirror of the Land Rover and caught his own reflection. The man staring back was a stranger. The puffy, tired look that had been his constant companion for years was gone. His skin had a healthy color. He looked... well. He looked like the version of himself from his wedding photos, a man with fewer worries and a lot more sleep.

The full, staggering weight of what had happened to them, of the secret they now carried in their very cells, settled over them. This wasn't just a story about survival anymore. This was something else entirely. Something much more complicated.

"The camera," Dave said suddenly, his mind snapping back to the practical, the tangible. The part of his brain that dealt with risk and assets was flashing red. "The GoPro. Where is it?"

"In the truck," Skot said. He went to the passenger side of the Land Rover and retrieved his dive helmet. He carefully detached the small, black camera. It felt impossibly small and fragile, yet it held a secret that could turn the world on its head. It was the only proof.

"We can't let anyone see that," Dave said, his voice low and urgent. "We can't let Buzz see that, not yet. Not until we know what we're dealing with. Not until we have a real plan. He'll see it as a product launch. We need to see it as evidence in our own weird trial."

"What do we do with it?" Skot asked, understanding immediately.

Dave thought for a moment, his CPA's mind, which was so good at hiding assets and managing risk, now working on a new kind of problem. "Your BCD," he said. "The pocket on the side. The one you kept the power bank in. It's the last place anyone would think to look. It just looks like a piece of dirty, useless junk."

It was a perfect solution. Skot took the camera and the power bank, zipped them securely into the waterproof pouch, and then tucked the pouch deep inside the side pocket of his filthy, water-logged buoyancy compensator. The most valuable piece of evidence on the planet was now hidden in plain sight, disguised as trash.

They sat back down on the wall, the empty Coke bottles at their feet, and watched the road. The sun dipped below the horizon, and the sky exploded into a brief, spectacular display of fiery color before giving way to the deep, velvety purple of dusk. The first stars began to appear. The air grew cooler.

And the aches returned.

It started as a dull throb in Dave's lower back, a familiar old enemy announcing its return. Then his knee began to protest, a low, grinding complaint that grew in intensity with every passing minute. The miracle was fading. The bill for their superhuman efforts on the Land Rover was coming due, right on schedule. He saw Skot wince as he shifted his weight, unconsciously rubbing his shoulder.

"You feel it too?" Dave asked, though he already knew the answer.

Skot just nodded, his face grim in the twilight. "Right on time. The magic's wearing off."

They looked at their BCDs, their last two doses of salvation. They had enough for maybe one good charge each. Maybe two smaller ones.

"Should we…?" Skot started to ask, his voice trailing off.

"No," Dave said firmly, though every screaming nerve in his body disagreed. "Not yet. We save it. We don't know what's coming. We don't know if Buzz will find us tonight or tomorrow morning. What if we have to help him change a tire on the way back? What if something else happens? We need to save it for when we really, truly need it."

It was a sensible, logical decision. And it was torture. They now had to consciously choose to inhabit their old, aching, broken bodies, knowing that relief, that youth, that perfection was just a few sips away. It was a new kind of hell, a psychological torment that was almost worse than the physical pain of the jungle. The jungle had been an honest enemy. This was a war with themselves.

They sat in the growing darkness, two ghosts at an outpost at the end of the world, wrapped in a universe of aches and pains. They listened to the strange, new symphony of the nocturnal insects, their enhanced senses now a curse, making every chirp and click sound unnaturally loud. They stared down the long, empty dirt road, watching for the faintest flicker of headlights, for the dust cloud that would signal the arrival of their loud, ridiculous, and desperately needed friend. The waiting was the hardest part. The waiting, and the slow, agonizing return of their own mortality.

Chapter 22: The Longest Mile

The asphalt ended fifty miles outside of Santa Marta. One moment, Buzz was on a relatively smooth, paved highway, making good time. The next, he was on a jarring, rutted dirt road that seemed determined to shake the teeth out of his head. The GPS on his phone, which had been his steadfast, reassuring guide, suddenly seemed less certain of itself. The blue dot representing his truck was now moving through a vast, featureless expanse of beige. The road he was on was just a thin, speculative line. The world, as far as the satellites were concerned, had run out of details.

Darkness had fallen hours ago, a sudden, heavy blanket that smothered the landscape in an impenetrable black. His headlights cut a lonely, trembling tunnel through the night, illuminating a chaotic dance of dust motes and the occasional, startled pair of animal eyes that would glow green for a second before vanishing back into the oppressive blackness. The anonymous Toyota pickup, which had felt so capable in the city, now felt like a tiny, fragile tin can adrift on a dark, empty ocean.

Buzz was running on a cocktail of stale gas station coffee, adrenaline, and a guilt so potent it felt like a physical presence in the passenger seat. He hadn't eaten since the steak dinner that felt like it had happened in another lifetime. His stomach was a tight, acidic knot of dread and anticipation. He gripped the steering wheel, his knuckles white, his eyes straining to see past the reach of his high beams.

Every fifteen minutes, his phone would buzz on the seat beside him. He knew without looking who it was. Jen. Or his sister, Sarah. Or his mother. The waves of concern from back home were relentless. He ignored them. Each unanswered call, each unread text, was a small, sharp stab of guilt, a reminder of the lie he was living. He imagined Jen, sitting by her phone, her hope dwindling with every passing hour of silence. The thought was a fresh torment, but he pushed it down. He couldn't afford to think about that now. He had to compartmentalize. He was the fixer. He had a mission. The emotional fallout would have to wait. He just hoped there would be a 'later' for it to wait for.

His mind, untethered from its usual distractions, began to play tricks on him. What would he find when he got there? The relief in Skot and Dave's voices on the phone had been real, but what did "okay" really mean? He pictured them injured, broken, sick from some jungle fever. He pictured himself having to carry them to the truck. He imagined the drive back, the silence filled with their pain.

Then the darker thoughts would come, slithering in from the corners of his mind. What if it was a trap? What if someone had found them first? The jungle was not an empty place. The story of the men in the journal, the ones who had gone mad from the "bad water," echoed in his head. What if his friends weren't his friends anymore?

He shook his head, trying to banish the thought. "Get a grip, Walker," he muttered, his own voice sounding loud and strange in the confined space of the cab. He turned on the radio, desperate for a human voice, but all he got was a crackle of static across the AM and FM bands. He was too far out. There was nothing out here.

The GPS chimed, a soft, digital sound that made him jump. "In one quarter mile, your destination will be on the right."

His heart hammered against his ribs. He slowed the truck, his eyes peering into the inky blackness. A quarter mile. It felt like the longest mile of his life. He was looking for a gas station, a point of light in this endless sea of darkness.

He saw nothing. Just the same dirt road, the same scrub brush illuminated in his headlights. Had he taken a wrong turn? Had they given him the wrong coordinates? Was this whole thing a massive, cruel joke?

And then he saw it. Not a bright, welcoming beacon, but a single, dim, yellow bulb, hanging naked and lonely in the distance. It was so faint it was barely visible, a dying star in a galaxy of black. But it was there.

He aimed the truck toward the light, his breath held tight in his chest. As he got closer, the outpost slowly resolved out of the darkness. A single, low cinder-block building. A rusted gas pump. And a dark, hulking shape parked next to it. A shape that, with a jolt of recognition, he realized was a vintage Land Rover, caked in mud and looking like it had been dredged from the bottom of a swamp.

He pulled his truck in, the engine's rumble sounding like an invading army in the profound silence. He cut the engine and the lights, and the world was plunged back into darkness, lit only by that single, pathetic, yellow bulb.

The door to the gas station creaked open, spilling a thin slice of light onto the dusty ground. An old man emerged, his silhouette framed in the doorway. He just stood there, watching.

Then, two other figures detached themselves from the shadows near the crumbling concrete wall. They moved slowly, stiffly, into the pool of dim light.

It was them.

Buzz stumbled out of his truck, his legs unsteady. He stared. They were a nightmare. Their clothes were in rags, filthy and torn. They were gaunt, their faces covered in a thick, scraggly beard growth. They looked haunted, their eyes wide and hollow in their grimy faces. They looked like men who had seen the end of the world and had somehow managed to crawl back.

But underneath the filth and the exhaustion, there was something else. Something strange. They stood with a stillness, a centeredness that was completely new. And their faces, what he could see of them under the beards, looked... he couldn't place it. Younger? It was impossible. It was a trick of the dim, yellow light.

He walked toward them, his feet crunching on the gravel. They walked toward him. The three of them met in the middle of the dusty lot, under the unblinking gaze of the old man and the single, buzzing light bulb.

For a long moment, no one spoke. What could they say? The chasm between their recent experiences was too vast to be bridged with simple words. Skot had been right. Buzz was scared. He was terrified. He was looking at his two best friends, and they were strangers.

It was Buzz who broke the silence, his voice a raw, cracked whisper. "Jesus, you guys look like shit."

Skot let out a sound that was half-laugh, half-sob. "You're not exactly a sight for sore eyes yourself, Buzz."

And then the dam of forced composure broke. Buzz lunged forward and pulled them into a fierce, clumsy, three-way hug. He buried his face in Skot's grimy shoulder, his own shoulders shaking. He could feel their bones through their tattered shirts. He could smell the jungle on them, the scent of damp earth and woodsmoke and something else, something wild and feral.

"I thought you were dead," Buzz choked out, his voice muffled. "They told me you were dead."

"Almost," Dave's voice rumbled from his other side. "We were almost dead."

They pulled apart, the raw emotion still hanging in the air. Buzz looked from Skot's face to Dave's, really looking at them now. The youthfulness wasn't a trick of the light. It was real. Their eyes were startlingly clear, impossibly vital against the backdrop of their ordeal. It was the most unsettling, inexplicable thing he had ever seen.

"We need to go," Dave said, his voice quiet but firm. "Now. Before someone else shows up."

Buzz nodded, snapping back into his role as the fixer. He had come prepared. He opened the passenger door of his truck and pulled out a duffel bag. "Clean clothes. Water. Some protein bars. It's all I could think of."

"You thought of everything," Skot said, his voice thick with a gratitude that made Buzz's guilt twist in his gut.

They left the Land Rover where it sat, a silent, rusting testament to an impossible story. They didn't even look back. They piled into the anonymous Toyota pickup, Skot and Dave in the back, Buzz back behind the wheel. The clean interior of the truck suddenly felt like a sterile operating room, their own filth a contamination.

Buzz started the engine and pulled out of the gas station, leaving the single yellow light and the outpost of ghosts behind them. He drove back onto the dark, empty road, heading toward the distant promise of the coast, of civilization.

The three of them were together again, enclosed in the small, humming space of the truck's cab. But the easy camaraderie, the decades of shared jokes and experiences, was gone, replaced by a heavy, charged silence. They were three strangers now, bound by a terrible secret, driving away from a miracle and toward a world that was going to want answers they could never possibly give. The longest mile wasn't the one that had brought him here. It was the one that was just beginning.

Chapter 23: The Shape of the Miracle

The cab of the Toyota pickup was a small, dark, moving world, an island of humming tires and stale air adrift in the vast, silent darkness of the Colombian interior. For the first hour, no one spoke. The road was a rough, uneven track that demanded Buzz's full attention, and Skot and Dave seemed to have retreated into a state of profound, bone-deep exhaustion in the back seat. The only sounds were the rattle of the truck's chassis, the low grumble of the engine, and the occasional, sharp inhale from one of the men in the back as a particularly nasty jolt sent a fresh spike of pain through their battered bodies.

Buzz drove with a cold, clear focus, but his mind was a chaotic storm. He kept glancing in the rearview mirror, his eyes flicking from the dark road ahead to the two shadowy figures behind him. They were ghosts. His ghosts. He had rescued them, but he didn't understand them. He had seen the Land Rover. He had smelled the foul smoke pouring from its exhaust. It was a dead machine, a rusted-out relic that belonged in a junkyard, not on a dirt road in the middle of nowhere. It simply wasn't possible. The image of the truck running, of his friends standing beside it, was a glitch in the matrix of his understanding of the world.

He couldn't hold it in any longer. The practical question, the one that bypassed the emotional chaos and went straight to the mechanical impossibility, finally burst out of him.

"Okay," he said, his voice loud in the quiet cab. "I have to ask. That piece of junk… that Land Rover. There's no way. I mean, there is just no possible way. How in the hell did you get it started?"

He watched their reflections in the mirror. Skot and Dave exchanged a look, a silent, heavy conversation passing between them in a single glance. It was the look of two men trying to decide how to describe a color to a person who has been blind from birth.

It was Dave, the pragmatist, who spoke first, his voice a low, tired rasp. "We, uh… we cleaned the engine."

"You cleaned the engine?" Buzz repeated, a note of incredulous sarcasm creeping into his voice. "You cleaned the engine. Of course. And I suppose you just happened to have a fully charged battery and four new tires in your back pocket? Come on. Don't handle me. I just drove five hours into the heart of darkness to rescue you. I think I've earned a little more than 'we cleaned the engine.'"

There was another long silence. Then Skot leaned forward, his arms resting on the back of the front seats. His face was close enough now that Buzz could see it clearly in the dim glow of the dashboard lights. The impossible youthfulness in his friend's eyes, the startling lack of weariness despite the ordeal, was deeply unsettling.

"You're not going to believe us, Buzz," Skot said, his voice quiet.

"Try me," Buzz shot back. "Right now, I'd believe you if you told me you were flown out of there by a UFO. It would make more sense than starting that truck."

And so, they told him.

Piece by painful, unbelievable piece, the story of the last three days unfolded in the dark, moving cab of the truck. Skot, the storyteller, would lay out the narrative, his voice a low, mesmerizing monotone. Dave, the accountant, would chime in with the facts, the data points, the things he knew to be true because he had measured them.

Buzz listened, his knuckles white on the steering wheel, his mind grappling with the impossible tale. He heard about the majestic beauty of The Cathedral, and he could picture it. He heard about the sudden, violent cave-in, and he felt a cold knot of secondhand terror form in his stomach. He heard about the desperate, claustrophobic swim through the escape tunnel, and he had to consciously force himself to keep breathing.

But then the story took a turn into the fantastical.

"The grotto was... glowing," Skot said, his voice filled with a lingering awe. "The water itself. A blue-green light, coming from the bottom of the pool. It was... alive."

Buzz's rational mind immediately began searching for an explanation. "A fungus," he said, nodding to himself. "Like a bioluminescent algae. That happens. I saw it on a nature show. You were hypoxic, you were panicking, you saw some weird glowing moss and your brains filled in the rest."

"My blood sugar was 92, Buzz," Dave's voice cut in, flat and absolute. "After being chased, trapped, and nearly buried alive. A fungus doesn't do that."

Buzz had no answer for that. He just drove, the silence stretching as he tried to process the data point that broke all the rules.

They told him about drinking the water, about the instantaneous surge of energy, the vanishing pain. They told him about their brutal, two-day trek through the jungle, their bodies failing and being reborn with every sip from their BCDs. They told him about Dave's injury and miraculous healing, their superhuman efforts on the Land Rover—lifting it from the mud, turning the seized engine by hand.

It was too much. It was a fairy tale, a myth. It was the kind of story you heard about a local legend, a "miracle spring" that turned out to be nothing but contaminated water and wishful thinking. But the evidence was sitting right behind him. He kept glancing in the mirror, at the two ragged men who should have been half-dead from exposure, dehydration, and exhaustion. But they weren't. They were alert. They were lucid. And underneath the grime, they looked healthier than he did.

He thought back to the story of the journal, the men who had drunk from the "bad water" and gone mad. "So you're telling me," Buzz said slowly, trying to get it straight, "that in the middle of a jungle that has poison water that makes you crazy, you just happened to stumble into a separate, secret cave that contains actual, literal magic water from the fountain of youth?"

"It sounds crazy when you say it out loud," Skot admitted.

"It sounds crazy when you say it in your head!" Buzz retorted. "It is the single most insane story I have ever heard."

But he was starting to believe them. Not because it made sense, but because nothing else did. The story, as impossible as it was, was the only explanation that fit the facts he had seen with his own eyes: the running truck, the impossible vitality of his friends.

As they got closer to the coast, the first hints of dawn began to stain the eastern sky a pale, sickly gray. A new, practical problem began to dawn on Buzz.

"I can't just drive you guys to the front door of the resort," he said, thinking out loud. "The place is going to be crawling with reporters by now. The second they see you, it'll be a global feeding frenzy. We'll never get through."

"So what do we do?" Dave asked.

The fixer, the man of logistics, took over. "The service entrance," Buzz said, a plan forming. "Around the back. It's where the laundry and food delivery trucks come in. Security is lighter there. We get you to my room, you get cleaned up, we get some food in you, and we figure out our next move. A real plan."

They followed the plan. Buzz drove them not to the grand, palm-lined entrance of the El Santuario, but to a grimy, concrete loading dock behind the kitchens. The sun was just beginning to rise, casting long, cool shadows. It was the hour of shift changes, of deliveries, of quiet, unseen work. In the controlled chaos, three men slipping through a side door went completely unnoticed.

They rode the service elevator up, a cramped, steel box that smelled of bleach and old food. They walked the plush, silent hallways of the fourth floor. Buzz swiped the key card, and the door to his suite swung open.

Chapter 24: Proof of Life

The hotel suite was a monument to a party that had ended badly. An empty champagne bottle lay on its side, a fallen soldier on the plush carpet. Discarded clothes formed a trail from the door to the bed, and a half-eaten room service cheeseburger sat on a tray, a sad, greasy relic of a forgotten impulse. In the center of this opulent mess stood three ghosts, their filthy, tattered forms a shocking contrast to the five-star luxury surrounding them. They weren't looking at the chaos of the room, however. Their eyes were fixed on the large, flat-screen television mounted on the wall.

On the screen, their own faces stared back. Skot's rugged, smiling selfie from a motorcycle trip. Dave's treasured family photo, his wife and kids happy and bright. The images were clean, perfect, ghosts from a life that felt a million miles away. Beneath them, in a stark, white, sans-serif font, were the words that negated their very existence, still there:

PRESUMED DEAD IN CAVE COLLAPSE

They stood in silence, watching themselves be eulogized. A somber-faced anchorwoman was talking about the "inherent risks of adventure tourism" and the "heartbreak for the families left behind." It was a surreal, out-of-body experience. They were attending their own funeral, uninvited.

For Skot, the feeling was one of profound, dizzying detachment. He saw his own face on the screen and felt nothing, as if he were looking at a picture of a stranger. He was an artist who had spent his life trying to capture moments, and now his own final moment had been captured, packaged, and broadcast to the world, and it was a complete fiction. The disconnect was so vast, so absolute, that his brain simply refused to process it.

Buzz's reaction was different. His mind, even in its exhausted state, was already moving past the shock and into the realm of damage control. He saw the news report not as a tragedy, but as a public relations catastrophe, a narrative that was spinning wildly out of his control. He saw the file photo of himself at the casino, a grinning, hedonistic fool, and he felt a fresh wave of nausea. He was a character in this drama, and he had been cast as the villain. The fixer in him was already calculating the angles, the threats, the sheer, unmanageable mess of it all.

But for Dave, it was simpler. It was pure agony. His eyes were locked on the photo of his family. He wasn't seeing a news report; he was seeing his wife's smile, a smile he now understood was gone, replaced by a grief he had personally inflicted. He saw his daughter's bright, innocent eyes, and he imagined them filled with tears and confusion. The weight of what their disappearance had done to the people they loved, the sheer, selfish terror they had unleashed, crashed down on him. He made a sound, a choked, guttural noise, the sound of a man's heart breaking.

"I have to call her," he whispered, his voice a raw, broken thing.

He turned, his movements stiff and robotic, and started toward the phone on the nightstand.

"Whoa, whoa, hold on there, chief," Buzz said, stepping in front of him, his hand held up like a traffic cop. "Hang on a second. Stop. Think."

"I don't want to think!" Dave's voice cracked, rising in volume and intensity. He tried to push past Buzz, his newfound strength surging with grief. "Get out of my way, Buzz. I have to call my wife. Now."

"Are you out of your mind?" Buzz shot back, holding his ground, his voice sharp with a new, authoritative edge. "You can't! The second you call her, what happens? She's going to scream, she's going to cry, she's going to be so relieved she's going to immediately call her sister, or your parents, or Skot's sister, and she's going to say 'They're alive!' And then what? That person will tell someone else. And in less than an hour, some cousin's best friend's neighbor who works for a local news affiliate will make a phone call, and the 'miraculous survival' story will leak. We will have reporters kicking down this door. We are in control of this situation for about another five minutes. We need a plan before we do anything!"

"I don't care about a plan!" Dave roared, his face contorted with pain. "I care about my wife, who thinks I'm dead! Do you have any idea what she's going through right now? Do you?"

The accusation hit Buzz square in the face. "Yes," he said, his own voice dropping, thick with a guilt that was still fresh and raw. "I do. I'm the one who had to listen to it. I'm the reason she's been going through it for the last twelve hours longer than she had to. Don't you dare throw that at me. I am trying to protect you. I am trying to clean up a mess that is bigger than you can possibly imagine right now."

Skot stepped between them, putting a hand on each of their shoulders. He was the mediator, the man in the middle, just as he had always been. "Okay. Both of you. Stop." He looked at Dave, his eyes full of a pained understanding. "I know, man. I feel it too. But he's right. We can't just call. What do we even say? 'Hi honey, I'm not dead, but I can't tell you why or where I am, and by the way, I look ten years younger'? That would be even crueler. That would sound like a prank, or like you've lost your mind. We have to be smart. For their sake."

Dave's furious energy seemed to drain out of him, replaced by a shuddering, hopeless sob. He stumbled backward and collapsed onto the edge of the unmade bed, burying his face in his hands. He was trapped. Trapped in the jungle, trapped in the cave, and now trapped by the consequences of his own survival.

Buzz took control. His mind, usually occupied with guest lists and party logistics, was now running a thousand different scenarios, calculating risks, managing the narrative. He was no longer the party animal. He was the producer of the most insane reality show in history.

"Okay," he said, his voice calm and firm, pacing the room like a caged animal. "Here's what we do. We need a story. A simple, believable story for now. A cover. Dave, you're going to call her. You have to. But you have to be coached. You have to know exactly what to say."

He knelt in front of Dave, forcing his friend to look at him. "You tell her you are alive and you are safe. You tell her you love her more than anything in the world. You let her cry, you let her scream, you take whatever she gives you. But then... then you have to tell her the first lie."

Dave looked up, his face a mask of misery. "A lie?"

"Yes," Buzz said, his expression grim. "A necessary one. You tell her that you were found by some... some local people. Prospectors or something. In a remote area with no communication. You tell her the situation is still... complicated. That these people are a little paranoid, and for your safety, you need her to be quiet. You tell her that if the authorities get involved before you're clear of the situation, it could be dangerous for you."

He paused, letting the weight of the words sink in. "You have to make her your co-conspirator, Dave. You have to swear her to absolute, total silence. Not her mom, not her sister, not Sarah. No one. Can you do that? Can you make her understand that your life depends on her silence?"

It was a terrible, impossible thing to ask. He was asking Dave to take his wife's immeasurable relief and immediately poison it with fear and secrecy. He was asking him to transfer the burden of this insane secret onto her shoulders.

Dave looked from Buzz's determined face to Skot's pained, conflicted one. He thought of Jen's voice on the phone, the grief that had hollowed it out. He couldn't leave her in that place for one second longer. But he also understood, with a cold, sickening clarity, that Buzz was right. A single leak would unleash a firestorm they couldn't control.

He wiped his eyes with the back of his dirty hand and took a deep, shuddering breath. He nodded, a single, jerky motion. "Okay," he whispered. "Okay. I can do it."

He stood up and walked to the phone on the nightstand. His hand trembled as he picked up the receiver. He dialed the long string of numbers for his home phone, a number he knew better than his own Social Security number. He put the phone to his ear and listened to the clicks and whirs of the international call connecting. He glanced at his friends. Skot gave him a supportive, heartbroken nod. Buzz just watched, his face tense, the fixer observing the most critical move of the game.

The phone rang. Once. Twice.

Then the line connected. "Hello?"

It was Jen's voice. But it wasn't her real voice. It was a dead voice. A voice thick with grief and exhaustion, the voice of someone who was just going through the motions of being alive.

Dave's own voice caught in his throat. He had to force the word out.

"...Jen?"

There was a sharp, broken gasp on the other end of the line. Then a sound that would haunt him for the rest of his life: a raw, animal wail of disbelief and a pain so deep it was indistinguishable from joy.

"Dave? Oh my God. Dave?"

He closed his eyes, tears streaming down his own face. "It's me, honey," he whispered into the phone. "I'm here. I'm okay. I'm so sorry."

He had given her proof of life. And now, he had to build her a prison of lies.

Chapter 25: The War Room

Dave placed the phone receiver back into its cradle with the slow, deliberate care of a man handling an unexploded bomb. The click of the plastic settling into place was the only sound in the room, a tiny, insignificant noise that felt as loud and final as a slammed prison door. He had done it. He had given Jen proof of life, and in the same breath, he had built a cage of lies around her and locked the door. The sound of her weeping, a raw, broken symphony of grief and impossible relief, was seared into his brain. He could still feel the weight of her silence after he had made her promise not to tell a soul, a silence filled with a terrifying, unspoken question: What have you gotten yourselves into?

He sank onto the edge of the ridiculously opulent, king-sized bed, the plush comforter offering no comfort. He was clean, he was safe, he was in a five-star hotel room. And he had never felt more trapped.

Skot watched him, his own face a mask of pained empathy. He understood the cost of that phone call. He walked over to the minibar, not for the alcohol, but just to do something, to create a sense of motion in the stagnant, emotionally charged air. He pulled out a bottle of overpriced Fiji water and handed it to Dave.

Buzz, however, was already in motion. The emotional gravity of the phone call had affected him, but his mind, a machine built for promotion and damage control, was already shifting gears. The immediate crisis of his friends' survival was over. Now, a new, far more interesting crisis was beginning, and it was one he felt uniquely qualified to manage. He started pacing the length of the suite, a caged tiger mapping the dimensions of its new territory. He saw the world in terms of problems and opportunities, and the situation they were in was the most spectacular, high-stakes combination of both he had ever encountered.

"Okay," Buzz said, his voice cutting through the heavy silence. "Okay. He did his part. Now we do ours." He stopped pacing and looked at his two friends. They were a mess. They had showered, scrubbing away the layers of jungle filth, and were now wearing an assortment of Buzz's clothes, which fit Skot like a tent and were comically tight on Dave. They were clean, but the haunted, hollowed-out look in their eyes remained. And the aches were returning. He could see it in the way Dave rubbed his lower back, the way Skot kept subtly trying to stretch his shoulder.

"First things first," Buzz announced, picking up the room service menu as if it were a tactical briefing. "We need fuel. Real fuel." He grabbed the phone and, with a flash of his old, performative self, began ordering with an authority that brooked no argument. "Yes, I need three of the El Santuario burgers, medium-rare. And three orders of the truffle fries. And a Caesar salad. No, three Caesar salads. And the seafood tower. And a bottle of your best Malbec. No, make it two bottles."

An hour later, their suite had been transformed into a bizarre, five-star refugee camp. A room service cart laden with a ludicrous amount of food sat in the center of the room. The smell of grilled meat and garlic replaced the lingering scent of stale celebration. For a while, they just ate, a primal, urgent need overwhelming everything else. They were fueling their broken bodies, replenishing calories burned in the jungle and in the impossible resurrection of the Land Rover.

It was during this meal that Buzz finally witnessed the miracle up close. He saw Dave wince as he reached for a bottle of water, a sharp, sudden pain flashing across his face.

"It's coming back," Dave muttered, his voice tight. "The pain. It's like clockwork."

Skot nodded, rolling his shoulder with a groan. "Mine too. We're running on fumes."

With a shared, grim look, they both reached for their BCDs, which they had rinsed out and now lay in a heap by the door like strange, deflated animals. They each unscrewed the valves and poured a small, carefully measured amount of the clear, magical water into a clean water glass from the minibar.

Buzz stopped eating. He watched, his fork halfway to his mouth. The fixer, the promoter, the man of action—all of that fell away, replaced by a pure, scientific curiosity. He watched as Dave, his face a mask of pain, lifted the glass and drank. He watched as the tension in his friend's shoulders eased. He saw the tight lines of pain around his eyes soften and then disappear completely. He saw a wave of vitality, of pure wellness, wash over him, as visible and undeniable as a light being switched on. The transformation took less than ten seconds.

Dave set the empty glass down and took a deep, easy breath. He rolled his back, and this time, there was no wince. There was only a look of profound, blessed relief. Skot repeated the process, with the exact same result.

Buzz was speechless. He had believed their story, on an intellectual level. But seeing it happen, right there, three feet away from a half-eaten seafood tower, was something else entirely. It was like watching someone turn lead into gold on your coffee table. It was real. Undeniably, terrifyingly, profitably real.

That was the moment the last vestiges of the frightened, guilty fixer died, and "The Buzz" was truly reborn.

He pushed his plate away, his appetite gone, replaced by a different kind of hunger. He grabbed the leather-bound notepad and pen from the hotel desk. "Okay," he said, his voice thrumming with a new, manic energy. "War room. Now." He drew a line down the middle of the page. "Problems on this side, opportunities on this side."

Dave looked at him, his expression wary. "Buzz, this isn't a business launch. This is a nightmare. The only plan we need is how to get home, talk to the police, tell them... I don't know, some version of the truth, and get our lives back." His goal was simple: retreat. He wanted normalcy. He wanted to go back to his spreadsheets and his family and forget this ever happened.

Buzz stared at him as if he had just suggested they set themselves on fire. "Get your lives back?" he said, his voice a squeak of disbelief. "Dave, you don't have a life right now. You're legally dead. And you can't just waltz into a police station and tell them this story. They'll think you're insane. They'll lock you up in a psych ward. Or worse, they'll believe you, and you'll spend the rest of your life in a government lab being poked and prodded by men in white coats."

He turned his attention to the 'Opportunities' column on his notepad and underlined it three times. "You guys aren't seeing this clearly. This isn't a problem to solve. This is the winning ticket to the biggest lottery in human history! You didn't just find a spring; you found a product. The product. The one every human being since the beginning of time has been searching for. This isn't a story; it's an IPO. It's a brand. It's everything!"

Skot, who had been listening quietly, leaned forward, his elbows on the table. He was the man in the middle, torn. "A product?" he asked, the artist in him intrigued by the sheer, world-changing scale of the idea, even as the friend in him was terrified. "Buzz, it's a puddle in a cave in the middle of nowhere."

"And Coca-Cola was just sugar water in a basement in Atlanta!" Buzz shot back, his eyes blazing with a zealot's fire. "It's all about the narrative! The marketing! We have the story—a survival epic! We have the proof—the 'before' pictures of two schlubby, middle-aged guys and the 'after' pictures of... well, whatever you are now! We control it. We own it. We can change the world. And get obscenely, filthy rich in the process."

"I don't want to be rich, Buzz!" Dave said, his voice rising. "I want to go to my daughter's soccer game on Saturday! I want this to be over!"

"It will never be over, Dave!" Buzz yelled, slamming his hand on the table, making the glasses jump. "Don't you get it? The genie is out of the bottle. Even if you wanted to, you can't put it back. The only choice you have is who controls it. Us, or them."

"Them who?" Skot asked quietly.

Buzz didn't have an answer for that yet. He just knew, with the primal instinct of a man who understood markets and desire, that something this valuable would not stay secret for long. Someone else would come looking.

....

Thousands of miles away, in a room that was the antithesis of their chaotic suite, a different kind of analysis was taking place. Damian Valis's home office was a masterpiece of cold, minimalist design. It was a space of glass, polished concrete, and brushed steel, devoid of any personal effects, save for a single, perfect orchid on his desk—a testament to nature's beauty, contained and controlled.

Valis was not watching the sensationalist 24-hour news. He was reviewing a private intelligence digest on a large, high-resolution screen that took up an entire wall. His intelligence network, a fusion of AI-driven data mining and human assets, was his real passion. It was his attempt to impose order on a chaotic world, to find the patterns in the noise.

An assistant, a young man with a face scrubbed clean of all emotion, presented him with a high-level anomaly report. The "Missing Divers in Colombia" story was a minor footnote, a blip of human tragedy that was statistically insignificant. But one detail, cross-referenced against a dozen other data points, had caused his system to flag it with a bright red, high-priority warning.

The official search had been terminated. The men had been declared deceased, their survival a "geological impossibility." Yet, in the hours that followed, their known associate, Keith Walker, had initiated a series of illogical and highly suspicious financial transactions. A large, untraceable cash withdrawal. A covert wire transfer to a rural outpost. The cash-only rental of a rugged vehicle. And now, that vehicle was moving rapidly away from the coast and back toward the very jungle where his friends had just been declared dead.

Valis stared at the data, his brilliant mind connecting the dots. Grieving friends did not behave this way. This was not the pattern of grief. This was the pattern of an extraction. An impossibility.

He felt the familiar, hated tremor begin in his right hand, a tiny, rebellious flutter of his own biology betraying him. He consciously stilled it, placing the hand flat on the cool, steel surface of his desk. He took a slow, deliberate breath, recalibrating his own failing machinery. Nature, his great adversary, had just presented him with an aberration, a beautiful, impossible data point that defied all the rules. He wasn't interested in the men themselves; their lives were irrelevant. He was interested in the why. Why had the pattern been broken? Why hadn't they died?

He turned his head slightly, his gaze falling upon a woman who had been standing silently in the corner of the room the entire time. Eva Rostova. His head of security. She was tall, severe, with the cold, coiled stillness of a predator. She was an extension of his own will, an instrument of absolute, unemotional efficiency.

He didn't raise his voice. He didn't need to. His quietest words carried the weight of an earthquake.

"I want to know why they didn't die," he said, his eyes fixed on the screen. "The official story is a lie. Find out what the truth is. Put our people on it." He paused, then added the final, chilling directive.

"I want eyes on them. Now."

Chapter 26: The First Post

The ghost of the news report lingered in the air of the hotel suite, a toxic, invisible cloud. The faces of their living selves, eulogized on international television, were seared onto the backs of their eyelids. The room, with its trashed luxury and half-eaten feast, felt less like a sanctuary and more like a mausoleum. They had survived the jungle only to find themselves buried alive by a different kind of rockslide—a global avalanche of misinformation.

Dave was pacing, a frantic, caged energy radiating from him. He couldn't stand still. The image of his wife's grieving face, a face he had only imagined but could see with perfect, agonizing clarity, was a torment. He had to fix it. He had to undo it.

"Okay," he said, his voice tight and strained, running a hand through his still-damp hair. "Okay. Here's the plan. We stay here. We lie low. Buzz, you find us a lawyer, the best damn international lawyer you can find. We have him release a quiet, simple statement. 'Skot Larson and David Bennett were lost following a diving accident but have been found alive and are recovering in a private location.' Something like that. No details. No press. Then we figure out how to get back home, and we never, ever talk about what really happened. To anyone. Ever."

He looked at his friends, his eyes pleading. His plan was a retreat, an attempt to shrink the story, to starve it of oxygen until it died. He wanted to crawl back into the anonymity of his old life, to pretend the last few days had been nothing more than a shared, waking nightmare.

Buzz stared at him as if he had just started speaking in tongues. He slowly lowered the burger he had been holding, his appetite gone, replaced by a look of profound, almost pitying disbelief.

"Dave," he began, his voice dangerously calm. "I love you like a brother. You know that. But that is, without a doubt, the single stupidest plan I have ever heard in my entire life. And I once watched you try to jump a dirt bike over a bonfire."

"It's not stupid, it's safe!" Dave retorted. "It protects my family! It protects us!"

"It protects nothing!" Buzz's voice rose, the promoter inside him roaring to life. "You think a quiet statement is going to stop this? You're the biggest news story on the planet right now! You are two guys who were officially declared dead by a foreign government! The search was called off! You think you can just show up alive and have everyone say, 'Oh, okay, cool' and just move on? No! They will descend on you like locusts! Every reporter, every government agency, every conspiracy theorist with a YouTube channel will dedicate their lives to finding out what really happened. A quiet statement is a bucket of chum in a shark tank. It doesn't make them go away; it makes them hungrier!"

"So what's your brilliant idea, Buzz?" Skot asked quietly from his chair. He was the fulcrum, caught between Dave's desperate need for privacy and Buzz's explosive vision. "We just walk out into the lobby and hold a press conference?"

"YES!" Buzz yelled, throwing his hands up in the air in a gesture of pure, ecstatic exasperation. "Well, not exactly. But yes! You don't run from a story like this. You get in front of it! You drive the narrative! You own it! You give them a story so big, so insane, so unbelievable that it makes their version look like a boring lie!"

"They'll think we're frauds," Dave muttered, shaking his head. "They'll say we faked the whole thing for attention."

"Of course they will!" Buzz said, a wild, manic grin spreading across his face. He was in his element now, the war room. "And that's fantastic! Controversy is engagement! Skeptics are just another demographic! For every person who calls you a fraud, two more will call you a hero, and a third will think you were abducted by aliens! And they will all be talking about you. We don't just tell the story, we become the story!"

"This isn't a brand launch, Buzz!" Dave yelled, his face flushed with anger and fear. "This is our lives!"

"This is BOTH!" Buzz shot back, his eyes blazing. He was pacing again, the caged tiger fully unleashed. "Your old lives are over! They ended the second you walked out of that jungle looking ten years younger! You can't go back to being a normal CPA, Dave! Your balance sheet now includes a line item for 'resurrection from the dead.' You have to accept that!"

The argument reached a stalemate. Dave, resolute in his terror, shook his head, unwilling to even consider Buzz's insane proposal. Buzz, equally resolute, saw their hesitation not as a roadblock, but as a failure of imagination. They didn't see what he saw. They didn't understand the power they were holding.

Skot, who had been watching the back-and-forth, finally stood up. He looked at Buzz, his expression a complex mixture of fear and dawning curiosity. "Buzz," he said, his voice quiet but firm. "You don't get it. You don't really understand what happened down there."

He walked over to where his dive helmet lay on a chair. He picked it up, then walked to the BCD and retrieved the small, waterproof pouch. He took out the GoPro and the power bank.

"You need to see this," he said.

He connected the camera to Buzz's high-end laptop, a sleek, silver machine that sat on the room's desk. A few clicks, and a video file was transferred. "Turn out the lights," Skot said.

Buzz, momentarily silenced, did as he was told. The room was plunged into a soft darkness, the only light coming from the brilliant, high-resolution screen of the laptop. The three of them huddled around it, their faces illuminated by the glow. Skot hit play.

For Buzz, the first part of the video was just a good adventure film. The swim through The Cathedral was beautiful, cinematic. The cave-in was terrifying, the shaky-cam footage making his own stomach clench with vertigo. He watched, fascinated, as his friends navigated the tight, claustrophobic tunnel, their breathing a ragged, panicked soundtrack.

And then it happened.

The lens broke the surface. And the screen was flooded with light. Not sunlight. A brilliant, impossible, turquoise light that pulsed with a life of its own. It was a color that shouldn't exist in nature. The footage showed his two friends, gasping, shocked, their faces pale. And then it showed Skot scooping the glowing water into his hands and drinking.

Buzz stopped breathing. He leaned closer to the screen, his eyes wide, his entire worldview dissolving in the face of the impossible image on the screen. This wasn't a story. This wasn't a fungus. This was real. He was watching a real, actual miracle.

"My God," he whispered, his voice cracking. "It's real."

He watched the rest of the footage in a stunned, reverent silence. When it was over, he just stared at the blank screen for a full minute. The promoter, the fixer, the party animal—all the different versions of himself were gone, burned away by the glowing light of the grotto. What was left was a true believer. A man who had just seen God, or something like it, on a laptop screen in a messy hotel room.

Then, slowly, a new look began to dawn on his face. The awe was replaced by a look of such ecstatic, greedy, world-conquering glee that it was almost terrifying. He looked at Skot and Dave, and his eyes were shining with the light of a thousand exploding suns.

"This…" he said, his voice trembling with the sheer, monumental weight of the revelation. "This isn't just a story. It's not just a product. It's proof. It's a damn movie. It's the biggest thing in the history of the world."

He didn't wait for their permission. He didn't ask for their input. He was a man possessed by a divine marketing plan. He sat down at the laptop, his fingers flying across the keyboard with a speed and precision they had never known. He opened a video editing program.

"We don't show them everything," he narrated, his voice a low, excited murmur, completely lost in his own creative process. "Not yet. We give them a taste. A teaser. We build the mystery."

He worked with the focus of a master surgeon. He pulled the most dramatic sixty seconds of footage. A flash of their faces, filled with terror. The violent, shaking roar of the cave-in. The claustrophobic darkness of the tunnel. And then, for the last five seconds, he slowed the footage down. A few cryptic, tantalizing, slow-motion frames of the impossible, glowing water, with no context, no explanation. He found a track of tense, dramatic, royalty-free music and layered it underneath.

Then he opened a web browser. He typed out the post. The title was a masterpiece of clickbait, a headline so perfect it was practically irresistible.

He turned to them, his face flushed, his eyes blazing. "Ready?"

Dave looked like he was about to vomit. Skot looked like a man watching his own execution. But they both knew, with a sinking, terrible certainty, that they had crossed a point of no return. They had no other choice. They nodded.

Buzz took a deep breath, positioned the cursor over the 'Upload' button, and clicked.

For a moment, nothing happened. The video just sat there, a thumbnail on a screen. Then the view counter appeared.

1

It stayed there for a second.

17

Then a jump.

412

Then another.

1,987

And then the numbers started to spin, a frantic, accelerating blur, like a slot machine hitting a jackpot. 10,000. 50,000. 100,000. The numbers were climbing so fast they couldn't keep up.

They stared at the screen, three men huddled in a dark room, illuminated by the glow of a single, catastrophic act of creation. They had lit the match. They had dropped it onto the gasoline-soaked floor of the entire world. And now, all they could do was watch it burn.

Chapter 27: The Shape in the Static

For the first sixty seconds after Buzz clicked 'Upload', the only sound in the hotel suite was the frantic, spinning number on the laptop screen. It was a digital tsunami, a tidal wave of human curiosity crashing against their small, isolated shore. The numbers climbed with a speed that defied comprehension, a blur of digits that represented individual people, all over the globe, their attention snagged by a sixty-second clip of a miracle wrapped in a nightmare.

Skot, Dave, and Buzz were no longer just men in a room; they were the epicenter of a seismic cultural event. They were a data point, an anomaly, a mystery, and they were going viral.

Dave watched the numbers, and with every hundred-thousand-view milestone, his face grew paler. He looked like a man watching a wildfire race toward his own home. This wasn't a victory; it was an immolation. He saw each view not as a person, but as a threat, a pair of eyes that would now be looking for them, a voice that would be judging them. He had wanted to crawl back into the quiet anonymity of his life, and instead, Buzz had pushed him onto the world's biggest, brightest stage.

Skot was mesmerized, caught somewhere between Dave's terror and Buzz's glee. He was an artist, a creator, and he had just participated in the most significant act of creation in his life. He had filmed the footage, and now it was taking on a life of its own, a story being told and retold millions of times a minute in a language of shares, likes, and comments. He was horrified and, in a small, secret part of his soul, he was thrilled.

Buzz, however, was in heaven. He was not watching a video go viral; he was watching his own genius be affirmed in real time. He had his hand on the throttle of a cultural rocket ship, and it was the greatest high he had ever known. No party, no drink, no woman had ever given him a rush like this.

"We're trending higher than the World Cup final in Brazil," he said, his voice a reverent whisper. He had his laptop open, a dozen windows tracking analytics, social media mentions, and news sites. "We're the number one search term on Google. In the world. They're already calling you guys 'The Grotto Men.'"

The first twenty-four hours were a blur, a claustrophobic siege conducted through digital wires. The hotel room, their supposed sanctuary, became a pressure cooker. The phones—Buzz's cell and the room phone—began to ring incessantly. News agencies from New York, London, and Tokyo. Old friends who had seen the video. Distant relatives. They were all clamoring for a piece of the story. Buzz, in his self-appointed role as gatekeeper, unplugged the room phone and silenced his own, letting the calls go to a voicemail that was already full.

They watched, huddled around the laptop, as the world began to react. The sixty-second clip was everywhere. It played on a loop on cable news. Pundits and experts were already being trotted out to offer their hot takes. The narrative was splitting, just as Buzz had predicted, into two fierce, opposing camps.

"This is a clear and obvious hoax," said one expert, a stern-faced man with a Ph.D. in visual effects, on a major news network. He pointed to a freeze-frame of the glowing water. "The light sourcing is inconsistent. The way it refracts in the water suggests a submersible LED array, probably battery-powered. It's a well-executed but ultimately amateurish fake."

Dave stabbed a finger at the screen. "See? I told you. They think we're liars. Frauds."

"Who cares!" Buzz shot back, his eyes gleaming. "He said our names, didn't he? He showed our video! He's helping us!"

On another channel, a woman who hosted a popular paranormal investigation show was looking at the camera with wide, sincere eyes. "What we are seeing here," she said, her voice filled with a hushed awe, "is something that defies our current understanding of science. This isn't a hoax. This is a revelation. This is proof that our world is filled with wonders we are only just beginning to rediscover."

The internet was where the battle was truly being waged. For every person calling them heroes, there were ten calling them con artists. Online sleuths began dissecting the video frame by frame. They analyzed the metadata of the file Buzz had uploaded, searching for signs of digital tampering. They cross-referenced the model of GoPro Skot used with its low-light capabilities. It was a global, crowdsourced investigation, and Skot and Dave were the prime suspects in their own miracle.

The pressure was immense. Dave retreated into a stony, terrified silence. Skot grew defensive, pointing out the flaws in the debunkers' arguments. Buzz just soaked it all in, a grin plastered on his face. He was scrolling through a Reddit thread on a subreddit called "Unsolved Mysteries," which had become the unofficial headquarters for the Grotto Men phenomenon.

"This is brilliant," Buzz chuckled, reading a comment aloud. "'My cousin's a geologist. He says that kind of bioluminescence is impossible at that depth. These guys are probably selling a new brand of crypto.'" He scrolled further. "Oh, listen to this one. 'It's a viral marketing campaign for a new James Cameron movie. Calling it now.'"

He was having the time of his life. And then he stopped.

"Whoa," he said softly.

"What now?" Dave asked, his voice laced with dread.

"Look at this," Buzz said, turning the laptop so they could all see.

He pointed to a post that was rapidly gaining traction, its title simple and intriguing: "Has Anyone Else Seen This? Frame 47.3 seconds."

The post contained a single image: a zoomed-in, heavily pixelated screenshot from their video. It was from the moment they were making their frantic ascent from the dark escape tunnel into the glowing grotto. The image was a chaotic, blurry mess of rising bubbles and murky, turquoise-lit water. But in the background, just behind where Skot's fins would have been, was a shape. It was utterly ambiguous, a phantom in the digital noise. It was a faint, elongated, humanoid form, its edges blurred and indistinct. It could have been a trick of the light reflecting off the rock formations. It could have been a swirl of silt. Or it could have been something else.

"What is that?" Buzz whispered, leaning closer.

Dave squinted at the screen. "It's nothing," he said dismissively. "It's a rock. People are seeing faces in the clouds, Buzz. It's meaningless."

But Skot didn't say anything. He just stared at the screen, his face draining of all color. He felt a cold dread wash over him, a memory from the edge of oblivion bubbling up to the surface.

Buzz noticed his friend's silence. "Skot? What is it?"

Skot swallowed hard, his eyes still locked on the blurry shape. He looked at Buzz, then at Dave, his expression haunted.

"I saw something," he said, his voice barely a whisper. "Just for a second. When we were coming up. I was right on the edge of blacking out. My vision was tunneling. I saw... a shape. In the water, watching us."

"What?" Dave said, sitting up straight. "Why didn't you say anything?"

"Because I thought I was hallucinating!" Skot said, his voice rising with a defensive edge. "I thought it was the hypoxia. My brain was playing tricks on me. It was the most logical explanation. It was impossible. So I buried it. I told myself it wasn't real."

A thick, heavy silence descended on the room. The impossible had just become impossibly stranger.

Dave looked horrified, as if a ghost from a nightmare had just been proven real. But Buzz... Buzz looked like he had just been handed the keys to the kingdom. The look of awe on his face was slowly replaced by the familiar, manic gleam of pure, unadulterated opportunity. He didn't see a terrifying, supernatural mystery. He saw content. He saw the hook for Season Two.

Without a word, he turned back to the laptop, a devilish grin spreading across his face.

"What are you doing?" Skot asked, a note of alarm in his voice.

"I'm engaging with our audience," Buzz said, his voice purring with delight. "I'm fanning the flames."

He created a new post, not on a forum, but on the new, official "SirenSpring" social media accounts he had created an hour earlier. He uploaded the blurry, ambiguous screenshot. And then he wrote the caption, a masterpiece of manipulative, mystery-building genius.

"The world is asking what happened in that cave. The truth is, we're still trying to figure it out ourselves. We are not scientists. We are not hoaxers. We are just two men who survived something we can't explain. We saw this in our own footage for the first time today, thanks to you. A trick of the light? A rock formation? Or something else? We don't know. What do YOU think this is? #SirenInTheSpring #GrottoGuardian"

He read it aloud, his voice dripping with self-satisfaction.

"Don't you dare post that, Buzz," Dave said, his voice a low growl.

But it was too late. Buzz's finger was already hovering over the mouse. He looked at them, his eyes gleaming. "Sorry, boys," he said. "The brand needs a narrative."

He clicked.

The post went live. And the fire they had started just twenty-four hours ago was suddenly doused with a fresh, volatile, and highly flammable gallon of gasoline. The mystery was no longer just about whether they were telling the truth. The mystery was now about what else was in the water with them.

Chapter 28: The Narrative

The moment Buzz clicked 'Post', a new kind of silence descended on the hotel suite. It wasn't the silence of exhaustion or fear; it was the charged, humming silence of a bomb that has been armed. Dave stared at the laptop screen, his face a mask of pale, horrified resignation. He looked like a man who had just watched his own confession be broadcast live on every channel. Skot stood behind him, a hand on his shoulder, though it was unclear if he was offering comfort or seeking it himself.

Buzz, however, was a coiled spring of pure, unadulterated energy. He leaned toward the screen, his eyes wide and manic, like a general watching his first volley of artillery hit its target. The post, with its provocative screenshot and its tantalizing hashtags, wasn't just a message; it was a declaration of war on the boring, predictable version of their story.

The reaction was not a wave; it was an explosion. The internet, which had been a churning sea of debate, was now a roiling, chaotic vortex. The #SirenInTheSpring hashtag began to trend globally within minutes. The ambiguous, blurry screenshot was suddenly everywhere, being analyzed, brightened, contrasted, and circled in red by a million amateur detectives. The debate was no longer about whether the footage was real or fake. That was yesterday's news. The new debate was about what else was in the water with them.

"They're losing their minds," Buzz whispered, his voice filled with a giddy, reverent glee. He was scrolling through the feed, a conductor marveling at the glorious, terrifying symphony he had just unleashed. "The cryptozoologists are fighting with the paranormal investigators. The marine biologists are calling it an undiscovered species of deep-sea cephalopod that got trapped in the cave system. My favorite so far is a guy who is absolutely convinced it's the ghost of a drowned conquistador."

"They think we're lunatics, Buzz," Dave said, his voice a low, defeated groan. He had collapsed into one of the armchairs, the fight seemingly gone out of him. "No one is ever going to believe we're just two normal guys ever again. We're part of the circus now. We're the freaks."

"Normal is boring!" Buzz shot back, spinning in his chair to face him, his eyes blazing with a promoter's fire. "Normal doesn't get a book deal! Normal doesn't get you a seven-figure Netflix special! Dave, you are grieving for a life that was already gone. You died on the news two days ago. That old you is a ghost. We have to embrace the new brand! 'The Grotto Men' isn't just a nickname; it's a registered trademark waiting to happen!"

"It's not a brand, it's my life!"

"It's both!"

Skot stepped in, his face a mask of deep conflict. He was the unwilling prophet of Buzz's new religion, the only one who had actually seen something, and the weight of that memory was a heavy burden. "Buzz, you have to slow down. This is… this is too much, too fast. We haven't even had a chance to process what happened, and you're selling merchandising rights."

"If we don't, someone else will!" Buzz insisted. "You think some T-shirt company in China isn't already mocking up a '#GrottoGuardian' shirt? You either control your narrative, or the narrative controls you. There is no in-between. Not anymore."

The phone on the desk, the one they had unplugged, suddenly began to ring. They all froze, staring at the blinking red light on the base as if it were a venomous snake.

"How is that possible?" Dave whispered.

"It means they're not just calling the room anymore," Buzz said, a slow, predatory smile spreading across his face. "It means they're calling the front desk and getting them to patch it through directly. They're getting smarter." He sauntered over to the phone and picked up the receiver. "Buzz Walker's Home for the Bewildered, you're on the air."

There was a pause. Buzz's flippant expression slowly faded, replaced by a look of intense, focused concentration. "I see," he said into the phone, his voice suddenly all business. "And what organization are you with?... Interesting... No, we are not currently entertaining offers, but I appreciate the call. You can submit a preliminary proposal to the email address you'll find on our new website, which should be live by tomorrow. Have a nice day."

He hung up the phone, his hand resting on it for a moment.

"Who was that?" Skot asked, his voice tense.

"That," Buzz said, turning to them, his eyes gleaming with the light of pure vindication, "was a senior literary agent from the most powerful agency in New York. They want to know who holds the exclusive rights to our story." He let the words hang in the air for a moment. "They think it could be the biggest nonfiction book of the decade. They want to call it Siren's Spring" he said with the huge grin of the cat who ate the canary.

The statement was eye opening to say the least. A book deal. It was an abstract concept that was suddenly, terrifyingly real. It was the first concrete sign that the gears of a massive, global media machine were beginning to turn in their direction.

Dave looked horrified. "Tell them no. Tell them we're not interested."

"Are you kidding me?" Buzz laughed. "I just created market demand! This is perfect!"

....

While they argued about the shape of their newfound fame, a different kind of professional was at work. Eva Rostova sat in the back of a nondescript black van parked across the street from the El Santuario resort's service entrance. The van was a state-of-the-art mobile surveillance unit, its interior a cold, clean nest of monitors and encrypted communication gear. She was not watching the sensationalist news reports. She was watching a live, high-resolution feed from a micro-drone currently hovering silently outside the fourth-floor window of Keith Walker's suite.

She had been there for hours. Her on-the-ground team in Santa Marta had moved with silent, lethal efficiency. They had identified Buzz's rental truck within an hour of her order. They had tailed it, unseen, on its journey back to the coast. They had watched as it bypassed the main entrance and slipped into the service area in the pre-dawn hours. And thermal imaging from the drone had confirmed the impossible: three distinct heat signatures in a room registered to one man. The anomaly was real. Her prey was in the cage.

"We have audio, ma'am," a technician in the front of the van said, his voice a low, professional murmur. A laser microphone aimed at the windowpane was picking up the vibrations and translating them back into sound.

Eva put on a headset. The sound was muffled, indistinct, but the emotional tenor was clear. She heard shouting, arguing. She could make out fragments. "...my life!"... "...biggest thing in the history of the world!"... "...book deal..."

It was noise. It told her nothing of substance. She was not interested in their petty squabbles. She was interested in the source of the anomaly. The why.

"The room service order," she said, her voice a placid, unemotional command. "What did they eat?"

The technician tapped on his keyboard. "Three burgers, three salads, three orders of fries, one seafood tower, two bottles of Malbec."

"And what did they drink from their own supply?"

This was the detail that fascinated her. Her team had intercepted the room service waiter, a young man who was easily bought, and had him plant a microscopic listening device on the cart. They had heard everything.

"They refer to it as 'the water,'" the technician reported. "Two of the subjects, Larson and Bennett, each consumed a small amount from what the waiter described as a 'dirty scuba vest.' The effect, according to the subject Walker, was an 'instantaneous visible physical change.'"

Eva's cold, analytical mind processed the information. It was absurd. It was impossible. And yet, it was the only data she had. The anomaly had a source. A specific, quantifiable source.

She looked at the thermal image of the room on her screen. Three bright, warm shapes, moving, arguing, completely unaware that they were being observed. They were loud, chaotic, and emotional. They were amateurs. And they were sitting on a secret that her employer would kill for, a secret that could rewrite the laws of biology.

"Maintain surveillance," she said, her voice a low whisper. "I want to know everything they do, everyone they talk to. I want to know what they had for breakfast in first grade. Do not engage. Do not be seen. Just watch."

She took off the headset and stared at the hotel, a glittering, five-star prison. The hunt was over. The observation phase had begun. And when the time was right, when she had learned everything she needed to know, she would move. And the loud, chaotic, viral story of the Grotto Men would come to a very quiet, very permanent end.

Chapter 29: Rules of Engagement

The call from the literary agent was a paradigm shift. It transformed the abstract, chaotic storm of their viral fame into something tangible, something with a price tag. The number of views on their video was no longer just a measure of curiosity; it was a measure of market value. The revelation hung in the air of the hotel suite, heavy and shimmering with possibility and dread.

Dave looked utterly horrified. To him, the agent's call wasn't an offer; it was an invasion. It was the first vulture circling, the first tangible proof that their story was no longer their own. It was a commodity, to be bought, sold, and packaged for mass consumption.

"Tell them no," he said, his voice a low, desperate growl. He was looking at Buzz, but his words were a plea to whatever forces were now in control of their lives. "Tell them we're not interested. Tell them to leave us alone."

Buzz looked at him with the kind of pity a financial advisor might reserve for a client who wants to put their life savings into lottery tickets. "Dave, you have to understand. That phone call is the sound of the starting gun. The race has already begun. Right now, there are a hundred other agents, a thousand producers, a million content creators all trying to figure out how to tell your story. If we don't get out in front and plant our flag, they will own it. They will create a version of you, and you will be forced to live with it for the rest of your life."

He turned and walked to the large, floor-to-ceiling window, which they had kept shrouded with the blackout curtains. He dramatically pulled one of the curtains back a few inches, revealing a slice of the resort's pristine, sun-drenched grounds. And, parked on the service road below, a white news van with a large satellite dish on its roof.

"They're already here," Buzz said, his voice grim. "They don't know we're in this room yet, but they're here. They're sniffing around. The second we walk out that door, we're public property." He let the curtain fall, plunging the room back into its gloomy, artificial twilight.

"He's right, Dave," Skot said quietly. He had been re-watching the GoPro footage of the grotto on his own, not on the laptop, but on the camera's tiny screen, as if trying to decipher a hidden message in the glowing pixels. "We can't put the genie back in the bottle. It's out. It's flying around, and it's causing a scene."

Dave sank into an armchair, the fight draining out of him, replaced by a weary, resentful acceptance. He was an accountant. He understood numbers, rules, and consequences. And he was beginning to understand that he was on the wrong side of a very, very unbalanced equation. "So what do we do?" he asked, his voice barely a whisper. "What's the plan, Buzz? Since you're the one who seems to have one."

The question was all the invitation Buzz needed. This was his moment. He grabbed the hotel notepad, which was already filled with his frantic scribbles, and a pen. He strode to the center of the room, a self-appointed general about to brief his two very reluctant troops.

"Okay," he began, his voice thrumming with an energy that was equal parts passion and mania. "This is no longer a rescue mission. This is now a media campaign. And every campaign needs rules of engagement. Rule number one," he said, scribbling a large '1' on the page, "is that from this moment forward, no one talks to anyone without my express permission. Not your wives, not your sisters, and especially not the guy who delivers the club sandwiches. We are on total communication lockdown. All information flows through me. I am the gatekeeper. I am the brand manager."

"We're not a brand, we're people," Dave muttered into his hands.

"You're both!" Buzz shot back without missing a beat. "And the people need to be protected by the brand. Rule number two: We establish a single, unified narrative. We agree on the story, and we stick to it. Every detail. The dive, the cave-in, the jungle, all of it. But we leave out the... the weird stuff for now. The healing, the strength... all of it. The story is 'miraculous survival.' We save 'superhuman side effects' for the sequel."

He was pacing again, the notepad in one hand, gesturing with the other. "Rule number three: We need to get ahead of the fraud accusations. They're our biggest immediate threat. And the only way to do that is to give them more proof. But we control the flow of that proof. We don't just dump the whole GoPro file online; that's amateur hour. We leak it, piece by piece. We give them a new clue every few days to keep the conversation going."

He was in his element. This wasn't just a plan; it was a performance. He was a maestro of hype, a virtuoso of viral marketing, and this was his magnum opus. Skot watched him, a look of grudging admiration on his face. He was horrified by the raw, naked commercialism of it all, but he couldn't deny that Buzz was a genius in his own strange, terrifying way.

Dave, however, was having none of it. "No," he said, his voice quiet but firm. He stood up, his gaze locked on Buzz. "I'm not a product. My family is not a marketing demographic. I will do this, because it seems I have no other choice. But I have one rule. One unbreakable rule."

He took a step closer to Buzz, his expression deadly serious. "My family. Jen and the kids. They are to be kept out of this. Completely. No pictures, no interviews, no 'heartwarming human-interest' stories. They are off-limits. They are a red line. If you cross it, I don't care about the book deals or the Netflix specials. I will burn the whole thing to the ground. Do you understand me?"

The raw, protective power in Dave's voice silenced Buzz for the first time. He saw the look in his friend's eyes, a look he had never seen before, and he knew it was not a negotiation. It was an ultimatum.

"I understand," Buzz said, his own voice sober now. "Red line. Absolutely. I'll hire a private security firm for them today. They'll be protected."

With the new, most important rule established, the tension in the room eased, replaced by a grim sense of shared purpose. They had a plan. A terrible, insane, high-stakes plan, but a plan nonetheless.

"So what's the first move?" Skot asked, finally closing the tiny GoPro screen.

"Phase One," Buzz said, his energy returning. "We need to do one interview. A single, exclusive, high-stakes interview with a major, credible news outlet. Someone serious. Not a late-night talk show, not a paranormal podcast. We need a respected journalist who can give our story a stamp of legitimacy. We tell our version, the one we control, and we make it the official record. We answer the tough questions, we look sincere, we build trust. We get ahead of the story for good."

He was already scrolling through the contacts on his phone, his mind sifting through a lifetime of schmoozing and networking. "I know a guy who knows a guy who works for Diana Sterling..."

"Diana Sterling?" Dave asked, his eyes wide. "The woman with the primetime news magazine show? The one who makes presidents cry?"

"The one and only," Buzz said with a wicked grin. "If you can survive her, you can survive anything. And the whole world will believe you."

In the back of the black surveillance van, Eva Rostova lowered the headset from her ears. She had heard everything. Every word of their frantic, amateurish strategy session. She had listened to Dave's emotional ultimatum, to Skot's conflicted silence, to Buzz's grandiose, ego-driven plans. It was like listening to a group of children planning a birthday party, completely unaware that a wolf was watching them through the window.

They were so predictable. So beautifully, wonderfully predictable. She had already identified their individual weaknesses. Dave, the protector, could be leveraged through his family. Skot, the artist, was the conscience, the one most likely to crack under moral pressure. And Buzz, the promoter, was the most dangerous and the most vulnerable. His ego was a massive, shining target. He could be manipulated with flattery, with offers of fame and access that would make his current plans seem laughably small-time.

A technician in the front of the van turned to her. "Ma'am, we have a flag. A new directive from Mr. Valis."

He handed her a tablet. A new message was on the screen, a single, chilling line.

The subjects have a product. I want to see a sample. Acquire a sample of 'the water.' Covertly. Do not engage.

Eva's cold, placid expression did not change. Her employer was growing impatient. He was a man who did not wait for products to come to market; he acquired them at the source.

She looked at the thermal image of the hotel room on her screen. She could see the three bright, warm shapes inside. She could see the two dark, sloshing shapes of the BCDs on the floor, their thermal signature identical to the bottled water in the minibar. That was it. The source. The product.

They were planning an interview. They were planning a book deal. They were planning a media empire.

And she was planning a simple, silent burglary.

Chapter 30: The Gilded Cage

Morning in the war room was not a gentle affair. It was an assault of ringing phones and the low, incessant hum of the 24-hour news cycle, which had been left on all night like a toxic, flickering nightlight. The initial, frantic energy of their strategy session had evaporated with the last of the adrenaline, leaving behind a thick, stagnant residue of boredom and a creeping, claustrophobic dread. The El Santuario suite, which had seemed like the height of luxury just days ago, now felt like a well-appointed prison cell. The velvet ropes had been replaced by blackout curtains, the open bar with a dwindling supply of room-service water bottles. They were fugitives living on a five-star expense account, and the novelty was wearing off with alarming speed.

Buzz was the only one who seemed to thrive in the chaos. He had been awake since dawn, a whirlwind of caffeinated energy, his phone practically fused to his ear. He was no longer just the promoter; he was the CEO, the legal department, and the chief of staff of their tiny, besieged nation-state. He paced the length of the suite, a bluetooth earpiece in his ear, speaking in a low, clipped tone that was a world away from his usual boisterous banter.

"No, I understand the liability," he said, his voice tight. "Of course I understand. Listen, David, I didn't hire you for your optimism, I hired you for your paranoia. Just keep the incorporation paperwork moving. And the NDAs.

I want an NDA so tight it would make a black hole claustrophobic."

He was talking to a lawyer in New York, a shark he had on retainer for his own, less world-altering business deals. The conversation was a sobering dose of reality. The lawyer had been blunt: their story, if true, was a legal minefield of unprecedented scale. If it was a hoax, it was international fraud. Either way, they were open to lawsuits from every direction, from the Colombian government for unsanctioned exploration to the families of the men who had died in the jungle decades ago, whose story they had inadvertently uncovered. The miracle had a million hidden liabilities.

Skot, meanwhile, was mainlining the poison. He sat on the sofa, Buzz's laptop open, scrolling through the endless, churning vortex of their own fame. He was the moral compass of the group, and he felt a deep, personal responsibility for the madness they had unleashed. He watched as the #SirenInTheSpring theory exploded. The blurry screenshot was now the subject of hour-long YouTube deep-dive analysis videos. "Experts" in CGI, marine biology, and paranormal phenomena were all weighing in, each projecting their own beliefs onto the ambiguous, pixelated shape.

He saw a CGI rendering an artist had created, a beautiful, ethereal, and slightly menacing-looking mermaid, her form superimposed over the original screenshot. The rendering was already going viral. He, Skot Larson, a freelance graphic designer who worried about making rent, had inadvertently created the most famous mythological creature of the 21st century. The thought filled him with a mixture of professional pride and profound, soul-deep horror. He had seen a flicker of something in the dark, and now the world was turning his private, terrifying hallucination into a global franchise.

Dave, however, was in his own private hell, a hell that had nothing to do with book deals or internet fame. He was focused on the one thing that mattered: the fallout at home. He was on the phone with Jen for the second time, his back to the room, his voice a low, pained murmur. This call was harder than the first. The initial, shocking relief had worn off, and in its place, a thousand terrifying, practical questions had taken root.

"No, honey, I can't tell you where we are," he whispered, his knuckles white as he gripped the phone. "It's not safe yet... No, I don't know when I'm coming home. Soon. I promise."

He listened, his face a mask of agony. Jen was struggling. She was a terrible liar, and the secret was a toxic presence in their home. Her sister had called, wanting to organize a memorial service. A neighbor had brought over a casserole, her eyes filled with pity. Jen was living a double life, grieving for the benefit of the outside world while secretly holding onto a hope that was terrifying in its vagueness. She was a prisoner, just like he was.

"I have to go," he finally said, his voice cracking. "I love you. Tell the kids... tell them I love them more than anything." He hung up the phone and stood with his forehead pressed against the cool glass of the window, the blackout curtain a shroud between him and the outside world. He had rescued her from grief, only to sentence her to an indefinite term of fear and isolation.

It was in this moment of peak tension, with each of the three men locked in his own private struggle, that a firm, authoritative knock came at the door of the suite.

They all froze. They looked at each other, their eyes wide with panic. It was too soon for room service. They hadn't ordered anything.

"Who is it?" Buzz called out, his voice a low, suspicious growl.

"Hotel management, Mr. Walker," a polite, tinny voice replied from the hallway. "I'm here with our head of security. We need to have a brief word with you, if you have a moment."

This was it. The bubble had burst. Buzz looked at Skot and Dave, a silent question in his eyes. They had no choice. He walked to the door and opened it, leaving the chain on.

Standing in the hallway was the hotel manager, his professional smile looking strained and brittle. Next to him was a large, imposing man in a sharp suit, whose expression was anything but smiling.

"Good morning, Mr. Walker," the manager began. "May we come in?"

Buzz undid the chain and opened the door. The two men stepped inside, their eyes taking in the scene—the messy room, the two other men who were supposed to be dead, the palpable atmosphere of a siege.

"There seems to be a significant misunderstanding," the manager said, his voice dripping with a forced, corporate politeness. "We were under the impression you were the sole occupant of this suite."

"My friends had a change of plans," Buzz said coolly.

"So it would seem," the man in the suit said, his voice a low, rumbling bass. He was the hotel's lawyer. "Mr. Walker, your... situation... has become a significant disruption to the hotel's operations. There are currently three international news vans parked on our service road. We have reporters attempting to bribe our housekeeping staff for information. The guests in the adjoining suites have complained about the constant phone calls. El Santuario prides itself on being a tranquil oasis for our patrons. This is... not that."

"I understand," Buzz said, though his posture was defensive. "We're trying to be discreet."

"Your time for discretion is over," the lawyer said, his tone hardening. "You have made our hotel the epicenter of a global media event without our consent. This is a breach of our guest conduct policy. And frankly, we cannot be held liable for your security, which appears to be... compromised."

The manager cleared his throat, stepping forward to deliver the final, polite blow. "What my colleague is trying to say, Mr. Walker, is that we must, with our sincerest apologies, ask you to check out. Immediately."

The words landed like a death sentence. Their sanctuary, their war room, their gilded cage—it was being taken away.

"You're kicking us out?" Skot asked, incredulous.

"We are terminating your stay," the lawyer corrected him. "For the security and comfort of our other guests. You have ninety minutes to vacate the premises."

While this tense, whispered confrontation was happening at the door, another, far quieter drama was unfolding behind them. A soft, deferential knock came from the open doorway. A housekeeper, a young woman with a timid smile, stood there with her cart.

"Housekeeping," she said in Spanish. "Servicio de habitacion?" She gestured to the room service cart with its load of dirty dishes from the night before.

Buzz, his attention completely focused on the manager and the lawyer, waved a dismissive hand over his shoulder. "Yes, yes, take it."

The housekeeper slipped into the room, her movements quiet and efficient. She began loading the dirty plates onto her cart. None of the three friends paid her any attention. They were too busy watching their entire world collapse.

As Buzz argued futilely with the lawyer, the housekeeper moved toward the pile of gear by the door. She reached for the two filthy, discarded BCDs. She picked one up, a look of mild disgust on her face, and placed it in the large canvas laundry bag hanging from her cart. She then reached for the second one.

But it wasn't the second one. From a hidden compartment in her cart, she produced a third BCD—an identical, decoy vest, weighted to feel exactly the same. In a single, fluid motion, she left the decoy on the floor and tossed Skot's real BCD, the one containing the precious, miraculous water, into her laundry bag, covering it with a pile of dirty towels.

The entire exchange took less than five seconds. It was a silent, flawless piece of tradecraft, executed in plain sight.

She pushed her cart back toward the door. "Gracias," she whispered, slipping out into the hallway as quietly as she had entered.

Up front, the argument had reached its conclusion. "Ninety minutes," the lawyer repeated, his tone leaving no room for negotiation. He and the manager turned and walked away, leaving the three of them standing in the doorway of a room that was no longer theirs.

Buzz closed the door, a look of stunned disbelief on his face. "Well," he said, the word falling flat in the silent room. "So much for the war room."

They were homeless. They were fugitives. They were trapped between a global media frenzy outside and a corporate policy that had just rendered them refugees. Their carefully laid plans, their rules of engagement, had just been vaporized by a simple checkout order.

And they were completely, blissfully unaware that they had also just been robbed. The last of their miracle, the very source of their impossible story, was now being silently wheeled down a service elevator in the bottom of a laundry cart, on its way to a woman in a black van who was waiting very, very patiently.

Chapter 31: Strategic Repositioning

The ninety-minute deadline hung in the air of the hotel suite like the blade of a guillotine. Dave was in a state of quiet, simmering panic, pacing the room like a caged animal. Skot was trying to methodically pack their meager, filthy belongings, but his movements were jerky and unfocused. The walls, which had been their sanctuary, were now closing in, the luxurious wallpaper seeming to mock them with its serene, repeating patterns. Their war room had become a trap, and the clock was ticking.

But Keith "Buzz" Walker was not panicking. He was alive. He was electric. The sullen, guilt-ridden fixer of the past few days was gone, sloughed off like a dead skin. In his place was the man he was always meant to be: the producer, the promoter, the four-star general in the army of his own ego. This wasn't a crisis; it was a challenge. It was a high-stakes, limited-time-offer, exclusive-access event, and he was the star.

"Okay, gentlemen, listen up!" he barked, clapping his hands together with a sound like a gunshot. He was a whirlwind of motion, his phone pressed to one ear, a hotel notepad in his hand. "The asset is compromised, the location is burned, which, by the way, is fantastic. We are officially in a strategic brand repositioning phase. It's exciting! It's dynamic! Think of it as a reboot, you know? The gritty, realistic reboot."

"A reboot? Buzz, we're being kicked out onto the street!" Dave said, his voice a half-octave too high. "There are reporters downstairs!"

"Whoa, whoa, back it up, Davey, back the whole truck up," Buzz said, holding up a hand while still listening to the phone. "Paparazzi. Okay? Let's get the lingo right, because it's all about the lingo. It's perception, it's reality, and right now the reality is those aren't just guys with cameras, that's the machine! And the machine isn't a threat, it's a tool! You just gotta know how to use it." He spoke into the phone. "Yes, hello? Concierge? This is Keith Walker in the Celestial Suite… Yes, the one you're kicking out, thanks for rubbing it in. Listen, I need a clean extraction. I'm talking about a helicopter. Rooftop. Now… What do you mean you don't have a helipad? What kind of five-star, third-world, fly-by-night operation are you people running? Do you have any idea who I have in this room? The talent! Fine!" He hung up with a theatrical slam. "Amateurs," he muttered, already scribbling a note on his pad. "Okay, chopper is a no-go, which is fine, it was too cliché anyway. Plan B."

He immediately redialed. "Front desk? Walker. I need a decoy vehicle at the main entrance in exactly seventy-five minutes. A black SUV, tinted windows, the whole nine. I want you to have a bellhop load it with my golf clubs, make a real show of it. And I want you to have your security team create a 'privacy corridor' from this suite to the service elevator in the east wing. We're moving the talent, and I want it done clean, like we're stealing the Declaration of Independence. Got it?" He didn't wait for an answer. He just hung up, a look of grim satisfaction on his face.

"The talent?" Skot asked, pausing in his attempt to stuff a muddy wetsuit into a designer laundry bag. He had seen Buzz doing his thing, but never on this kind of high before.

"That's you!" Buzz said, pointing at him with the pen. "You're the talent. I'm the management. He's the nervous money guy," he added, gesturing at Dave. "It's a classic Hollywood setup. Try to keep up."

The central conflict of the next seventy-four minutes now presented itself: where, exactly, were they going?

"We need a motel," Dave said, his voice firm with the conviction of the sensible. "A cheap, anonymous motel on the absolute farthest outskirts of the city. We pay cash, we check in under a fake name, we keep our heads down, and we wait for this to blow over."

Buzz stopped his frantic pacing. He turned to face Dave, and his expression was one of such profound, pitying contempt that it was almost comical. He slowly lowered his phone.

"Davey, listen to me, and listen good, because I'm dropping truth bombs here and you gotta catch 'em," he said, his voice dropping into a rapid-fire, confidential tone. "A motel? A motel? Are you actively trying to hurt me? Because that hurts me. That's not just a bad idea, that's a career-ender. That's like showing up to the Super Bowl and deciding to play in your flip-flops. It's brand suicide, my friend. Total self-sabotage! The optics are a catastrophe! A complete and utter train wreck!"

"I don't care about optics, Buzz! I care about not being found!"

"It's the same thing! It's two sides of the same beautiful, high-stakes coin!" Buzz was back in motion, a shark that had to keep moving to breathe. "We can't give our first, exclusive, multi-million-dollar interview from a place with bedbugs and a flickering neon sign that says 'EAT'! Diana Sterling is not going to meet you at a Motel 6! This is a pivotal moment! We are defining the visual language of the Siren Spring brand!"

He whipped out his phone again, his thumbs a blur. He turned the phone around, displaying a series of glossy, architectural photos. They showed a stunning, ultra-modern villa perched on a cliff overlooking the ocean. It was a palace of glass, white concrete, and polished steel, with a shimmering infinity pool that seemed to melt into the horizon.

"This," Buzz announced with a presenter's flourish, "is our new safe house."

Dave stared at the picture, his mouth hanging open. "That's not a safe house, Buzz, it's a fishbowl! It's got glass walls! We'll be completely exposed!"

"See, this is the thing, you're playing checkers, but I'm playing 3D chess in another dimension," Buzz said, his words tumbling over each other. "It's a total head-fake! They're looking for little mice, right? Hiding in the dark corners, the cheap motels with the flickering signs, the shadows. So what do we do? We don't hide. We peacock! We get the biggest, brightest, most ridiculously expensive fishbowl on the cliff and we jump right in, do a little dance. It's so wrong it's right! It's beautiful. It's money. Plus," he added, zooming in on a photo of a cavernous, art-filled living room, "the natural lighting in there will be fantastic for the interview."

"He's gone insane," Dave said to Skot, a statement of simple, objective fact.

"He might have a point," Skot said, a small, intrigued smile playing on his lips. The sheer, breathtaking audacity of the plan appealed to the artist, the adventurer, the part of him that was just as crazy as Buzz.

"Thank you, Skot," Buzz said, preening. "At least one of you understands the importance of production value. It's all about the sizzle." He made a few more taps on his phone. "Done. It's booked. For a week. You guys owe me. Big time."

With their destination decided, the frantic packing began in earnest. Dave, having lost the argument, resigned himself to the madness, stuffing his few belongings into a backpack Buzz had produced from a cavernous closet. It was Skot who made the discovery.

He walked over to the pile of gear by the door, reaching for his B-C-D. It was the most important piece of equipment they had left. It held the GoPro, their only proof. It held the last, precious, life-saving dregs of the water.

He picked it up. And he froze.

"What's wrong?" Dave asked, seeing the look on his friend's face.

"This isn't mine," Skot said, his voice a low, confused murmur. He ran a hand over the fabric. "Mine had a tear on the left shoulder strap from where it snagged in the tunnel. This one... this one's perfect."

He frantically fumbled with the side pocket, the one where he'd hidden the waterproof pouch. He unzipped it. His face went white.

He turned the B-C-D upside down and shook it. Nothing came out.

The pocket was empty.

"No," Skot whispered, his eyes wide with a dawning, sickening horror. "No, no, no."

"What is it?" Buzz demanded, his fast-talking energy finally screeching to a halt.

"The camera," Skot choked out. "The pouch. The power bank. It's gone."

Panic, cold and absolute, ripped through the room. They tore the suite apart. They upended the laundry bags, threw cushions off the sofa, looked under the beds. Nothing. They checked Dave's B-C-D. It was still there, untouched. But it was Skot's that had held the proof.

And then the second, even more terrifying realization hit them. Skot picked up the decoy B-C-D and held it up. He looked at the oral inflator valve, then at the main bladder. He tried to get water out of it. It was dry. Bone dry.

"The water," Skot said, his voice barely a whisper. "Dave, the rest of the water is gone."

The truth shook the room. The housekeeper. The quiet, timid young woman who had slipped in and out while they were arguing with the manager. It wasn't a mistake. She hadn't accidentally taken the wrong vest. It was a switch. A professional, flawlessly executed swap.

Buzz stood completely still, the blood draining from his face. The manic energy evaporated in an instant, replaced by a cold, genuine fear, the kind he hadn't felt even when he thought his friends were dead. The game he thought he was producing, the narrative he thought he was controlling, was a lie. There was another player, a silent, invisible professional who had been in their room, who had walked among them, who had stolen their most precious secrets from right under their noses.

The phone on the desk buzzed, a summons from the front desk. The decoy car was ready. Their 90-minute clock was almost up.

They were no longer just viral sensations. They were no longer just fugitives from the media.

They were targets of someone, or many someones. Only God knows who.

Chapter 32: The Copy

The realization landed in the center of the room with the silent, concussive force of a bomb. The water was gone. The camera was gone. The last vestiges of their miracle, the physical proof and the supernatural power, had been snatched from them in a single, flawless act of professional theft. For a moment, the only sound in the suite was the frantic, useless hum of the air conditioning. The ninety-minute deadline, the reporters downstairs, the angry hotel manager—all of it evaporated, replaced by a new and infinitely more terrifying reality.

Dave's face was a mask of pure, unadulterated terror. He looked at the empty pocket of the decoy BCD, then at his own hands, as if expecting them to suddenly wrinkle and age before his eyes. The magic was gone. Their safety net had been cut. "They were in the room," he whispered, his voice a dry rustle of panic. "They were in here with us."

Skot was in a state of shock, turning the useless decoy vest over and over in his hands, his mind refusing to process the violation. The camera, his footage, the unblinking witness to their impossible story—it had been stolen by a ghost.

But it was the change in Buzz that was the most profound. The manic, fast-talking, energy drained out of him in an instant. The promoter, the producer, the hype-man—they all vanished, leaving behind a man he hadn't been since the first terrible hours in the lobby: the fixer. His face went pale, his jaw tightened, and his eyes, for the first time, were filled not with glee or arrogance, but with a cold, clear, and genuine fear. The game he thought he was playing had just been revealed to be something else entirely, something with rules he didn't understand and stakes he was only just beginning to comprehend.

"They didn't just take the gear," he said, his voice a low, dangerous murmur that was more chilling than any of his previous shouting. "They took the source code. They knew what they were looking for. This wasn't a random snatch-and-grab. This was a targeted acquisition." He walked to the window and, this time, he wasn't looking for news vans. He was scanning the rooftops, the other balconies, the spaces in between. He was looking for hunters.

"What do we do?" Skot asked, his voice shaking slightly.

Buzz turned from the window, and the manic energy was back, but it was different now. It was no longer the joyful chaos of a man on a high; it was the frantic, high-speed energy of a man who has just realized he's in a car with no brakes, heading downhill.

"What do we do? We get the hell out of here, is what we do!" he said, his words a rapid-fire staccato. "The plan is still the plan, it's just that the plan is now on fire and being chased by wolves! Which is fine! It adds a little spice, a little pizzazz! Let's go! Grab your stuff! Whatever's left! We're moving!"

He was a whirlwind of motion, grabbing their few belongings, stuffing them into bags. The impending checkout was no longer an insult; it was an escape hatch.

"Buzz, they have the footage!" Dave said, his voice cracking with despair. "It's over! They have the proof!"

"Wrong!" Buzz shot back, not even breaking his stride. "Wrong, wrong, wrong! They have a camera, a little piece of plastic and glass! They have a memory card! You think I would let the single most valuable piece of intellectual property in human history exist on one, single, stealable device? What am I, an amateur? This isn't my first rodeo, boys!"

He grabbed his laptop from the desk, patting it like a beloved pet. "I secured the asset, Davey! The second you guys gave it to me, I backed up the entire raw file. Two hours of glorious, high-definition, world-changing truth. It's right here." He tapped the laptop. "They stole the Mona Lisa's frame, but I've got the painting. Which, by the way, just got a hell of a lot more valuable because now it's the only copy. Scarcity, baby! It's the first rule of economics!"

The revelation was a lifeline. Skot and Dave stared at him, their expressions a mixture of shock and profound, dumbfounded relief.

"You made a copy?" Skot breathed.

"Of course I made a copy!" Buzz yelled, now grabbing the last of their things and shoving them toward the door. "What kind of monster do you think I am? Now let's go! The decoy is in position, the clock is ticking, and I, for one, would like to get out of here before our new, very quiet friends decide to come back for the master file!"

Chapter 33: Hiding in the Light

The escape from the El Santuario resort was not a covert operation. It was a chaotic, high-energy, and deeply embarrassing piece of performance art, directed by a madman. The moment they stepped out of the service elevator and into the concrete belly of the resort, Buzz transformed from a man gripped by cold fear into a frantic, fast-talking field marshal executing a plan that seemed to be inventing itself in real time.

"Okay, listen up!" he hissed, his voice a rapid-fire whisper that was louder than most people's normal speaking voice. He herded them behind a large, humming laundry dryer, the air thick with the smell of bleach and warm linen. "The decoy is in play. The paparazzi are chasing a set of Big Bertha golf clubs down the main drive. That gives us a window. A beautiful, glorious, tactical window. We move on my signal. Stay low, stay quiet, and for the love of God, try to look like you belong here. Think of it as a movie. You're not fugitives; you're character actors. Now, let's go make some magic!"

He crept from behind the dryer with a theatrical stealth that was completely undone by his bright yellow polo shirt. He scurried from one pillar to the next, gesturing frantically for them to follow. Skot and Dave exchanged a look of pure, mortified resignation and did as they were told, two grimy, bearded men trying to look inconspicuous while skulking through the bowels of a five-star resort behind a man who looked like he was auditioning for a spy movie parody.

They made it to the rented Toyota pickup without being stopped, their hearts hammering in their chests. They threw their bags in the back and piled into the cab, the clean interior a shocking contrast to their own disheveled state.

"See?" Buzz said, panting as he started the engine, a triumphant grin plastered on his face. "Clean as a whistle! A beautiful extraction! It's like we were never even here! We're ghosts, baby, ghosts in the machine!"

As he peeled out of the service area, his phone, which he had plugged into the truck's charger, lit up. It was an alert from a news site, the one he had been monitoring. He glanced at the headline.

"DEVELOPING: Chaos at Colombian Resort as Friends of Missing Divers Attempt to Flee."

He turned the phone around to show them. A live video feed from the front of the hotel showed a crowd of reporters and photographers swarming a black SUV, their cameras flashing like a strobe light. A bellhop was struggling to load a set of golf clubs into the trunk.

He drove with a renewed, manic energy, leaving the resort and the city of Santa Marta behind, heading up the coast toward the coordinates he'd plugged into the GPS. He was on a high, a pure, uncut rush of adrenaline and success. He had faced down the hotel management, he had outsmarted the media, and he had his boys back. In his mind, he wasn't just a fixer; he was a hero.

For the first few miles, they just drove, the adrenaline slowly receding. The reality of their new situation began to set in. They had the footage, but they had no more magic.

"So, that's it?" Skot asked, his voice quiet. He touched his shoulder, as if expecting the old ache to return at any second. "The water... it's really gone?"

"The last of it, anyway," Dave said grimly. "Whatever that stuff did to us, I guess this is as good as it gets."

"What do you mean?" Buzz asked from the front seat, his good mood momentarily forgotten. "You mean you're not going to stay all... you know, young and fabulous forever? Don't tell me the product has a shelf life. That's a marketing nightmare."

"We don't know what's going to happen," Skot admitted. "But the 'overdrive,' the instant healing... that's gone. We're on our own now."

The statement hung in the air, a sobering reminder of their new vulnerability. They were no longer gods. They were just two remarkably healthy, middle-aged men with a very dangerous secret, a secret that was currently saved on a single, uninsured laptop.

They drove on, heading for the cliffs, for the absurdly beautiful and completely indefensible glass villa that was their new safe house. Buzz, his confidence returning, was already planning his next move, talking a mile a minute about NDAs and interview prep and the importance of having a good B-roll package. Skot was staring out the window, a look of deep, existential dread on his face.

And Dave, the numbers guy, was doing the math. He was calculating the odds, weighing the assets against the liabilities. And he knew, with the cold, unshakeable certainty of a man who has spent his entire life looking at the bottom line, that they had just made a terrible, terrible trade. They had escaped the jungle, but they had just walked into a whole new kind of hell, one made of glass and paranoia and the unblinking eye of a world that was now hunting them for a miracle they no longer possessed.

"Okay, so, new business," he said, his mind already moving on to the next phase. "We need to address the elephant in the room. The branding. It's a mess."

"The branding?" Dave asked, his voice a flat monotone of disbelief. "Buzz, we were just robbed by what I can only assume is a covert operative from a Bond movie, and you're worried about the branding?"

"Of course I'm worried about the branding! The branding is everything!" Buzz shot back, gesturing wildly with one hand while steering with the other. "The branding is the armor that protects the product! And our product has a name problem. A big one. 'The water.' It's boring. It's a utility. You pay a bill for water. This isn't a utility, it's a luxury good! It's a miracle! You don't call a Ferrari a 'car,' you call it a Ferrari."

He paused for dramatic effect. "From this moment forward, for all strategic and media purposes, we refer to it as… The Potion."

"The Potion?" Skot repeated, a hint of a smile in his voice.

"The Potion!" Buzz confirmed, his voice booming. "It's got sizzle. It's got mystery. It sounds like something a wizard would cook up in a secret tower, not something you'd find in a cave next to a bunch of bats. It's perfect! Words matter, gentlemen. Words are the paint we use to create the masterpiece."

They drove on, following the winding coastal highway. The scenery was stunning—dramatic cliffs plunging into a turquoise sea—but none of them noticed. They were trapped in their own moving bubble of paranoia and absurd marketing strategy.

An hour later, the GPS instructed them to turn off the main highway and onto a narrow, private road marked with a simple, elegant sign that read "FINCA PRIVADA." They followed the road as it snaked its way up a steep cliff. And then they saw it.

The villa was exactly as it had appeared in the pictures: a breathtaking, audacious structure of glass and white concrete, cantilevered over the edge of the cliff. It didn't look like a safe house; it looked like the lair of a villain in a superhero movie. The infinity pool seemed to spill directly into the sky.

"Welcome," Buzz said with a grand, sweeping gesture, "to the new corporate headquarters."

They parked in the pristine, white gravel driveway and got out, their grimy, exhausted forms a stark contrast to the sterile beauty of the architecture. The place felt less like a home and more like a modern art museum. It was beautiful, and it was completely, utterly indefensible.

"We're going to die here, Buzz," Dave said, his voice a quiet statement of fact as he stared at the floor-to-ceiling glass walls. "This isn't hiding in the light. This is hiding in a giant, expensive light bulb."

"Relax, Davey, relax!" Buzz said, clapping him on the back. "It's about the psychology of the thing! No one would be stupid enough to hide in a place this obvious, which is why it's the perfect place to hide! It's a double-bluff! Now come on, let's go check out the screening room. I need to see what we're working with on the master file."

....

Miles away, in a location that was the polar opposite of the sun-drenched villa, a different kind of analysis was taking place. The black surveillance van was now parked in the cool, subterranean garage of a nondescript warehouse on the industrial outskirts of Santa Marta. The celebratory chaos of the villa was replaced by a cold, silent, and ruthlessly efficient focus.

Eva Rostova stood before a portable, sterile workstation that had been set up in the back of the van. On a stainless-steel tray lay the prize: Skot's stolen BCD. A technician wearing latex gloves was carefully using a syringe to draw the last few, precious drops of liquid from the bladder. There was less than an ounce left.

He carefully deposited the clear liquid into a vial and placed it into a small, humming centrifuge. Another technician was dissecting the waterproof pouch they had recovered from the side pocket. He pulled out the GoPro, the power bank, and the charging cable. He plugged the camera into his own laptop, his fingers flying across the keyboard.

"The camera is a standard Hero 10," he reported to Eva, his voice a low, professional murmur. "The memory card is a 256-gigabyte SanDisk." He paused. "The card has been wiped. Professionally. There's no recoverable data."

Eva's placid expression did not change. She had expected as much. The associate, Walker, was a fool, but he wasn't a complete amateur. Of course he would have secured the data. It didn't matter. The physical proof was a secondary objective. The real prize was in the vial.

The centrifuge spun down with a soft whir. The technician took the vial, placed a single drop of the liquid onto a slide, and put it under a powerful digital microscope. An image of the sample, magnified a thousand times, appeared on a large monitor on the wall of the van.

Eva stared at the screen. The technician, a brilliant young biochemist poached from a Swiss pharmaceutical giant, just stared, his mouth slightly agape. What they were seeing was impossible. It wasn't just water. It was a complex, living soup of previously unknown extremophilic bacteria and a unique, stable protein chain that seemed to act as a universal catalyst.

"The cellular regenerative properties are…" the biochemist began, his voice trailing off as he struggled to find the right words. "They are off the charts. It's not just accelerating the healing process; it seems to be actively rewriting damaged cellular code, reverting it to its base state. It's… it's a biological reset button. I have never seen anything like this. It defies our current understanding of cellular biology."

Eva felt a flicker of something she rarely allowed herself to feel: a professional satisfaction. This was it. This was the source of the anomaly. This was the why.

Her satellite phone buzzed. It was Valis. She stepped to the back of the van, affording herself a small measure of privacy.

"Report," his voice commanded, thin and reedy from halfway across the world.

"We have the sample, sir," she said, her voice a placid, unemotional whisper. "And we have a preliminary analysis. Your hypothesis was correct. It is a biological accelerant of an unknown type. Its potential is… significant."

There was a long silence on the other end of the line. She could hear his faint, labored breathing. "And the subjects?" he finally asked.

"They have relocated to a private villa up the coast. They are isolated. And they believe they are safe."

"They are fools," Valis rasped. "And they have something that belongs to me. You have your orders, Eva. I want the source. Not a sample. The source. Find it. And then, erase the anomaly."

"Understood, sir," she said.

The line went dead.

Eva stood in the cool, humming silence of the van, the order echoing in her mind. Erase the anomaly. The mission parameters had just changed. The observation phase was over. The hunt had just become an extermination.

Chapter 34: The Pre-Production

The day of the interview dawned with an obscene, postcard-perfect beauty. The sun rose out of a calm, turquoise sea, flooding the glass villa with a warm, golden light that made the polished concrete floors and designer furniture gleam. It was a day designed for leisure, for sipping mimosas by an infinity pool, for feeling smug about one's life choices. It was, in other words, a terrible day to be staring into the abyss of your own impending global fame.

Dave felt like he was going to throw up. He stood by the massive, floor-to-ceiling window, a cup of coffee held in a trembling hand, and stared out at the perfect view. It felt like a mockery. His back was a knot of dull, throbbing pain, a familiar enemy that had returned with a vengeance. His knee ached with a familiar, grinding rhythm. The absence of the Potion was no longer a fresh shock; it was a constant, nagging reality, a background hum of his own mortality. He was just a man again, a tired, aching, forty-seven-year-old CPA who had somehow found himself on the wrong side of a miracle. And in a few short hours, he was going to have to lie about that miracle, on camera, to the most famous and feared journalist on the planet.

He found Skot in the villa's massive, open-plan living room, nursing a cup of coffee and staring out at the ocean with a similarly grim expression. The artist's posture, usually so energetic, was stiff and guarded. He was sketching furiously in a notebook he had found in a desk drawer. It was a habit, a way to process the world, to impose lines and order on chaos. He wasn't sketching the beautiful landscape. He was drawing dark, claustrophobic, abstract shapes—the memory of the cave, of the tunnel, of the terrifying, crushing pressure.

Into this tableau of quiet, middle-aged anxiety, Buzz descended like a category five hurricane of pure, unadulterated hype.

"Gentlemen! Good morning! Rise and shine, you glorious, resurrected sons of bitches!" he boomed, striding into the room. He was already dressed in a crisp linen shirt and expensive-looking shorts that were probably worth more than Dave's first car. He was wearing his designer sunglasses indoors. His bluetooth earpiece was firmly in place. He was holding a tablet in one hand and a steaming mug in the other. He was not in pain. He was not in doubt. He was in his element.

"I hope you've been visualizing success, because today, we are not just telling a story, we are birthing a legend! And the delivery is going to be flawless! Flawless, you hear me?"

"I think my spine is trying to divorce my pelvis," Dave muttered, finally managing to produce a shot of espresso from the complicated machine, which looked like it belonged on a spaceship.

"Pain is temporary, Davey, but a successful brand launch is forever!" Buzz declared, waving his tablet. "You're thinking about the aches. The pains. The boo-boos. That's yesterday's thinking! That's small-time! You're looking at the problem. Me? I'm looking at the opportunity! And the opportunity, my friends, is a tidal wave, and we, we are the surfers! We are the Big Kahunas of the biological apocalypse!"

He set his tablet down on the giant, polished concrete kitchen island and turned to face them, his eyes wild with a manic, caffeinated energy. "Okay, so, the interview. The big show. The whole enchilada. We know what's coming. Diana's not just gonna ask about the cave-in, she's gonna ask about the spooky stuff. The main event. The Grotto Guardian. The mermaid. The moneymaker! And we need to be ready to knock that pitch out of the park."

"I'm not pitching anything, Buzz," Skot said quietly, not looking up from his sketchbook. "I'm just going to tell her I don't know what I saw."

Buzz rushed over and slammed his hands down on the island, making the coffee cups jump. "Whoa, whoa, whoa, back it up, Rembrandt, back the whole truck up," he said, his voice a rapid-fire staccato. "You can't just say 'I don't know.' 'I don't know' is boring! 'I don't know' is a narrative dead end! It's the truth, maybe, but it's terrible television! It's like ending a movie with 'and then they all went home and filed their taxes.' Nobody wants that! You gotta give her the mystery! You gotta be the reluctant witness! The man of science who saw a ghost, and it's tearing you apart! It's beautiful!"

Dave just stared at him, aghast. "You are literally scripting a hallucination."

"I'm scripting a billion-dollar intellectual property, Davey!" Buzz shot back. "There's a difference! Look, we need to get our heads in the game. And that starts with looking the part. It's about the visual narrative. The unspoken story. Wardrobe! My suite, five minutes! Let's go, let's go, let's go!"

The next hour was one of the most surreal of Dave's life. He and Skot were subjected to what Buzz called a "style-out." Buzz's suite was larger than their first apartment, and his walk-in closet was a terrifying, color-coded temple to his own vanity. He began pulling out clothes, tossing them onto the massive bed with the frantic energy of a madman.

"Okay, Skot, you're the artist, the mystic, the reluctant prophet," Buzz narrated, his mind a whirlwind of branding clichés. "We need something earthy, something soulful. The Henley? No, too casual, too 'I'm about to chop some wood.' The cashmere sweater? Too 'billionaire on his yacht after a hostile takeover.' Ah! Perfect!" He produced a simple, dark, long-sleeved shirt made of some kind of ridiculously soft, heathered material. "It's understated. It's mysterious. It says 'I've seen things you people wouldn't believe.' It's perfect. It makes you look sensitive, but also like you might have a knife hidden somewhere."

He then turned his attention to Dave. "Davey, my man. You're the everyman. The bedrock. The audience's anchor in this sea of madness. You're the relatable one. You're the guy who was just trying to manage his numbers, and then boom, you get a face full of miracle. We need you to look... haunted. But hopeful. Grounded, but changed." He held up two shirts. "This button-down says 'accountant.' This slightly-more-expensive button-down in a slightly darker shade of blue says 'accountant who has just survived a harrowing ordeal and is questioning the very nature of his own existence.' We go with that one. It's a subtle but crucial distinction. It's all in the subtext, baby!"

Dressed in their new, Buzz-approved costumes, they were herded back into the living room for their final prep session. This was no longer a friendly chat; this was media training. Buzz sat opposite them on a ridiculously uncomfortable-looking designer chair, playing the role of Diana Sterling.

"Okay, first question," he said, his voice shifting into a mock-serious, journalistic tone. "Mr. Larson, the internet is on fire with this image, this so-called 'Siren in the Spring.' You were there. What did you see?"

Skot hesitated, then recited the line Buzz had been drilling into him. "Diana, I was on the edge of blacking out. I was hypoxic. My mind was playing tricks on me. But… I saw something. A shape. It was there, and then it was gone. I can't explain it. I probably never will."

"Brilliant!" Buzz yelled, dropping the character and clapping his hands. "Perfect! A masterpiece of reluctant testimony! You see? You give them the mystery, but you wrap it in a responsible, scientific disclaimer! It's bulletproof! They'll go crazy!"

He then turned to Dave. "Okay, Mr. Bennett. Your friend here is seeing sea monsters. Your story is that you miraculously survived being buried alive. And yet, news outlets have reported you look significantly younger than recent photos. How do you explain that?"

Dave took a deep breath. "Diana, I don't know. I just know that I stared death in the face, and I'm just grateful to be here, to have a second chance to see my family."

"YES!" Buzz screamed, jumping to his feet. "That's it! The pivot! He uses the pivot! He goes from the weird, unexplainable science stuff to the heartwarming, relatable human stuff! It's a classic media judo move! It's beautiful! You guys are naturals! You're gonna be stars!"

It was in the middle of this bizarre rehearsal that they heard it. A low, thumping sound, faint at first, then growing steadily louder. A sound that did not belong in this tranquil, cliffside paradise.

Whump. Whump. Whump. Whump.

They all froze, the color draining from their faces. They walked slowly to the massive glass wall of the living room, which offered a panoramic view of the cliffs and the sea. The sound was louder here, a rhythmic, percussive beat that was vibrating through the floor, through the soles of their feet.

A helicopter.

It crested the edge of the cliff, a sleek, black machine, like a predatory insect against the bright blue sky. It wasn't a news chopper. It was a private, corporate-looking aircraft with no visible markings. It circled the villa once, a slow, deliberate survey, as if assessing its target. Then, it began a slow, controlled descent toward the large, flat lawn area near the front of the property.

They stood frozen, three men in their carefully selected costumes, and watched as the machine of their new reality descended from the sky. The interview was no longer a distant, theoretical concept. It was here. The world, in the form of a woman armed with a microphone and a million-dollar production budget, was at their door.

"Okay, boys," Buzz whispered, his voice a tight, nervous squeak, his own carefully constructed bravado finally cracking. He smoothed the front of his shirt, a gesture of pure, unadulterated terror. "It's showtime."

Chapter 35: The Close-Up

The sleek, black helicopter settled onto the manicured lawn of the villa with a final, percussive whump of its rotors, the sound vibrating through the glass walls and up through the soles of their feet. The engines whined down, and for a moment, the world was filled with an unnerving, expectant silence. They stood frozen in the living room, three men in their carefully selected costumes, watching as a side door slid open and a small staircase unfolded.

The first person out was a burly man in a dark suit, a classic security type with a thick neck and an earpiece, who immediately began scanning the perimeter. The second was a younger man with a wiry frame who hefted a large, professional-grade television camera onto his shoulder with practiced ease.

And the third was Diana Sterling.

She was smaller than she appeared on television, but her presence was immense. She wore a simple, elegant pantsuit, her silver hair cut in a sharp, no-nonsense style. She didn't look around at the stunning view or the absurdly luxurious villa. Her gaze, sharp and analytical, was fixed on the three men standing behind the glass wall. She wasn't a guest arriving at a party; she was a predator entering a new territory, assessing the local fauna.

"Okay, it's showtime, baby, showtime!" Buzz whispered, his voice a frantic, high-pitched squeak that betrayed the terror underneath his bravado. He smoothed the front of his shirt for the tenth time. "Remember the plan! Stick to the script! We are the heroes of this story! Be charming, be haunted, be relatable! Let's go make some magic!"

He strode toward the massive glass doors that led to the patio and pulled them open, a wide, practiced, and completely fraudulent smile plastered on his face. "Diana! Welcome! Welcome to our humble abode!" he boomed, his arms spread wide. "Buzz Walker. I'm the guy who's been wrangling these two wild men. Can I get you a drink? A water? A mimosa?"

Diana Sterling walked toward him, her hand extended. Her handshake was firm, her eyes unblinking. "Thank you, Mr. Walker. Water would be fine. And I'd prefer to speak with Mr. Larson and Mr. Bennett." Her voice was exactly as it was on television: a calm, confident, and slightly gravelly instrument that had dismantled politicians and brought corporate titans to their knees. She dismissed Buzz with a single, polite sentence, her focus shifting entirely to Skot and Dave, who were now standing awkwardly in the doorway.

The power dynamic in the room had shifted instantly and irrevocably. Buzz, who had been the director, the producer, and the star of his own show for the past two days, had just been relegated to the role of a glorified production assistant. The look on his face was one of stunned, wounded pride.

The next hour was a swift and efficient invasion. Diana's tiny team, just her, the cameraman, and a quiet, intense young woman who was her producer, transformed the minimalist living room into a television studio. They didn't ask permission; they simply rearranged the expensive designer furniture to create the perfect shot. They set up two small, powerful LED light panels that threw a clean, clinical light onto the two chairs where Skot and Dave were instructed to sit. The massive glass wall with its stunning ocean view was now their backdrop.

Dave sat down, the leather of the chair cool against his skin. His heart was a frantic, trapped bird in his chest. The camera lens, a single, black, unblinking eye, was pointed directly at him. He could see his own terrified reflection in it. He felt like a specimen under a microscope, his entire life about to be dissected for the entertainment of a global audience. He thought of Jen, of his kids, and he tried to channel the protective anger he had felt before, but all he felt was a cold, liquid terror.

Diana sat opposite them, in a chair they had just moved, so that she was slightly off-camera. She held a small notepad, but she rarely looked at it. Her focus was entirely on them, her gaze a physical weight.

"Thank you both for doing this," she began, her tone calm and disarming. "I know this has been an unimaginable ordeal. I just want you to tell me what happened. In your own words. Skot, let's start with you. Take me back to the morning of the dive. What were you hoping to find in that cave?"

And so it began. Skot, his voice a little shaky at first, started to tell the story. He told the rehearsed version, the one they had practiced with Buzz. He talked about the spirit of adventure, the lure of the unknown, the geological beauty of the cenotes. He was good. The artist in him was a natural storyteller, and he painted a vivid picture of their excitement and their meticulous preparation.

Dave chimed in, playing his part as the cautious everyman, the one who was there for his friend but who had a healthy respect for the risks. He talked about checking the gear, about their dive plan, about the trust he had in Skot's experience. It was all true, but it was a curated truth, a story stripped of its impossible, unbelievable heart.

They described the swim into The Cathedral. They described the sudden, violent horror of the cave-in. They described their desperate, claustrophobic escape. Diana listened patiently, her expression a mask of professional empathy, interjecting only with small, clarifying questions. "How long were you in the tunnel?" "What were you thinking at that moment?"

They were doing it. They were sticking to the script. Buzz, who was hovering just out of frame, gave them a subtle, encouraging nod.

Then, Diana Sterling leaned forward, a subtle shift in her posture that signaled a change in the temperature of the room. The softballs were over.

"Dave," she said, her voice still calm, but with a new, sharper edge. "The world has been watching this story. We've all seen the file photos from your driver's license, from your family's social media. And we've seen you now. And frankly, you look remarkably well for a man who spent three days lost in a jungle with no food and almost no water. You look healthier than most men your age who haven't just been declared legally dead. How do you explain that?"

This was it. The question Dave had been dreading. He felt a hot flush of panic. He could feel Buzz's eyes on him, practically screaming the rehearsed lines into the back of his head. He took a breath.

"Diana," he began, his voice thick with an emotion that was not entirely faked. "I don't know. I can't explain it. All I know is that I was in a place where I was sure I was going to die. I was never going to see my wife or my kids again." He looked directly into the camera, just as Buzz had instructed, picturing Jen's face. "And when you come that close to losing everything... it changes you. I don't know what I look like. I just know that I am so incredibly grateful to be here, to have a second chance to see my family."

He had done it. He had delivered the pivot. It was a beautiful, heartfelt, and completely evasive answer.

Diana's expression didn't change. She just held his gaze for a long, uncomfortable moment before nodding slowly. "A second chance," she repeated, the words hanging in the air. She then turned her sharp, analytical gaze to Skot.

"Skot," she said. "Your associate, Mr. Walker, has been very active online, promoting a certain screenshot from your footage. The so-called 'Siren in the Spring.' He has built a global mystery around it. I want to hear it from you. You were the one with the camera. You were the one on the edge of consciousness. What did you really see in that water?"

Skot felt his throat go dry. This was his performance. His lie. He looked off into the distance, toward the perfect, blue horizon, just as Buzz had coached him. He let the silence stretch, creating a moment of dramatic tension.

"Diana," he began, his voice a low, haunted whisper. "I was on the edge of blacking out. I was hypoxic. My brain was playing tricks on me. I know that. Logically, that's what was happening." He paused, then turned to look her in the eye. "But... I saw something. A shape. It wasn't a rock. It was there, and then it was gone. I can't explain it. I probably never will."

It was a masterful performance of reluctant testimony. He had given them the mystery, but he had wrapped it in a responsible, scientific disclaimer.

"So you're not saying you saw a mermaid?" Diana pressed, her voice laced with a hint of steel.

"I'm saying I saw something I can't explain," Skot replied, his gaze unwavering.

The final act was the footage itself. "I understand you have the video," Diana said. "The full, unedited file. We've all seen the clip. I'd like to see the rest."

This was Buzz's moment to reassert his control. "Of course, Diana," he said, stepping forward with his laptop. "But we've agreed that our broadcast partner gets the exclusive first look. We'll be providing your team with a watermarked, high-resolution copy for your story."

Diana just looked at him, and her faint, almost imperceptible smile made his own confident grin feel cheap and brittle. "That will be fine."

They played the key sections of the raw footage on the massive television screen. Diana didn't gasp. She didn't act shocked. She watched with a chilling, analytical intensity, her eyes missing nothing. She had them play the clip of the grotto, the glowing water, three times. She watched the moment of the "siren" in slow motion, her expression unreadable. She wasn't just watching a story; she was absorbing data.

When it was over, she stood up. Her team, as if on a silent cue, began to efficiently break down the set, the lights, the camera. The interview was over.

"Thank you for your time," she said, shaking their hands again. Her hand was cool, her grip firm. "You have a remarkable story."

She and her team walked back toward the waiting helicopter. As she was about to board, she turned back to them, her sunglasses on, her face an impassive mask.

"Be careful, gentlemen," she said, her voice almost lost in the rising whine of the helicopter's turbines. "You have no idea what you've started."

The door slid shut. The helicopter lifted off, its rotor wash tearing at the perfect lawn, and banked out over the sea, disappearing into the vast, blue sky.

They were left standing in the sudden, deafening silence, the pristine living room of their glass house now feeling like a crime scene. They had done it. They had survived the interview. They had told their story, their carefully crafted, edited, and packaged version of the truth.

But Diana Sterling's final, ominous words hung in the air, a cold and terrifying prophecy. They hadn't ended the mystery. They had just given it a global stage. And they were standing directly in the spotlight.

Chapter 36: The Broadcast

The silence that descended after Diana Sterling's helicopter vanished over the horizon was heavier and more oppressive than any they had yet experienced. The living room, with its rearranged furniture and the lingering, clinical scent of professional lighting equipment, felt like a crime scene. They were the victims, the perpetrators, and the star witnesses all at once, and they had just given their full confession to the world's most formidable prosecutor.

Buzz was the first to break the spell. A slow, wide grin spread across his face, and he let out a whoop of pure, unadulterated triumph that echoed in the cavernous room.

"Boom!" he yelled, slamming a fist into his palm. "That's a wrap, baby! We crushed it! We absolutely crushed it! You guys were incredible! Sincere, haunted, relatable... you were money! Absolute money! I was watching from the sidelines, and even I almost believed you!" He strode to the oversized, stainless-steel wine fridge. "We are celebrating. This is a champagne moment. No, this is a 'drink-the-champagne-straight-from-the-expensive-bottle' moment!"

Neither Skot nor Dave shared his enthusiasm. They felt drained, hollowed out, and profoundly unclean. They had just spent two hours performing a carefully curated, heavily edited version of the most traumatic and miraculous experience of their lives. It felt less like a victory and more like a violation.

"I feel like I need another shower," Dave said, his voice a low, weary murmur. He collapsed into one of the designer chairs, the one he had just been interrogated in, and put his head in his hands. "I just lied. On what is about to be international television. I lied to millions of people."

"It's not a lie, Davey, it's a narrative pivot!" Buzz corrected him, wrestling with the cork on a bottle of Dom Pérignon. "It's a strategic omission for the purposes of brand integrity! You think Coca-Cola puts 'cavity-causing sugar water' on the label? No! They sell happiness! We're not selling lies; we're selling wonder! And wonder, my friend, is a growth market!"

"He's right, you know," Skot said, his voice grim. He was staring at his own hands, at the faint, pink line on his shin where a six-inch, bone-deep gash had been just a few days ago. "We can't ever tell the whole truth. Who would even believe it?"

The champagne cork flew across the room with a loud pop, but the celebratory mood fell flat. They drank the expensive champagne, but it tasted like ash. The interview was over, but now a new, more insidious form of torture was beginning: the waiting.

The show was scheduled to air the following evening. They had a little over twenty-four hours to exist in a state of suspended animation, trapped in their glass house on the cliff, waiting for the world's judgment.

Buzz, predictably, thrived in the vacuum. He was a machine, a one-man media startup operating out of a borrowed villa. He spent the entire day on his laptop and phone, his voice a constant, low, rapid-fire murmur. He finalized the incorporation of "Siren Spring, LLC." He hired, via a series of curt, non-negotiable phone calls, a private security firm to watch over Dave's house back in the States, a move that terrified and reassured Dave in equal measure. He bought the domain names for SirenSpring, TheGrottoMen, and GrottoGuardian. He was building the infrastructure of an empire whose sole product was a story.

Dave, on the other hand, descended into a personal hell of quiet, anxious misery. He spent most of the day on the phone with Jen. The calls were excruciating. He was trying to be a husband, to offer comfort and reassurance, but he could only speak in the vague, frustrating platitudes of the lie they had concocted. He couldn't tell her about the villa, about the interview, about the terrifying, exhilarating madness of their new reality. He could only say, again and again, "It's complicated, honey. We have to be careful. I'll be home soon, I promise." Every word felt like a fresh betrayal, another layer of insulation between his new life and the one he was desperate to reclaim.

Skot retreated into himself, into the silent, internal world of his art. He filled page after page of the notebook with sketches. He drew the grotto, trying to capture the impossible quality of its light. He drew the jungle, its menacing, suffocating beauty. And he drew, over and over again, the shape. The blurry, ambiguous form from the water. He was trying to define it, to give it form, to understand if it was a trick of his own oxygen-starved mind or something else, something real that had looked back at him from the darkness.

The hours crawled by. That evening, the night of the broadcast, the tension in the villa was a palpable, physical thing. Buzz had the screening room prepped, the massive screen dark and waiting. He had ordered another obscene amount of room service, but no one could eat.

They sat there, in the plush, reclining leather chairs, three men waiting for their own public execution.

"Okay, boys," Buzz said, his own fast-talking bravado finally showing some cracks. His leg was bouncing nervously. "Whatever happens, we're in this together. The brand is strong. The narrative is ours."

The show began. Diana Sterling's face filled the screen, her expression a mask of somber, journalistic authority. They watched, their hearts pounding, as she masterfully set the stage—the tragic story of the two missing American adventurers, the frantic search, the grim conclusion.

Then came their faces. They looked good. The lighting was perfect. They looked haunted but sincere, just as Buzz had coached. They watched themselves tell the story of the cave-in, of the survival trek. It was a compelling, heroic tale.

Then Diana pivoted. "But when they emerged from the jungle," she narrated, her voice taking on a new, skeptical edge, "questions began to arise."

She showed the before-and-after photos, the contrast stark and undeniable on the high-definition screen. She played the clip of Dave's heartfelt, emotional, and completely evasive answer about his second chance. She didn't editorialize. She just let his non-answer hang in the air, a beautiful, suspicious question mark.

Then came the Siren. She showed the clip from the online forums, the red circles, the frantic speculation. Then she played Skot's masterful performance of the reluctant witness. He was incredible. He was believable. He was a man torn apart by an unexplainable vision.

"It was a masterpiece," Buzz whispered in the darkness, a tear of pure, professional pride in his eye.

Diana wasn't finished. "A fantastic story," she said on screen, her voice a purr of journalistic steel. "A tale of survival, a hint of the supernatural. But it might not be the first story to come out of that dark and mysterious jungle."

And then came the blow they never saw coming.

A new face appeared on the screen, a stern-faced historian from a university in Bogotá. An image of the rusted, water-damaged journal they had found in the Land Rover filled the screen.

"We provided Diana's team with exclusive access to the journal recovered from the vehicle," the historian said. "While much of it is illegible, what we can decipher tells a grim story. A story of a different group of men, decades ago. Prospectors, perhaps, searching for gold."

Fragments of the journal, enhanced and translated, flashed on the screen. "...fever... Ramirez is delirious... the bad water... it makes the rage come..."

"These men also seem to have found a spring," Diana's voice narrated, a cold, chilling counterpoint to the images. "But their discovery did not lead to a miraculous tale of survival. It led to madness. And death."

The camera cut back to Diana in her studio, her expression a perfect, calculated mixture of curiosity and concern. She looked directly into the camera, into the eyes of a hundred million viewers.

"Two stories," she said, her voice a low, captivating whisper. "From the same stretch of unforgiving jungle. One, a modern miracle of survival and unexplained phenomena. The other, a dark, forgotten tale of poison, madness, and death. Which leads to the final, chilling question: Did Skot Larson and David Bennett find a one-of-a-kind miracle? Or did they just get a luckier dose of the same jungle poison that drove other men to their doom?"

The screen faded to black.

The three of them sat in the screening room, in the absolute, crushing silence. They were stunned. Utterly, completely stunned. They had been played. Masterfully. Diana hadn't just told their story; she had co-opted it, reframed it, and wrapped it in a much older, darker, and more sinister narrative.

Buzz was on his feet, his face a mask of pure, apoplectic rage. "That son of a bitch!" he screamed into the darkness. "She sandbagged us! She never mentioned the journal! She used us to build a whole new mystery! She stole our narrative!"

They had thought they were controlling the story. But Diana Sterling had just shown them that they weren't even the main characters. They were just the latest chapter in a much more frightening book.

And then, as if on cue, all three of their phones, which had been sitting silently on the console, began to buzz and chime at once. A frantic, discordant symphony of incoming alerts, texts, and calls. The world wasn't just watching anymore. The world had questions. And the story was no longer about whether they were heroes or frauds. It was about whether they were blessed... or cursed.

Chapter 37: The New Narrative

The screening room was a tomb, the silence absolute, the air thick with the ghost of Diana Sterling's final, damning question. The broadcast was over, but the story she had unleashed was just beginning. They sat in the plush leather chairs, three men staring at a blank, black screen, each trapped in his own private vortex of shock and horror. They had walked into that interview thinking they were the main characters, the heroes of their own survival epic. They had walked out as a subplot, a footnote in a much older, darker tale of madness and death in the jungle.

Buzz was the first to move, a puppet whose strings had been violently cut. He shot to his feet, his face a mask of pure, apoplectic rage. The cool, calculated professional was gone, replaced by the raw, wounded ego of a man who had been publicly and masterfully outplayed.

"That woman is a ninja!" he screamed into the darkness, his voice a raw, strangled sound. "A media ninja! She comes in, she smiles, she eats your complimentary cheese plate, and then she guts you with a smile on national television! She sandbagged us! She never mentioned the journal! She used us to build a whole new mystery! She stole our narrative!"

"She didn't steal it, Buzz," Skot said, his voice a low, hollow murmur. "She just added the chapter we didn't know existed." He was staring at the blank screen, but he was seeing the rusted, water-damaged journal, the frantic, faded script. The bad water... it makes the rage come...

He felt a cold, creeping dread that had nothing to do with reporters or book deals. What if their miracle wasn't a different spring? What if it was just a different dose?

Dave said nothing. He was curled in on himself, his arms wrapped around his stomach as if he'd been physically punched. He had gone through the ordeal of lying to his wife, of scripting his own harrowing experience, all to protect his family. And for what? For Diana Sterling to turn him into a lab rat, a potential carrier of a jungle plague. The word "poison" now hung in the air, a toxic, invisible cloud. He imagined Jen watching, hearing that word, and the thought was a fresh, agonizing torment.

And then, as if on cue, the world began to knock. All three of their phones, which had been sitting silently on the console, began to buzz and chime at once. It wasn't the slow trickle of calls from before; it was a deluge. A frantic, discordant symphony of incoming alerts, texts, and calls, a digital avalanche that signaled the world was no longer just watching; it was reacting.

Buzz, his rage momentarily forgotten, scrambled for his phone. The screen was a blinding, strobing wall of notifications. His eyes widened. "Oh, boy," he whispered. "Okay. We have a situation."

The tenor of the conversation had changed completely. The messages weren't just from friends and family anymore. They were from strangers. Thousands of them. The #GrottoMen hashtag was now trending side-by-side with a new, more sinister one: #JunglePoison.

He read a few of the comments aloud, his voice a mixture of horror and a kind of perverse, professional admiration.

"'My brother's a doctor,' this one says. 'He thinks it's a neurotoxin. The 'youthful' look is just the first stage. Next comes paralysis and dementia. These guys are ticking time bombs.' Wow. That's vivid."

"Stop," Dave croaked, his face pale.

"Wait, wait, listen to this one!" Buzz insisted, a manic energy returning to his voice. "This is from a conspiracy subreddit. 'It's not a mermaid. The 'Siren' is a metaphor for a hallucinogenic bacterium. The government has known about this for years. They're not survivors; they're Patient Zeros.'"

"Buzz, for the love of God, shut up!" Skot snapped, his own composure finally cracking.

But Buzz wasn't listening. A strange, wild light was dawning in his eyes. His initial rage at being outmaneuvered was being replaced by a promoter's grudging respect, and then by a flash of brilliant, opportunistic insight. He started pacing the screening room, the phone in his hand, a general surveying a battlefield that had just changed in a fascinating and unexpected way.

"Don't you see?" he said, his voice beginning to regain its rapid-fire cadence. "You guys are looking at this like a disaster! A P.R. nightmare! But you're thinking small! You're thinking checkers! This isn't a disaster; it's a plot twist! And it's a damn good one!"

He spun to face them, his arms spread wide. "She didn't ruin the brand; she gave it an edge! A dark side! We're not just the Grotto Men anymore, we're a mystery box! A beautiful, terrifying, can't-look-away mystery box!

Are they heroes? Are they ticking time bombs? Did they find God in a cave, or did they find the Devil? Tune in next week to find out! It's a built-in cliffhanger! You can't buy this kind of engagement!"

"It's our lives, Buzz!" Dave yelled, finally finding his voice. "It's not a TV show!"

"It's both now, Davey, it's both!" Buzz shot back, his excitement overriding all sense of empathy. "And we don't run from it! We double down! We lean into the crazy! We are the custodians of the weird, the curators of the creepy! We are the only ones who know the truth, and that, my friends, is called leverage!"

He was about to launch into a full-blown marketing sermon when a different kind of alert sounded, this one from his laptop, which was still open on the console. It was a sharp, electronic chime he hadn't heard before.

"What's that?" Skot asked.

Buzz's face went from manic glee to a sudden, cold sobriety. He walked over to the laptop. "That," he said, his voice a low murmur, "is the security system I had installed at your house, Dave."

He opened the laptop. A live feed from a series of discreet, high-definition security cameras appeared on the screen. They saw Jen's minivan in the driveway. The lights were on in the living room. Everything looked normal. But a small, red icon was flashing in the corner of the screen.

"Motion alert," Buzz said, his fingers flying across the trackpad. "Perimeter breach. Back of the property."

He switched camera views. The new image was from a night-vision camera, showing the back fence of Dave's suburban yard. The image was grainy, rendered in shades of eerie green and black. And it was not empty.

Two figures, dressed in dark clothing, were moving with a silent, economic grace along the fence line. They weren't teenagers looking for a shortcut. They moved with a purpose, with a professional, practiced stealth that was utterly out of place in this quiet, suburban landscape. One of them paused, looking directly at the location of the hidden camera, and pointed a small, cylindrical device at it. The screen fizzled into a shower of static, then went black.

"Signal jammed," Buzz whispered, his voice barely audible. The blood had drained from his face.

Dave was on his feet, his heart a frantic, hammering drum. He stared at the dead screen, at the last, ghostly image of the intruders in his yard. They were there. The nameless, faceless "them" that Buzz had been talking about were no longer a theoretical threat. They were real. And they were at his home.

"Call Jen!" he screamed, lunging for his phone. "Call her now! Tell her to get the kids and get out of the house!"

"No!" Buzz yelled, grabbing his arm, his grip surprisingly strong. "Don't! They're not there to hurt them! Not yet! If they were, they would have just kicked in the door. This is a message. This is a warning. They're showing us they can get to our families. They're telling us they're in control."

The reality of their situation crashed down on them with a new and terrifying force. This wasn't about media narratives or book deals anymore. The professional, silent hunters had finally shown themselves. The glass walls of the villa, which had felt like a fishbowl, now felt like the crosshairs of a sniper scope. They had been so focused on the loud, chaotic battle for public opinion, they had never even seen the real enemy, the one that moved in the shadows.

Buzz's phone rang again. But this time, it wasn't a news agency or a curious fan. The caller ID was a string of zeroes, an anonymous, untraceable number.

He looked at Skot, then at Dave, his own face a mask of pale, dawning terror. The game he thought he was playing was over. A new one had just begun, and the other players were not playing by his rules.

He answered the phone.

Chapter 38: The Quiet Game

The anonymous, untraceable number on Buzz's phone screen was a black hole, a void that threatened to swallow the last of the manic, defiant energy that had been keeping them afloat. The frantic buzzing of a hundred media alerts was just noise; this was a signal. A single, clear, and terrifying signal that someone else was in control of their story.

Dave stood frozen, his eyes locked on the phone in Buzz's hand. He could still see the ghostly, green-tinged image of the two figures moving with a silent, predatory grace along his back fence. They were there. The nameless, faceless "them" had a face now, a shadowy form that was at that very moment just yards away from his wife and children.

Skot moved closer to Buzz, his posture coiled and tense, like an animal sensing a predator it cannot see. The bravado, the arguments about branding and narrative, had evaporated in the harsh, electronic glare of the security alert, leaving behind only the raw, primal reality of their situation.

Buzz, for his part, was a statue. The fast-talking promoter, the man who had a clever analogy for every crisis, was gone. The blood had drained from his face, leaving it a pale, waxy mask. He looked at the phone as if it were a venomous snake, poised to strike. He had played a loud, chaotic, public game, and he had just realized, with a certainty that chilled him to the bone, that he had been playing on the wrong board the entire time.

The phone stopped ringing. The silence that followed was somehow worse, thick with unspoken threats. Then, it started again, a persistent, patient summons. They weren't going away.

With a trembling hand, Buzz answered the call. He put it on speakerphone, his eyes never leaving the faces of his two friends.

"Hello?" Buzz said, his voice a dry, tight croak, all the swagger and confidence gone.

The voice that answered was not what he expected. It wasn't a gravelly, menacing movie-villain voice. It was a woman's. It was calm, cool, and utterly devoid of any discernible accent or emotion. It was a voice that was as sterile and precise as a surgeon's scalpel.

"Mr. Walker," the voice said, the sound quality so perfect it was as if she were standing in the room with them. "This is a courtesy call. I suggest you listen very carefully."

"Who is this?" Buzz demanded, a flicker of his old defiance returning.

"That is not important," the voice replied, unruffled. "What is important is that you and your associates understand the new rules of the game you have decided to play. We have been watching your recent media activities with great interest. The performance has been... amateurish, but effective."

A cold dread washed over Dave. *We have been watching.*

"We are in possession of a GoPro Hero 10 camera," the voice continued, each word a carefully placed stone, building a wall of intimidation around them. "And a buoyancy control device containing a small, residual sample of a unique biological agent. A sample of… 'The Potion,' as you have so cleverly branded it."

Buzz felt his knees go weak. They knew. They knew everything. The theft wasn't just a random act of espionage; it was a message. They were demonstrating their reach, their capability.

"We also know," the voice went on, a hint of something that might have been amusement in her placid tone, "that you were clever enough to make a digital copy of the footage. A wise, if ultimately futile, precaution. This brings us to the present."

The sterile, calm voice paused, letting the weight of her knowledge settle over them. The message was clear: We are professionals. You are children. And we are tired of your games.

"Here are your instructions," she said, her tone shifting from informative to directive. "Effective immediately, you will cease all media engagement. Your social media accounts will go dark. You will not answer any more calls from reporters or book agents. You are to become ghosts."

"And if we don't?" Skot asked, his voice a low growl.

"The next part of your instructions," the woman continued, completely ignoring his question, "is that within the next twelve hours, you will release a formal statement through a reputable lawyer. The statement will express your deep regret for perpetrating a hoax. It will claim that the entire 'miraculous survival' story was a fabrication, an elaborate viral marketing stunt designed to gain fame and attention. You will discredit yourselves. You will become a cautionary tale about the dangers of online misinformation. You will, in essence, destroy the brand you have worked so hard to build."

"You're insane," Buzz breathed, the words escaping his lips before he could stop them.

"After you have done this," the voice said, her calm utterly unshakable, "you will remain in your current location and await further instructions. If you follow these steps precisely, Mr. Bennett's family will remain safe and unmolested. Their privacy will be respected. The assets we have watching his home will be withdrawn."

The threat was no longer veiled. It was a clean, sharp, and perfectly delivered stiletto to the heart.

"What do you want from us?" Dave asked, his voice choked with a mixture of rage and terror.

For the first time, there was a slight pause on the other end of the line. When the woman spoke again, her voice was even colder, if that was possible. "We want the one thing you can no longer provide. We want the source. And until you are prepared to give it to us, you will do exactly as you are told. The quiet game starts now, Mr. Walker. I suggest you learn the rules quickly."

The line went dead.

The three of them stood in the center of the luxurious living room, the silence of the dead phone a screaming, deafening void. The game wasn't just over; the entire board had been flipped. Their manic, public spectacle had been answered with a single, silent, and utterly dominant move.

Dave was the first to explode. He lunged at Buzz, grabbing the front of his ridiculously expensive shirt. "This is your fault!" he roared, his face a mask of pure, unadulterated fury. "You and your stupid brand! Your hashtags! Your narrative! You led them right to my door! You put a target on my family's back!"

"I didn't know!" Buzz yelled back, trying to push him away, his own face pale with terror. "How could I know?"

"Because this is the real world, Buzz!" Dave screamed, shoving him backward. "It's not a game! It's not a brand launch! There are real consequences! And now my wife and my kids are the ones who have to pay for it!"

"Stop it!" Skot yelled, getting between them, his arms outstretched. "This isn't helping! She's listening! They are probably listening to us right now!"

The thought sent a fresh wave of ice through the room. They looked around at the pristine, minimalist space, at the elegant, designer furniture. The glass walls of the villa no longer just felt like a fishbowl; they felt like the transparent walls of a laboratory cage. They were specimens, being observed, their reactions being recorded.

Dave stumbled back, collapsing onto a sofa, his rage dissolving into a shuddering, hopeless despair. He was trapped. He had to choose between his own freedom and his family's safety. It was no choice at all. "We do it," he whispered, his eyes vacant. "We do what she says. We release the statement. We kill the story. We give them whatever they want."

"No," Skot said, his voice quiet but firm. He was looking at Buzz, his expression grim. "We can't."

"Why not?" Dave asked, looking up, his face a mess of confusion and fear.

"Because it won't end there," Skot said, his artist's mind seeing the shape of the whole, terrible picture. "She said it herself. They want the source. They want The Potion. And they think we know where it is. If we do what she says, if we discredit ourselves and go quiet, we lose all our leverage. We'll just be three discredited hoaxers that no one is looking for anymore. And then they can do whatever they want to us, quietly, to get the information they think we have. They won't just make us disappear; they'll take us apart, piece by piece, until we tell them a secret we don't even know."

The chilling logic of Skot's words settled over them. Surrender was not an option. It was just a slower, more private form of execution.

They were completely and utterly on their own. They couldn't go to the police; who would believe the story of the three legally dead men who claimed they were being hunted by a shadowy, all-powerful organization? They couldn't fight; their enemies were ghosts, professionals who could steal a miracle from a locked room and jam a security feed from a suburban street. And they couldn't run; their hunters knew where they were, and more importantly, they knew where their families were.

Buzz walked slowly over to the laptop, the one that held their only remaining asset. He closed it with a soft, final click. The fast-talking promoter was gone. The manic energy was gone. All that was left was the cold, hard weight of a reality he had helped create.

"Okay," he said, his voice a low, somber whisper he didn't recognize as his own. "Okay. We can't win their game." He looked at his two oldest friends, his eyes filled with a terror and a resolve they had never seen before. "So we have to change the rules. We have to start our own."

Chapter 39: The Dead Man's Switch

The silence in the villa was the sound of a game board being flipped, the pieces scattered, the rules rendered meaningless. The calm, sterile voice of the woman on the phone echoed in the vast, minimalist space, a ghost of a threat that was now terrifyingly real. They were caught. They were exposed. And their families were hostages in a game they didn't even know they were playing.

Dave was a wreck, a man hollowed out by a terror so profound it had burned past anger and left only a shuddering, hopeless despair. The first thing he did was call Jen again. He had to. He had to hear her voice, to confirm that the silent threat had remained just that—a threat. He stood on the far side of the villa, his back to his friends, his forehead pressed against the cool, unyielding glass of the wall, creating a small, private bubble of agony.

The call was torture. Jen, bless her heart, was trying to be strong for him. She was telling him about their daughter's day at school, about a funny drawing their son had made. She was trying to build a bridge of normalcy across an ocean of chaos, and Dave could hear the immense strain in her voice. He listened to the sounds of his life happening without him—the distant chime of the doorbell, the dog barking—and each normal sound was a fresh stab of guilt. He was a ghost haunting his own home, a disembodied voice on a phone, and he was the reason it was all in jeopardy. He couldn't tell her that men were watching her house. He couldn't tell her to run. All he could do was listen, and lie, and feel a piece of his own soul chip away with every forced, reassuring word.

Skot, meanwhile, was the grim analyst, the artist trying to find the shape in the chaos. He had the laptop open, not to track their fame, but to descend into the digital rabbit hole of their new enemy. He wasn't just a guy with a search engine; his senses, his focus, everything was still operating at a higher level than normal. He wasn't just reading articles; he was inhaling data, finding patterns, connecting dots. He typed in phrases like "corporate espionage," "private intelligence firms," "extractive security." He found a series of articles about the ruthless, often lethal, world of biotech acquisitions. He read about scientists who had disappeared, research that had been stolen, small, promising companies that had been bankrupted or bought out by a shadowy, dominant player in the field. And at the periphery of several of these stories, like a ghost in the machine, was a name: Aevum Therapeutics.

The company's public profile was pristine, a beacon of medical innovation. But in the dark corners of the internet, on encrypted forums for disgruntled ex-employees and investigative journalists, a different story was being told. A story of a company that operated with the ruthless efficiency of an intelligence agency, a company whose CEO, a reclusive and brilliant man named Damian Valis, was rumored to be obsessed with cracking the code of human mortality. Skot was looking at the face of the monster that was hunting them, and it was a monster with a global reach and a bottomless bank account.

It was Buzz who finally broke the spell of paralysis. He had been standing perfectly still for ten minutes, his back to them, staring out the massive glass wall at the indifferent, blue sea. The manic energy was gone, the fast-talking promoter silenced. When he finally turned around, his face was pale, his eyes were bloodshot, but there was a new, strange light in them. It wasn't the glee of a hype-man; it was the cold, hard glint of a man who had been backed into a corner and had decided to chew his way out.

"Okay," he said, his voice a low, gravelly whisper that was more intense than any of his previous shouting. "Okay. So that's the game. The quiet game. We go dark, we discredit ourselves, we become boring, forgotten frauds. And then, when the world stops looking, they come for us. They take us apart, piece by piece, until we tell them where to find a treasure map we don't have. It's a checkmate. A beautiful, elegant, cold-blooded checkmate."

He started to pace, no longer the swaggering showman, but a caged, calculating animal. "We can't win their game. It's their board, their rules. We play quiet, we lose. We try to play loud again, we lose, and our families pay the price. So what do we do?" He stopped, a dangerous idea beginning to form behind his eyes. "We get a new board. We start a new game. A game they don't know how to play. We change the stakes so completely that their old rules don't matter anymore."

"What game, Buzz?" Skot asked, looking up from the laptop, his face a mask of weary skepticism. "The one where we learn to fly?"

"Close," Buzz said, a flicker of his old, manic self returning, but darker now, sharper. "The game is called 'Mutually Assured Destruction.' It's a classic! Cold War 101. The only way to stop a bully with a nuke is to get a nuke of your own and aim it right back at him. And we," he said, tapping the closed laptop on the counter, "have a nuke."

He grabbed the laptop and strode into the screening room. Skot and Dave followed, drawn in by the sheer, desperate certainty in his voice. He plugged the laptop into the projection system, and the two-hour, high-definition raw footage of their miracle filled the massive screen. The glowing grotto pulsed with its impossible, silent power.

"This is our weapon," Buzz said, his voice a reverent murmur. "They think they have the only sample. They're wrong. They think they can control the story by intimidating us into silence. They are about to find out how spectacularly wrong they are. We're not going to play the quiet game. We're going to build a bomb so loud it will deafen the entire planet if it goes off."

The plan that spilled out of him over the next hour was a masterpiece of paranoid, high-stakes, digital warfare. It was the culmination of his entire life's experience—his understanding of hype, of technology, of the media's insatiable hunger, all sharpened to a razor's edge by a new and unfamiliar terror.

He found the service online. A secure, encrypted, automated data-delivery system based in a country with no extradition treaty with anyone. It was designed for journalists and whistleblowers. A digital dead man's switch.

"Okay, here's how it works," he explained, his old, fast-talking energy returning, but now with a deadly focus. "We upload the entire package. The whole nuke. The two-hour raw footage file, unedited. A written, signed testimony from each of you, detailing the entire story, from the cave-in to the Land Rover, to the impossible healing of your leg, Davey. We scan every page of that damn journal. We add the before and after photos. Scans of your old driver's licenses, your passports. Everything. We build a complete, undeniable dossier of the truth."

He was already creating a distribution list, a massive, sprawling network of recipients. Every major news outlet on the planet—Reuters, Al Jazeera, CNN, BBC. Every significant wire service. Every major newspaper. And, for good measure, every WikiLeaks-style whistleblowing site he could find.

"And then," he said, a grim, triumphant smile on his face, "we put it on a timer. A twenty-four-hour clock. Every twenty-three hours, we have to log in with a series of rotating, encrypted passwords that only the three of us know a piece of, and reset the clock. If we fail to reset it—if we're captured, if we're killed, if we're just too busy being tortured to get to a keyboard—the system automatically blasts the entire package to everyone on this list. The truth bomb goes off."

Dave stared at him, his initial, panicked resistance being replaced by a slow, dawning understanding. This wasn't a media stunt. This was a shield. A way to protect his family by making himself the most dangerous hostage in the world.

"They wouldn't dare touch us," Skot whispered, the logic of the plan settling over him. "If we disappear, their secret gets blown wide open."

"Exactly!" Buzz said, pointing at him. "Their greatest strength—their secrecy, their ability to operate in the shadows—becomes their greatest weakness! We are chaining our safety to their secrecy. It's a beautiful, terrifying paradox! They can't kill the story without killing their own anonymity!"

The final piece was the most dangerous. They had to tell the hunters that the bomb had been armed. They had to send a message.

This was Buzz's true test as the fixer. He spent two hours constructing a chain of digital misdirection, using a series of encrypted VPNs that bounced his signal from servers in Iceland to Singapore to Brazil, finally routing it through a public library's unsecured Wi-Fi in a city he'd never been to. He used a temporary, encrypted messaging app to send a single, untraceable text message to the anonymous number that had called them.

The message was five words long.

The switch is now active.

He hit send, his finger hovering over the screen for a moment before pressing down with a sense of terrible finality.

They stood in the dark screening room, the three of them, illuminated by the faint glow of the laptop screen. A small, digital clock in the corner of the dead man's switch application was counting down.

23:59:58

The bomb was armed. The clock was ticking. They had just taken back control of their lives by chaining themselves to a perpetual, 24-hour doomsday machine. Every day for the rest of their lives, they would have to check in, to reset the clock, to prove to their own automated defense system that they were still free.

The quiet game was over. They had just started a new one. The game of survival had become a game of mutually assured destruction. And the first move was theirs.

Chapter 40: The Hunter's Response

The message arrived without a sound. It was not a notification, not a chime, just five simple words that appeared in a sterile, encrypted messaging window on the tablet Eva Rostova was holding:

The switch is now active.

She sat in the cool, humming silence of the mobile surveillance van, the message glowing in the dark. She stared at it for a full thirty seconds, her face a mask of placid neutrality. Her team, a collection of quiet, focused professionals monitoring a bank of screens, did not speak. They knew better than to interrupt her when she was processing.

To an outside observer, her expression was unchanged. But inside, her mind was working with the speed of a supercomputer, recalculating variables, reassessing threat levels. This was not a move she had anticipated. Not from these opponents. The subjects—the artist, the accountant, the promoter—were amateurs. They were loud, emotional, and predictable. Their previous actions had been driven by panic, then by a clumsy, ego-driven attempt to control a narrative they didn't understand.

This, however, was different. This was a sophisticated, asymmetrical response. It was clever. It was desperate. And it was a profound, infuriating complication.

They had taken the one thing her employer valued above all else—secrecy—and they had turned it into a weapon aimed directly at his head. The quiet game she had initiated, the slow, methodical process of observation and intimidation, was now obsolete. The amateurs had just forced a stalemate.

She closed the messaging window, the five words burning a psychic afterimage in her mind. Her protocol was clear. A change in mission parameters this significant required immediate consultation with the client. She rose from her chair, the sleek, black pantsuit making no sound, and moved to the secure communications station at the back of the van. The technician, without being asked, initiated the encrypted video link. He knew the procedure.

The face that appeared on the main screen was not the one the world knew from the rare, decade-old file photos. The Damian Valis in those pictures was a titan, a man with a gaze of piercing, arrogant intelligence. The man on the screen was a ghost, a flickering, digital echo of that power, trapped in a failing machine.

He was in his private medical suite, a room that was more sterile than a hospital operating theater. The walls were a soft, neutral white, and the only color came from the myriad of glowing, multi-colored lines on the biometric monitors behind him. Those lines, a constant, silent testament to his heart rate, his blood oxygen levels, his brain activity, were the true wallpaper of his life.

His illness, the Accelerated Cortical Decay, was winning. The tremor in his right hand was more pronounced now, a constant, frustrating vibration that he tried to conceal by keeping the hand flat on the table in front of him. His speech, once so precise and cutting, was now slightly slower, each word chosen with a deliberate, effortful care, as if he were having to manually override a faulty connection between his brain and his mouth.

"Eva," he said, his voice a dry, reedy rasp. "Report."

"Sir," she began, her own voice a calm, steady counterpoint to his frailty. "We have a development. The subjects have not responded as predicted. They have not released a statement discrediting themselves. Instead, they have armed a digital failsafe."

She explained the dead man's switch with a cold, clinical precision, outlining the nature of the uploaded file, the automated distribution list, and the 24-hour timer. She finished her report and waited, a silent, patient instrument.

Valis was silent for a long time, his eyes, sunken and shadowed, fixed on something beyond the camera. He was processing the new data, his brilliant, decaying mind wrestling with the implications. When he finally spoke, his voice was a low, guttural snarl of pure, intellectual rage.

"A stalemate," he hissed, the words laced with a venomous contempt. "They think they can force a stalemate. With me." He attempted a laugh, but it came out as a dry, painful cough that shook his frail frame.

"They are insects," he continued, his voice rising, gaining a measure of its old, terrifying power. "Insignificant, random variables who stumbled into an equation they can't possibly comprehend. And they think they can hold me hostage with their little digital toy."

"The threat is credible, sir," Eva said, her tone unwavering. "If the file is released, the anonymity of the project will be compromised. The source will become the subject of global, governmental-level scrutiny. We would lose any chance of securing it quietly."

"Quietly?" Valis spat, his good hand clenching into a fist. "Do I look like a man who has time for 'quietly,' Eva? Look at me." He held up his trembling right hand, a look of profound self-loathing on his face. "This is the random chaos I have spent my entire life trying to conquer. This is God, or nature, or whatever you want to call it, telling a joke at my expense. The punchline is that the cure is finally within my grasp, but the clock is running out."

He leaned closer to the camera, his eyes burning with a feverish intensity. "The sample your team acquired… the preliminary analysis is more promising than I could have ever imagined. It's not just a cure; it's perfection. It's evolution. It is my victory. And it is being kept from me by a glorified party planner and two middle-aged thrill-seekers."

"A direct assault is a high-risk option," Eva stated calmly, presenting the counter-argument as was her duty. "The villa is a glass house, but it is defensible. They are on high alert. And if we fail, if even one of them escapes to reset the clock…"

"Then we will have failed," Valis interrupted, his voice dropping to a deadly, final whisper. "And failure is not an option. Not for me. Not anymore." He looked directly at her, and the command in his eyes was absolute. "The stalemate is unacceptable. A 24-hour clock is an eternity I do not have. The mission parameters have changed. Your previous orders are rescinded."

He took a slow, rattling breath. "Your new directive is simple. You will acquire the laptop containing the master file. You will acquire the subjects, alive. You will bring them to a secure location, and you will extract from them the location of the source. And you will force them to disarm their little doomsday machine. I do not care what methods you have to employ. I do not care about the noise. I do not care about the mess. This ends. Now."

It was a reckless order, born of desperation and ego. It went against every one of Eva's professional instincts for clean, silent, invisible operations. An assault was loud. It was messy. It was… amateurish. But the client was the client. And the client was a dying man who had just ordered her to burn the world down to get what he wanted.

"Understood, sir," she said, her placid expression betraying nothing of her own assessment.

"I want a status report in twelve hours, Eva," Valis said, a note of finality in his voice. "And I expect that report to include the words 'assets secured.'"

The screen went black.

Eva stood in the humming silence of the van. The game had changed. Her employer's desperation had just become her problem. She turned to the technician at the communications station.

"Get me a line to the tactical team lead," she said, her voice a low, calm command that was colder than any of Valis's raging. "I want them mobilized. Full assault gear. Non-lethal rounds for the subjects, lethal for anyone else who gets in the way. I want a full schematic of the villa's power and communication lines. I want to know every way in, and every way out."

She walked to the large monitor displaying the live, thermal feed from the drone outside the villa. She could see the three bright, warm shapes inside, moving around, completely unaware of the storm that was about to break over their heads. They thought their clever little switch had made them safe. They thought they had time.

"And get me the weather forecast," she added, her eyes fixed on the screen. "I want to know when it gets dark."

Chapter 41: The Siege on the Glass House

The twenty-four-hour clock was a tyrant. It was a small, digital countdown in the corner of Buzz's laptop screen, and it had become the malevolent, ticking heart of their new existence. With every passing minute, its power grew, a constant, nagging reminder that their safety was a subscription service, and the bill was due every single day.

They spent the day in a state of high-strung, anxious limbo. The stunning, sun-drenched villa was no longer a safe house; it was a cage, a beautiful, transparent prison where they were both the inmates and the zookeepers. They watched the clock. They watched the perimeter. And they waited.

Buzz, incapable of sitting still, had reverted to his default setting: frantic, fast-talking, and pathologically overconfident. The initial, cold fear from the phone call had been metabolized into a manic, strategic energy. He was the producer of the world's most dangerous show, and he was deep in pre-production.

"Okay, so, the endgame, the big picture, we gotta think about the endgame!" he said, pacing the length of the living room, a fresh cup of espresso in his hand. "Because this is beautiful, this is a beautiful stalemate, a real work of art. But it's not sustainable. We can't just reset a doomsday clock every day for the rest of our lives. That's not a lifestyle, that's a job! And the benefits package is terrible!"

Dave, who was huddled over a different laptop at the kitchen island, didn't look up. He was watching the live feed from the security cameras Buzz had set up at his house, his eyes flicking between the four camera angles with an obsessive, paranoid intensity. "I don't care about the endgame, Buzz. I care about the two guys in the dark suits who were in my backyard last night."

"Details, Davey, details! That's the micro, I'm talking about the macro!" Buzz shot back, not breaking his stride. "We have the ultimate leverage. The nuke. So what do we want? We don't just want them to go away. That's playing for a tie. We play to win! We want a payout. A big one. We want them to set us up with new identities, clean passports, and a trust fund so big our great-grandchildren will be able to complain about being bored on their space yachts. It's a negotiation, baby! It's the ultimate negotiation!"

"They tried to have us killed, Buzz," Skot said, his voice a low, grim rumble. He was standing by the glass wall, his arms crossed, his gaze fixed on the jungle that bordered the villa's property. He hadn't stopped watching the perimeter since they woke up. "I don't think these guys are interested in a negotiation."

"Everybody's interested in a negotiation!" Buzz insisted. "It's just a question of finding their pain point! And their pain point is that we have a video of their corporate Holy Grail and we're threatening to show it to the entire planet! It's a beautiful thing! We hold all the cards!"

As dusk began to settle, the character of the villa changed. The golden afternoon light, which had made the place feel like a luxury resort, was replaced by long, creeping shadows. The glass walls, which had offered a stunning panoramic view, now felt like a terrifying, one-way mirror. They could see out, but more importantly, the entire, dark, unseen world could see in. The glass house had become a deatrap.

Buzz's manic energy finally began to falter. His jokes fell flat in the heavy, expectant silence. Even he couldn't deny the palpable sense of dread that was settling over the house with the setting sun. The bravado was a flimsy shield against the primal fear of being hunted in the dark.

"Maybe we should turn some of these lights off," Dave said, his voice a nervous whisper. He was still staring at the security feed from his home, a world away. All was quiet. The dark figures were gone. But their absence was somehow more menacing than their presence.

The first sign came at 8:17 PM. The power did not go out. It flickered. A single, almost imperceptible dip in the current that made the recessed lights in the ceiling dim for a fraction of a second before returning to full strength.

"What was that?" Skot asked, his body instantly coiled and tense.

"Probably just a brownout," Buzz said, though his voice lacked its usual conviction. He walked over to his laptop, the one with the ticking clock. A small, red banner was flashing at the top of the screen.

CONNECTION LOST. ATTEMPTING TO RECONNECT...

"The Wi-Fi is down," Buzz whispered, the blood draining from his face.

The dead man's switch was offline. They were being isolated. They were being cut off from their only weapon.

"It's a coincidence," Dave said, though the look on his face said he didn't believe it. "The storm last night, it probably messed with the lines…"

His words were cut short by a sound from the patio. A soft, scraping noise, like a shoe dragging on stone.

They all froze, their eyes locking on the massive glass wall that separated them from the darkness. The infinity pool was a placid, black mirror reflecting the dim interior lights of the living room. Beyond it, there was only the impenetrable black of the night.

And then, a figure rose from the darkness. A man, dressed head-to-toe in black tactical gear, his face obscured by a balaclava, emerged on the far side of the pool. He moved with a silent, fluid grace, a ghost rising from the abyss. He held a small, black object in his hand. He was not looking at them. He was looking at the glass wall.

Before any of them could even shout a warning, a second figure appeared. And a third. They materialized from the shadows on the patio, moving into a coordinated, triangular formation.

"Get down!" Skot roared, his voice a raw, primal cry of pure adrenaline.

He tackled Dave, throwing both of them behind the massive, solid concrete kitchen island just as the glass wall imploded.

It did not shatter with a loud crash. There was a high-pitched, almost inaudible hiss, and then the entire, massive pane of glass simply dissolved into a million tiny, sparkling cubes that cascaded inward, a silent, deadly waterfall of shattered crystal.

Three figures, armed with sleek, black carbines, stepped through the now-empty frame and into the living room.

Chaos erupted. Skot, fueled by a surge of pure, desperate power, came up from behind the island. He didn't have a weapon. He was the weapon. He grabbed a ridiculously heavy, solid marble accent table and hurled it at the closest intruder. The man, surprised by the sheer, impossible speed and strength of the attack, was knocked off his feet, his weapon clattering across the floor.

A second intruder raised his carbine, but it didn't fire a bullet. There was a soft thwip sound, and a small, finned dart embedded itself in Skot's shoulder. He grunted, a look of shocked surprise on his face, and then his legs buckled beneath him. He was still conscious, but his body was no longer listening to his brain.

Dave, his mind screaming, knew he had one job. He scrambled on his hands and knees toward the screening room, toward the laptop. The "nuke." It was their only hope. He was halfway there when the third intruder rounded the island, raising his weapon.

But then the room was plunged into a strobing, disorienting chaos. The lights began to flash on and off with a frantic, seizure-inducing rhythm. The automated blinds began shooting up and down. And from the high-end, invisible speakers in the ceiling, a blast of Vivaldi's Four Seasons erupted at a deafening, eardrum-shredding volume.

It was Buzz. He wasn't a fighter, but he was a technician of chaos. He was crouched behind the bar, jabbing frantically at the villa's master control tablet, which he had commandeered the moment they arrived. He had turned their luxurious prison into a high-tech haunted house.

The diversion gave Dave the second he needed. He launched himself into the screening room and grabbed the laptop. As he turned, he saw one of the intruders, disoriented but focused, aiming his weapon at him. There was another soft thwip, and a searing, electric pain shot through Dave's leg. He collapsed, the laptop clattering to the floor but still blessedly intact. His leg was on fire, his muscles spasming uncontrollably.

It was over. They were outnumbered, outgunned, and outmaneuvered.

But Skot was not done. The tranquilizer dart had paralyzed his limbs, but it hadn't extinguished the fire. He was lying on the floor, watching the scene unfold in a horrifying slow motion. He saw Dave go down. He saw the intruders closing in on Buzz, who was now just cowering behind the bar. He knew, with a final, desperate clarity, what he had to do. He had to save the asset. Not the laptop. The man.

With a roar that was pure, primal will, he used the last of his strength, the last of the Potion's residual miracle, to move. He didn't stand. He lunged, a low, powerful tackle, wrapping his arms around Dave's paralyzed body. He got his feet under him and stood, hauling his friend's dead weight over his shoulder in a fireman's carry. It was an act of impossible, Herculean strength.

Buzz, seeing his chance, scrambled from behind the bar, snatched the laptop from the floor, and ran. He ran toward the back of the villa, toward the only possible escape route he had seen on the architectural plans. A small, secondary service door that led out onto the dark, undeveloped side of the cliff.

Skot followed, his lungs burning, his own muscles beginning to fail as the tranquilizer took full effect. He could hear the shouts of the intruders behind them, the sound of boots on the polished concrete floor.

They burst through the service door and into the cool, black night. They were on a narrow, rocky path, the jungle on one side, a sheer, hundred-foot drop to the sea on the other. There was no escape.

But they didn't have to escape. They just had to disappear.

With the last of his strength, Skot, still carrying Dave, launched himself off the path, not toward the jungle, but toward the cliff's edge. He threw himself, and his friend, over the side.

Buzz, seeing them go, didn't even hesitate. He clutched the laptop to his chest like a holy relic and followed them, leaping out into the black, empty air.

They fell, a chaotic tumble of three bodies and a single, precious laptop, plunging down into the darkness, toward the cold, waiting, and mercifully deep waters of the Caribbean Sea below. The siege was over. The hunt had just begun.

Chapter 42: The Long Fall

The fall was a silent, chaotic eternity. For a split second after they launched themselves into the black, empty air, there was a moment of pure, terrifying weightlessness. Dave, his body a leaden, unresponsive prison due to the tranquilizer dart, felt a strange sense of calm. This was it. The end. A hundred-foot drop onto unseen rocks or into the unforgiving sea. He was vaguely aware of Skot's iron grip on him, a final, futile act of friendship. He saw Buzz, a wide-eyed silhouette against the distant stars, clutching the laptop to his chest like a holy text, his mouth open in a silent scream. And then the world, which had been a slow-motion tableau, slammed into them at a hundred miles an hour.

The impact with the water was not a gentle splash; it was a blow that felt as hard and unyielding as concrete. The cold was a shocking, violent explosion that seized Dave's lungs and jolted his paralyzed body with a jolt of pure, agonizing sensation. He was sinking, tumbling head over heels in the churning, inky blackness, his limbs refusing to obey the frantic, screaming commands from his brain. The water was a crushing weight, pulling him down, and he was completely, utterly helpless. This was a drowning, pure and simple.

Buzz hit the water like a cannonball, the impact knocking the wind out of him in a single, painful gasp. He swallowed a lungful of saltwater, the searing, briny taste a jolt to his system. His first instinct, the one that had been drilled into him by a lifetime of poolside horseplay, was to panic. But the cold, hard terror of the last two days had forged something new in him. He kicked for the surface, his mind a frantic, screaming checklist. Laptop. Skot. Dave. Laptop. Skot. Dave.

He broke the surface, sputtering and gasping, treading water with a desperate, clumsy energy. He was still clutching the laptop, which he had managed to shove into a waterproof dry bag he'd grabbed in the chaos of their escape. The asset was secure. For now.

"Skot! Dave!" he yelled, his voice a raw croak that was swallowed by the sound of the waves crashing against the base of the cliff.

He saw a head bobbing in the water ten feet away. Skot. He was conscious, but his movements were sluggish, uncoordinated. The tranquilizer was in full effect.

"Dave…" Skot gasped, his teeth chattering from the cold and the shock. "Can't… can't find him…"

A new, more potent terror seized Buzz. He scanned the dark, churning water, his eyes wide with panic. And then he saw it. A flash of a pale blue shirt, just below the surface, sinking slowly into the black.

Buzz didn't think. He took a deep breath, kicked down, and swam. He grabbed a fistful of Dave's shirt and pulled, his muscles screaming with the effort. Dave was a dead weight, his body completely limp. Buzz kicked for the surface again, his lungs burning, dragging his unconscious friend with him. They broke the surface with a violent, desperate gasp. Dave's head lolled back, his eyes closed.

"I got him!" Buzz yelled, looping an arm under Dave's chest. "I got him! Now what the hell do we do?"

They were in the water at the base of a sheer, hundred-foot cliff of black rock. There was no beach, no ledge, nowhere to go. Behind them, the vast, empty sea. Above them, a house full of professional killers who were, at that very moment, realizing their prey had vanished.

It was Skot, his mind still working despite the drug, who saved them. "The cliff..." he slurred, his words thick. "Look... at the base..."

Buzz, while trying to keep both Dave's head and the laptop out of the water, squinted through the darkness. He saw what Skot was pointing at. Not a beach, but a shadow. A shadow within the shadow of the cliff. A dark, jagged crack in the rock at the waterline, just big enough for a person to fit through. A sea cave.

It was their only chance. It was a one-in-a-million shot, a feature they could never have seen from the top.

"Okay," Buzz panted, his body screaming with a level of physical exertion it had never known. "Okay, baby, okay. We can do this. It's just a little swim. A little midnight dip." He was talking to himself now, his old, fast-talking bravado returning as a desperate coping mechanism. "It's like a water ride at a theme park, a very exclusive, very high-stakes theme park! Let's go!"

The swim to the cave was a ten-minute nightmare. Buzz, with the laptop bag clenched between his teeth, had to half-drag, half-push his two incapacitated friends through the choppy water. Skot kicked weakly, trying to help, but his limbs were clumsy and unresponsive. They finally reached the opening, a jagged, toothy maw that smelled of salt, brine, and ancient, wet stone. A surge of a wave pushed them through the opening and into the relative calm inside.

Their feet touched a sandy, sloping floor. They stumbled out of the water and collapsed in a heap in the absolute, pitch-black darkness of the cave. For a long time, the only sounds were their own ragged, shuddering breaths and the gentle lapping of the water at the cave's entrance.

They had survived the fall. They had survived the water. They were alive. And they were trapped.

An hour passed. The effects of the tranquilizer darts slowly began to recede, replaced by a deep, bone-chilling cold and a full-body ache that was a universe of misery. Dave finally came to, his first conscious act a violent, wracking cough that expelled a lungful of saltwater.

"You're okay," Skot's voice said from the darkness beside him. "You're okay. We're safe. For now."

Buzz, fumbling in the dry bag, found one of their dive lights. He switched it on, and the powerful beam cut a brilliant, white cone through the darkness, illuminating their new, temporary home. It was a small, high-ceilinged sea cave, the walls slick with moisture and covered in strange, otherworldly-looking anemones.

They took stock. They were alive. The laptop, thanks to Buzz's foresight and the high-quality dry bag, was wet on the outside but seemed to be functional. They were cold, they were weak, and they were completely, utterly on their own.

It was from the mouth of their dark, dripping sanctuary that they saw the hunters. A brilliant, white searchlight suddenly sliced through the night from the top of the cliff, its beam cutting a sharp, clinical path across the surface of the churning water below. Then another. They were sweeping the area, looking for bodies.

A few minutes later, they heard the low, guttural roar of a boat engine. A small, inflatable Zodiac with two dark figures in it began a grid search of the water, its own powerful spotlight playing across the waves.

The three of them scrambled back into the deepest, darkest corner of the cave, their hearts pounding. They were like mice in a hole, watching the cats prowl outside. The search was methodical, professional. It was terrifyingly efficient.

It was Dave, the man who had been a whimpering, terrified mess just a few days ago, who found his voice first. The experience of the jungle, of facing death and coming back, had forged something new in him. The cautious accountant was gone, replaced by a man with a cold, clear, and terrifying understanding of their new reality.

"They're not going to stop," he said, his voice a low, steady whisper in the dark. "Not ever. As long as we have that," he gestured to the laptop, "and as long as they think we know where to find more of The Potion, they will never, ever stop hunting us. Or our families."

"So what do we do?" Buzz asked, his own voice small, stripped of all its usual bravado. "The dead man's switch is our only card. If we let that clock run out…"

"They'll just assume we died in the fall and the system went off automatically," Skot reasoned, his mind clearing as the last of the drugs wore off. "They'll weather the media storm, and the secret will be out. Valis will have a hundred other teams in that jungle, looking for the source. We don't stop him; we just make the race public."

"And if we keep resetting the clock," Dave continued, the terrible logic of their situation becoming clear, "we just live like this forever. Hiding. Looking over our shoulders. A life sentence of resetting a damn clock every twenty-three hours until they finally find us."

He looked from Skot's grim face to Buzz's terrified one. "There's only one way to win. We can't hide the prize. We can't just threaten to reveal the prize. We have to destroy it."

"Destroy it?" Buzz squeaked. "Davey, that laptop is our golden goose! It's our leverage! It's our only damn card to play!"

"It's not the prize, Buzz," Skot said, a new, strange light dawning in his eyes. He was seeing the shape of it now, the one, true, final move on the board. "The footage isn't the prize. The Potion is. The Grotto. As long as it exists, he will never stop. We have to take it off the board. For good."

A long, heavy silence filled the cave. The plan was insane. It meant going back. It meant voluntarily re-entering the green hell that had almost killed them, and this time, they were being actively hunted by a team of professionals.

"We can't," Buzz said, shaking his head. "We can't find it. It was a fluke. A one-in-a-billion shot. It's impossible."

"No," Skot said, his voice quiet but certain. He closed his eyes, his artist's mind replaying the footage, the memories, the sensations. "No, it's not. I can find it." He opened his eyes, and they were filled with a new, terrifying resolve. "When we came out of the exit cenote... for just a second, before the trees blocked the view... you could see the peak of the mountain to the west. And there was a rock formation on it. It was shaped like a jaguar's head. I remember it because I thought about sketching it."

He looked at his friends. "I saw it in the footage from the drone that first day, too. From a different angle. If I have a real map of this region, a topographical map... I can cross-reference the two sightings. I can triangulate the position. I can find that cenote."

The plan was a desperate, long shot, a gamble based on a half-remembered glimpse and a flicker of artistic inspiration. It was the most dangerous idea any of them had ever had. And it was their only way out.

Dave, the man who had once been defined by his fear of risk, was the first to agree. He looked out at the searchlights slicing through the darkness, a symbol of the life of paranoia that awaited them. "Okay," he said, his voice firm. "Let's go back. Let's finish this."

Buzz just stared at them, his mouth agape. These were not the men he had known his whole life. They were harder, stranger, more dangerous. They were survivors. And they had just decided to go back to war.

Chapter 43: The Price of the Ticket

The decision, once made, settled in the small, dark sea cave with the weight of a tombstone. Go back. Go back to the green hell that had almost swallowed them whole. Go back to the place that had birthed their miracle and their curse. It was a plan born of pure, distilled desperation, a suicidal long shot that was somehow, inexplicably, their only logical move.

They huddled in the deepest recess of the cave, three shivering, soaking wet men, and watched the clinical, sweeping beams of the searchlights slice through the night outside. The Zodiac inflatable boat moved back and forth with a patient, methodical persistence, its spotlight tracing intricate patterns on the churning surface of the sea. The hunters were efficient. They were thorough. And they were not going away.

"Okay, so, new plan," Buzz whispered, his voice a shaky, chattering thing that was a million miles away from his usual booming confidence. The bravado had been completely extinguished by the cold, salty reality of the Caribbean Sea. "And I'm just spitballing here, just throwing some spaghetti at the wall to see what sticks. Maybe we don't go back. Maybe we find a nice, quiet fishing village, we grow beards, we learn to live off the sea. I could get into fish tacos. I really could."

"They have our names, Buzz," Dave said, his voice a low, steady rumble in the dark. The transformation in him was profound. The cautious, anxious accountant was gone, replaced by a man who had been stripped down to his essential components: a father and a husband with a singular, protective focus. "They have our families' names. There is no fishing village on this planet where they won't find us. This doesn't end until we make it end."

"I hate it when you're the logical one," Buzz muttered, hugging the waterproof dry bag with the laptop in it to his chest like a teddy bear. "It's very off-brand for you."

They waited for what felt like an eternity, the minutes stretching into an hour, then two. The tranquilizer darts had worn off completely, leaving behind a deep, cellular exhaustion and a full-body ache that was a constant, nagging reminder of their newfound mortality. They were just men again—cold, weak, and painfully human.

Finally, the engine of the Zodiac grew fainter. They watched as the boat, having found no bodies and no debris, made one final, sweeping pass and then turned, heading back up the coast. The searchlights from the top of the cliff clicked off one by one, plunging the world back into a profound, star-dusted darkness.

"It's now or never," Skot said, his voice quiet but firm. He was already moving toward the mouth of the cave. "They're not gone. They're just regrouping. They'll be back with a full-scale land search at dawn. We have to be gone before then."

The swim was a brutal, punishing ordeal. They stayed in the deep shadow of the cliff, the rock face a rough, unforgiving guide against their shoulders. The water was cold, and the waves, which had seemed merely choppy from the cave, were a relentless, heaving force that threatened to slam them against the rocks. Buzz, the least athletic of the three, struggled, his movements a clumsy, inefficient thrashing. Skot and Dave had to flank him, each taking an arm, half-dragging him through the water. They were a single, three-headed, shivering organism, fighting for every inch of progress.

After a half-hour that felt like a lifetime, they found it. A small, hidden cove, invisible from the top of the cliff, with a narrow strip of sandy beach. They stumbled out of the water, their legs barely able to hold them, and collapsed onto the sand, their chests heaving, their bodies trembling with cold and exhaustion.

They had escaped the immediate vicinity of the villa, but they were in no better shape. They were soaked, freezing, and had no shelter. And their doomsday clock was still ticking.

"The laptop," Dave said, his teeth chattering. "Buzz, is it okay?"

Buzz, with trembling, numb fingers, unsealed the dry bag. He pulled out the sleek, silver laptop. It was dry. He pressed the power button. A faint, hopeful chime sounded, and the screen lit up, its bright, clean light a shocking intrusion in the natural darkness of the cove. A small icon in the corner of the screen showed the battery was at less than twenty percent. But more importantly, the clock was still visible in the corner of the desktop.

12:47:16

They had less than thirteen hours to find a secure internet connection and reset the switch.

"Okay," Dave said, taking charge, the pragmatist now a field commander. "We need a plan. A real one. Skot, your jaguar head. How sure are you?"

Skot was staring at the laptop, his eyes distant. "I'm sure I saw it. From two different angles. But to triangulate it, I need a real map. A good one. A topographical survey map of this entire region. Not just some tourist thing."

"And I need to get us a new vehicle," Buzz added, his teeth still chattering. "And supplies. Food. Dry clothes. Burner phones. This whole 'living off the land' thing is not my style. I'm more of an 'ordering room service from the land' kind of guy."

They looked at each other. The answer was obvious, and it was terrible. One of them had to go into town.

"It has to be me," Buzz said with a groan, the realization dawning on him. "Of course it has to be me. You two look like you just wrestled a bear and lost. You're too conspicuous. Me? I just look like a slightly disheveled tourist who had a really, really bad night at the casino. It's my natural state. I can blend."

The plan was simple, and it was terrifying. As soon as the sun came up, Buzz would make his way to the nearest coastal highway. He would have to hitchhike or catch a local bus to the nearest town of any size. There, he would have to find a place that sold detailed maps, buy supplies, and somehow acquire another untraceable vehicle, all without raising any suspicion. It was a true spy mission, a role he had been joking about for years, and the reality of it was making him physically ill.

They found a small, shallow cave at the back of the beach, a hollow in the rock that offered minimal protection from the wind but was at least out of sight. They huddled together for warmth, the laptop between them, its screen a small, precious fire. Skot, using the last of the battery, was already sketching the jaguar-head rock formation from memory, his artist's mind capturing every detail, every angle.

As dawn approached, painting the eastern sky a pale, hopeful gray, Buzz prepared to leave. They gave him the last of their cash.

"Be careful, man," Skot said, clapping him on the shoulder. "Don't be a hero."

"Are you kidding me?" Buzz said, a flash of his old, terrified persona returning. "The second I hit that road, I'm not a hero, I'm a ghost! I'm a whisper! I'm going to be so discreet, so low-profile, you'll think I was never even here! I'm just a humble tourist, looking for a good cup of coffee and maybe a souvenir poncho. Nobody will even see me."

He turned to go, then paused. He looked back at his two friends, huddled and shivering in the dim light of the cave. "Just, you know… try not to die while I'm gone, okay? It would make this whole trip a total waste of time."

He gave them a weak, unconvincing grin, and then he was gone, scrambling up the sandy slope toward the road, a reluctant, terrified spy on the most important mission of his life. Skot and Dave were left alone, with a dying laptop, a half-remembered landmark, and the chilling knowledge that their enemies were hunting them, the world thought they were frauds, and their only hope was currently in the hands of a man whose primary survival skill was knowing how to order the right kind of champagne.

Chapter 44: A Humble Tourist

The sun was an accusation. It was bright, hot, and unforgiving, and as Buzz scrambled up the last few feet of the sandy incline from the hidden cove to the coastal highway, it seemed to be doing everything in its power to expose him. He crouched behind a thick, dusty bush, his heart hammering against his ribs like a trapped bird. He was a mess. His ridiculously expensive linen shirt was stained with salt water and grime. His hair was a wild, wind blasted disaster. He looked less like a high-powered media consultant and more like a man who had just lost a drunken argument with a pelican.

"Okay, Walker, get a grip," he whispered to himself, his voice a frantic, shaky patter. "You got this. You are a ghost. You are a whisper. You are just a humble tourist, a man of the people, out for a morning stroll to admire the local... flora. Yeah, that's it. You love flora. You're a flora enthusiast. Nobody's looking for you. Why would they be looking for you? You're just a guy. A normal, regular, completely unsuspicious guy. Who happens to be the most famous accomplice on the planet right now. It's beautiful. It's perfect. No pressure."

He took a deep breath, plastered what he hoped was a casual, touristy smile on his face, and stepped out from behind the bush onto the shoulder of the road. The highway was a two-lane strip of sun-bleached asphalt that hugged the coastline, with the glittering, turquoise sea on one side and the dense, green jungle on the other. A car whizzed past, then another. He stuck out his thumb, feeling like a complete and utter fraud.

This was not his world. His world was one of ubers with black leather seats, of private drivers who magically appeared when you needed them. Hitchhiking was something that happened in movies, usually right before the main character was murdered by a guy in a hockey mask.

After ten minutes of humiliating failure, an ancient, rattling pickup truck, its original color long since lost to a patchwork of rust and faded blue paint, slowed and pulled over. The back of the truck was filled with wooden crates that were clucking and squawking. Chickens. Of course it was chickens.

The driver, an old man with a face as wrinkled as a walnut and a single, formidable eyebrow, leaned across the seat and pushed the passenger door open. He grunted something in Spanish that Buzz took to mean, "Get in before you melt."

"Gracias, my friend, thank you, you are a lifesaver, a true gentleman of the road!" Buzz said, climbing in, the cab smelling powerfully of chicken, dust, and diesel fuel. He slammed the door shut and flashed his most charming, non-threatening smile.

The old man just stared at him, then at his fancy, water-stained loafers, then back at his face. He grunted again and pulled the truck back onto the road. The silence was thick and awkward. Buzz, a man who could not tolerate a conversational vacuum, felt compelled to fill it.

"So!" he began, his voice a little too loud. "Great day for a drive, huh? Beautiful country. Absolutely beautiful. I'm just, you know, out exploring! Taking in the sights. I'm a big fan of the local... topography. Yeah, that's the word. The topography. Which brings me to a question. You wouldn't happen to know where a guy, a humble tourist like myself, might be able to find a really, really detailed map of this whole area, would you? A topographical map. For... birdwatching! Yeah, birdwatching. Big birds. Very specific birds that only live on, you know, certain elevations. It's a whole thing."

The old man glanced at him, his single eyebrow arching in what could have been curiosity or profound, world-weary pity. He grunted a single word. "Santa Catalina."

"Santa Catalina! Great!" Buzz said. "Is that a big town? Lots of... you know... stores? Places a man could get a few things? A new phone, maybe? Some supplies? And, uh, maybe rent a car? From a place that isn't too picky about, say, paperwork?"

The old man gave him a long, slow, assessing look. Then, a slow, toothless grin spread across his face. He nodded once. He understood.

They drove for another half hour, the clucking of the chickens a frantic, hypnotic soundtrack to Buzz's rising anxiety. He kept checking his watch. The dead man's switch. The dying laptop battery. The clock was ticking.

The town of Santa Catalina was not a tourist trap. It was a real place, a dusty, sun-baked fishing village with a small, bustling central square, a few cantinas, and a collection of cinder-block buildings painted in faded, cheerful pastels. The driver dropped him in the center of the square, pointed to a building with a faded sign that read "OFICINA GUBERNAMENTAL," and then, with a final, conspiratorial wink, pointed to a dusty, grease-stained garage at the far end of the square before rattling off down the road.

First, the map. The government office was a small, stuffy room that smelled of old paper and bureaucratic indifference. The woman behind the counter looked at him with a deep, profound suspicion. He repeated his birdwatching story, laying it on thick this time, inventing a rare, mythical species called the "Cliff-Dwelling Emerald Toucan" that he was writing a book about. He could tell she didn't believe a word of it, but after a tense twenty minutes and a "research donation" that was suspiciously the exact price of the map, he walked out with a large, rolled-up, beautifully detailed topographical survey map of the entire coastal region. He felt a surge of triumph. He had his treasure map.

Next, supplies. He found a small general store, a cluttered wonderland of hardware, fishing tackle, and dusty groceries. He moved through the aisles with the frantic energy of a contestant on a game show, grabbing items with a single-minded purpose. Two cheap, untraceable burner phones. A pile of protein bars and bags of dried fruit. A multi-tool. A basic first-aid kit. A powerful flashlight. He paid in cash, the shopkeeper barely looking up from his newspaper.

The car was the final, most dangerous piece of the puzzle. He walked to the garage at the end of the square. It was less of a business and more of a collection of automotive carcasses in various states of decay. A young man with slicked-back hair and a swagger that far outstripped the quality of his inventory sauntered out to meet him.

"You're the American," the young man said in surprisingly good, movie-inflected English. "My Tío called me. Said you might be stopping by. You need a ghost."

"A ghost?" Buzz asked, his heart pounding.

"A car that doesn't exist," the young man said with a grin. "Clean plates, temporary registration. You drive it for a week, you leave it somewhere, it disappears. For a price."

The price, once again, was extortionate. But Buzz was in no position to negotiate. He handed over a thick stack of cash, and in return, he was given the keys to a beat-up, twenty-year-old sedan whose only redeeming quality was that it was so profoundly, unforgettably boring that it was practically invisible.

He had done it. He had the map, the supplies, the ghost. He threw his bags in the back, the precious map roll on the passenger seat, and pulled out of the town, his hands trembling with a mixture of terror and exhilaration. He had survived. He was the hero. He was the fixer. He was the man.

He turned on the car radio, twisting the dial until he found a news station. He needed a dose of the real world, a reminder of what he was fighting for. A newscaster was speaking in the rapid, melodic cadence of Colombian Spanish. Buzz didn't understand most of it, but his blood ran cold as he heard three distinct, universally understood words.

"Larson."

"Bennett."

And then, a name he had just learned a few days ago, a name that had no business being on a local news report.

"Aevum Therapeutics."

He didn't need to understand the rest of the sentence. He knew, with a sudden, sickening certainty, what it meant. He fumbled for his new burner phone, his fingers clumsy, and used its basic web browser to search the company's name. A recent press release, translated into Spanish, was the top result.

"AEVUM THERAPEUTICS PLEDGES SUPPORT IN SEARCH FOR MISSING AMERICAN DIVERS."

He read the article, his heart sinking with every word. The global biotech giant, in a gesture of "corporate citizenship and humanitarian concern," was offering to lend its "considerable private resources, including advanced geological survey technology," to the Colombian government to aid in the official investigation into the tragic disappearance of Skot Larson and David Bennett.

Buzz felt a wave of nausea so profound he had to pull the car over to the side of the road. He sat there, the engine idling, the Spanish news report a meaningless buzz in the background.

The game had just escalated in a way he could never have imagined. The enemy was no longer a shadowy hunter moving in the dark. They had just stepped directly into the light. They had wrapped themselves in the flag of legitimacy. They were no longer the villains of the story; they were the heroes, the benevolent corporation helping to solve a tragic mystery. They weren't just hunting them anymore. They were now officially leading the hunt. And they were using the full power and resources of a national government to do it.

He looked at the map on the passenger seat, the beautiful, detailed map that was supposed to be their path to salvation. It no longer looked like a treasure map. It looked like a target.

He slammed his fist on the dashboard, a single, sharp crack of plastic and rage. The brief, glorious moment of triumph was gone, replaced by a new and much more profound terror. He threw the car back into gear and floored the accelerator, kicking up a cloud of dust as he sped down the lonely road. He was no longer just a spy. He was a fugitive, racing against a clock that was being run by an enemy who had just rewritten all the rules.

Chapter 45: The Long Wait

The moment Buzz disappeared over the sandy rise, a new kind of silence descended on the small, hidden cove. It was a heavy, profound quiet, no longer filled with the frantic energy of planning or the adrenaline of escape. It was just the rhythmic, eternal sound of the waves sighing against the shore and the distant cry of a gull. For Skot and Dave, it was the sound of being utterly, completely alone.

They retreated into the shallow cave at the back of the beach, a damp, cramped hollow in the rock that offered little comfort but was at least out of the direct line of sight from the sea. The sun began its slow, merciless climb into the sky, heating the air, but it did little to chase away the bone-deep chill that had settled into them during their night in the water.

The pain came back first. It wasn't a sudden attack, but a slow, creeping tide. For Dave, it started in his lower back, the familiar, grinding ache of a lumbar disc that had been complaining for fifteen years. Then his knee, the one that had been miraculously healed, began to throb with a dull, phantom memory of its old injury. It wasn't the searing agony of the initial wound, but it was a constant, nagging reminder that the miracle had a shelf life. He was a machine whose warranty had just expired.

Skot felt it in his shoulder, a deep, rotational ache that had been his constant companion after a climbing fall in his twenties. The Potion had erased it so completely he had almost forgotten it existed. Now, it was back, a ghost repossessing its old haunts. They moved stiffly, their bodies a cacophony of groans and winces. They were no longer the superhuman survivors who had resurrected a dead truck; they were just two beat-up, middle-aged men who had spent the night in a cold ocean and were now paying the price.

"This is a new kind of hell," Skot muttered, trying to find a comfortable position on the cold, sandy floor of the cave. He couldn't. Every position just introduced a new and interesting angle of discomfort.

"Tell me about it," Dave grunted. He was trying to stretch his back, a movement that produced a series of pops and cracks that sounded like a small branch being broken. "You know what the worst part is? I can remember not feeling it. For a few days, I was living in a body that didn't hurt. I'd forgotten what that was like. And now... now the memory makes the pain worse."

He was right. The Potion hadn't just healed them; it had shown them a world they had forgotten existed, a world without the constant, low-grade static of chronic pain. To have that world snatched away was a special kind of cruelty.

As the morning wore on, a new enemy made its presence known: boredom. A profound, soul-crushing, and deeply terrifying boredom. In the jungle, they had been driven by the constant, immediate need to survive. Every step was a challenge, every moment a calculation of risk. Here, in the relative safety of the cove, there was nothing to do but wait. And waiting was a vacuum that was quickly filled by their own anxieties.

They watched the laptop battery. It had become the focal point of their existence, a small, green icon on the screen that represented their connection to their only weapon. The percentage ticked down with an agonizing slowness: 19%... 18%... They knew they had to conserve it. They dimmed the screen to its lowest setting. They shut down every non-essential program. They treated every single percentage point like a precious, non-renewable resource.

"We should turn it off," Dave said after an hour of watching the number drop to 15%. "Just turn it off completely until we need it to reset the switch."

"No," Skot argued, his voice sharp with a new, frayed tension. "What if it doesn't turn back on? It took a bath in the ocean last night. It's working now, but what if something's corroding in there? If we shut it down, we might be shutting it down for good. We can't risk it."

"We can't risk the battery dying before the clock runs out, either!" Dave shot back. "The clock is the only thing that matters, Skot! It's the only thing keeping those guys away from my family!"

"I know that, Dave!"

The argument was sharp, ugly, and born of pure fear. They were two men at the end of their rope, their nerves rubbed raw by exhaustion and terror. In the end, they compromised. They put the laptop to sleep, a state of low-power hibernation that was a terrifying gamble in itself. The screen went dark, and the cave was plunged back into a dim, natural light, their single, digital lifeline now dormant.

With the laptop off, the silence returned, heavier this time. To fill it, they began to talk, their conversation a meandering, desperate attempt to distract themselves from the slow, agonizing passage of time. They talked about their kids, about their wives. They talked about the first time they had ever gone on a "thrill tour" together, a ill-advised white-water rafting trip when they were barely out of their teens. They talked about everything except the one thing that was consuming their thoughts: the very real possibility that Buzz was not coming back.

What if he got caught? What if he, in his usual, conspicuous way, drew attention to himself and was picked up by the police, or worse, by them? What if he just… gave up? The thought was a disloyal one, but it was there, lurking in the back of their minds. Buzz was their friend, their brother, but he was not a man built for this kind of pressure. He was a creature of comfort, of leisure. And they had just sent him on a solo spy mission into the heart of a country he didn't know, with the fate of their entire world resting on his very broad, very unreliable shoulders.

By midday, hunger had joined the party. It was a deep, hollow ache in their stomachs that made the physical pain in their joints seem like a distant cousin. They were dehydrated, their mouths dry and sticky. They had the last of their Potion, a few precious swallows in Dave's BCD, but they had made a silent pact not to touch it. That was for a true, life-or-death emergency. It was their last resort, their final get-out-of-jail-free card, and this gnawing hunger wasn't it. Not yet.

It was Skot, the eternal adventurer, who found a solution. He remembered seeing mussels clinging to the rocks at the far end of the cove. He spent an hour painstakingly prying the small, black shells from the rocks with his dive knife, returning with a handful of slimy, unappetizing-looking shellfish.

"Lunch is served," he announced, his voice a grim parody of a cheerful waiter.

Dave looked at the mussels, then at Skot. "You want us to eat those? Raw? Skot, we'll get sick. We'll get parasites."

"You got a better idea?" Skot shot back, his own patience worn thin. "You want to wait for Buzz to show up with a pizza? This is it. This is what we have."

They ate them. They forced down the raw, salty, metallic-tasting morsels, the texture a slimy, gag-inducing horror. But it was protein. It was fuel. It was a small, disgusting victory against the creeping despair.

The afternoon was the worst. The heat was at its peak, and the small cave offered little respite. They were lethargic, their bodies shutting down, conserving energy. They dozed in fitful, nightmare-filled bursts, only to be woken by the crash of a wave or the sharp cry of a seabird. Every sound, every shadow, was a potential threat.

Dave woke with a start, his heart pounding. "Did you hear that?" he whispered, his eyes wide.

Skot, who had been dozing against the rock wall, was instantly awake. "Hear what?"

"A car," Dave said. "On the road. I thought I heard a car slow down."

They crawled to the mouth of the cave, peering out from behind a rock. The highway above was empty. There was nothing but the heat haze shimmering off the asphalt.

"You're hearing things," Skot said, but his own voice was tight with tension.

They didn't sleep again after that. They just sat, and they waited, and they watched the clock in their heads. 12 hours left. 11. 10.

The sun began to dip toward the horizon, painting the sky in the same brilliant, mocking colors as the day before. And with the fading light came the fading hope. He wasn't coming. Something had gone wrong.

They woke the laptop, a desperate, final act. The battery was at 9%. The clock on the switch read 04:17:32. They had four hours left. Four hours until their secret was blasted to the world. Four hours until their enemies knew their only leverage was gone. Four hours until the hunt would begin again, this time with no pretense, no games.

It was in this moment of ultimate, rock-bottom despair that they heard it. A real sound this time. The crunch of footsteps on the sandy path leading down from the highway.

They scrambled back into the deepest shadow of the cave, their hearts in their throats. They held their dive knives, the cold steel a pathetic comfort. They waited, their breath held tight in their chests, as the footsteps grew closer. A figure appeared at the top of the path, a dark silhouette against the dying, purple sky.

The figure paused, then started down the slope.

"Guys?" a familiar, frantic voice called out, a loud whisper that echoed in the quiet cove. "It's me! Don't stab me! I come bearing gifts! And a whole new set of horrifying problems! It's a whole thing!"

It was Buzz.

Relief, so powerful and absolute it was nauseating, washed over them. They stumbled out of the cave to meet him as he half-slid, half-ran down the sandy path. He was carrying two large, heavy-looking bags. He looked terrible. His face was pale, his eyes were wide with a new and unfamiliar terror, but he was there. He had made it.

He dropped the bags on the sand. "Okay," he panted, bending over to catch his breath. "Good news. I have food, I have water, I have burner phones, I have a ghost car that runs on sadness and rust, and I have your treasure map." He pulled the rolled-up topographical map from one of the bags with a flourish.

"What's the bad news?" Dave asked, his own voice trembling with relief.

Buzz stood up straight, and the frantic, comedic energy was gone, replaced by a cold, hard sobriety that was more terrifying than any of his previous panic.

"The bad news," he said, his voice a low, grim whisper, "is that the game has changed. The quiet little company that was hunting us? They're not so quiet anymore. They just officially and publicly joined the search for you. They've partnered with the Colombian government. They're the good guys now."

He looked from Dave's shocked face to Skot's. "They're not just hunting us in the shadows anymore," he said, the words landing like stones. "They're now hunting us in the light. With helicopters, and soldiers, and the full blessing of an entire country."

Chapter 46: The Good Samaritans

The news, delivered in Buzz's low, grim whisper, landed in the small, dark cave with devastating force. Aevum Therapeutics. The Good Samaritans. The benevolent, humanitarian corporation, lending their "considerable private resources" to the official search. It wasn't just a move on the chessboard; it was a complete upending of the game. Their silent, shadowy enemy had just stepped into the brightest, most unimpeachable spotlight on the planet.

Dave felt a wave of nausea so profound he had to sit down on the cold, damp sand. He stared at Buzz, his mind struggling to process the sheer, diabolical brilliance of the move. "So they're not just hunting us anymore," he said, his voice a hollow echo of itself. "They're leading the hunt. They'll have access to police reports, to military-grade satellite imagery, to everything."

"Worse," Skot added, his face a grim mask in the dim twilight. He was staring out at the dark sea, but his artist's mind was seeing the shape of their new reality. "They control the narrative. Completely. Anything we do, any move we make, can be framed as uncooperative, as suspicious. We're not just fugitives anymore; we're ungrateful, paranoid lunatics who are hindering our own heroic rescue."

"It's a checkmate," Dave whispered, the finality of it settling over him like a shroud. "It's over. We have nowhere to run."

Buzz, who had been standing there, a statue of stunned disbelief, suddenly started to laugh. It was not a happy sound. It was a wild, unhinged, slightly crazed bark that was halfway between a sob and a snarl.

"Over?" he said, his voice cracking with a new, manic energy. "Over? Are you kidding me? It's not over! It's just getting interesting! This is beautiful! This is a masterclass in corporate villainy! I mean, you have to respect the artistry, the sheer, breathtaking audacity of it! They didn't just flip the board; they redesigned the whole damn game in the middle of a play! It's inspiring, is what it is!"

He was back. The terror of the last few hours had been alchemized into a new, more potent, more desperate form of his mania. He started pacing the small stretch of sand, a caged tiger who had just been informed the cage was now on fire and also shrinking.

"Okay, okay, okay, so, the situation has been recontextualized," he said, his words a rapid-fire staccato, a verbal machine gun of thought. "It's a new paradigm. We're no longer the scrappy underdogs; we are now the designated villains in a story where the bad guys are pretending to be the Avengers. Which is fine! It's fine! It gives us a clearer objective! We just have to be better, smarter, and a whole lot crazier than they are!"

"Crazier is not a problem for you," Dave muttered, rubbing his throbbing temples.

"Thank you!" Buzz said, taking it as a compliment. "But first things first. Before we can even begin to formulate our brilliant, counter-insurgency media campaign, we have a much more pressing, much more digital problem." He pointed a trembling finger at the laptop, which sat on a rock, its screen glowing with the single most important number in their world.

03:58:12

Less than four hours until the dead man's switch went off. Less than four hours until their nuke was launched, their secret was blown, and their last piece of leverage was gone.

"And," Skot added, gesturing to the small battery icon next to the clock, "we're at nine percent. We probably have an hour of life left on this thing, tops. The clock is ticking faster than the battery is dying. We're in a race we can't win."

The weight of their immediate, technical problem silenced Buzz's manic monologue for a moment. He stared at the dying laptop, his face a mask of sudden, cold panic. "Okay," he said, his voice a low, serious whisper. "Okay. New top priority. Forget Aevum. Forget the map. We have one job: we need to find a secure Wi-Fi connection and a power outlet in the next ninety minutes. That's it. Nothing else matters."

"And where are we supposed to find that, Buzz?" Dave asked, his voice laced with a weary sarcasm. "At the Starbucks in the middle of the Colombian wilderness?"

"Don't be ridiculous, Davey, their Wi-Fi is terrible!" Buzz shot back, the frantic energy returning. "No, no, no. We need something better. We need a place with fiber optic! A place with a password-protected, high-speed connection! We can't risk the upload failing halfway through! This is a matter of national security! Our national security!" He was pacing again, his mind a whirlwind of insane, desperate logistics. "We need a hotel. A good one. Not a five-star place, that's too hot now. But like, a solid, three-star business hotel. The kind of place with a reliable internet connection and an anonymous, transient clientele. A place where three slightly-disheveled guys checking in late at night wouldn't look too out of place."

"And how do we pay for that?" Skot asked. "We're out of cash. And I'm pretty sure my credit card has been flagged by every intelligence agency on the planet by now."

Buzz just grinned, a flash of his old, promoter's brilliance. "We don't pay. Not yet." He pulled one of the burner phones he had bought from his bag, a cheap, plastic flip phone. "I have a Platinum Amex with a credit limit that could probably fund a small war. I'm going to call them. I'm going to report my card stolen. I'm going to tell them I lost my wallet last night at a casino in Santa Marta. They'll cancel the card, and they'll ask if I want them to book me a hotel for the night while they courier me a new one. I will say yes. I will tell them to book a room for me and my two 'business associates' at a nice, reliable, business-class hotel in the next major city down the coast. It'll be booked under my name, but it'll be paid for by Amex's travel insurance. It's a beautiful little loophole. It's clean. It's untraceable. And it gets us online."

The plan was so audacious, so quintessentially Buzz, that Skot and Dave could only stare at him in a kind of stunned, horrified admiration. It was insane. It was brilliant. It was their only shot.

While Buzz was on the phone, a thirty-minute performance of award-winning charm, distress, and gratitude with an unsuspecting customer service representative in a call center in Utah, Skot got to work. The urgency of the situation had a clarifying effect. He grabbed the topographical map and the powerful flashlight Buzz had brought and spread the large, crinkled paper out on the sandy floor of the cave.

The map was a dizzying, intricate web of contour lines, elevation markers, and tiny, blue veins representing rivers and streams. To Dave, it was an incomprehensible mess. But to Skot, it was a canvas.

He closed his eyes, his artist's mind accessing a different kind of memory. He wasn't just remembering a shape; he was remembering a composition. The way the light had hit the peak of the mountain. The angle of the sun. The specific, jagged silhouette of the jaguar's head rock formation against the sky. He had seen it from the drone footage, an aerial view. He had seen it from the cenote, a low-angle, ground-level view.

He opened his eyes and began to trace the lines on the map with his finger, his movements slow and deliberate. He found the mountain range that ran parallel to the coast. He found the cluster of unnamed peaks. And then he saw it. A single, distinct peak with a cluster of rock outcroppings on its western face that, when viewed from the correct angle on a topographical map, formed a shape that was undeniably, unmistakably, like the head of a stalking jaguar.

His finger then traced a path down from the peak, following the natural watershed, the path that a subterranean river would most likely take. It led to a small, flat, unassuming patch of green nestled between two low hills, about five miles inland. There was no mark on the map. No label. Just an empty space.

"There," he whispered, his voice filled with a quiet, certain awe. "That's it. That's where we came out." He looked at Dave, his eyes shining with a new, fierce hope. "I can get us back."

Just as he said it, Buzz snapped his flip phone shut with a triumphant click. "Boom!" he announced. "We are in business! A triple-occupancy room has been booked and paid for at the very respectable, very boring, and very-well-connected-to-the-internet Hotel Intercontinental in Barranquilla. Check-in is in my name. We are officially legitimate, insured, and about to become very, very busy."

He looked at his friends, a wild, crazed grin on his face. "So, what do you say, boys? Ready for a little road trip?"

They gathered their meager supplies. The precious, dying laptop. The treasure map that now pointed the way to their last, desperate act. And the ghost car that was their only transport. They were a mess. They were exhausted, they were in pain, and they were being hunted by a benevolent, globally-applauded corporation that wanted to dissect them for their secrets. But for the first time in days, they had a plan. A ridiculous, high-stakes, probably-going-to-get-them-killed plan.

They piled into the beat-up sedan, the engine turning over with a reluctant, sputtering cough. Buzz took the wheel, Skot navigated with the map, and Dave held the laptop in his lap, guarding the last few percentage points of its battery as if it were the last ember of a dying fire. They pulled out of the hidden cove and onto the dark, empty highway, a desperate, broken, and newly determined team on the most important road trip of their lives.

Chapter 47: The Digital Ghost

The ghost car was a symphony of suffering. It was a twenty-year-old sedan whose shocks had given up the will to live somewhere around the time its first owner had named it. Every pothole and ripple in the asphalt was a percussive event, a jarring, full-body assault that sent a fresh wave of agony through Dave's and Skot's aching joints. The car smelled of stale cigarettes, old coffee, and the faint, sweet scent of desperation. It was, in other words, the perfect vehicle for their current predicament.

"She's a beauty, isn't she?" Buzz said from the driver's seat, his voice a chipper, booming counterpoint to the car's rattling death throes. He was in his element. This wasn't a desperate flight; it was a road trip movie, and he was the charismatic, fast-talking star. "The guy I bought it from, he called her 'La Cucaracha.' The Cockroach. Because you can't kill her. See? She's got character! She's got a backstory! It's beautiful!"

"I think I just felt one of my kidneys come loose," Dave grunted from the back seat. He was hunched over the laptop, guarding it with the fierce, protective energy of a mother hen. The screen was dark, the machine in a deep, battery-saving sleep. He had become the Keeper of the Clock, a role he had not asked for and did not want.

"That's just the car telling you you're alive, Davey!" Buzz shot back, expertly weaving around a truck that was carrying a precarious, teetering load of sugar cane. "It's visceral! It's real! We're not in the five-star bubble anymore, my friends! We are on the ground! We are in the trenches! This is where the magic happens!"

Skot, in the passenger seat, was not listening. He was completely absorbed by the topographical map spread across his lap, his finger tracing a path, his eyes scanning the intricate web of contour lines. He was the navigator, the cartographer of their own insane quest. "There's a town coming up," he said, his voice a low, focused murmur. "Ciénaga. We need to bypass it. Go around. We can't risk a police checkpoint."

"A checkpoint? Fantastic!" Buzz declared. "Adds a little spice, a little dramatic tension! But you're right, you're right. The talent needs to stay under wraps for now. We take the scenic route. The road less traveled. The path of maximum tactical advantage!" He cranked the wheel, turning onto a smaller, less-maintained road that ran through a sprawling banana plantation. The rattling of the car was now accompanied by the rhythmic slapping of giant green leaves against the windows.

The two-hour drive to the city of Barranquilla was the most tense and bizarre road trip of their lives. Dave stared at the dark screen of the laptop, a man in a prayer vigil for a dying battery. Skot navigated, his mind lost in the geography of their impossible goal. And Buzz provided a running, non-stop monologue, a stream-of-consciousness performance that was equal parts strategic briefing and stand-up comedy routine.

"Okay, so, the hotel," he began, his eyes scanning the road ahead, the rearview mirror, the side mirrors, a constant, paranoid sweep. "The Intercontinental. It's a beautiful choice. It's the perfect kind of anonymous. It's not a tourist trap, it's a business hotel. It's full of sad, lonely men in suits who are just trying to close a deal and get home to their families. We'll be invisible. We'll be ghosts. Digital ghosts. It's a beautiful metaphor, isn't it? I just came up with that. Write that down, somebody."

"Nobody is writing that down," Dave said from the back.

"Fine, I'll remember it," Buzz said, undeterred. "So, here's the play. I go in alone. The advance scout. The point man. You guys stay in the car, in the parking garage. Keep your heads down. I walk in, cool as a cucumber. I'm just a guy, a guy whose wallet was tragically stolen by a beautiful but treacherous woman at a baccarat table. It's a sad story, a classic tale of woe. The clerk at the front desk, she's gonna feel pity. She's gonna feel sympathy. I'll be charming, I'll be a little broken. I'll probably make her laugh. I'll get the keys, and I'll be back before you can even start to miss me."

They finally reached the sprawling, concrete outskirts of Barranquilla as the sun began to set. The city was a different world, a noisy, energetic beast of traffic, lights, and people. Buzz navigated the chaotic streets with a surprising skill, the ghost car weaving through the traffic like it belonged there. He found the Hotel Intercontinental, a tall, modern, and profoundly anonymous-looking glass and steel tower.

He pulled into the underground parking garage, the air suddenly cool and smelling of concrete and exhaust fumes. He found a dark, secluded corner and killed the engine. The sudden silence was deafening.

He looked at the laptop in Dave's lap. "Status report, Mr. Spock."

Dave woke the machine. The screen flickered to life. The battery icon was a tiny, terrifying sliver of red. 4%. The clock on the dead man's switch read 01:22:47. An hour and twenty-two minutes.

"Oh, boy," Buzz whispered, his own face going a little pale. "Okay. Okay. The clock is hot. That's fine. I work best under pressure. It focuses the mind." He took a deep breath, adjusted the collar on his shirt, and put on his sunglasses, even though they were in a dark, underground garage. It was a costume. It was armor.

"Don't do anything stupid, Buzz," Skot said, his voice tight with tension.

"Stupid is my middle name, Skotty, but tonight, I'm all business," he said. He got out of the car. "I'll be back in ten. Don't talk to anyone. Don't look at anyone. And for the love of God, try not to look like two legally dead men hiding in a stolen car."

He strode toward the elevator, a man on a mission. The moment he was gone, the silence in the car became a living entity, a suffocating presence. Skot and Dave just sat there, listening to the hum of the garage lights, watching the battery percentage on the screen. 3%.

Buzz's walk from the parking garage elevator to the front desk was the longest walk of his life. The lobby was a bright, clean, sterile space of polished floors and recessed lighting. It was filled with the low, pleasant murmur of business travelers checking in, of colleagues meeting for a drink at the lobby bar. It was a world of absolute, soul-crushing normalcy, and he was a Trojan horse, smuggling a world of chaos and madness inside his own head.

He approached the front desk, a young woman with a warm, professional smile looking up at him. "Good evening, sir. Welcome to the Intercontinental. How can I help you?"

"Hi, yes, hello," Buzz began, his voice a masterpiece of weary, slightly-embarrassed charm. "My name is Keith Walker. I believe my corporate travel service, American Express Platinum, called ahead for me? I had a bit of a... situation in Santa Marta. A little too much fun at the casino, a wallet gone missing. You know how it is. It's a whole thing."

The clerk's smile was full of practiced sympathy. "Of course, Mr. Walker. I have your reservation right here. A suite, two king beds. I just need to see a piece of photo ID."

Buzz's heart stopped. The one thing he hadn't planned for. The one thing he didn't have. His own wallet was back at the villa, a casualty of their chaotic escape. He was dead. It was over.

"My ID?" he said, letting out a laugh that he hoped sounded charming and not like the shriek of a terrified animal. "Honey, that's the whole problem! The wallet is gone! Poof! Vanished into the ether! The ID, the credit cards, a very sentimental picture of my first dog, everything. It's a tragedy. A real tragedy."

The clerk's smile tightened a fraction. "I understand, sir, but hotel policy requires a photo ID for all check-ins. For security."

"Of course, of course, security, it's the most important thing, I get it, I'm a big security guy," Buzz babbled, his mind racing, searching for an exit, a new narrative. He leaned in, lowering his voice conspiratorially. "But you know who else is a big security guy? My contact at Amex. A lovely woman named Brenda. She personally guaranteed this reservation. She probably sent you an email, a fax, a carrier pigeon, I don't know. She's very thorough. Maybe you could just check?"

The clerk hesitated. Buzz gave her his most winning, most pathetic, "man-at-the-end-of-his-rope" look. It was a look he had perfected over a lifetime of talking his way out of trouble.

She sighed, a small puff of air that was a tiny, beautiful victory. "Let me just call the manager, sir."

The next five minutes were the most excruciating of Buzz's life. He stood there, trying to look casual, while the clerk had a whispered conversation on the phone. He could feel the eyes of the other guests on him. He felt like a fraud, a con man, a character who had just forgotten his lines in the middle of a play.

Finally, the clerk hung up. She looked at him, her professional smile back in place, but with a new, weary resignation in her eyes. "My manager has made a one-time exception, Mr. Walker, given the circumstances of the pre-paid booking," she said, her voice crisp. She slid two plastic key cards across the counter. "Welcome to the Intercontinental. You're in room 1214."

Buzz wanted to weep. He wanted to vault over the counter and kiss her. Instead, he just gave her a weak, grateful smile. "Brenda will be very pleased," he said. "You're a lifesaver."

He practically sprinted back to the garage, his heart a triumphant drum. He slid back into the driver's seat of the ghost car, holding up the key cards like a trophy.

"We're in business!" he whispered.

They took the service elevator, a slow, rattling ride that seemed to take an eternity. They found room 1214, a profoundly anonymous and blessedly clean hotel room at the end of a long, silent hallway.

They burst inside. The laptop battery was at 1%. The dead man's switch clock read 00:07:14. Seven minutes.

What followed was a frantic, slapstick ballet of pure panic. Skot snatched the laptop from Dave and sprinted for the desk, looking for an outlet. Dave was fumbling with the Wi-Fi password, which was printed on a small, laminated card. Buzz was just running in circles, whispering, "Oh, boy, oh, boy, oh, boy."

Skot found the outlet, plugged in the power cord, and the laptop chimed, a happy, life-affirming sound. The battery was charging.

Dave, his hands trembling, typed in the long, complex Wi-Fi password. The connection icon spun for a heart-stopping second, then turned a solid, beautiful blue. They were online.

"The password!" Buzz yelled. "The password!"

It was a three-part code, a piece of paranoid genius they had concocted in the villa. The first part, an alphanumeric string, was from Skot. The second, a series of symbols, was from Dave. The third, a nonsensical phrase from a song he'd heard in a casino, was from Buzz.

They typed it in, their three heads huddled together, their fingers fumbling over each other.

The screen changed. A new button appeared: RESET CLOCK.

The timer read 00:00:09.

Dave's finger stabbed at the trackpad. He clicked.

The screen refreshed. A new clock appeared, its green numbers a beacon of glorious, life-affirming relief.

23:59:59

They had done it.

They collapsed, a tangle of limbs and gasping breaths, onto the floor of the anonymous hotel room. Skot was laughing, a weak, wheezing sound. Dave had his face buried in the surprisingly clean carpet, his shoulders shaking with silent, shuddering sobs.

And Buzz... Buzz just lay on his back, staring at the textured white ceiling, a single, happy tear tracing a path through the grime on his cheek.

"I love this job," he whispered to the empty room.

Chapter 48: The Logistics of the Impossible

The aftermath of the adrenaline was a brutal, punishing silence. The green, life-affirming numbers of the newly reset clock on the laptop screen were the only things in the hotel room that seemed to have any energy. Skot and Dave were sprawled on the floor, two discarded marionettes whose strings had been cut. The superhuman effort, the terror, the desperate, high-stakes race against time—it had all been cashed in, and the payment was a deep, cellular exhaustion that felt like it had settled into their very bones. The aches were back, not as a gentle reminder, but as a loud, insistent screaming.

Dave lay with his eyes closed, his face a pale, waxy gray under the hotel room's unforgiving fluorescent lights. He was trying to will the pain in his back to subside, a futile exercise in mind over matter. He was no longer the heroic survivor; he was just a forty-seven-year-old man with a bad lumbar, lying on the floor of a strange hotel in a country that wasn't his, with a group of professional killers somewhere outside and the weight of a world-changing secret pressing down on him. It was, he decided, not his best Tuesday.

Skot sat with his back against the wall, the topographical map spread out before him like a sacred text. He was the only one with a flicker of purpose. He was a cartographer of miracles, his mind already trying to solve the next impossible puzzle, but his body was a traitor.

Every time he shifted his weight, a low groan escaped his lips as his shoulder sent a fresh bolt of fire through his system.

Into this tableau of quiet, middle-aged suffering, Buzz was a category five hurricane of misplaced triumphalism.

He was on his feet, pacing the room, a ball of pure, uncut, victorious energy. He had faced down the system, he had won the race, he had saved the day. In his mind, he wasn't just the fixer; he was a damn action hero.

"Beautiful!" he declared to the room at large, his voice a booming, cheerful sound that made Dave wince. "A beautiful piece of work, gentlemen! A symphony of tactical precision! They zigged, we zagged! They played checkers, we invented a whole new game involving quantum physics and, I don't know, psychic espionage! It was a masterpiece!"

He grabbed the room service menu from the desk. "Okay, first things first. We need to refuel the machine. I'm thinking steaks. Big ones. The kind of steaks that have their own zip code. And lobster. We deserve lobster. And what's the most expensive bottle of red wine you have? Don't tell me, just send up three of them! We are celebrating! This is our victory lap!" He was already on the phone, his voice a torrent of joyous, non-negotiable demands.

An hour later, their anonymous hotel room had been transformed into the most depressing and paranoid victory party in history. A room service cart laden with an obscene amount of food sat in the middle of the room, most of it untouched. Buzz was the only one eating, devouring a steak with a primal, celebratory vigor. Skot and Dave just picked at their food, their stomachs a tight, acidic knot of anxiety.

"Okay, so, the victory lap is over," Buzz announced, pushing his plate away and wiping his mouth with a linen napkin. He was all business again, the manic CEO ready to brief his board of deeply traumatized directors. "Time to talk about the next phase of the operation. The counter-offensive. The part where we take the fight to them. Metaphorically, of course. I am not a fighter. I am a lover. And a strategist. Mostly a strategist."

It was Skot who took the lead. He gestured to the map spread on the floor. "This is the next phase," he said, his voice quiet but firm. "This is the only phase that matters."

He, Dave, and Buzz huddled around the map, a strange, mismatched trio of fugitives. Skot, with the last precious dregs of the laptop's battery, pulled up the screenshots he had saved—a grainy image from the drone footage, a freeze-frame from the GoPro. He placed them next to the map.

"Look," he said, his finger tracing a line on the paper. "The drone showed the mountain range from the east. When we came out of the cenote, we were looking at it from the west. From that angle, you can see this." He pointed to a tight cluster of contour lines on a specific peak. "The Jaguar's Head. It's a unique rock formation. It's unmistakable. Once you know what you're looking for."

His finger then moved down the map, following the natural, invisible lines of the watershed. "A subterranean river would follow the path of least resistance. It would flow down from the highlands, through this valley here." His finger finally came to rest on a tiny, unmarked, and completely insignificant-looking patch of green, nestled between two low hills, miles from any marked road.

"And it would surface... right there," he said. He looked up at them, his eyes shining with a startling, absolute certainty. "That's it. That's the cenote. I'm sure of it."

The declaration hung in the air, a statement of such profound and impossible hope that it felt dangerous.

It was Dave, the risk assessor, who shattered the moment. "Great," he said, his voice flat and devoid of any hope. "You found a dot on a map. Fantastic. Now tell me how we get to it. Because I'm looking at that dot, Skot, and what I'm not seeing is a road. I'm not seeing a convenient parking lot or a friendly little visitor's center. That dot is in the middle of a giant, green ocean of 'you're-going-to-die-here.' How do we get there? We can't just walk. It's a hundred miles inland. We'd need supplies, gear, a whole damn expedition."

He wasn't finished. His voice rose, a crescendo of pragmatic despair. "And the clock, Buzz! What about the damn clock? We have to find a Wi-Fi connection and reset that switch every twenty-three hours! Are we going to find a Starbucks in the middle of your magical dot on the map? Is there a hidden jungle Marriott with a good business center we don't know about? The plan is impossible. It's a fantasy."

The sheer, crushing weight of the logistical nightmare settled over the room. Dave was right. They were trapped in a paradox. To stay in civilization meant they could be found. To go into the wilderness meant their dead man's switch would go off, and their secret would be exposed anyway. It was a perfect, elegant trap.

Buzz was silent for a long time, staring at the map. He wasn't looking at the dot. He was looking at the thin, blue lines. The rivers. A strange, wild light began to dawn in his eyes.

"A car," he said softly. "Davey, you're thinking about a car. That's where you're wrong. You're thinking on the ground. You're thinking like a landlubber. But we're not landlubbers. We're Grotto Men! We were born in the water! We need to get back to our roots!"

He was on his feet now, the monologue building, the insane, brilliant solution taking shape in real time. "A car is too loud, too traceable! They're looking for a car! They're looking for guys on a road! So we don't use a road! We go off-road! We go off-grid! We don't go by land; we go by water!" He stabbed a finger at the map, at the largest blue line that snaked its way from the coast deep into the interior. "The Magdalena River! It's a highway, baby! A big, muddy, beautiful highway with no traffic cameras! We buy a boat! A crappy, old, forgettable fishing boat! We become river rats! We sail deep into the heart of darkness, completely invisible! It's classic! It's cinematic! It's Heart of Darkness meets The A-Team! It's the most brilliant plan I've ever had!"

"And the clock, Buzz?" Skot asked, his own eyes starting to gleam with the sheer, mad audacity of the plan.

"The clock is the beautiful part!" Buzz roared, now in a full-blown frenzy of creative genius. "The clock is the part that makes us legends! We don't just need gear; we need a mobile command center! A floating fortress of solitude! We're not just buying a boat; we're outfitting an expedition! We buy a small, portable satellite internet dish. You can get them anywhere! We buy a couple of heavy-duty marine batteries to power it! We turn our crappy little fishing boat into a damn floating, Wi-Fi-enabled, ghost-in-the-machine headquarters! We can reset the clock from the middle of the Amazon if we have to! It's beautiful! It's money! It is the single greatest idea in the history of desperate, on-the-run ideas!"

The plan hung in the air, audacious, ridiculous, and undeniably their only path forward.

Miles away, in the cool, humming silence of the mobile surveillance van, Eva Rostova was looking at a different kind of map. It was a digital chart of the city, overlaid with a spiderweb of data points and financial transactions. She had lost them. The amateurs had slipped through her net. Their ghost car had been found abandoned in the parking garage of a downtown hotel, wiped clean. Their hotel room, booked under a fake name, was empty. They had vanished.

She was not angry. Anger was an inefficient emotion. She was a professional, and this was simply a new phase of the problem.

She turned to her lead analyst. "They have gone to ground in the city," she said, her voice a calm, precise whisper. "They are no longer reacting; they are planning. They believe their next move is to go back to the source. They will need supplies. They will need transportation. A man like Walker, a creature of comfort, he will not be buying a single backpack. He will be outfitting an expedition. He will over-purchase. It is in his psychological profile."

She looked at the analyst, her eyes cold and clear. "So we are no longer looking for three men. We are looking for a transaction. A large, off-the-books, cash-heavy purchase of specific, high-end equipment. Scan every outfitter, every charter boat captain, every marina, and every private satellite equipment vendor in a two-hundred-mile radius. I want a flag on any cash transaction over five thousand dollars for survival gear, nautical equipment, or satellite hardware. Widen the net. They are amateurs, but they are not stupid. They will try to be clever. We will be smarter."

She turned back to her map. "They are planning a journey," she said, almost to herself. "And every journey begins with a ticket. We will find the man who sells them that ticket."

Her phone buzzed. A new directive from Valis. Status?

She typed back a simple, confident reply.

The prey is choosing its own trap. I will be ready when it does.

Chapter 49: The Shopping Trip

Dave and Skot were a wreck. The physical relief of a night in a real bed was completely negated by the psychological torment of their situation. They were in pain, their bodies a constant, aching reminder of their lost miracle. They were also bored. A profound, soul-crushing boredom that was somehow more terrifying than the jungle. They were two adrenaline junkies, two men of action, who had been ordered to sit in a room and do absolutely nothing. It was a special kind of hell.

Buzz, on the other hand, was a live wire. He was vibrating with a mixture of terror and pure, uncut, professional exhilaration. He had slept for maybe two hours, his mind a frantic whirlwind of logistics, contingencies, and potential branding opportunities. He was wearing the same clothes as the day before, but he wore them with the rumpled, sleepless authority of a man running a covert operation.

"Okay, gentlemen, listen up, the sun is up, the birds are chirping, and the enemy is probably using military-grade satellites to read the brand of jam I'm putting on my toast!" he began, his voice a rapid-fire monologue. "So we have to be smart, we have to be fast, and we have to be beautiful. Today, I go shopping. And this isn't just any shopping trip. This is the most important, most high-stakes, most tactically significant shopping trip in the history of retail. We are outfitting a revolution, and the revolution needs supplies."

He grabbed a piece of hotel stationery and a pen. "Skotty, my man, my rugged, jungle-surviving artiste. Talk to me. What do we need to not die in a very unpleasant way in the middle of nowhere? Hit me."

Skot, who had been staring blankly at the wall, seemed to come to life. This, at least, was a problem he understood. "A good machete," he said, his voice a low, practical murmur. "Two of them. A water purifier, a real one, not just tablets. A comprehensive medical kit, heavy on antibiotics and anti-venom. Tarps. Rope. A good compass. A fire starter. And fuel. As many full cans of gasoline as we can carry."

"Beautiful! Practical! I love it!" Buzz said, scribbling furiously. "Davey, my favorite CPA, my beloved voice of doom and gloom, what am I missing? What's the variable that's going to get us killed?"

Dave, who had been massaging his aching back, looked up. "The money, Buzz. The money. You can't just walk into a store and buy all that with a duffel bag full of cash. It's a red flag the size of a planet. They're looking for a transaction. You said it yourself. One big, conspicuous purchase, and we're done."

"Exactly!" Buzz said, pointing his pen at Dave as if he'd just solved the final equation. "That's the beauty of it! That's the head-fake! We don't make one big purchase. That's for amateurs! That's checkers! No, no, no. We're playing 3D chess, baby! We break it up. We spread the love. A little here, a little there. They're looking for a whale, we're gonna give them a school of minnows. They'll never see us coming!"

He took a deep breath, his eyes gleaming with the light of his own perceived genius. "And one more thing," he said, adding an item to the bottom of the list with a dramatic flourish. "A very good cooler. For the cervezas. It's a morale thing. It's non-negotiable."

An hour later, Buzz was on the street. He looked nothing like the man who had checked in the night before. He had traded his linen shirt for a faded, nondescript t-shirt he'd found in the bottom of his bag. He wore a baseball cap pulled low over his eyes and a cheap pair of sunglasses he'd bought from a street vendor. He was no longer Keith "Buzz" Walker, international man of leisure. He was just a guy. A tourist. A ghost.

His first stop was not a high-end outfitter. It was the Mercado Publico, a sprawling, chaotic, and beautiful labyrinth of sights, sounds, and smells. It was a city within the city, a place where you could buy anything from a freshly caught fish to a counterfeit watch. It was the perfect place to disappear.

He moved through the crowded aisles, a man on a mission. He bought two heavy, well-balanced machetes from a guy in a hardware stall who also sold live chickens. He bought tarps and rope from a different stall that seemed to specialize in nautical supplies. He bought the medical kit, piece by painful piece, from three different pharmacies, pretending to be a concerned father stocking up for a family camping trip. He haggled in his terrible, broken Spanish, a performance of such earnest, touristy incompetence that no one gave him a second glance. He was just another gringo, lost and slightly overwhelmed. It was the perfect cover.

The satellite dish was the hard part. The most dangerous part. He couldn't just walk into an electronics store. He had to go deeper. Following a tip from the ghost-car salesman, he found himself in a grimy, back-alley neighborhood far from the tourist districts. He found the "importer," a man with a single gold tooth and the dead, watchful eyes of a shark, in the back of a small shop that ostensibly sold cell phone cases but seemed to do very little actual business.

The negotiation was a tense, whispered affair. Buzz, his heart hammering, explained what he needed, using vague, technical terms he had memorized from a website. A portable, auto-aligning satellite dish. High-bandwidth. Encrypted uplink. The man with the gold tooth just stared at him, his expression unreadable. He made a phone call, a short, guttural conversation in a dialect Buzz didn't recognize.

Finally, the man nodded. He named a price that was easily three times the retail value. Buzz didn't even try to haggle. He just pulled out a thick, pre-counted stack of cash. The transaction felt illicit, dangerous. He felt like a spy trading secrets in a Cold War movie. He half-expected to be arrested. But twenty minutes later, he was walking out with a large, heavy, and completely anonymous-looking hard-shell case.

He was on fire. He was a natural. He was Jason Bourne with a better sense of humor and a much higher credit limit.

The boat was the final piece of the puzzle, the climax of his shopping trip. He took a taxi down to the city's working docks, a gritty, salt-stained world of peeling paint, diesel fumes, and the constant, screaming cry of gulls. This wasn't a marina for yachts; this was where real work happened. Small, sturdy fishing boats, their hulls scarred from years of battling the sea, were tied up to weathered wooden piers.

He found what he was looking for almost immediately. It was perfect. A small, ugly, but sturdy-looking vessel with a small cabin and a reliable-looking outboard motor. It was called the Esperanza Perdida—The Lost Hope. The irony was so perfect, so beautiful, he almost wept.

The owner was a grizzled fisherman named Hector who was mending a net on the pier. Buzz put on his best performance yet. He was a rich, clueless American tourist who had decided, on a whim, that he wanted an "authentic" Colombian fishing experience. He wanted to buy a boat, right now, for cash.

Hector looked at him with a deep, profound suspicion. But the cash was real. After an hour of negotiation, of Buzz pretending to be a fool and Hector pretending to be a shrewd businessman, they settled on a price. As Buzz was counting out the final stack of bills, he felt it. A cold prickle on the back of his neck. The feeling of being watched.

He didn't turn his head. He didn't make any sudden movements. He just let his eyes drift, a casual, touristy glance across the bustling dock. And then he saw them.

They were standing near a stack of lobster traps, pretending to be in a conversation. Two men. They were clean, too clean for this place. They wore simple, practical clothes, but their shoes were too new, too expensive. And they weren't looking at the boats or the fishermen. They were scanning. Their eyes were constantly moving, taking in everything, assessing, analyzing. They were hunters. They were Eva's people.

They weren't looking at him. Not yet. But they were here. Their net was out. And he had just swum right into it.

The blood in his veins turned to ice. The thrill of the spy game evaporated, replaced by the cold, hard terror of a man who has just realized the game is real, and the stakes are his life.

He had to get out. Now.

He shoved the rest of the money into Hector's hand. "The boat," he said, his voice a low, urgent hiss. "I need it now. And the fuel. All the fuel you have."

He spent the next twenty minutes in a state of pure, adrenaline-fueled panic, helping Hector load a dozen full fuel cans onto the boat. He could feel the eyes of the two men on his back. He didn't dare to look. He just worked, his hands clumsy, his mind screaming at him to run.

Finally, it was done. He had the boat. He had the supplies. And he had been seen.

He didn't even bother with a taxi. He ran. He ran through the back streets of the dock district, his heart a frantic, hammering drum. He found his ghost car and threw the last of his supplies in the back. He drove back to the hotel, his hands shaking so badly he could barely keep the car on the road.

He burst into room 1214, dropping the bags of gear on the floor with a loud crash. Skot and Dave jumped to their feet, their faces a mask of alarm.

"Pack your bags, boys!" Buzz yelled, his voice a wild, terrified, triumphant shriek. "The store is officially closed! We are checking out! Now!"

"What happened?" Skot demanded. "Did you get it all?"

"I got it all and then some!" Buzz said, his chest heaving. "I got the boat, I got the map, I got the magic internet dish! And I got a big, fat, steaming side order of 'we are completely and utterly screwed!' They were there, guys! At the docks! They saw me! They're on to us! The quiet game is over! The loud game is over! The only game left is the 'get-the-hell-out-of-Dodge' game, and it starts right now!"

Chapter 50: The Burner

The anonymous hotel room, which had briefly served as a planning office and a psychological torture chamber, was now the scene of a frantic, high-speed evacuation. Buzz's panicked declaration sucked all the oxygen out of the air, replacing it with a thick, potent cocktail of adrenaline and pure, uncut terror. The theoretical threat, the shadowy "they," had been given a face—two of them, in fact, clean-shaven and professional, standing by a stack of lobster traps. The game was no longer a chess match of digital countermeasures; it was a desperate, physical scramble for the exit.

"Pack it up! Pack it all! Go, go, go!" Buzz was a blur of motion, a human tornado of fear. The cool, confident fixer was gone, replaced by the original Buzz—a man of immense, chaotic, and deeply loud energy. "They were there, guys! At the docks! Just standing there, pretending to be interested in crustacean futures or whatever! But they weren't! They were hunting! I saw the shoes! The shoes were too clean! It's always the shoes! It's the first rule of spycraft, you learn that on day one!"

He was throwing their meager belongings into the bags he had just unpacked. Skot and Dave, jolted from their own weary paralysis, moved with a new, desperate urgency. They were a team again, their individual anxieties momentarily forgotten, fused together by a singular, unifying purpose: flight.

"Did they follow you?" Skot asked, his voice a low, tight growl as he shoved the precious, rolled-up map into a long, protective cardboard tube Buzz had miraculously procured.

"I don't know! I don't think so!" Buzz shot back, his words tumbling over each other in a frantic rush. "I went full Jason Bourne back there! I took three left turns when I should have taken a right, I went down a one-way street the wrong way—which, by the way, the locals don't even seem to notice—I think I drove through an open-air fruit market at one point! I was a ghost! A beautiful, terrified, fruit-splattered ghost! But we can't assume anything! The car is burned."

"What do you mean, burned?" Dave asked, zipping up a bag with a final, angry tug. "We just got it!"

"It's a burner car, Davey, a burner!" Buzz explained, his eyes wide with the paranoid logic of a man who has seen too many spy movies. "They saw me at the docks, they probably saw the car I was driving before that. They'll be looking for this one. It's compromised. It's dirty. We have to ditch it. We have to shed our skin! It's beautiful! It's a metaphor!"

They were out of the room and in the hallway, moving with a speed that drew a curious look from a woman pushing a housekeeping cart. Buzz gave her a dazzling, high-wattage smile. "Big business meeting! You know how it is! The early bird gets the worm, or in this case, the multi-billion-dollar international distribution deal! Have a great day!"

They took the service elevator down to the parking garage. The ghost car, their trusty, invisible steed, now looked like a trap.

"Okay, new plan," Buzz whispered, huddling them together behind a concrete pillar. "We can't just drive out of here. They'll be watching the exits. They'll have the license plate. We have to create chaos. We have to be the chaos."

He handed Dave the keys. "Davey, you're up. You're the most normal-looking one. You're going to get in the car, you're going to drive it to the exit, and you're going to cause a small, believable, and deeply inconvenient accident."

"What?" Dave said, his eyes widening in horror.

"Just a fender-bender!" Buzz insisted. "Find some rich guy in a Mercedes who isn't paying attention. Tap him. Just a little love tap! You're a tourist, you're confused by the signs, it happens all the time! You get out, you argue, you exchange insurance information you don't have! You create a scene! A beautiful, traffic-snarling, attention-grabbing scene! While you're doing that, Skotty and I, we're going to slip out the pedestrian exit on the far side and grab a taxi. It's a classic misdirection play! It's the old okie-doke!"

"You want me to crash a car and then abandon it to flee the scene of an accident?" Dave asked, his voice a squeak of pure, law-abiding terror.

"Yes! It's perfect!" Buzz said, his face alight with the sheer genius of his own terrible idea. "It's the last thing they'll expect! Now go! Be the mild-mannered, slightly incompetent driver you were always meant to be!"

Dave looked at Skot, a silent plea for sanity. Skot just gave a grim, resigned shrug. Buzz's plan was insane, but it was also their only plan.

With a look of profound, spiritual agony, Dave got behind the wheel. He drove the ghost car up the ramp toward the exit, his heart a frantic drum against his ribs. Skot and Buzz, weighed down with their gear, slipped through a side door and out into the bright, hot, and noisy chaos of the city.

They didn't have to wait long. Five minutes later, they heard the unmistakable sound of a car horn blaring, followed by the crunch of metal on metal and a torrent of angry, rapid-fire Spanish. The decoy had worked.

Buzz flagged down a taxi, a tiny, yellow deathtrap with a cracked windshield. He threw their bags in the back and gave the driver a destination, a busy public market on the other side of the city. As they pulled away, they could see the traffic at the entrance to the parking garage already backing up. Dave, bless his heart, was in the middle of a very animated, very believable argument with a man in a very expensive suit. He was a natural.

The rest of the day was a blur of calculated, paranoid motion. They took the first taxi to the market, got out, walked through the entire, sprawling labyrinth of stalls, and emerged on a different street, where they immediately got into another taxi. They took that one to a bus station, where they bought tickets for a local bus that was heading south, down the coast. They rode the hot, crowded, chicken-filled bus for ten miles, then got off in a small, anonymous-looking town. From there, it was a third taxi, this one hired for an exorbitant cash fee, to take them the final, long leg of the journey back to the docks of Barranquilla, arriving from the south, the opposite direction from which they had left.

It was a shell game, a deliberate, frustrating, and exhausting attempt to erase their own trail. By the time their taxi finally pulled up to a quiet, deserted side street a few blocks from the marina, night had fallen. The city was a glittering tapestry of lights against the dark velvet of the sea.

"Okay," Buzz whispered, his voice hushed and conspiratorial. "This is it. The final leg. We go in on foot. We move fast, we move quiet. We find the boat, we load the gear, and we disappear into the night. We are ninjas. We are whispers on the sea breeze. Any questions?"

"I have to pee," Dave said, having finally rejoined them after his own harrowing, multi-taxi journey from the scene of his staged accident.

"There's a whole ocean for that in about twenty minutes, Davey, hold it in!" Buzz snapped.

The docks at night were a different world. The daytime chaos of fishermen and vendors was gone, replaced by a quiet, menacing stillness. The only sounds were the gentle creaking of the boats straining against their ropes and the lapping of the dark water against the wooden piers. The air was thick with the smell of salt, diesel, and fish. Every shadow seemed to hold a threat. Every stray cat that darted across their path made them jump.

They found her, moored at the very end of the longest pier, bobbing gently in the darkness. The Esperanza Perdida. The Lost Hope.

"She's beautiful," Buzz whispered with a reverence that was completely unearned by the ugly, utilitarian boat.

They worked in a state of high-strung, silent efficiency, passing their gear from the pier to the deck. The satellite dish in its hard-shell case was heavy and awkward. The fuel cans were a dead weight. Finally, it was all aboard.

Skot was the only one with any real boating experience. He moved with a quiet confidence, checking the lines, priming the outboard motor. Dave and Buzz just tried to stay out of his way.

"Cast off the bow line," Skot whispered. Dave fumbled with the thick, wet rope, his fingers clumsy in the dark. He finally got it undone.

"Stern line," Skot said. Buzz untied the final rope that connected them to the land, to the world of men and rules and consequences.

Skot took a deep breath and pulled the cord on the outboard motor. It sputtered once, a pathetic, gasping cough, and then died. The silence that followed was deafening.

"Oh, no," Buzz whimpered. "No, no, no. Don't do this to me, you beautiful, magnificent rust bucket. Don't do this to me."

Skot pulled the cord again, harder this time. The engine coughed, sputtered, and then, with a loud, rattling roar that sounded like a squadron of angry hornets, it caught. The sound was a violation in the quiet night. It felt like they had just set off a flare.

"Go!" Dave hissed. "Get us out of here!"

Skot put the engine in gear, and the Esperanza Perdida chugged slowly away from the pier, leaving the world of solid ground behind. They motored through the dark, quiet harbor, past the ghostly silhouettes of larger, sleeping fishing vessels. They were a small, insignificant boat, slipping out into the vast, black emptiness of the sea.

As they cleared the breakwater and the city of Barranquilla spread out behind them like a carpet of scattered jewels, they saw it. A pair of headlights swept across the pier they had just left. A dark, official-looking SUV, the kind that was conspicuously absent of any markings, pulled to a stop exactly where their taxi had dropped them off. Two figures got out and stood at the end of the pier, staring out into the darkness where a small, noisy fishing boat had just been.

They were too late. By minutes.

Skot pushed the throttle forward, and the small boat picked up speed, its engine a defiant roar in the night. They weren't heading for the open sea. They were turning, following the coastline, aiming for a new shadow, a new darkness. The wide, black, and utterly unknown mouth of the Magdalena River.

The race had begun. And they had a head start. But as Dave looked back at the receding lights of the city, at the two, small, patient figures standing on the pier, he knew, with a certainty that chilled him to the bone, that a head start was not the same as an escape.

Chapter 51: The River of Ghosts

The mouth of the Magdalena River was not a gentle transition; it was a border crossing. One moment, they were on the vast, open, and relatively clean expanse of the Caribbean Sea, the next, they were swallowed by a different world. The water changed color, from a deep, clear blue to a thick, opaque, and muddy brown. The fresh, salty air was replaced by a heavy, humid atmosphere that smelled of wet earth, decaying vegetation, and the rich, loamy scent of a million years of life and death. The wide-open horizon was gone, replaced by two towering, impenetrable walls of solid green. The jungle pressed in on both sides of the wide, sluggish river, a silent, watchful audience to their desperate, upstream journey.

The Esperanza Perdida, which had felt so small and vulnerable on the open sea, now felt like an impossibly loud and conspicuous intruder. The sputtering roar of its outboard motor echoed off the dense foliage, a brazen announcement of their presence in a world that preferred whispers.

Skot was at the helm, a small tiller in his hand, his eyes constantly scanning the dark water ahead for sandbars and submerged logs. He was the captain now, a role he had not asked for but had assumed with a grim, quiet competence. His face, illuminated by the dim glow of the boat's single compass light, was a mask of intense concentration. He was no longer just an artist; he was a river pilot, navigating them deeper into the abyss.

Dave was in the small, cramped cabin, which smelled faintly of fish and gasoline. He had the topographical map spread out under the beam of a flashlight, trying to match the winding curves of the river on the paper with the dark, featureless reality outside. He was the navigator, the man trying to impose a grid of logic onto a world that defied it. The pain in his back and knee had settled into a low, constant throb, a miserable, rhythmic counterpoint to the engine's drone.

And Buzz… Buzz was the self-appointed "Director of Tactical and Communications Operations," a title he had invented for himself about ten minutes into their river journey. He was in the middle of the small, open deck, surrounded by the spoils of his shopping trip, a manic, sleep-deprived, and terrified king surveying his strange, new kingdom.

"Okay, boys, a little status report from the comms deck," he said, his voice a loud, rapid-fire monologue that was clearly designed to keep his own terror at bay. "The good news is we are officially off the grid. We are ghosts. We are whispers in the wind. The bad news is we are in the middle of a giant, muddy snake-filled ditch in a boat that I'm pretty sure is held together with duct tape and good intentions. But that's fine! It's fine! It adds to the production value! This is our third-act location change! It's gritty, it's real, it's beautiful!"

He kicked the large, hard-shell case that contained their salvation and their biggest headache. "The problem, as I see it," he continued, his voice dropping into a conspiratorial whisper, "is the clock. The big, scary, 'we're-all-gonna-die' clock. Davey, my man, my keeper of the sacred timeline, give me the bad news. What are we looking at?"

Dave shuffled out of the cabin, his movements stiff and pained. He held the laptop, its screen a dim, precious glow in the darkness. The green numbers were a stark, digital threat. 19:32:04.

"Nineteen and a half hours," Dave said, his voice flat. "And the laptop battery is at sixty-eight percent. We had to use it to get a look at the map."

"Nineteen hours!" Buzz declared, running a frantic hand through his hair. "That's nothing! That's a long nap! That's a Quentin Tarantino movie! We need to find a spot to pull over, to set up the magic internet dish, to phone home to the doomsday machine. We need to do it before lunch! This is a crisis!"

"We can't just pull over, Buzz," Skot's voice cut through the darkness from the stern. "Look around. It's a wall of jungle. There's no shore. We need to find a tributary, a small, hidden creek where we can get out of the main channel and drop anchor without being seen by a passing fishing boat."

"A tributary! Great! I love it!" Buzz said. "It sounds tactical! Find us a tributary, Skotty! A beautiful, secluded, high-speed-internet-capable tributary!"

They motored on through the night, the jungle a living, breathing entity on either side of them. The sounds were a constant, unnerving symphony. The deep, guttural roar of a howler monkey. The splash of something large and unseen sliding into the water from the muddy bank. The air was thick with the buzz of a million insects, their tiny bodies forming a halo around the boat's single dim light.

It was nearly dawn when Skot finally found what he was looking for. A narrow break in the jungle wall, a dark, black ribbon of still water that fed into the main river. He steered the Esperanza Perdida into the tributary, the engine's roar now muffled by the dense, overhanging canopy. After a hundred yards, the creek opened into a small, secluded lagoon, a perfect, hidden circle of water surrounded on all sides by the jungle. It was a secret place, a pocket of silence in the noisy green hell. Skot cut the engine.

The sudden, absolute silence was deafening.

"Okay," Buzz whispered, his voice a reverent hush. "This is it. The comms center. Let's go, let's go, let's go. We're losing precious seconds."

What followed was a scene of such profound, high-stakes absurdity that it bordered on performance art. Buzz, with the frantic energy of a man trying to assemble a barbecue in the middle of a hurricane, opened the hard-shell case and began to unpack the satellite dish. It was a sleek, futuristic-looking piece of equipment, a small, self-aligning dish connected by a thick cable to a modem and a power converter.

"Okay, so the instructions," he said, pulling out a small, folded piece of paper, "are in Mandarin. Which is a problem. A big problem. But that's fine! It's fine! How hard can it be? It's just... space stuff! Point it at the sky, plug it in, and we're surfing the web with Elon Musk, right? Right?"

It was not that easy. For the next hour, Buzz, with Dave and Skot offering useless, contradictory advice, struggled with the device. He had to connect it to the heavy marine battery he'd bought, a process that involved a shower of sparks and a string of curses that was truly epic in its creativity. He had to position the dish on the roof of the small cabin, where it had a clear view of the sky.

And all the while, Dave was calling out the time.

"Five hours left on the clock!"

"The laptop is at forty percent!"

"Come on, Buzz!"

"I'm working on it! I'm working on it!" Buzz shrieked, his hands a blur of cables and connectors. "This is not my skillset! My skillset is in the schmoozing arts! In the subtle dance of social lubrication! I'm not an IT guy! I'm a people person!"

Finally, after connecting and reconnecting the cables in every possible permutation, a small, green light on the modem flickered to life. A signal.

"Yes!" Buzz screamed, a cry of pure, triumphant relief. "We have contact! The eagle has landed! I am a god of technology!"

They scrambled into the cabin, a cramped, humid space that now smelled of sweat and terror. Skot powered on the laptop. The battery was at a terrifying 22%. Dave, his hands trembling, opened the browser and connected to the satellite's Wi-Fi network. The connection was slow, agonizingly slow, but it was there. He navigated to the dead man's switch website.

The clock read 00:54:12. Less than an hour.

The three of them huddled around the small screen, their faces illuminated by its glow. They typed in their three separate, ridiculously complex parts of the password, their fingers fumbling over each other.

The screen changed. The RESET CLOCK button appeared.

Dave clicked it. The screen refreshed. And the beautiful, life-affirming green numbers appeared.

23:59:59

A collective, shuddering sigh of relief filled the small cabin. They had done it. They had survived another cycle. They were safe, for another twenty-three hours and fifty-nine minutes.

They collapsed back, the tension draining out of them, leaving them weak and giddy.

"I think I'm going to have a heart attack," Dave said, his voice a weak whisper.

"A beautiful job, team," Buzz declared, his bravado returning in a rush. "A flawless execution of a high-risk, high-reward digital maneuver. I think we all deserve a raise. And a beer. Definitely a beer."

It was in that moment of triumphant, exhausted relief that they heard it.

It was a sound that did not belong in their secret, silent lagoon. It was a low, powerful thrum, coming from the direction of the main river. A sound that was getting steadily, rapidly louder.

The sound of a high-speed boat engine.

They looked at each other, the color draining from their faces. The relief was gone, replaced by a sudden, cold, and absolute terror.

They weren't alone on the river. The hunters were here. And they were closing in.

Chapter 52: Echoes on the Water

The relief was a beautiful, fragile thing, a soap bubble in a hurricane. For a glorious thirty seconds, they were victorious. They had beaten the clock, they had outsmarted the system, they were masters of their own digital destiny. They were legends.

And then they heard the sound.

It started as a low, deep thrum, a vibration that seemed to travel through the water itself and up into the hull of the Esperanza Perdida. It was a sound of power, of speed, of something modern and efficient and utterly out of place in this ancient, sluggish world of mud and mangroves.

"What was that?" Dave asked, his head snapping up, the brief, giddy relief on his face instantly replaced by a mask of cold, primal fear.

Skot was already moving. He lunged for the engine, his movements economical and swift, and killed it with a single, decisive twist of the key. The sputtering, rattling roar of their own motor died, and in the sudden, profound silence that followed, the new sound became terrifyingly clear. It was a high-speed boat engine, and it was on the main river, and it was getting closer.

"Oh, no," Buzz whimpered from the deck, his eyes wide with a terror that was almost comical in its intensity. "No, no, no, no, no. That's not supposed to happen! We're ghosts! We're whispers! We're off the grid! You can't be off the grid if the grid comes looking for you with a very large, very fast, and very angry-sounding boat! That's not in the rulebook!"

He scrambled into the small cabin, a frantic, panicked crab-walk. "Kill the lights! Kill all the lights!" he hissed, fumbling with the switch for the single, dim compass light, plunging them into an even deeper darkness.

The thrumming grew louder, a steady, predatory thump-thump-thump that was vibrating in their teeth, in their bones. It was the sound of a wolf approaching in the dark, and they were a small, ugly, and very lame sheep trapped in a watery pen.

"They can't see us in here," Dave whispered, though he didn't sound convinced. "The tributary is too narrow. The trees are too thick."

"They don't have to see us, Davey!" Buzz shot back, his voice a frantic, high-pitched whisper. "They're not using their eyes, they're using their ears! Our beautiful, magnificent rust bucket of a boat sounds like a heavy metal concert in a library! They probably heard us from five miles away! We just sent up a giant, sputtering, two-stroke smoke signal!"

Skot was at the bow of the boat, peering through the dense foliage toward the main river. He was the captain again, the man of action, his mind working with a cold, clear focus in the heart of the panic. "He's right," Skot said, his voice a low, grim murmur. "They'll slow down when they get to this creek. They'll check it out. We're sitting ducks right here."

He scanned the small, hidden lagoon. It was a perfect circle of black water, surrounded on all sides by the impenetrable wall of the jungle. But on the far side, it wasn't just a wall. It was a maze. A thick, tangled, and utterly menacing forest of mangrove trees, their roots like a thousand gnarled, skeletal arms plunging into the dark water. It was a place a boat was not meant to go.

"There," he said, pointing. "It's our only shot."

"The spooky tree-swamp?" Buzz squeaked. "The place where horror movies go to die? Skotty, that's not a hiding place, that's a tomb! There are probably snakes in there the size of school buses! And spiders! I have a thing about spiders! A very well-documented and legitimate thing!"

"You got a better idea?" Skot snapped back, his voice a low, urgent command. He was already at the stern, grabbing a long, wooden pole from the deck. "We can't start the engine. We have to pole our way in. Now. Move."

What followed was a scene of silent, desperate, and profoundly clumsy labor. Skot was in the stern, using the long pole to push them off the muddy bank and guide them toward the mangroves. Dave was at the bow, using a short, splintered boat hook to fend off low-hanging branches and submerged roots. And Buzz, after a brief, furious argument, was tasked with the most important job of all: being quiet. He was crouched in the middle of the deck, clutching the laptop to his chest, his eyes wide with terror, his mouth, for the first time in his life, clamped firmly shut.

The boat slid into the mangrove forest with a soft, scraping sound, the branches of the ancient trees closing in around them like the bars of a cage. It was a different world in here. The air was still and smelled of salt and decay. A thick, green canopy blotted out the last of the pre-dawn light, plunging them into a primal darkness. The only sounds were the gentle sloshing of the water, the creak of the boat, and the frantic, ragged sound of their own breathing.

They were just in time.

The thrumming on the main river grew to a deafening roar. They could see flashes of a powerful, white searchlight cutting through the trees. The high-speed boat had reached the mouth of their tributary. And it was slowing down.

They froze, every muscle in their bodies tensed. Skot had managed to wedge the Esperanza Perdida between the thick, gnarled roots of two massive mangrove trees, a position that offered almost complete cover from above. They were completely blind, able to do nothing but listen, and pray.

The powerful engine of the other boat idled down, its deep, throaty rumble a menacing purr just a hundred yards away. They could hear voices, muffled by the trees, speaking in a calm, professional, and unidentifiable language. They couldn't make out the words, but the tone was clear. They were searching.

A beam from the searchlight sliced through the canopy above them, a brilliant, white dagger that momentarily illuminated their hiding spot in a terrifying flash. They all flinched, ducking lower, convinced they had been seen. But the beam moved on, continuing its slow, methodical sweep.

The minutes stretched into an eternity. They sat there, three men in a leaky fishing boat, holding their breath, while a team of professional hunters prowled just outside their hiding place. It was the most intense, most terrifying silence of their lives.

And then, just as suddenly as it had arrived, the powerful engine roared back to life. The thrumming grew louder, then began to recede as the boat picked up speed and continued its journey up the main river.

They waited, not daring to move, for a full ten minutes after the sound had completely faded, leaving behind only the natural, chirping silence of the waking jungle.

They were safe. They had survived.

Buzz was the first to let out his breath, a long, shuddering, whistling sound. "Okay," he whispered, his voice trembling. "Okay. I think I'm going to need a new pair of shorts. A whole new wardrobe, actually. We should probably just burn these clothes. For sanitary and psychological reasons."

But Dave wasn't listening. He was staring at the satellite dish, which was still sitting on the roof of the small cabin, a silent, futuristic-looking mushroom in the middle of this ancient, primeval forest. The little green light, the one that had been their salvation an hour ago, was still blinking. The little green light that was connected to a global network of satellites. The little green light that was, at this very moment, sending and receiving data.

A new, cold, and terrible thought began to form in his mind. The accountant, the man who understood systems and patterns, was putting the pieces together.

"That was too close," he said, his voice a low, thoughtful murmur. "That wasn't a random patrol. They knew we were here. Or they knew we were somewhere in this sector."

"What are you talking about?" Buzz asked. "We're ghosts! We're invisible!"

"No, we're not," Dave said, his eyes still locked on the blinking green light. He looked at Skot, then at Buzz, and the dawning horror on his face was more terrifying than the sound of the approaching boat had been.

"Don't you see?" he said, his voice a quiet whisper of pure, dawning dread. "How do you think a satellite dish works? It doesn't just receive a signal. To get a connection, it has to send one. It has to tell the satellite where it is. It's a handshake."

He pointed a trembling finger at the dish. "That thing," he said, his voice cracking. "That beautiful, magical, life-saving thing… it's a beacon. It's a damn tracking device. Every time we turn it on to save our lives, we are sending up a giant, digital flare that tells the hunters exactly where in the world we are."

The realization settled over the small boat, a new and infinitely more terrible silence than any that had come before. Their lifeline was a leash. Their brilliant, last-ditch plan was the very weapon being used against them. They weren't just being hunted anymore. They were actively, unknowingly, leading the hunters right to their door. And the clock was already ticking down to the next time they would have to turn it on.

Chapter 53: The Beacon

The realization, once spoken, was a poison. It seeped into the humid air of the mangrove forest, more toxic and paralyzing than any snake venom. Dave's words hung in the small, cramped cabin of the Esperanza Perdida, a perfect, elegant, and utterly devastating summary of their own fatal stupidity. The satellite dish. Their brilliant, high-tech, last-ditch lifeline. It was a beacon. It was a homing device. And they had just fired it up like a giant, digital flare in the middle of a global game of hide-and-seek.

For a long moment, nobody moved. They were three statues in a tableau of dawning, absolute horror. Skot was frozen at the bow, his hands still gripping the wooden pole. Dave stood in the doorway of the cabin, his face a pale, ghostly mask in the pre-dawn gloom. And Buzz... Buzz looked like a man who had just been told that his winning lottery ticket was, in fact, a bill for a billion dollars.

He slowly, with the deliberate care of a man handling a live explosive, reached up and touched the satellite dish on the cabin roof. He traced the smooth, futuristic curve of its surface.

"A beacon?" he whispered, the words a puff of air, his voice completely stripped of its usual booming, manic energy. "A beacon. Of course it's a beacon. It's a two-way street. You can't just listen to space, you have to talk back to it. It's a handshake. A digital... handshake." He looked at his own hands as if they had personally betrayed him.

And then the meltdown began.

It started as a low, guttural groan and quickly escalated into a full-blown, classic monologue of pure, uncut, self-loathing panic.

"I'm an idiot!" he shrieked, his voice a frantic, cracking thing that sent a flock of unseen birds scattering from the canopy above. "An absolute, world-class, hall-of-fame-level idiot! I thought I was a ghost! A whisper! A beautiful, tactical phantom slipping through the digital cracks! It turns out I'm a foghorn! A big, loud, obnoxious, 'hey-the-miracle-is-over-here-come-and-get-it' foghorn! I didn't just give them our location; I sent them a damn engraved invitation with an RSVP and a plus-one! This isn't a strategic repositioning; it's a catastrophic, brand-ending, we're all gonna die in a swamp level screwup!"

He was pacing the small, cluttered deck of the boat, a caged, terrified animal. "They weren't just hunting us! They were following the breadcrumbs! And I'm the idiot who was leaving a trail of gourmet, artisanal, gluten-free breadcrumbs with a big, flashing neon sign that said 'Free Miracles This Way!' This is a disaster! A beautiful, epic, career-ending disaster!"

"Get a grip, Buzz," Skot said, his voice a low, steady growl. He had poled the boat deeper into the mangroves, the thick, leafy branches now forming a nearly solid roof over their heads. He was all business, his mind already moving past the mistake and onto the next, more pressing problem. "Panicking isn't going to help. They know our rough position. That's a fact. What do we do now?"

"What do we do now?" Buzz squeaked, his voice a full octave higher than usual. "I'll tell you what we do! We pray! We find a local religion, and we convert! Immediately! I don't care what it is! Snake gods, tree gods, moss gods, I am open to any and all theological options right now!"

"The boat is a trap," Dave said, his voice quiet but clear. He had moved past the initial shock and into a state of cold, pragmatic analysis. The new Dave, the one who had been forged in the jungle, was back in control. "They know we're on this river. They'll set up a blockade downstream, and they'll have patrols sweeping upstream. We stay on the water, we're finished. It's a dead end."

His words, calm and logical, finally seemed to penetrate Buzz's hysterical fog. Buzz stopped pacing and looked at him, his mouth agape. "So what are you saying? We just… get out and walk?"

"That's exactly what I'm saying," Dave replied, his gaze firm.

The new plan was not a plan at all; it was a forced march, a desperate, last-ditch sprint into the green hell they had only just escaped. The river was no longer their highway; it was a deathtrap. Their only option was the jungle. They had to abandon the boat and make their way to Skot's magical dot on the map on foot.

The next hour was a scene of grim, determined preparation. The sun was rising, its first, weak rays filtering through the dense canopy, painting the dark water in shifting patterns of green and gold. They were no longer outfitting a leisurely river trip; they were packing for a forced march through hostile territory.

They laid out their supplies on the deck. The machetes. The water purifier. The medical kit. The tarps and the rope. Buzz's ridiculously expensive cooler, which now seemed like a relic from a different, stupider civilization. And, of course, the two most important, and most cumbersome, pieces of equipment: the laptop, and the satellite dish with its heavy marine battery.

"We have to take it with us," Dave said, pointing to the dish. "It's the only way to reset the clock. It's our shield and our curse, all in one."

The sheer, brutal weight of their new reality was crushing. They had to haul a delicate, 50-pound piece of electronic equipment through a hundred miles of unforgiving jungle, all while being hunted by a team of professionals.

They began to load the backpacks Buzz had bought. The mood was somber, the silence broken only by the rustle of gear and the constant, buzzing hum of the insects. They were no longer a team of miraculous, superhuman survivors. They were just three tired, aching men, their bodies a constant, painful reminder of the Potion they no longer had.

It was Buzz who made the final, crucial contribution. He looked at the dozen full cans of gasoline they had loaded onto the boat, the fuel that was supposed to take them up the river.

"We can't just leave those," he said, a new, dangerous glint in his eye. "If they find the boat, they'll know we went on foot."

"So we dump them in the river?" Skot asked.

"No," Buzz said, a slow, wicked grin spreading across his face. The promoter was gone, replaced by a budding, amateur demolitions expert. "No, we don't dump them. We use them. We create one last, big, beautiful, and deeply confusing distraction."

The final act was one of calculated, desperate sabotage. They took four of the full gasoline cans and wedged them in the small cabin of the Esperanza Perdida. Buzz, using a length of rope and a strip of oil-soaked rag, fashioned a crude, time-delayed fuse. It was a stupid, dangerous, movie-inspired idea, and it was perfect.

They loaded the rest of the fuel cans, the laptop, the satellite dish, and all their other gear into their backpacks, the weight a punishing, immediate reality. They were ready.

Skot took his machete and, with a few, powerful, and deeply reluctant swings, punctured the hull of the boat below the waterline. The sound of the metal giving way was a painful, final sound. The muddy river water began to trickle, then gush, into the hold. Their beautiful, stupid, hopeful little boat was dying.

With a final, coordinated heave, they pushed the Esperanza Perdida out of the mangroves and back into the center of the small, secluded lagoon. Buzz lit the fuse. It caught, a small, sputtering flame.

"Go!" he yelled.

They didn't wait to watch. They turned and scrambled onto the muddy bank, plunging into the thick, waiting jungle. They didn't look back.

They were about a hundred yards in, the sounds of their own frantic, crashing progress a roar in their ears, when they heard it. A low, dull whoomp that was more of a feeling than a sound, a pressure wave that vibrated through the damp earth and the thick, humid air. It was followed a second later by the sound of a secondary, much larger explosion, a sharp, cracking roar that sent a shockwave of panicked birds screaming up from the canopy.

They stopped, turning to look back in the direction they had come. Through the thick, green latticework of the trees, they could see a plume of thick, black, oily smoke rising into the clear, morning sky. It was a funeral pyre. It was a smoke signal. It was a final, defiant, and deeply desperate middle finger to the people who were hunting them.

They stood on the muddy bank of the jungle, weighed down by impossibly heavy packs, and looked at the smoke. Their last sanctuary was gone. Their last plan was in ashes. All they had left was a map, a dying laptop, a 20-hour clock, and a hundred miles of unforgiving wilderness between them and their goal.

The final, desperate sprint had begun.

Chapter 54: The Weight of the World

The smoke from the burning Esperanza Perdida was a thick, black, oily finger pointing directly at them from the sky. It was a funeral pyre, a smoke signal, and a formal declaration of war all rolled into one. For a moment, they just stood there, a hundred yards into the jungle, and watched their last, best, and most idiotic plan go up in flames. The sound of the explosion, a deep, satisfying whoomp, was the starting gun for a race they were already losing.

"Well," Buzz panted, his hands on his knees, his face a pale, sweaty mask of terror. "On the plus side, that was a truly spectacular special effect. The production value was top-notch. On the negative side, we just sent up a giant, flaming, 'we-are-right-here' arrow for the guys who are, and I cannot stress this enough, trying to kill us."

"Move," was all Skot said. His voice was a low, hard growl. He turned his back on the smoke and plunged deeper into the suffocating green.

And then, the pain began.

It wasn't the slow, creeping return of their old aches and pains. This was a new, more brutal, and immediate agony. The backpacks were instruments of pure, medieval torture. Dave's, weighed down with the heavy, awkward satellite dish and its marine battery, felt like it was actively trying to tear his spine from his body. Every step was a fresh, searing jolt of pain in his lower back, a grinding protest from his knee. He was no longer a man with a bad back; he was a bad back that happened to have a man attached to it.

Skot's pack was loaded with the fuel cans, a dead, sloshing weight that threw his balance off with every step and pulled at his damaged shoulder with a merciless, grinding insistence. The miracle of the Potion was a distant, beautiful memory. This was the consequence. This was the bill.

But it was Buzz who was truly in hell. He was a man whose primary form of physical exertion was the walk from a valet stand to a restaurant hostess. He was now being asked to carry fifty pounds of survival gear through a sweltering, hostile jungle. His pack, filled with the food, the tarps, and the ridiculously heavy cooler he had insisted on bringing, was a monument to his own poor life choices.

"Guys," he wheezed, not ten minutes into the march, his face already a blotchy, alarming shade of crimson. "We need to talk about the… the strategic pacing of this… this tactical advance. I'm thinking maybe a more… leisurely… approach might be better for morale. You know? A little siesta? A water break? Maybe a light snack?"

"We stop, we die, Buzz," Skot grunted from the front, not even breaking his stride. He was the leader now, the reluctant captain of their miserable, three-man platoon. He was the only one with a map, both on the paper in his pocket and in his head. He moved with a grim, relentless purpose, his machete a blur as he hacked at the thick, grasping vines that blocked their path.

The first few hours were a descent into a special kind of misery. The jungle was not a quiet, beautiful place. It was a loud, aggressive, and deeply personal enemy. A cloud of buzzing, biting insects formed a personal halo around each of them. The mud was a greedy, sucking thing that tried to pull their boots off with every step. The air was so thick and humid, it felt like they were breathing hot soup.

And Buzz complained. He complained with a creativity and a stamina that was, in its own way, almost as impressive as their own impossible survival.

"I have bugs in places I didn't even know I had places!" he yelled, swatting at the back of his own neck. "This is a design flaw! The human body! We should have come with a bug zapper! And this humidity! My shirt isn't just wet, it's a whole new state of matter! It's like a liquid I'm wearing! This is not what I signed up for!"

"You didn't sign up for anything, Buzz!" Dave shot back, his own patience worn to a threadbare nub by the pain and the exertion. "You just sort of... showed up!"

"And I'm regretting that decision with every single, agonizing, sweat-drenched step!"

By midday, they were on the verge of collapse. They had covered maybe five miles, a pathetic distance that had cost them an ocean of sweat and a universe of pain. They found a small, slightly-less-miserable patch of ground and collapsed, their packs falling from their shoulders with a series of heavy, final-sounding thuds.

They were a pitiful sight. Three broken, middle-aged men, drenched in sweat, covered in mud and insect bites. But they were still moving. And the clock was still ticking.

Dave pulled out the laptop. The battery was at a respectable ninety-eight percent, having been charged in the hotel. But the dead man's switch clock was now the enemy. 14:02:45.

"We're not going to make it," Dave said, his voice a flat, defeated statement of fact. "There's no way. We can't keep this pace. And we still have to stop for an hour to set up the dish and reset the clock before this time tomorrow. We'll be lucky to cover ten miles a day. We're not going to make it to the cenote in time."

The brutal, simple math of their situation settled over them, a new and more terrible kind of exhaustion. They were in a race they had already lost.

It was in this moment of rock-bottom despair that Skot, who had been studying his map with a fierce, quiet intensity, looked up. "He's right," he said. "We can't make it. Not like this."

He pointed at their backpacks. "We're carrying too much weight. We're moving too slow. We're trying to be a self-sufficient expedition. But we're not an expedition. We're prey. And prey has to run fast." He looked at Buzz, his expression grim. "The cooler has to go."

"The cooler?" Buzz shrieked, his voice cracking with a genuine, heartfelt pain. "You want to get rid of the cooler? Skotty, that's not just a cooler, that's a symbol! It's a symbol of hope! It's a symbol of the civilization we're fighting to get back to! It's a symbol of cold, refreshing, morale-boosting beer!"

"It's fifty pounds of dead weight, Buzz," Skot said, his voice cold and hard. "And so is most of this other stuff. The extra tarps. Half the food. We're not planning a camping trip. We're in a race. We take what is absolutely essential to survive the next forty-eight hours, and we ditch the rest."

The argument was brief and brutal. In the end, logic, and the raw terror of their situation, won out. They performed a ruthless triage on their own supplies. The cooler was the first to go, a bright blue monument to a luxury they could no longer afford. They jettisoned half the food, extra clothes, anything that wasn't absolutely critical to the mission: reset the clock, find the grotto.

They repacked, their new, lighter packs a small, blessed relief. They were about to set off again when they heard it. Faint, but unmistakable. The distant, rhythmic thump-thump-thump of a helicopter.

They froze, their blood turning to ice. They scrambled for cover under the dense canopy of a giant fig tree, their hearts pounding in their chests. The sound grew louder, a mechanical heartbeat in the jungle's wild symphony. It was coming from the direction of the river. From the smoke.

The helicopter, a sleek, dark green machine with the markings of the Colombian military, appeared over the treetops. It wasn't looking for them. It was circling the site of their burning boat, a vulture investigating a kill. They were out of sight, but the message was clear. The hunters knew where they had been. And they knew the direction they were heading. The net was closing.

They waited until the sound of the helicopter had completely faded, leaving behind only an even more profound sense of dread.

"Okay," Buzz whispered, his face pale, all the jokes gone. "New, new plan. We are officially in panic mode. And I, for one, am leaning into it. We need to move. Now. And we need to be a lot faster."

He looked at his two friends, at the pain etched on their faces, at the grim resolve in their eyes. The party animal was gone. The fixer was gone. All that was left was a man who was terrified of dying in a jungle with two guys who were the only real thing in his life.

"So here's what we do," he said, his voice a low, desperate growl. "We forget the pain. We forget the bugs. We forget everything except the clock and the dot on that map. And we run. We run like our lives depend on it. Because for the first time in my very pampered, very ridiculous life, I'm pretty sure they actually do."

Chapter 55: The Jaguar's Head

The jungle did not get easier. It was a lie that adventurers told themselves, a comforting fiction that the human body would adapt, that the mind would harden. The jungle did not allow for adaptation. It was a relentless, grinding force that simply wore you down, one insect bite, one thorny vine, one mud-filled boot at a time. After three days of a forced, panicked march, they were no longer just tired; they were being systematically dismantled.

Their bodies were a roadmap of misery. Every muscle ached with a deep, liquid fire. Their feet were a raw, blistered mess. They were covered in a latticework of angry red insect bites and festering scratches. The Potion's residual miracle was a distant, beautiful memory. They were just men now, fragile and breaking.

The psychological toll was worse. They moved in a state of paranoid, exhausted silence, the only sounds the wet suck of their boots in the mud and their own ragged, labored breathing. The jungle was no longer just a place; it was a predator, a living, breathing entity whose sole purpose was to consume them. Every shadow was a threat. Every rustle in the undergrowth was an enemy.

And through it all, there was the clock. The tyrant. The digital god to whom they were now slaves.

Their final reset of the dead man's switch was an act of pure, desperate faith. They found a small, slightly-less-miserable clearing as dusk began to fall on their third day. The laptop battery was at a terrifying 5%. They had one shot at this.

"Okay, boys, last dance," Buzz whispered, his voice a raw, cracked thing that bore no resemblance to his usual booming delivery. The jungle had stripped him of his bravado, leaving behind a core of pure, chattering terror. "Let's just... you know... not screw this up. Because I, for one, do not want the last thing I ever see to be the inside of a crocodile's mouth. It's a bad look. It's off-brand."

They worked with the frantic, fumbling energy of a bomb disposal team that has forgotten its training. Skot set up the satellite dish, his hands shaking with exhaustion. Dave booted up the laptop, his heart pounding with every slow, agonizing second it took for the operating system to load. They connected to the network, the signal weak and intermittent under the thick canopy.

The clock on the switch read 00:12:45.

They typed in their codes, their fingers slipping on the keys. They hit 'RESET'. The screen spun, the connection flickered, and for a heart-stopping, eternal second, nothing happened. Then, the screen refreshed. 23:59:59.

A collective, shuddering sigh of relief filled the small clearing. They had bought themselves another day. But the cost was immense. The moment the clock was reset, Dave shut the laptop down. The battery was at 1%. It was done. Their digital shield was now a dead piece of plastic and silicon. From this moment forward, they were truly on their own. They were ghosts, with no way to tell the world if they were alive or dead.

"So that's it, then," Dave said into the gathering gloom. "We just... hope we make it before the next clock runs out?"

"No," Skot said, his voice quiet but infused with a new, strange energy. He was staring past them, through the trees, his eyes fixed on something they couldn't see. "We're already there."

He had been tracking their progress on the topographical map with a single-minded, almost religious focus. He was no longer just navigating; he was communing with the landscape, his artist's mind seeing the shapes, the patterns, the hidden logic of the terrain.

"The ridge," he whispered, his voice filled with a quiet, reverent awe. "We've been following this ridge for the last two days. The map says it should be right... here."

He pushed his way through a final, thick curtain of vines, and the world opened up. The dense, claustrophobic jungle suddenly gave way to a rocky, windswept promontory. They had climbed higher than they realized, and now, for the first time in days, they could see.

The view was breathtaking. A vast, rolling ocean of green jungle stretched out before them, all the way to the distant, shimmering line of the Caribbean Sea. But they weren't looking at the ocean. They were looking at the mountain peak to the west, the one that now dominated the horizon.

And there it was.

It was unmistakable. A massive, natural rock formation on the side of the peak, carved by a million years of wind and rain into a shape that was so perfectly, uncannily like the head of a stalking jaguar that it felt like a deliberate sign, a piece of ancient, divine cartography.

"The Jaguar's Head," Skot breathed.

They had found it. Their impossible, half-remembered landmark. It was real. A surge of pure, unadulterated hope, an emotion so foreign and powerful it was almost painful, washed over them.

"You did it, Skotty," Buzz whispered, a single, happy tear tracing a path through the grime on his cheek. "You magnificent, crazy son of a bitch, you actually did it."

The rest of the journey was a blur, fueled by a fresh, last-ditch surge of adrenaline. The landmark was their guide, their North Star. They scrambled down the other side of the ridge, their movements no longer a weary, shuffling trudge, but a frantic, forward-moving fall. They were no longer just wandering; they were homing in.

After another hour of brutal, punishing descent, they found it. A small, flat, unassuming patch of green nestled between two low hills, just as Skot had predicted. They pushed their way through a final wall of broad, waxy leaves and stepped into a clearing.

And there it was.

The cenote. A perfect, circular pool of crystal-clear water, the walls draped in vines and moss. It was the place from their memories, the gateway from their nightmare. They had made it. They were back.

For a moment, they just stood at the edge, their chests heaving, their bodies screaming, a strange, triumphant, and deeply broken trio. They had walked through hell and had come out the other side.

"We did it," Dave said, his voice cracking with an emotion he couldn't name. He was laughing, a raw, unhinged sound of pure relief. "We actually did it."

It was in this moment of pure, unguarded, victorious joy that they heard the sound.

It wasn't a jungle sound. It wasn't the screech of a monkey or the buzz of an insect. It was a clean, sharp, and utterly out-of-place sound.

Click.

The sound of a rifle's safety being disengaged.

They all froze, the laughter dying in their throats. They turned slowly, their eyes scanning the dense, shadowy wall of trees on the other side of the cenote.

And then she stepped out.

Eva Rostova emerged from the shadows as if she were a part of them. She was dressed in practical, dark gray tactical gear, her face a mask of calm, professional neutrality. She was not alone. Two other figures, similarly dressed, armed with sleek, black carbines, emerged on either side of her, their movements silent and economical. They fanned out, creating a perfect, inescapable kill zone.

Eva was holding a small, suppressed pistol, and it was aimed not at them, but at a spot on the ground a few feet in front of them. She wasn't threatening to kill them. She was just announcing, with a chilling, absolute certainty, that she could.

"Good morning, gentlemen," she said, her voice a calm, placid murmur that carried easily across the quiet clearing. It was the same voice they had heard on the phone, the sterile, unemotional voice of their own personal ghost. "I must commend you. Your wilderness survival skills are… surprisingly adequate."

Dave stared at her, his mind a blank, white-hot sheet of pure, uncomprehending terror. Skot instinctively moved in front of him, a futile, protective gesture.

But it was Buzz who finally found his voice. The blood had drained from his face, leaving it a pasty, grayish color. The triumphant hero of a moment ago was gone, replaced by a man who was looking at the physical embodiment of all his worst fears.

"How?" he squeaked, the single word a pathetic puff of air. "How did you find us?"

Eva allowed herself a small, almost imperceptible smile. It was the smile of a master chess player explaining the final, elegant move to a novice.

"You were never lost, Mr. Walker," she said, her voice as cool and clear as the cenote water. "Not to us." She gestured to the sky, a small, almost casual wave of her hand. "The drone has been tracking your heat signatures for the past thirty-six hours. We weren't hunting you. We were simply waiting for you to arrive at your destination."

The final, brutal truth of their situation crashed down on them like the avalanche that began their ordeal. The race hadn't been a race at all. It had been a carefully observed procession, a long, painful, and ultimately futile march into a cage that had been waiting for them all along.

"Now," Eva said, her voice losing its conversational tone and taking on a new, hard, and absolute edge. "The game is over. My employer is a very impatient man. You are going to lead us to the source. And you are going to do it now."

Chapter 56: The Standoff

The silence in the clearing was a living thing, a thick, heavy blanket woven from the threads of their own terror. The three men stood frozen, a tableau of captured prey, their brief, triumphant joy now a bitter, mocking memory. Eva Rostova stood on the opposite side of the cenote, a vision of calm, lethal efficiency. Her two operatives were ghosts, their black carbines held in a low, ready position, their movements so minimal they seemed to be a part of the jungle itself.

"I'm glad we understand each other," Eva said, her voice a placid, conversational murmur that was somehow more terrifying than a shout. "This doesn't have to be unpleasant. My employer is a man who values efficiency above all else. You have something he wants. You will give it to him. It's a simple transaction."

Dave, his mind a frantic, screaming engine of pure, protective rage, found his voice first. "Stay the hell away from my family," he growled, taking a half-step forward, a move that caused the two operatives to raise their weapons a fraction of an inch.

"Mr. Bennett," Eva said, her tone still maddeningly calm. "Your family is perfectly safe. For now. They are a point of leverage, not a target. Their continued well-being is entirely contingent upon your cooperation. So let's cooperate, shall we?" She gestured with her pistol toward the crystal-clear water of the cenote. "The source. The Grotto, as you call it. You're going to take us there. Now."

Skot let out a short, bitter, humorless laugh. "You think it's that easy? You think it's a walk in the park? You think there's a secret door with a welcome mat?" He pointed a trembling finger at the water. "The only way back to that place is through a two-hundred-foot, pitch-black, underwater tunnel. A tunnel we barely survived coming out of, with the current at our backs and a miracle in our veins. Going back in? Against the current? In our condition? That's not a journey. It's a suicide mission. We'd drown before we got fifty feet."

Eva's placid expression didn't flicker, but a new, cold light entered her eyes. She saw their exhaustion, their pain. But she interpreted it as a negotiation tactic. A lie.

"I appreciate your attempt at subterfuge, Mr. Larson," she said. "But we are not fools. We have a sample of the Potion. We have a preliminary analysis. We know what it does. You are not two broken-down men. You are... enhanced. Now, stop wasting my time."

"She thinks we're still full of the magic juice!" Buzz suddenly shrieked, his voice a high-pitched squeak of pure, unadulterated terror. He had been a silent, trembling statue until now, but the direct threat seemed to have rebooted his system into its default state: frantic, high-speed babbling. "She doesn't get it! The tank is empty! The miracle has left the building! We're running on fumes, lady! Fumes and a very questionable diet of raw mussels and protein bars! We're not superhuman anymore, we're just... super-tired! And super-screwed!"

Eva ignored him. Her gaze was locked on Dave, the one she had correctly identified as the emotional weak point. She raised the small, encrypted satellite phone she held in her other hand.

"Perhaps you require a more tangible incentive," she said, her voice dropping a half-octave. She dialed a number. "I have a team outside your home, Mr. Bennett. A very professional, very quiet team. All I have to do is speak a single word into this phone, and they will enter your house. They will not harm your family. Not initially. They will simply… wait with them. Until you see reason."

This was it. The final, brutal move. Dave felt the world tilt on its axis. He could see Jen's face, her confusion turning to terror. He could see his children, their happy, innocent world shattered by the intrusion of these quiet, efficient monsters. He broke.

"Okay!" he yelled, his voice a raw, ragged cry of surrender. "Okay, you win! We'll do it! We'll try! Just… leave them alone. Please."

"No, Dave, don't!" Skot yelled, grabbing his arm. "We can't! We'll die!"

"It doesn't matter!" Dave screamed back, his face a mess of tears and fury. "Don't you get it? Nothing matters but them!"

It was a perfect, elegant checkmate. Eva had won.

But she hadn't accounted for the chaos factor. She hadn't accounted for Buzz.

"Wait!" Buzz shrieked, stumbling forward, his hands held up in a gesture of frantic surrender. "Wait, wait, wait! You can't kill us! You don't understand! We're the only ones who can reset the clock! The big one! The digital one! The whole world will know! It's mutually assured destruction, baby! It's the nuke! You kill us, you get a face full of nuke! You think your boss wants his face on the front page of The New York Times next to a picture of a magic mermaid? That's bad for business! That's a real hit to the stock price!"

Eva just stared at him, her expression a mixture of confusion and contempt. But there was a flicker of something else in her eyes. A flicker of professional curiosity. The digital failsafe was a variable she hadn't fully accounted for. It was the one part of their amateurish plan that was genuinely sophisticated. She knew the threat was credible. She couldn't kill them. But that didn't mean she couldn't take them.

"Your digital ghost will not protect you forever, Mr. Walker," she said, her voice a low, cold purr. "A twenty-four-hour clock is a very long time. Long enough for a professional to extract a password. Or a location." Her plan shifted in that instant. She gestured with her pistol to her two operatives. "Sedate them. All of them. We're taking them with us."

The two men began to move forward, their carbines raised, the barrels now aimed directly at them. This was the end. Capture. Torture. A quiet, anonymous disappearance from the face of the earth.

It was in this moment, with the intruders closing in and the last of their hope evaporating, that Skot, the artist, the dreamer, the man who had been sketching the impossible shape from the water over and over again, made a final, desperate, and completely insane gamble. He had nothing left to lose.

He looked at the calm, crystal-clear water of the cenote. He thought of the journal. The spring was a demon. He thought of the pirate, Calico Jack, and the legend Buzz had read to them. A legend of a crew that had vanished, of ghosts trapped in the jungle. He thought of the shape. The silent, watching shape in the glowing water.

And he yelled.

He yelled not at Eva, not at her men, but at the water itself. He screamed into the quiet clearing, his voice a raw, primal roar of pure, desperate faith.

"IS THIS WHAT YOU WANT?" he shrieked, his voice cracking. "YOU SHOWED YOURSELF TO US! ARE YOU JUST GOING TO LET THEM TAKE IT?"

It was the cry of a madman. Eva's operatives paused, a flicker of confusion in their eyes. Buzz and Dave just stared at Skot as if he had lost his mind.

"What are you doing?" Dave whispered, aghast.

"I don't know," Skot breathed, his eyes locked on the placid surface of the cenote.

For a moment, nothing happened. The jungle was silent. The only sound was the faint, mocking chirp of a bird somewhere high in the canopy. Eva let out a small, contemptuous sigh. The subjects were cracking under the pressure. It was predictable.

And then, the water changed.

It wasn't a big change. It was subtle. A low, resonant hum, a vibration that seemed to come from the very depths of the earth, vibrated up through the rock and into the soles of their feet. The surface of the cenote, which had been as smooth as glass, began to shimmer, as if a giant tuning fork had been struck in the depths below.

And then, a light.

From the deepest part of the pool, a faint, turquoise glow began to pulse. It was the light they had seen in the grotto. The light of the Potion. But it was here. In this cenote. The miracle wasn't just in the grotto; it was connected. It was the same system.

Eva and her men froze, their professional cool finally shattering in the face of the impossible. They stared at the glowing water, their weapons momentarily forgotten.

The light grew stronger, a pulsating, hypnotic beat. And with it, the hum intensified, a low, powerful thrum that was felt more than heard. It was the sound of something ancient, something powerful, and something that was waking up.

It was the only chance they would get.

"NOW!" Skot roared.

He didn't run from the hunters. He ran toward the miracle. He launched himself off the rock ledge and into the glowing water of the cenote.

Dave, without a second's hesitation, followed him.

Buzz, after a single, heart-stopping moment of pure, abject terror, looked at the armed, stunned professionals behind him, then at his two friends splashing into a pool of glowing, magical mystery water. He let out a high-pitched shriek that was half-scream, half-war cry.

"I'M WITH THE LUNATICS!" he yelled, and he grabbed the laptop, clutched it to his chest, and took a running, clumsy, and completely unathletic leap into the abyss.

They hit the water, the strange, glowing, and impossibly powerful liquid closing over their heads, a final, desperate baptism in the heart of the jungle. They were plunging back into the world that had started it all, not as explorers, but as refugees, seeking sanctuary in the one place on earth their enemies would never, ever dare to follow.

Chapter 57: The Heart of the Siren

The world dissolved into a silent, brilliant, turquoise explosion. The moment Dave plunged into the glowing water of the cenote, the pain vanished. It wasn't a slow fade; it was an instantaneous, digital deletion. The fire in his back, the grinding ache in his knee, the deep, cellular exhaustion that had been his constant companion for days—it was all just gone, erased by the cool, energizing embrace of the Potion. He felt a surge of pure, clean power, a wave of impossible vitality that was even more potent than what he had experienced in the grotto. This was not a diluted sample; this was the source code.

He opened his eyes. Underwater, the world was a cathedral of light. The turquoise glow seemed to emanate not from the bottom of the pool, but from the water itself, every molecule a tiny, shimmering star. He saw Skot a few feet away, his movements no longer the stiff, pained gestures of a broken man, but the fluid, graceful strokes of a powerful swimmer. He saw Buzz, his eyes wide with a mixture of terror and pure, dumbfounded awe, dog-paddling with a clumsy but newfound strength, the precious laptop still clutched to his chest. They had been recharged. The miracle was back online.

On the ledge above, the world was in chaos. Eva Rostova, for the first time in her meticulously controlled professional life, was completely and utterly stunned. She stared at the glowing, pulsating water, her mind, a machine built on logic and predictability, struggling to process the impossible data flooding her senses. Her two operatives were equally frozen, their weapons momentarily forgotten, their faces a mask of disbelief.

It was a standoff between the rational and the impossible. And it was Skot who broke the spell.

He surfaced, his head breaking the shimmering, glowing water, and looked at Dave and Buzz. "The tunnel!" he yelled, his voice echoing in the clearing. "It's the only way!"

His words jolted Eva from her stupor. The professional, the hunter, reasserted control. The asset was not the men; it was the water. And the men were swimming in it.

"After them!" she commanded, her voice a sharp, cutting bark that sliced through the awe. "Do not let them get away! The subjects are secondary! Secure the source!"

But her men hesitated. They were professional soldiers, trained for every conceivable combat scenario. But their training manual had no chapter on "engaging with a glowing, possibly sentient, supernatural body of water."

As Skot and Dave took a deep, final breath and kicked down toward the dark, waiting mouth of the tunnel at the bottom of the cenote, Eva's lead operative took a tentative step into the water. The moment his boot touched the surface, the low, resonant hum that had been vibrating through the ground intensified, rising in pitch to a deep, guttural, and distinctly angry thrum. The water around his boot seemed to recoil, to shimmer with a new, agitated energy.

It was enough to make him stop. That single, half-second of hesitation was all the head start they needed.

Skot, Dave, and Buzz plunged into the tunnel, a familiar, terrifying darkness that now felt like a sanctuary. This was their world. They knew its contours, its dangers. They were no longer prey fleeing into the unknown; they were natives, returning to their home turf.

Behind them, Eva, her face a mask of pure, cold fury at her team's insubordination, made a decision. She wouldn't be defeated by superstition. She drew her sidearm and fired two, sharp, clinical shots into the water near her operative's feet. It wasn't a threat; it was a command.

The message was received. The two operatives, their fear of their commander outweighing their fear of the unknown, plunged into the glowing water and swam for the tunnel in hot pursuit.

The journey back through the tunnel was a disorienting, high-speed flight. They were swimming against the current now, but their newly restored, Potion-fueled bodies were machines. They kicked with a strength and an endurance that was utterly inhuman. Buzz, surprisingly, was keeping up, the terror of being captured a more powerful motivator than any personal trainer could ever be.

They were halfway through the dark, winding passage when the hunters caught up. They saw the beams of their powerful, military-grade dive lights cutting through the water behind them, two sharp, probing cones of white that were closing the distance with an alarming speed.

It was then that the tunnel itself seemed to come alive. The low, resonant hum they had felt in the cenote was now a physical, vibrating force. The water around them grew colder, the current stronger, more chaotic. Skot, in the lead, felt a strange, primal sense of being watched, a feeling that had nothing to in with the men behind them.

He glanced over his shoulder. The hunters' lights were just a few yards back. And then he saw it.

It wasn't a blurry shape this time. It wasn't a trick of the light. For a single, heart-stopping, impossible second, the beam of one of the hunter's lights illuminated it. A form, massive and ancient, seemed to uncoil from the very rock of the tunnel wall. It wasn't a mermaid. It wasn't a monster. It was something older, stranger. A flash of pale, smooth skin, a suggestion of a long, serpentine body, and a single, large, luminous eye, like a pearl in the darkness, that regarded the intruders with a look of cold, intelligent, and deeply alien indifference.

The Guardian. It was real.

The sight was so shocking, so fundamentally reality-breaking, that Skot almost stopped swimming. The hunters saw it too. They faltered, their steady, professional pursuit breaking in an instant of pure, primal terror.

The Guardian did not attack. It acted. A powerful, invisible wave of force, a blast of pure kinetic energy, erupted from the wall of the tunnel. It wasn't an attack on them; it was an attack on the water itself. A chaotic, violent current tore through the passage, a subterranean whirlpool that sent the two hunters tumbling head over heels, their lights spinning wildly, their bodies slammed against the rock walls.

Skot, Dave, and Buzz were caught in the edge of the vortex, but the main force was directed at the intruders. It was a clear, unambiguous, and terrifyingly effective act of defense. The Siren was protecting its own.

They didn't wait to see what happened next. They kicked with the last of their adrenaline-fueled strength and burst out of the end of the tunnel, into the familiar, beautiful, glowing sanctuary of the grotto.

They surfaced, gasping, their minds reeling from the impossible thing they had just witnessed. They scrambled onto the familiar rock ledge, their safe harbor, their refuge.

"You saw it, right?" Buzz shrieked, his voice a high-pitched hymn of terror and vindication. "The big, spooky, calamari-looking thing! The ghost squid! I am not crazy! You all saw it!"

"We saw it," Skot breathed, his own face a mask of awe and fear.

Their safety was a temporary illusion. They didn't know if the hunters were alive or dead, but they knew they couldn't just stay here. Eva was still out there. And she would not give up.

"We have to end it," Dave said, his voice quiet but absolute. He looked around the grotto, at the glowing water, at the beautiful, impossible source of all their joy and all their misery. "We have to take it off the board. For good."

The plan was insane, but it was the only one they had. The original cave-in that had trapped them in The Cathedral had also weakened the structure of this entire section of the cave system. They could see long, deep fissures in the ceiling of the grotto, evidence of the immense geological stress.

"If we can cause a new collapse," Skot said, his artist's mind now thinking like a demolition expert, "right here... we can seal this place forever."

They went to work. Fueled by the full, potent power of the Potion, they were no longer men; they were forces of nature. They found a massive, partially dislodged column of limestone at the edge of the grotto, a casualty of the original collapse. It was a colossal piece of rock, weighing tons, and it was a keystone. If they could move it, the whole ceiling might come down.

They put their shoulders to it, their three bodies a single, unified machine. They pushed, their muscles screaming, the Potion singing in their veins. The column groaned, a deep, grinding sound of rock on rock. It moved. An inch. Then another.

It was in the middle of this Herculean effort that a new light appeared at the mouth of the tunnel they had just exited. A single, sharp, white beam. A figure, sleek and dark, emerged from the water.

It was Eva.

She was alone. Her gear was torn, and there was a dark, bleeding gash on her forehead, but she was alive. And she was furious. Her professional calm was gone, replaced by the raw, cold rage of a predator that had been wounded. She raised her pistol, its black form a stark, ugly shape in the beautiful, glowing light of the grotto.

"It's over," she said, her voice a low, ragged hiss. "You are not leaving this cave."

But before she could fire, a deep, cracking roar echoed from the ceiling above. The column was giving way. A shower of dust and small pebbles rained down around them.

"NOW!" Skot roared.

They gave one final, convulsive, superhuman shove. The massive limestone column shifted, teetered for a single, heart-stopping, eternal second, and then plunged into the glowing pool below with a deafening, catastrophic crash.

The chain reaction was immediate. The ceiling screamed, the fissures widened, and the entire grotto began to implode. Massive slabs of rock plunged into the water, sending huge waves crashing against the walls.

Eva, her face a mask of pure, unbelieving horror as her prize was destroyed before her very eyes, was knocked off her feet by the first wave, her gun flying from her hand as she was swept back into the tunnel.

Skot, Dave, and Buzz scrambled away from the collapse, toward the other side of the grotto, toward the original, claustrophobic squeeze they had used to escape The Cathedral. The collapse, in a final, beautiful act of irony, had shifted the rock in a new way. The tiny, impassable crack was now a wider, survivable passageway. It was a new, unknown path to the surface.

With the roar of the collapsing world at their backs, they plunged into the new tunnel, swimming for their lives, not knowing or caring where it led. All they knew was that it led up, toward air, toward life, toward a world that was finally, blessedly, free of the Siren's song. They were mortal again. But they were free.

Chapter 58: The Echo

The tunnel was a rebirth in reverse, a frantic, desperate scramble out of the womb of the earth and back into the harsh, unforgiving light. It was a tight, dark, watery passage, but it was different from the others. It was blessedly short. They swam with the last, ragged dregs of their adrenaline, their bodies screaming in protest, the memory of the Potion's power now a cruel, taunting ghost. They were just men again, fragile and breaking, and the pain was a profound, shocking reminder of their own mortality.

They surfaced not in a pristine, beautiful cenote, but in a small, muddy, and profoundly unremarkable jungle river. They burst through the surface, gasping, choking, and flailing, their lungs burning with the need for real, unfiltered air. They stumbled onto a muddy bank, three half-drowned rats who had just been spat out by the planet's angriest plumbing system.

They lay there for a long time, a tangle of limbs on the damp earth, the sounds of the jungle a familiar, unwelcome chorus. They were alive. They were free from the cave. They were free from the hunters. And they were hopelessly, completely, and utterly lost one last time.

"Well," Buzz croaked, his voice a raw, wet rasp. He rolled over and spat out a mouthful of muddy river water. "On the plus side, I don't think they'll be following us. On the negative side, I have no earthly idea where we are, what we're going to eat, or how we're going to get out of here.

Also, I think a fish may have tried to build a nest in my shorts. So, you know. Pros and cons."

The journey out was different this time. It wasn't a frantic, panicked race. It was a slow, agonizing, and strangely peaceful march. The constant, gnawing fear of being hunted was gone, replaced by the simpler, more honest challenges of survival. They were in pain, their bodies a symphony of aches and groans. They were hungry. They were exhausted. But there was a lightness to their step, a freedom they hadn't felt since they first stepped off the plane. The terrible, crushing weight of the secret, of the laptop, of the doomsday clock, had been lifted. They were no longer the custodians of a world-changing miracle. They were just three guys trying to find their way home.

Skot, with his uncanny, almost supernatural sense of direction, took the lead. He found a tributary, and with the simple, unshakeable logic of a man who understands the wilderness, he knew that all water eventually leads to people. They followed the small, winding river for two days, their progress a slow, painful crawl. They ate the last of their protein bars. They used their water purifier. They moved with the grim, quiet determination of men who had been to the edge and back and had decided they quite liked not being on the edge.

It was on the third day that they stumbled out of the jungle and onto a small, dusty, sun-baked dirt road. It was the most beautiful thing they had ever seen. They stood at the edge of the trees, three bearded, tattered wild men, and just stared at this simple, profound symbol of civilization.

They didn't have to wait long. An ancient, rattling pickup truck, its bed piled high with yuca, came bouncing down the road. The driver, a kind-faced farmer, slowed down, his eyes wide with a mixture of pity and alarm at the sight of them. They didn't have to say a word. He knew the jungle gave up its ghosts from time to time. He gestured to the back of the truck.

The ride was bumpy, uncomfortable, and glorious. They sat on the rough wooden planks in the back, the wind in their hair, the dust in their faces, and they laughed. A real, honest, and slightly unhinged laughter of pure, unadulterated relief.

The driver dropped them at the edge of a small, forgotten-looking town, a collection of cinder-block buildings and faded paint that was, to them, the most beautiful city on earth. He refused their money, just shook his head, made the sign of the cross, and drove away, leaving them in a cloud of dust and the full, shocking glare of the modern world.

They found a small, dusty cantina with a single, flickering fluorescent light and a sign in the window that offered "Cerveza Fria." More importantly, it had a second, hand-written sign that offered "Wi-Fi Gratis."

This was it. The final move. Their last act as the Grotto Men.

They sat at a rickety table in the back corner, the laptop open between them. The battery was at less than 1%. The clock on the dead man's switch read 02:14:32. It was time to end the game.

"Okay, boys, last dance," Buzz said, his voice a low, serious whisper that was completely devoid of his usual manic energy. This wasn't a performance. This was the end of the show. "We do this, and it's over. No book deal. No Netflix special. No brand. We just... go away. You guys sure about this?"

Dave looked at Skot. Skot looked back at him. They had discussed it a hundred times on their long walk out. There was no other way. A life of resetting a clock was just a different kind of cage.

Dave nodded. "We're sure."

Buzz took a deep, shuddering breath. He had dreamed of this moment, of the global launch, the media empire. He was about to voluntarily kill the greatest story he would ever have. It was the hardest, and the best, thing he had ever done.

He logged into the dead man's switch website. But he didn't reset the clock. He went to a different screen, the one that allowed him to edit the message that would be sent out if the clock ever reached zero.

They drafted it together, three men leaning over a dying laptop in a dusty bar at the end of the world. They chose their final words to the planet with a quiet, somber care.

When they were done, Buzz read it aloud one last time.

"'Everything you have seen is true. We are not hoaxers. But we will not be hunted, and this discovery will not be weaponized or exploited. The full, unedited footage, along with our personal testimony and medical data that proves our biological changes, has been uploaded to an automated, decentralized system. As long as we, and our families, remain safe and anonymous, the full file will remain sealed. If any harm comes to any of us, or if any attempt is made to find us, the system will automatically release everything to every news outlet and government on the planet. The story is over. We are now disappearing. Do not come looking for us.'"

It was perfect. It wasn't a threat; it was a promise. A permanent, unsolvable state of mutually assured destruction.

Buzz's fingers moved across the keyboard. He disabled the 24-hour timer. He typed in a final, complex authorization code. And then he clicked the button that said 'ACTIVATE & SEAL'.

A small, green checkmark appeared on the screen. It was done. The files were locked away in their digital vault, the key thrown away forever. Their part of the story was officially over.

The laptop, as if on cue, chimed a soft, sad little tune and the screen went black. The battery was dead.

They stood up. Buzz left a small pile of cash on the table. They walked out of the cantina and into the warm, dark night. Without a word, Dave took the laptop, walked to a nearby drainage ditch, and, with a final, cathartic heave, threw it in. They heard a faint splash.

They walked to the edge of the town, where a single, beat-up, and completely anonymous-looking sedan was waiting for them. Buzz had made one last call, to one last shady contact, their final ghost car.

They got in, three men with no past and a completely unknown future. Dave took the wheel. He looked at his friends, at their grimy, exhausted, and impossibly familiar faces. And for the first time in what felt like a hundred years, he felt a flicker of something he had thought was gone forever. Peace.

He started the car, and they drove off into the night, away from the jungle, away from the miracle, away from the world that would now tell their story in a thousand different ways, but would never, ever know the truth. They were finally, truly, and completely free.

Epilogue: The Long Jump

The wind was a clean, cold, living thing. It rushed past his face with a sound like a sigh, a perfect, alpine symphony. Below, the world was a masterpiece of impossible, jaw-dropping beauty. A patchwork of emerald green valleys, dotted with tiny, storybook villages, was framed by the jagged, snow-dusted peaks of the Swiss Alps. A river, the color of glacial melt, snaked its way through the landscape like a ribbon of pure turquoise. It was a view that made you feel both infinitesimally small and infinitely alive.

Sonny Bullard, who had once been a man named David Bennett, banked his hang glider into a gentle turn, the colorful wing dipping with a practiced, easy grace. He looked over at the glider flying a hundred yards to his left. He could see the familiar, wiry frame of his friend, Angus Lowery, once known as Skot Larson. Angus gave him a thumbs-up, a wide, joyful, and completely un-haunted grin on his face.

This was their life now. It was five years after their disappearance, five years since the world had briefly obsessed over, and then largely forgotten, the strange, unsolvable mystery of the Grotto Men. The permanent, biological gift of the Potion was a quiet, humming miracle inside them. The aches and pains of their old lives were there, just barely. Dave's diabetes was a distant, bad memory. Skot's shoulder only flared up in bad weather; otherwise it was perfect. They were men in their early fifties who had been given the priceless, impossible gift of feeling thirty again. And they were not wasting a single second of it.

They had new names, new passports, new histories, all meticulously crafted and paid for by a very small fraction of the seed money Buzz had insisted they all take from his own accounts before they vanished. Dave—Sonny—had moved his family to a quiet, beautiful town in the Pacific Northwest, where he coached his daughter's soccer team and ran a small, successful accounting firm under his new name. He was a pillar of his new, anonymous community. Jen was happier than he had ever seen her, the shadow of his old anxieties gone, replaced by a man who was present, who was calm, who understood with a profound, bone-deep certainty what was truly important. He was, finally, the man she had always deserved.

Skot—Angus—had found his peace in a small, windswept town on the coast of New Zealand's South Island. He painted. He surfed. He lived a quiet, solitary life, but it was not a lonely one. His art, which he sold under a pseudonym, was gaining a reputation for its vibrant, almost violent energy, its obsession with the interplay of brilliant light and crushing darkness. He was a ghost, but he was a happy one.

Twice a year, they would meet. The thrill tours. It was the one, non-negotiable condition of their new lives. They would pick a spot on the globe, a place of stunning beauty and exhilarating risk, and for one week, they would be Skot and Dave again, two adrenaline junkies chasing the high.

They landed in a wide, green field, their descents smooth and professional. They shed their harnesses, their bodies moving with an easy, youthful athleticism that belied their chronological age. They were laughing, the pure, uncomplicated laughter of old friends who have just shared a perfect moment.

They were packing up their gliders when they heard the sound of a car approaching on the small, gravel access road. It was a profoundly boring, silver rental sedan, the kind of car that was specifically designed to be forgotten. It pulled up, and the driver's side door opened.

A man got out. He was wearing a ridiculous, wide-brimmed fishing hat, a pair of oversized sunglasses, and a loud, garish floral shirt. It was Buzz. He moved with a kind of comical, exaggerated stealth, as if he were a spy in a very bad movie. He didn't just look at them; he scanned the entire perimeter, his head on a constant, paranoid swivel.

"Are we clear?" he whispered, his voice a loud, conspiratorial hiss as he scurried over to them. "I took the scenic route. The long way. I think I shook them. I made three unscheduled stops to buy cheese. It was a beautiful piece of misdirection. They'll never think to look for a man buying that much Gruyère."

"Who's 'them,' Buzz?" Sonny asked, a wide, easy grin on his face.

"Who do you think, Sonny boy, who do you think?" Buzz shot back, his voice a rapid-fire patter. "The men in black! The spooks! The corporate goons! They're always watching! Always! You guys think this is a game? This is my life now! I have to live like a ghost! A very well-dressed, very important ghost with an excellent credit score, but a ghost nonetheless!"

Buzz, predictably, had thrived. He had never been able to stomach the quiet anonymity that his friends craved. He had found the loophole. He couldn't talk about the Potion, but he could talk about his role in the story. He had become a world-renowned media consultant and "crisis manager," a guru of the narrative. He had written a best-selling, and intentionally vague, book called The Narrative, a self-aggrandizing memoir about his experience managing the "biggest secret in the world." He was richer and more famous than ever, a regular on the talk-show circuit, still winking at the world, the keeper of a flame he could never fully reveal.

But twice a year, he would disappear. He would cancel his appointments, ghost his own life, and execute a comically elaborate travel plan that involved multiple airlines and burner phones, all to join his friends for their reunion.

"Did you bring it?" Angus asked, his eyes gleaming.

"Did I bring it? Did I bring it?" Buzz said, a look of mock offense on his face. "Does a bear defecate in the woods? Of course I brought it!" He opened the trunk of the boring sedan. Inside, nestled amongst his designer luggage, was a large, top-of-the-line cooler.

That evening, they sat on the wooden deck of the small, secluded chalet Buzz had rented, a bottle of impossibly expensive single-malt scotch open on the table between them. The sun was setting behind the jagged peaks, painting the sky in fiery, impossible colors. They were just three friends, their easy, familiar banter a symphony that had been playing for over forty years. They talked about their new lives, about their families, about the sheer, ridiculous beauty of the world.

Buzz was in the middle of a long, rambling, and mostly fictional story about a tense negotiation with a Hollywood studio head when he suddenly paused. He looked at his friends, his expression for once stripped of all its usual bravado and irony.

"You know," he said, his voice quiet and serious. "I can't post anything. That's the deal. No pictures, no check-ins, no witty, self-aggrandizing captions. It's killing me. My brand is taking a serious hit. My followers think I'm on a juice cleanse in Malibu."

He picked up his glass, a rare, genuine smile on his face. "But you know what? It's worth it."

He raised his glass. Sonny and Angus raised theirs to meet it. The three glasses clinked together, a small, perfect sound in the vast, alpine silence.

"To the new rules," Buzz said, his eyes twinkling. He looked from Skot's face to Dave's, a look of profound, unspoken love passing between the three of them. He grinned, a final, perfect, celebratory flash of the old, magnificent Buzz.

"What happens on the thrill tour," he declared, "stays on the thrill tour."

And in the quiet of the setting sun, surrounded by the silent, watching mountains, the three friends drank their toast, their long, impossible, and beautiful secret finally, and forever, safe.

Acknowledgements

First and foremost, to my family and frends, my deepest thanks for your endless patience and support. You are the bedrock of all my adventures, and your encouragement is the fuel that makes any journey possible. Thank you for tolerating the late nights, the distracted conversations, and for sharing our time on the lake and at the beach so I could bring this story to life.

To my friends, Dennis, David, and Skot, this book is a testament to a friendship that has spanned decades. Thank you for a lifetime of real-life adventures, from the entrepreneurial to the open road. The bond between the characters on these pages is a direct reflection of the one we share, and this story would not exist without you.

A special thanks to my agent and my editor at Hearthstone Press, whose guidance and sharp insights helped shape this novel from a rough idea into a finished story. Your belief in this project was invaluable.

And finally, to you, the reader. Thank you for taking this journey with Skot, Dave, and Buzz. I hope their adventure reminds you that youth is a state of mind, and the greatest thrill of all is the time spent with good friends.

About the Author

Brian Wallace is a professional mechanical engineer from Birmingham, Alabama, where he designs industrial machinery. He lives on Lewis Smith Lake, north of the city, and spends his free time boating and swimming with his family. An avid fan of college football, he can be found cheering for his alma mater, the University of Alabama, every fall. His adventures often take him to the Gulf Coast beaches of Alabama and the Smoky Mountains of Tennessee. Siren's Spring is a story born from decades of real-life adventures and enduring friendships.

A Conversation with Brian Wallace

Q: What was the spark for a story that combines a high-stakes thriller with a miraculous discovery like the fountain of youth?

A: The heart of the story really comes from the friendship between the main characters. I grew up riding motorcycles with my own friends, David and Skot, who were the direct inspiration for the characters in the book. David and I still take motorcycle trips to the mountains. Skot is a very talented artist, and we've shared our own real-life entrepreneurial adventures for the last thirty years. The thriller plot was a way to raise the stakes on that friendship—to ask what would happen if the thing that could save their adventures was also the thing that could destroy them.

Q: The bond between Skot, Dave, and Buzz feels incredibly authentic. How much of their dynamic is pulled from your own experiences?

A: A huge amount of it. That dynamic of the dreamer, the pragmatist, and the guy who brings the energy is something I know well. When you have friendships that last for decades, you develop a kind of shorthand, a rhythm to the way you interact. I wanted to capture that feeling—the inside jokes, the arguments, the unconditional loyalty. The impossible situation they find themselves in is just a pressure cooker for that lifelong bond.

Q: Beyond the adventure and the danger, what's the one idea you hope readers are left thinking about after they finish Siren's Spring?

A: That youth is a state of mind, especially when you are enjoying time with friends. The Potion is the catalyst in the story, but it's not the real magic. The real magic is in the shared experiences, the loyalty, and the decision to keep seeking adventure together, no matter your age. The Potion gives them a second chance at life, but it's their friendship that tells them how to use it.